ETCHINGS OF POWER

AEGIS
OF
THE GODS
BOOK 1

TERRY
C.
SIMPSON

Also By Terry C. Simpson

AEGIS OF THE GODS
Prequel: The Shadowbearer
Book 1: Etchings of Power
Book 2: Ashes and Blood (Coming Soon)

Copyright

Find out more about the author and upcoming books
online at Terrycsimpson.com, Ramblings of a Fantasy Author or
@TeeSimps, or TCSimpson on Facebook
Second Print Edition
ISBN: 978-1-939172-03-7

Dedication

This book is dedicated to my wife Marie, and my daughter Kai. Without you this would not be possible. You motivate me in ways I didn't think were possible.

Acknowledgements

First, thanks to the man upstairs. And again, thanks to my wife Marie for being there to support me and for giving me the most wonderful gift in our daughter, Kai. Kai, you inspire me to write every time I see you pick up one of my huge epic fantasy hardcovers and say "Daddy, read for me."

A big thanks to my Speculative Collective Writing Group. Leighland J Feinman, for your the good, bad and ugly crits. Ted Anderson, your crits have been priceless in getting me here, and you are often first to see plot and story flaws and taught me much about pacing and reveals. Edward Hoefer, always so supportive yet firm, and never pulling a punch. Elisa Hansen, your pointers on structure, dislike for gerunds and purple prose and ability to see the little things kept me grounded. Katie Garrigan, the grammar goddess, who helped keep my wayward writing in check.

To my editor D Kai Wilson–Viola. Funny how life works that I meet an editor with the same name as my daughter. Thanks for putting up with my unending questions about your suggestions and changes. You helped to bring about a certain life in my work by encouraging me to be true to my descriptive half and not be too bland. You helped bring my characters to life. Your workshop on social media and help on facebook, twitter etc. has been amazing. If only there were more people as selfless as you are.

To my Novel Review Group at writing.com. Tamara, Milhaud, LJPC, MsJ, Vampyr14, you all taught me much of what I needed to get this done.

To my best friend Hughey. A big thank you for telling me this was my calling.

Map of Denestia

Carnas Area and The Wilds

Eldanhill to Randane

CHAPTER 1

Ryne Waldron wondered if he should kill the woman. Blood, bodies, and screams rolled across his mind with the thought of her and those she represented. The stink of something dead or worse hung in the air. He expelled a great breath, chest heaving with the hope the stench was only death.

An old, familiar feeling, like heat seeping into a cold hearth, stirred deep within his eight–foot frame. In response, the vibrant tapestry of tattoos covering his body from foot to chin writhed. Seamless replicas of the same artwork decorated his armor, they too twitching in unison with those on his body. Ryne flinched, his muscled arms and broad back clenching, the scars under his leather armor drawing taut. Frowning, he stopped himself from reaching to his hip for his greatsword's hilt. His bloodlust had never risen before unless he touched his power. He shut away the craving to kill with practiced ease.

Unable to shrug off the lapse of control, Ryne stepped to the rear of one of Carnas' many rosewood and teak homes and glanced out across the Orchid Plains. Shimmering heat rose in waves, and yellowed grass and flowers bowed under the sun's rays as if praying for relief, but sure enough, there she stood.

Mariel—if that was even her real name—kept her gaze trained in his direction. Dark hair hung to her shoulders, and she was dressed in a short–sleeved shirt and close–fitting trousers, her slight body and paler skin color the opposite of the native Ostanians. As usual, she stayed beyond the range where he could read her aura.

Ryne turned his head to the noise of a boot scraping on the wooden stairs next to him.

"See here?" Dren craned his head to peer at Ryne, his leather boot poking at a dried bloodstain. "This is where they took Miss Corten last night."

Looming over Dren, although the sinewy man stood two stairs higher, Ryne inspected the scuffmarks. Rust colored splotches stained the wood. Next to the steps, several flattened flowers were the only other signs of a struggle. Ryne's brow wrinkled. "Nowhere near enough blood to have been anything serious."

"Exactly." Dren nodded, scarred hands rising to stroke his short beard. "Miss Corten can hunt as well as any one of us scouts. But no one heard her sound an alarm or even cry out."

Ryne gauged the proximity to the other adjoining homes. Despite the space between houses afforded here at Carnas' outskirts, someone should have heard Miss Corten. With the recent hot weather and lack of rain, the shuttered windows on these houses would've been open. Neither the sturdy structures nor the wooden tile roofs would have kept out the sounds of the struggle or a cry for help. Not even the gales that often howled during one of the frequent thunderstorms could have drowned out Miss Corten's cries. However, there hadn't been any such wind, not the past few days. The weather had remained as it was now, hot, still, and silent with not much more than an inconsequential breeze.

Shifting uncomfortably in his fitted leather armor to sample the air once more, Ryne flicked his thumb across his nose as the whiff of something long dead, of decay and unwashed dog fur curdled his insides. "Have you noticed the smell, Sakari? It's faint, but it's there."

Sakari glided forward, his nostrils flaring. The silver flecks dominating the whites of his eyes flashed as he sniffed the air. At near seven feet—almost reaching Ryne's shoulder—today he was the opposite of Ryne in girth, his body svelte, each part fit in near perfect proportions under his scaled leather armor. "Yes," Sakari answered after a final scrunch of his nose, "Rot. Old fur. Something not quite dead."

Dren's brows drew together, his eyes narrowed, and sweat beaded his forehead. His hand eased down to his sword hilt as he glanced around, his gaze searching the woods across the expanse of pastures. "Master Waldron, you think it's a beast from the Rot?" the scoutmaster whispered, his head shifting from left to right as if to make sure no one overheard.

Indeed, Dren had cause for his fear. If any beast had crossed the Rotted Forest, there would be reason to worry for everyone. "Maybe. We'll know soon enough. Take us to the body," Ryne ordered.

Dren gave a tentative nod and set off at a jog, his hand on the pommel of his sheathed short sword. Under too clear skies and a burning sun, they cut across the Orchid Plains with its grasses and namesake blue and red flowers that lit up the air with the sweet scent of their blooms. In places, the brush and plants around them not only drooped and were becoming sickly yellow but were a dying brown.

Ryne spared a look over his shoulder, and the muscles along his neck formed a tight rope of tension. As usual, Mariel followed. He smirked. She wouldn't escape him today.

Seeing her usual dogged pattern brought questions rising within Ryne again. Why did she seek him? Why did she maintain the distance from him that she did, yet still followed wherever he went? Could she know of his ability to see auras? No. He dismissed the thought. Besides Sakari, no one else knew.

Brow creased from both curiosity and worry, he wondered if she recognized him. If she did, and she reported his identity to her masters, life would become even more dangerous for Carnas' residents. There wouldn't be just eight villagers who went missing over the last few weeks since she appeared; the Granadian Tribunal would wipe Carnas from the map. The fact he still lived was an embarrassment that reeked of their failure, a weakness for others to exploit.

Or so they would see it.

As soon as the thought crossed his mind, a memory bloomed. Garbed in golden armor of interlocking plates, five–foot greatsword in hand, ebony hair tied in a ponytail, Ryne stood atop a mound of dead people. Skulls and ruptured bodies by the hundreds spread all around a smoke–shrouded village square. He plunged the Tribunal's Lightstorm battle standard through a corpse, into the ground, and roared a challenge. He was the Tribunal's instrument of vengeance and none could stand before him. Not even the Tribunal's own. Then he was running, and running, and running, chased by the Tribunal's assassins. The vision shifted. He was on his knees in chains, unable to use his power, his body covered in blood, torn flesh and half–mended scars from lashes. The whip struck again. Pain seared through his body with the memory. Ryne clenched his sword's hilt. *Never again. Never again will I suffer at the hands of the Tribunal's kind.*

"I see Mariel is still following you. When last you tried to catch her?" Dren's words broke Ryne from his thoughts.

Ryne gave a shake of his head and grunted before he shortened his strides in an effort not to outpace the much shorter man. "Two days ago." Counting his steps, Ryne pictured where Mariel would be behind them. The moment needed to be perfect.

"She's better at hiding than anyone I ever met." The admiration in Dren's voice was clear. "In my years as a scoutmaster, I've yet to meet one as skilled as she who wasn't an Alzari. It's almost like she uses the shade to hide. I wonder if she wields the elemen—"

Ryne veered off from the path the scoutmaster set and broke into a full out sprint, his hand on his scabbard to keep it in place. To his right Sakari kept pace, sandy hair bouncing to match his languid strides, a constant shadow hovering somewhere near, eyes seeing everything but revealing nothing. As Ryne expected, Mariel turned tail and sped toward the Fretian Woods.

With the path clear ahead, Ryne opened his mind and linked with Sakari. Ryne's vision doubled. In one sight, he was in his own body, tearing through the brush. In the other, he saw through Sakari's eyes as if he ran in his companion's boots, each step a glide that barely touched the ground.

"Whatever we do, we must catch her before she reaches the woods," Ryne said under his breath.

"As you wish."

Ryne closed the link, and his vision receded to his alone once more. Ponytail slapping against his back, he ate up the distance between him and Mariel. Frightened birds flapped from his path, their morning song interrupted, protesting squawks coming in discordant jangles.

Dren's unfinished question had brought up another issue Ryne had considered. Suppose Mariel did use the elements to hide? That would make her more than the high ranked priestess she claimed since she arrived in Carnas. Lips curling, Ryne snarled and pumped his massive legs faster. The old pain from his torture by the Tribunal rose anew. If she did possess the ability to use the same power as he, then he would force her to do so. When she did, she would confirm his suspicions of her intent. And he would kill her.

Deep inside himself, Ryne's bloodlust flared to life. In response, his Scripts—the tattoos covering his body— roiled like living things.

Down a gentle slope they ran, the occasional tree a blur as they pursued. On the opposite incline, Mariel crested the hilltop before she disappeared down the other side.

As he rushed to the top of the hill, Ryne's strides faltered and slowed. He'd chosen what he thought was the perfect moment and the best path to cut her off. Somehow, the woman had anticipated his move. Not only had she opened up more distance since the chase began, but she fled at an angle that made sure she would reach the woods long before he managed to catch her. So clear was her path and wide her distance, not only was catching her near impossible, but he wouldn't be able to close the gap to read her aura.

Unless…

He growled in frustration, and his bloodlust surged.

"*Embrace your power,*" a deep voice, steeped in malevolence, whispered in his head. "*Capture her. Kill her.*"

"*No. Remember what* that *has cost you in the past,*" warned a soothing voice in a low whine. "*The blood, the bodies, the innocents slaughtered.*"

"*Yessss,*" the first voice encouraged in trembling tones of a creature savoring its pleasure. "*Remember the past. How your power saved you. Our power. Kill for usss. Feed ussss. And none can escape you.*"

The opposing voice pleaded, "*No, please, no. If you do so, you will lose yourself yet again. Is that your wish? To see all you love covered in blood by your hands, steeped in despair that you wrought?*"

On and on the voices warred. Ryne closed his eyes and inhaled deeply, the argument a buzz in the background. As he had practiced the last few years, he listened to the latter voice. If he touched his power now, not only would he kill Mariel, but if he lost control, those he'd come to love in Carnas would suffer a similar fate. Shuddering with the effort, he fought down his lust and shut it off yet again. He heaved a sigh. This sudden rise of his urges didn't bode well. Suspicion of Mariel's ill intentions was all well and good, but without proof, he was no better than those in Carnas who blamed the woman for the missing villagers or the recent bodies they'd found.

What was he thinking? Regardless of her capacity in her work for Granadia's Tribunal, should anything happen to her, Carnas' inhabitants would pay. The Tribunal's price was always absolute. Ryne squeezed his eyes shut for a moment. Picturing those he loved in Carnas lying dead under the Tribunal's banners, crushed by the boots of their military might brought bile rising to his throat.

"Sakari, stop," Ryne shouted. He churned to a halt, his breathing heavy with exertion.

Sakari slowed to a walk. He turned and glided back to Ryne in those smooth strides of his. As he drew close, Sakari shook his head. "You make this more difficult than it needs to be." The green pupils of his eyes were deep pools of nothingness.

Ryne ignored the man. He'd heard the same more than enough times. Well ahead of them, Mariel reached the woods' rosewood and mahogany trees and vanished among the dappled shadows cast by trunks and branches. Ryne spared a glance for the footsteps thudding behind him.

Breaths coming in harsh gasps, Dren caught up with them. "W–What was that all about?" His chest heaved as he gathered himself. "Why chase her now?"

Ryne shrugged." I thought I'd be able to get her before she reached the woods."

Dren wheezed a laugh. "I've seen that bitch easily outrun our dogs. Forian and the others have been whipping the village into a frenzy since you been gone the last two days." He sucked in a breath. "He been saying the things she does proves she's evil. They say she follows the path of the shade."

"And the mayor has been allowing him as usual," Ryne concluded.

Dren nodded. "There's others who think differently, but sooner or later they're going to attack Mariel. May be a good idea for you to speak to them before it gets any worse. They're meeting at Hagan's right now."

"Yes. I might have to," Ryne said, expression thoughtful,

his gaze focused on the area where Mariel had fled. She reappeared at the forest's edge. "Lead us to the body," he said to Dren.

Gesturing toward where Mariel now stood, Dren grunted and shook his head. "She sure is persistent." He turned to lead them back the way they'd come.

After one last look at Mariel, Ryne followed Dren with Sakari in tow. Within an hour, the wood–tile roofs and sturdily built homes of Carnas dwindled behind them to the south as they passed the sparse trees dotting this section of the plains. Dren called for them to stop at a small stand of trees. Ryne glanced back. From the edge of the copse, the lone sandstone structure of Hagan's Inn stuck up from the dip in the land where Carnas was located. Near the slope's crest behind them, Mariel watched, but made no attempt to venture closer.

"The body's just in there." Dren pointed to a few stunted kinai trees. The sweet fruit from the misshapen branches dotted the ground, their color yellowed and pale instead of their normal red.

Hand on his sword, Ryne strode toward the kinai orchard with Sakari flanking him. Ryne picked out an old blood trail and smelled the stink of death before he saw the body. Ravaged beyond recognition like the others, the corpse had been stripped naked, limbs twisted at odd angles. From the mess for a face and the torn torso, he could barely tell the person was a man.

Grinding his teeth, his nose upturned at the stench of offal, Ryne inspected the death wounds without touching the remains. The shredded flesh across the corpse's face made Ryne brush the old scars that striped the left side of his own. What did this? Could Mariel be responsible like some suggested? And if so, how? He knew every creature within the woods. None came to mind that could have torn a person in such a way. Something from the Rotted Forest, maybe? No. His Scripts hadn't warned him that his wards had been triggered.

He longed to touch his power to see if any malevolence existed within the gashes or the body, but the potential consequences stopped him. Until he figured out why his control appeared to wane, he needed to resort to relying on his physical gifts. Old habits died hard, and this dead body reminded him too much of his past, of the War of Remnants, of the years before when he'd seen beasts ravaged in even worse ways totter to their feet and attack. A simple method existed for him to make certain no such darkness existed here.

Ryne unsheathed his greatsword with a rasp of metal on leather. Runes and glyphs etched into the five–foot silversteel weapon glinted from the sun's penetration through the trees. In a smooth motion, he stepped forward and swung. The wide, double–edged blade passed through the corpse's neck without resistance. Blood pooled onto the soft dirt and leaves.

With a flick of his sword to the side, Ryne rid it of any residue, and sheathed the weapon. "May Ilumni and his Battleguards keep you safe," he said in reverence.

Dizziness swirled through him for a brief moment, and he swayed. Sakari stepped forward to help, but Ryne waved him off. He'd grown used to these bouts of lightheadedness over the past few years. This one he could handle.

"What do you think?" Ryne nodded toward the corpse.

"No beast from the Rotted Forest delivered those wounds. And the only stench here is just death," Sakari said.

"A weapon?"

"None I can think of."

Ryne grunted his agreement. "And I see no auras around the body so no elements were used. Come let's see what else we find."

They searched the area but found nothing else out of place. Still baffled by what could have caused such grievous wounds, they left the stand and headed for home with Mariel still trailing them. With the sun beating down on them, they made a straight line for the sandstone edifice that marked Hagan's Inn.

"Let me guess," Dren said, an eyebrow arched. "You're going to let them know the error of their ways if this foolishness with Forian continues."

"Something like that," Ryne admitted, his voice even. "I think Mayor Bertram has downplayed just what kind of response the Tribunal would have if Mariel was harmed."

In short order, they reached the low wooden wall surrounding the village.

Dren slowed to a walk, his eyes focused toward the woods. He pointed. "Who's that out there?"

In that instant, a bestial roar pierced the humid afternoon

air. Ryne's head whipped toward the sound, the same direction in which Dren, foot raised in an unfinished step, still pointed.

A boy stood frozen amongst the brush and long grass. The large teak, mahogany, and rosewood trees in the forest before him shook with such violence a rain of leaves fell.

"Kahkon?" Ryne said under his breath, cold fingers of dread slithering down his spine as he squinted at the skinny youth.

A huge beast, at least five the times the size of a large wolf, leaped from the dark woods. The aura about the creature shone with an obsidian blackness instead of its normal gray. Fluids dripped from raw, pink flesh and dark fur splotched black with decay. The infected lapra reared up on four of its six legs like a mantis preparing to attack. A wide, snout of a muzzle and forepaws tipped with sharp claws flashed. Before Kahkon could react, the beast snatched him by a leg. Kahkon screamed. A sound that brought shivers sliding down Ryne's back. With the same speed it struck, the lapra disappeared back into the trees, the boy a ragdoll in its mouth.

CHAPTER 2

Screams and cries from the villagers who witnessed the taking jarred Ryne into action. "Go!" he yelled to Sakari and Dren. "Fetch Lenka and Keevo. And gather several other hunters from the woods."

"What about Mariel?" Sakari gestured toward the woman.

"I'll deal with her. Go! Go!"

"No, Master Waldron. The elders, the villagers…you have to calm them," Dren implored, his eyes frantic.

"The boy comes first," Ryne snapped. He rounded on Dren, towering over him like a great cliff, his eyes steel. "I'll be damned if I have his blood on my hands. If I ever had a son, he'd be like Kahkon. I won't stand by—"

Dren grabbed at Ryne's arm. His hands trembled. "You don't understand, Master Waldron. The way Forian been going at them the last few days, they'll attack Mariel for sure with this. You know how it was during the War of Remnants. The Tribunal will kill everyone if we harm Mariel. I have a wife, sons…Master Waldron. Please. Look, if we're to save Kahkon, we can't afford for them to go traipsing into the Fretian now anyway. We'd be sure to lose the lapra's tracks. And if they go after Mariel, there'll be nowhere to hide from the Tribunal's wrath." Tears welled up in the scoutmaster's eyes.

Agonized by the need to save Kahkon, Ryne clenched his fists. Deep down, he knew Dren was right. Kahkon's survival meant a lot to him, but so did the rest of Carnas. He couldn't dream of sacrificing one for the other. Both needed him. As harsh as it sounded to himself, right now, staving off whatever malice resided in Carnas must take precedence. He needed to rely on Sakari and the others to find the tracks in time.

Torn, Ryne pulled his arm away from the scoutmaster. "Fine, fine," he whispered, his voice hoarse. "You two go. Gather the others. I'll inform the elders and settle the people down before I come. Sound the horn when you find the tracks. Sakari." Their gazes locked. "Do not fail."

"Thank you, Master Waldron," Dren said reverently.

Without a word, Sakari bowed and ran off with Dren following on his heels. Sakari weaved his way amongst frantically pointing villagers who'd crowded the hard–packed dirt road surrounded by Carnas' wooden homes. As he raced by, he gestured to two men in armor that matched his. One was a gray–haired, wiry man with a horn at his hip, and the other, a grizzle–faced hunter whose arms were all sinew. They ran after Sakari toward the woods.

Broad back and legs stiff from fighting the urge to chase after them, Ryne turned and stalked in the opposite direction toward Hagan's Inn. Villagers still pointed and a few young boys had climbed onto a roof and were gazing out toward the Fretian Woods. Concerned chatter flowed among the throngs on the road.

The door to Hagan's Inn burst open. Mayor Bertram, Hagan, and several other members from Carnas' village Council rushed outside the three–storied sandstone building. Ryne strode to meet them.

"What's happening?" Bertram's scarred face was gaunt and grim. His one good eye scanned the panicked crowd. His left arm, which ended at the elbow, moved on its own accord.

Hagan waddled just behind him, chest heaving, shirt so tight about his barrel–shaped belly it appeared as if it would burst open with his next breath. "Has another body been found?" He popped his pipe into the corner of his mouth and kneaded giana leaves into the bowl.

A flurry of questions spilled from the other Council members. Ryne lifted his hand, and a reluctant silence followed as villagers gathered in a respectful band around the elders.

"No, there hasn't been another body," Ryne said, feeling

a great weight on his chest as he thought about the boy's small shape hanging from the beast's jaws. "But an infected lapra took Kahkon."

Gasps sounded from all around. Standing well over everyone, Ryne took in their wide–eyed expressions and animated gestures.

"An infected lapra?" Bertram repeated. "Here? You certain? How…What's it doing here? The Rot is hundreds of miles away. And the wards…"

Several other elders seconded Bertram's opinion.

Ryne shook his head. "It doesn't need to make sense. That's what took the boy. You can ask anyone who saw." Some Council members did as he suggested. In turn, Ryne graced them with a glare. "Listen, you can stay here and continue to squabble about Mariel's intentions. Or who or what killed those men we found near the kinai orchards. Or about what took the other eight villagers. I'll have none of it. Before Kahkon ends up like them, I'm going after the boy. I've already sent Sakari to gather a few others for the task."

A gravelly voice called from the crowd, "Mariel sent the beast." All eyes shifted to the baldheaded man. Baker Forian wiped greasy hands on an apron dark with stains. "She took those who we be missing too."

Ryne raised his brow. "You have proof of this?"

Forian sucked in his paunch as he held himself erect. "I seen her speak to plains lapras with my own two." He pointed at his beady eyes. "They ran off without bothering the woman once. If that not be proof then what be?"

Several people gave doubtful grumbles, while others sounded as if they expected such an occurrence. Forian's face flushed, but from his eyes, Ryne could tell the man believed what he said. Ryne frowned. Could Mariel have taken the villagers? The thought had crossed his mind before, but he'd yet to find proof. Yet, what made him more uncertain was the chance she might have an ability to commune with beasts similar to Sakari. He'd never seen anyone who possessed a skill comparable to his companion.

Despite his doubts, Ryne decided on caution. If he left now without knowing where the beast headed, the last mistake he needed was to unwittingly lead Mariel to the hunters' location.

Not to mention the consequences if he didn't find a way to calm the murderous intent Forian had stirred up.

"But she's a Devout," someone from the gathered crowd shouted.

"If she be a Devout, she wouldn't be involved in such things," Forian insisted.

Mayor Bertram scoffed. "If, indeed. We've argued all day about whether she's a Devout. I tend to believe differently. If only they would see it." He regarded the other elders with his good eye narrowed. "I've yet to see a high priestess without their guards or their uniform." All, except Hagan, avoided his gaze.

The innkeeper blew a puff of perfumed giana smoke into the air. "She bears the Lightstorm insignia. And—"

A wail broke out from the back of the crowd. Murmurs drifted through the villagers. A path opened between them to reveal a middle–aged woman stumbling toward the elders—Kahkon's mother, Lara. Several men helped hold up the weeping woman. Dark circles ringed her eyes. Her disheveled clothing appeared as if she'd thrown on any scrap she could find when she received the news.

Lara's body convulsed. "My Kahkon. My poor Kahkon," she bawled.

One man bent close and spoke into Lara's ear. Her head rose, and her gaze ran over the Council. They regarded her with pity. She scrubbed at her tear–streaked face as she shambled into the circle of village elders. When she saw Ryne, a faint, hopeful expression spread across her face before more sobs tore from her throat, and she swooned.

Ryne stepped forward and caught her. In her hand, she cradled one of the books he'd given to Kahkon—the boy's favorite—*When the Gods Walked Among Us*, the title read. Kahkon had a love for the old stories and would often say he dreamed of being one of the gods. In his dreams, he said Ryne was one of his Battleguards, protecting him as he did Carnas. Ryne's chest tightened with the memory.

"I'll return your boy safely, Miss Lara. I promise. As soon as Sakari sends word he's found the beast's trail." Ryne held her upright so he could peer down into her grief–ridden eyes.

Lara's legs steadied, and she craned her neck. Her bloodshot eyes darted back and forth, peering into his, hope radiating from them. "I, I know you will, Master Waldron," she said, her voice tremulous. "He's my only boy. I told him, you know. I told him about the dead men they been finding. I told him stay away from the woods, but you know Kahkon. He loves the trees. Why me, Master Waldron? Why my boy?"

"I don't know, but I intend to find out." Ryne released his hold on Kahkon's mother.

"It be Mariel's fault all this be happening," another person yelled from the crowd.

"Look at the kinai crops. It's her fault we haven't had constant rains the last few months for a proper harvest. In the middle of the rainy season. And this year's fruit been sour besides. The storm gods punish us like in the days of the Shadowbearer."

Ryne eyed the large warehouse a few feet from where they stood. The normally fist–sized kinai fruit stacked in buckets in front the building were withered and brown.

A second voice joined in. "The old blood still runs strong among us in Ostania. We'd never lay with daemons or wolves like the Granadians do."

"Praise be to the true god, Humelen," a third voice yelled.

"It's because they partake in flesh instead of the purity of the land," another villager shouted.

"The Granadians brought ruin to Ostania twice," Forian announced. "And they will again. Let them keep their lecherous ways across the sea. It be them made all manner of monsters descend upon our lands. I say burn that bitch, Mariel, before she can make half–wolf children or any other daemon spawn who grow up worshiping the shade. Who be with me?"

Bloodthirsty shouts ruptured the air until the uproar grew to an incomprehensible din. Lara began wailing again. Men and women reached for swords or clubs, and metal rasped on leather. Those who did not already clench weapons shook their fists.

"Just head on out, Master Waldron," old, toothless Sanada pleaded. "Sure as fleas to a dog, she follows you. My sons can go before you do. The rest of us can trail her. You all turn back and she be ours for the taking."

Ryne ignored the man and the nods and murmurs of approval.

A smile curled onto Mayor Bertram's lips. Ryne's Scripts shifted like the tentative brush of a new lover's fingers against his skin. For an instant, Ryne thought he saw the man's aura flash to a darker shade, but it was gone so fast he dismissed the sight as a trick of the day's heat. Bertram's and Forian's gazes met for a brief instant before Forian gave a subtle nod.

Ryne wanted nothing more than to make his way to the woods to help in the search for the boy. Yet, he'd seen this coming for weeks now. He'd hoped the Council meetings would have given Bertram pause in his efforts to stir up the people. But the hateful seeds sown by Bertram through Forian had taken stronger root. If he did nothing, and they continued to grow, someone would indeed be bold enough to attack Mariel. If only Bertram wasn't so blinded by hate.

"Stop!" Ryne's basso voice thundered over the riotous crowd. The din dwindled to a murmur. A few village folk standing close to him retreated several steps. "Listen to yourselves. When have any of you seen what you speak of? When have you seen any man control the weather? Daemon spawn? When have any of you seen a Granadian or a Devout give birth to or create a shadeling?" He met their heated expressions with an icy scowl, daring anyone to answer.

"Because you don't see a thing doesn't mean it didn't happen," Baker Forian yelled.

Ryne gave the man a stare that could curdle milk. "Forian, when has anyone you've known witnessed any such occurrence? What is it but poison you've been spreading for years? Now even more so when this woman has shown up. You claimed to have proof of her ill intentions, but you provided none beyond your word. And that, in itself, can be called to account due to your own ways. Believe me, if you can prove to me here and now she's involved, I'll deal with her myself."

"Her speaking to lapras not be proof?" Forian retorted.

"You've seen Sakari speak to all manner of beasts, does that make him evil? A child stealer? A creator of shadelings?" Ryne shook his head at the absurdity of his own questions. Everything he'd read agreed the shade's beastly minions couldn't be created in this realm. When Forian didn't answer, Ryne carried on. "Miss Corten often spoke to her flowers. Old Sanada speaks to his dogs and the rats and pheasants." Sanada shifted uneasily as Ryne continued. "Hagan likes to chatter to the birds. Are they evil? Does it mean they were involved in the creature taking the boy?"

Red–faced, Forian dipped his head and avoided Ryne's cold stare. "All I know be what I saw her do. And it be said when the rot leaves the forest, the shade will walk the land." He peered at the faces around him. "Well, the rot left the forest. An infected lapra. If what she did not be of the shade then what be?" He paused for effect. "This be the first time I seen any beasts leave the Rot. And it happens when she be here, after she speaks to the same type of creature." He turned his hands palms up as if the conclusions were inescapable. "I don't call that chance." A few in the crowd nodded their agreement.

Concerned mutters followed from the elders before Hagan spoke up. "You should be careful what you say, Forian." He kept his voice low, but it still carried. "We wouldn't want wind of words she might consider blasphemy to get back to her ears." He peered in the direction of Mariel's last camp.

"Why should we care what she thinks is blasphemy?" Bertram shrugged, his one–eyed gaze taking in everyone. "Even if she is a Devout, none of us here worship her gods."

Murmurs of agreement joined the nods, steadily increasing. Someone else yelled Humelen was the true god.

Glowering, Ryne drew himself up, causing those nearby to take a few steps back as he loomed even larger. "Most of you here have been a part of the War of Remnants. You helped drive the last of the shadelings from your lands. Yet, your lands wouldn't be your own right now if not for the same people you rebuke. Take a look around you." He pointed at the rolling plains, then he gestured to the squat wooden buildings along the alleys and lanes within Carnas. "Look at your children, your neighbors, your friends." He kept his eyes fixed on the villagers until they did as he commanded. "Without Granadia's help, without the Devout," he grimaced even before he said the next bit, "without the Tribunal, you may not be here today. They saved you from the shade. Remember that."

The unrest died down.

"You be the reason we be here today," Hagan said, his voice quiet.

Bertram cocked his head to regard Ryne with his good

eye. The burn scar tissue covering the left side of Bertram's face puckered, but he said nothing.

Ryne ignored Bertram's expression and continued, "The most important thing right now is seeing Kahkon to safety. Debate these outlandish stories and accusations another time. Return to your homes. Make sure your children are safe. No one is to venture near the Fretian Woods."

Few grumbled protests followed, but after a look at Ryne's hulking form and hardened face, the villagers dispersed in small groups. Ryne waited to make sure the village square was clear.

"A moment if you will, Master Waldron," Bertram said. "Hagan and I would like to speak with you." He gestured toward the door of the inn.

"I've more important things to do," Ryne snapped. "As do you. You should be seeing to your people." He took in the mayor's glare with a look akin to frozen steel.

Bertram growled something under his breath and spun on his heels. The elders followed.

Ryne signaled to Vana and Vera. The serving women ambled over to him. "I need you two to take Miss Lara home. See to her needs and make sure she's comfortable."

"Yes, my Lord," Vana said.

Vera held out her hand. "Lord Waldron, take this with you." She handed a pouch to him, and he leaned forward to see what it contained. "It's the best kinai we could find. We had the mender make a paste just for you. It may also be useful when you find the boy."

"You should eat some now too," Vana added. She tiptoed and brushed her hand on the scars that striped the left side of his face. "There's never anything wrong with a little extra energy." She gave him a sweet smile.

Ryne sighed. He almost told them again he was no lord, but he knew his words would come and go like a fluttering breeze. Instead, he accepted their gift, acknowledged them both with a nod, and admired their shapes as they curtsied and hurried off with Miss Lara in tow.

A hunter's horn wailed from within the woods.

Ryne dashed off toward the sound. Villagers scrambled out of his way as he bounded along the main road before he veered off into one of the many alleys, startling a few dogs foraging among garbage, the foul odor of piss and other undesirable waste permeating the air—the result of almost two weeks without rain. He leaped over the clogged drains and past the homes that lined the alleys, his leather boots making soft, rhythmic thuds as he ran. More than once, children at play jumped from his path. Emerging from Carnas' eastern exit, he dodged past the gate in the low wooden wall. When he glanced out to his left, he growled.

Mariel watched him from across the plains. As usual, she maintained a distance where he couldn't see her aura.

Ryne focused ahead and made a straight path toward the Fretian Woods. As he ran, he took a quick peek over his shoulder. Mariel followed.

CHAPTER 3

Irmina Nagel studied the giant man racing across the grassy dips and slopes of the terrain. Just watching the giant with the sun beating on him while only the slightest of breezes whispered through the air made her wish for a drink of water. With the back of her hand, she flicked away dark strands of hair stuck to her face and wiped at sweat streaming down her brow.

The thick fescue and blue and red flowering brush of the Orchid Plains offered little resistance to the man's massive legs. His two–handed greatsword's wide scabbard bounced on his thigh before he brought his hand down and kept it in place. He ate up the distance in great strides, three times a normal man's full stretched leap.

She kept a careful eye on him and his tattoos. With his every move, they glinted like precious stones where they caught the sunlight. Any change in direction could be an attempt to capture her again. He'd tried three times since she came to Carnas, and she'd quickly learned to add more distance than her master had advised.

Birds fluttered from his path into the sparse trees, their sharp squawks announcing their displeasure. The one time he'd looked over his shoulder was his only acknowledgment of her existence, but she knew better than to think he forgot about her presence. As he closed in on the woods, Irmina's vigilance increased. The man's strange bodyguard and two others had passed that way. Soon after, she'd heard the horn from the same direction.

Are they trying to save the boy or hunt the creature down? She frowned. Even she wouldn't want to confront the infected lapra within the forest's confines. Her brief peek into the creature's head revealed a mind as decayed as the rest of its body. The beast refused her attempt to command it to release the boy. Despite the day's warmth, a shiver ran through her.

When she saw the lapra spring from the woods, she'd been tempted to try save Kahkon in a more direct manner. She almost did, before she realized it would be a fatal mistake. The giant man would see the power she used. High Shin Jerem had been explicit in his orders. At no time should she reveal herself to the man. Not if she wished to live.

Another question nagged at Irmina. What was the boy doing near the woods anyway? She'd sent a warning to the mayor about the golden–haired woman and the lapra's presence. Why would they still allow the children—or anyone unprotected for that matter—to venture near the forest after those who already went missing? Her brow puckered. *Unless Kahkon didn't deliver my message. Maybe he forgot? No, he wouldn't. Maybe, he didn't understand?* But that didn't seem likely.

Two things surprised her since coming to Carnas in her guise as Mariel the Devout. The first was many of the Ostanian youth in the village spoke Granadian to some extent. The second was the giant man had taught them. Her stories about the gods mesmerized Kahkon, and he never missed a chance to visit her each day. She'd promised him more stories if he took her message directly to the mayor. He hadn't returned since.

She wondered if the reason for Kahkon's absence bore any relation to the odd way the villagers acted of late. When she first arrived, most paid proper reverence to her Devout title, although without the typical uniform, she had nothing but her insignia of the sun encased in a halo to show as proof of her stature. Over the last few weeks, their outlook changed. She noticed a peculiar, abrasive attitude from the village folk since they found the last few dead bodies in the kinai glades and their own people disappeared. Each day since, the number of visitors dwindled until only Kahkon frequented her campsites in secret. *Do they think I'm somehow responsible for the deaths or the missing villagers?*

At first, she thought it might be someone among them who knew she was not who she claimed to be. She'd entertained the notion someone had contacts within the Tribunal and informed the villagers she didn't represent the Tribunal's interests here in Ostania. She'd quickly dismissed the idea as ludicrous. High Shin Jerem assured her no one in Granadia would know of her presence here. One did not doubt the High Shin.

That left the recent murders and disappearances. Surely, they didn't think she killed those men or took the others. If so, why? Could the village folk believe a Devout capable of carrying out such crimes? The savagery of Granadian politics was a thing long dead, with nothing amounting to more than petty squabbles over the last three decades. That past was the very reason the Tribunal ruled and Devout were appointed. The Tribunal's rise and Streamean worship ensured all in Granadia walked the path of light. The idea of a Devout engaging in such heinous actions was so foreign to her as to be unfathomable. If they knew her true identity, she could've understood this train of thought. But her disguises had never failed on any mission.

All this brought her to the golden–haired woman in the woods. Irmina had only gained a glimpse of her twice, but several bodies were found in the same general vicinity soon after. She'd ruled out coincidence and sent a warning to the mayor. If only she could confirm its delivery.

Regardless, she would be even more careful. She needed to keep in mind these people were less civilized than she was accustomed. Who knew what other strange beliefs they entertained? If the giant and his bodyguard were a good guide, these Ostanians possessed capabilities she would be a fool to underestimate.

Irmina licked her lips at the salty taste of sweat as she picked her way through the brush and sparse trees. A light breeze blew, but offered little relief from the humid air. Ahead, the giant man continued his run toward the woods, his strides steady, the sun and the hot air appearing to have little to no effect.

"Find the man, the High Shin says. When you do, you must convince him of your need, he says. He must return with you to Granadia. Pwah. I should've known it wouldn't be so simple when you told me I could never allow him to see me use my abilities." Irmina ground her teeth.

As if this wasn't difficult enough, Jerem had assured her the time would come here in Ostania when she would face the hardest decision she would ever make in her life. He'd warned her whatever she chose would prove crucial in what path she took and would scar her for life. As if she didn't already bear enough scars. Every moment spent in this backward land made her regret taking on this mission. If not for Jerem's insistence that this was a required step in the completion of her training, she may have refused. For her, graduation meant another toehold toward vengeance.

The thought brought a shudder through her and sparked a memory of her as a child when she received the news of her family's murder—her mother, father, brothers and her sister lying face down in pools of blood. The despair and loneliness she felt before the Dorns adopted her arose fresh and raw. She brushed tears from her eyes as she remembered the blinding rage she burned with a year ago when she discovered the part the Dorns played in her family's demise.

Thinking of her lost family and the Dorns served to prompt her feelings for Ancel. He was part of the reason she'd cried then. For the love the Dorns had taken from her not once but three times. Despite her hatred for Ancel's parents, a longing for his touch, to see his emerald eyes, to see his carefree smile, eased through her. With any luck, he'd gotten over her by now. It wouldn't make what she needed to do much easier, but it might help.

She squeezed her eyes tight as she wished she could rewrite her last words and instead tell him how much she loved him. She wished she could have told him the truth of her mission. She wished she could've told him the truth about his parents.

Her last thought grated her insides. The people who raised her as their own, who she'd come to love and care for since she lost her family, had been revealed as frauds. Murderous frauds, who, to this day, clung to their plots. How many others knew what occurred? How many more were involved? She would weed them out one by one for as long as she lived. And let them feel the pain she endured.

Life and love are brutal teachers. Learn, adjust, and survive. Or die. Those are your choices. I choose life. She repeated Jerem's mantra to herself as she did every day since her discovery.

Irmina grasped at the slim sword in its sheath at her waist. Her hand shook with strain. The weapon was not what a priestess typically carried, and although not quite as effective as a regiment of guards, it served its purpose to deter most bandits. More than that, the sword was once her mother's weapon. Those foolish enough to ignore her blade because she was a woman soon learned their mistake. Remembering her training, she opened the cold place deep in her mind and shoved her emotions there until they dwindled. For this mission, she could afford no distractions.

Her master had given her so little information, and the villagers even less. None she interviewed gave up the names of either the giant or his bodyguard with the disconcerting silver eyes. Not even the children. Their faces became guarded every time she mentioned the two men.

When she first saw them, she hadn't given the giant's companion much thought. He appeared of no consequence. He had typical Ostanian swarthy skin and sandy hair, his height well over six feet. This was before she saw him move. He never appeared to touch the ground, his sinuous frame gliding like oil across a smooth surface. His eyes too, were odd, like silver flashes of frictionless mercury.

His master, the eight–foot giant with the tattoos, appeared to live up to her master's description as the more dangerous of the two. To some extent, she agreed. She'd observed them in their daily sparring sessions when the giant would win three fights for each one he lost. They fought with a grace and skill that would shame the best Weaponmasters in Eldanhill. Yet, for all the bigger man's skill, something about his guardian made her skin crawl.

Irmina found herself peering toward the tree line ahead as she thought about Silvereyes. As she did, she noticed the glint from the tattoos no longer bounced rhythmically.

The giant stood at the forest's edge staring at her.

Irmina ducked and slid behind a tree. If he entertained any thoughts to chase after her once again, she would make sure he realized she was not easy game.

CHAPTER 4

A ncel Dorn brushed his hand against his beige coat's
breast pocket. Despite knowing the words by heart,
the letter he kept there tempted him to take it out and read for
the thousandth time. He clenched his reins tighter in his fist. *Nine
hundred and ninety nine is good enough.*

His mare crested the hill lined on both sides by small
fields and the Greenleaf Forest that dominated this part of the
Whitewater Falls region. Miles to the right and north, beyond the
forest, the Kelvore Mountains stretched their broad shoulders
and snowcapped peaks. Straight ahead on the rutted road,
Eldanhill spread before him and Mirza Faber.

The town's white and yellow brick buildings glinted in
the early morning sunlight. Dominating the town's center, the
square clock tower of the Streamean temple jutted up at least ten
stories above the slate and tile roofs of the other sandstone and
granite structures. Townsfolk bustled down the wide, yet already
crowded, Eldan Road, appearing more like small colorful insects
than people.

The distant buzz of a thousand conversations, clopping
hooves, trundling wagon and dray wheels, and hundreds of daily
activities played a familiar rhythm. Among them rang the clang
of smithies and stonemasons, the whir and rattle of the many
windmills along the Kelvore River, the receding roar from the
Whitewater Falls to the northeast, and the bird song and chatter
of small animals within the Greenleaf.

The clamor and his surroundings brought a soothing
sensation along Ancel's shoulder and neck. An unusually chill

wind that smelled of rain streamed his cloak out behind him. Ancel shivered and glanced to Mirza who rode the chestnut stallion thudding a slow rhythm a few feet away.

Mirza tilted to one side, grabbing at the pages of the book he'd been reading as the wind whipped at the pages. He snatched for his reins and pommel, barely managing to prevent himself from falling. Ancel chuckled.

"That wasn't funny," Mirza said as he righted himself. His skinny legs, in the narrow pants he favored, squeezed against the stallion's side. The fitted coat he wore matched Ancel's own except for the book and pen insignia stitched to the lapel. Ancel's emblem was a silver sword.

"Not funny to you," Ancel replied. "But if you sat where I am and saw your arms and legs fly all over you'd be laughing too."

Mirza passed a hand through his rust–colored hair. "I guess I would." He smiled.

"You know, if you studied at night you wouldn't need to cram the next day."

"I did study," Mirza protested. "But I'm not like you. I need to refresh the morning of a test so I don't forget anything."

Ancel shrugged. "The test will be simple enough."

"Easy for you to say," Mirza grumbled. "You've taken it already."

"It was simple then too."

"Well, if it's so easy, how about helping? Ask me a few questions." Mirza leaned over to hand him the book.

Ancel shooed him off. "I don't need it. Just tell me what you want me to ask."

Mirza straightened his back. He rubbed a thumb on the reddish stubble growing from his chin. "How about the gods? And Mater?"

Seeing Mirza touch his beard made Ancel's own prickly growth itch. "You know, that's a pretty broad area." Ancel scratched at the offending sprigs of hair under his chin. "Here, I'll try to be specific and start with something easy."

Mirza nodded, hands fidgeting on the pommel of his saddle.

A few moments passed. Ancel said nothing. He stared off to the east where he could make out the rust colored Red

Ridge Mountains beyond where the land dipped toward the Kelvore River.

Frowning, Mirza eyed him. "Well?"

"Well, close that," Ancel said, his head gesturing to the still open book in his friend's hand.

"Oh!" Mirza flipped the book shut.

"Uh, huh." Ancel gave his friend a wry look. "You just happened to have the chapter on religion open."

Mirza glowered at him. "Ask your questions already."

"Name the gods and their titles." Ancel's lips twitched ever so slightly.

Eyes widening, Mirza stammered, "A–All their titles, and all the gods?"

"Fine. Name the major gods and the elements of Mater they represent."

"That's easy." Mirza beamed.

"Really?" Ancel lifted his brow.

Mirza's smile changed to a scowl. "Ilumni, Amuni, Bragni and Rituni, the gods of Streams. Humelen, Liganen and Kinzanen, the gods of Forms. Hyzenki and Aeoli, the gods of Flows. There."

"Good, but not quite right" Ancel said, feeling a little sorry for his earlier sarcasm.

"What? They're all correct."

"Aeoli's a goddess," Ancel said with a bemused smirk.

Mirza groaned.

"Here, I'll ask you the first question you will see on the test, but you need to answer exactly as Teacher Calestis wrote or else she'll mark it wrong."

Intense concentration creased Mirza's brows.

"What's Mater?"

Mirza squinted and stroked his stubble with his thumb. After a few more moments, he said, "Mater is the core elemental power which exists within everything. It makes up the three elements the gods represent and their individual essences." He looked over for Ancel's approval.

"Go on," Ancel encouraged.

"Mater is more than just the elements driving our world. It drives all worlds," Mirza said with an air of finality. His face lit up.

Ancel smiled. That last bit was Teacher Calestis's favorite saying. "Excellent. What's the most important thing to practice and master before learning how to touch your Matersense?"

"Control. Emotional and physical."

"Perfect. Now—"

"Ancel," Mirza said, his smooth voice becoming serious. "Why're you back in the same class as me?"

Ancel absently brushed his breast pocket. "I told you. I failed the end of term test. They decided I needed to take religion and principles again."

"They're saying you failed it on purpose."

Ancel's eyes became slits. "Who?"

"The other students," Mirza said before he quickly averted his gray eyes. "They're saying you failed on purpose. Just so you could be in the same class where Irmina used to come meet you."

Ancel clenched his jaw, against both Mirza's words and the image of Irmina's golden brown eyes, her raven black hair, and her lithe form and shrugged. "They can say what they want. I failed. It's as simple as that. And what did I tell you about saying her name?"

"I, I'm sorry." Mirza scrunched up his face and shook his head. "I mean, no, I'm not."

Ancel glared at his friend. His hands tightened on his reins.

"Listen," Mirza pleaded. "You're my best friend. If I don't tell you, then who will? You've always been the smartest of us all. You'd have to be, to become the youngest trainee since… well ever. But after she left, you stopped caring. I hate watching you throw everything away."

"You don't know shit," Ancel spat.

"Burning shades, Ancel. I watch you every day. You practice the sword for the women. You bed as many as you can, and you daydream through class. That's not who you are. It's about time you moved on. She did. A year you said, remember? But you still pine over her. Now you risk failing classes again. All the things we dreamed about when we were young, playing at becoming Knights, of going off to join the legions, maybe one day crossing the Vallum of Light to help defend Granadia. It's all there for you. Why—"

"Just shut it," Ancel said his voice like ice. Another chill wind kicked up. This time he didn't shiver.

A sudden multitude of colors like miniature rainbows swirled through Ancel's vision as he stared toward Eldanhill. The hues appeared to jump across people and animals. They even stood out on the flock of birds in the near cloudless sky. He closed his eyes and rubbed his thumb and forefinger across his lids. When he opened his eyes, the colors were gone.

Ancel glanced toward Mirza, but his friend showed no reaction to what he'd seen. Instead, Mirza drew his cloak around himself, and his eyes focused on the rutted road ahead. Mirza ground his teeth, obviously still upset.

A soft coo made Ancel look toward the field to his right. Charra, his daggerpaw, loped through the short grass and shrubs. He stood as big as a bull, his head reaching almost to the withers of Ancel's mare. His shaggy, whitish fur was stained brown with whatever mischief he'd gotten himself into. Charra shook his broad muzzle, sending slobber flying into the air. The soft bone hackles, which extended around his neck and down his back in a bushy mane, swished.

"Where've you been, boy?" Ancel shouted, his mood a little lighter at seeing his pet.

Charra's golden–eyed gaze swept to Ancel as he responded with a growl, crossed to the field on the other side road, and trotted a few feet ahead of their horses. Ancel shook his head. There was no accounting for Charra's moods.

Ancel returned to studying Mirza who still rode in silence. *If only you knew how right you are.* Ancel took a deep breath. Try as he might, he couldn't think without Irmina crossing his thoughts. His hand found its way to his coat pocket again.

"She wrote me the day she left, you know," Ancel said, his voice low.

Mirza looked at him from the corner of his eyes. "You mean the letter you read every day?"

Ancel cocked an eyebrow. "When'd you notice?"

"Hard not to," Mirza replied with a shake of his head. "We're only together every day. When you aren't touching that pocket of yours, you're lost in thought. Then sometimes when you think no one's watching, you pull the letter out and start reading."

"Why didn't you ask?"

Mirza gave him a rueful smile. "You promised to run me through if I ever mentioned her name."

"I'm surprised you listened for so long."

"You've never seen your own face when someone mentions the woman."

Ahead, Charra stopped to stare into the Greenleaf Forest. Ancel peered toward the tree line, but saw nothing. He dismissed it as part of Charra's recent habit of growling at shadows when he was in a foul mood.

"So what's in the letter?" Mirza asked.

"Not much. We'd spent the night together. When I woke, she was gone, and the letter was next to my pillow," Ancel answered absently, his gaze fixed on his daggerpaw. "The letter said she had to leave. That there was another." Ancel's chest throbbed with an almost physical pain. "She said she may never return to Eldanhill. That one day when I completed my studies and passed the trials, I'd understand. She just left me, as if I never mattered."

An uncomfortable silence followed. Somewhere among the trees, a bird began a mournful lament.

"Life and love are brutal teachers. Learn, adjust, and survive. Or die. Those are your choices. I choose life," Ancel said. He shrugged at Mirza's frown for his sudden statement. "Those were the words she repeated several times before she left. I think I'm now beginning to understand."

Ancel reached for the letter. At the same time, Charra growled, low and hard. His bone hackles rose into a ridge of hardened spikes, their edges sharp as a newly forged dagger, the ones about his neck almost a foot long before growing less dense and shorter as they tapered off near his tail. Ancel's gaze flitted from Charra to the woods. Brambles and bindweed snarled through the undergrowth and across stone outcrops beneath the trees. Red cedar and oak thrived. Except for the occasional sunlit patch, their canopies kept the forest in deep shadow.

"What's gotten into him now?" Mirza nodded to Charra.

"I don't know. He's been moodier than usual the last few days, growling at shadows and the like. But this…" Ancel stopped his mare. The horse pranced, and he rubbed its neck until it calmed. This had to be more than just Charra's mood.

"I've only seen him like this when we're hunting wolves." Mirza brought his mount next to Ancel's.

"Wolves wouldn't come this close to town," Ancel said.

Charra raised a shaggy foot and took one tentative step forward. He growled again, louder this time. The sound vibrated through Ancel. The horses' eyes rolled, and the animals whickered.

Stomach aflutter as he peered into the woods, Ancel frowned.

"Listen," Mirza said, his voice almost breathless.

Ancel did. His brow knitted tighter.

No birds sang. No animals chattered. The only sounds reaching them came from Eldanhill.

The wind rose again, a little stronger than before. A faint smell from some animal, long dead, reached them. This time Ancel found himself rubbing his arms from the chill.

Did a shadow just pass through that patch of sun? Ancel squinted at the spot within the woods, but he saw no other movement.

"Did you see that?" Mirza whispered, his question confirming what Ancel thought he saw.

Ancel nodded.

The breeze passed, and the air stilled. The silence remained for another moment before birdsong rose and other sounds from the woods resumed.

Charra whined, bone hackles softening and receding until they once again lay flat against his fur. He turned and loped toward Eldanhill.

Ancel and Mirza sat there for a moment more, their gazes still riveted on the dappled shadows.

Mirza broke their silence. "What do you think it was?"

"I don't know. But I wouldn't worry about it now." Ancel nodded toward Charra who continued toward Eldanhill. "He isn't."

"I guess." Mirza flapped his reins and started his stallion down the road.

Ancel followed, troubled by Charra's reaction and Mirza's earlier words about Irmina. As much as he wanted to return to his old self, he was not sure he could. *It's not like I asked to feel this way about her. It just happened. Somehow, I'll work this out. I think.*

Charra, on the other hand, was another issue. With his erratic behavior increasing, Ancel hoped his father wouldn't listen to the townsfolk and ask him to leave the daggerpaw at the winery. Not being able to bring him to school was one thing. To do without him in Eldanhill altogether was another entirely. Given a choice, he would rather not come to town at all if it meant leaving his daggerpaw behind.

Of course, not going to Eldanhill presented another set of problems. His need for female companionship would suffer. The thought made him remember today's rendezvous.

"By the way," Ancel said, "I'm supposed to meet with Alys after school."

Mirza looked over his shoulder. "Is this your way of telling me you're shirking your duties again? We're supposed to be gathering kinai for Soltide and your father's winery later."

"I know," Ancel said. "But in case I lose track of time, I wanted you to know where to find me."

"Which means I *will* have to come find you."

Ancel snorted. "If that's what you think, then—"

"Here's what," Mirza interrupted. "I'll do it if you're willing to make a wager."

"If you want to lose more coin to me," Ancel shrugged, "Who am I to argue? So what's the bet?"

"Simple. I bet you'll think more with your cock than with your head. I know you won't be able to hold back. Not with Alys. So if I have to come get you, it'll cost you a gold hawk. If you manage on your own, I owe you two."

Ancel grinned. "There's no way I'll lose."

"We'll see."

They continued on their way to their classes at Eldanhill's Mystera.

CHAPTER 5

Ryne sprinted through the woods, tingles running through his body in tiny bursts.

Did Mariel have anything to do with the lapra's attack as Forian suggested? He wasn't sure, but if so, he needed to keep her at bay. He couldn't afford to take an unnecessary risk while trying to save Kahkon. When Sakari located the beast's lair, the last thing they needed would be her interference.

As he thought about the woman, his bloodlust boiled through his insides once more. The feeling conjured up images he knew too well over the years since he woke. Him, as he slammed the banner displaying the sun with a lightning storm striking in front of it into the ground. Towns and villages razed. The dead stacked in mounds. His Scripts as they roiled about his body more akin to living things than detailed tattoos when they drew on the elements of Mater. How that power had driven him to kill repeatedly to feed its hunger.

"Our power is yours to use," the vibrant voice edged with darkness urged. *"Take it. Abuse it as you will. Revel in the victory our power can bring you."*

No. Ryne slammed his mind shut against the voice. *I cannot afford to lose control now. Not when Carnas's people may be in danger. Not when Kahkon's life depends on me.* Concentrating, Ryne held the urge to kill at bay the way he'd practiced the last twenty years. He forced back the murderous intent by sheer will. A deep breath escaped his lips. *Why has my control waned? Why now after all these years?*

Ryne cast a glance behind him. Mariel's form disappeared

among the trees. He knew the pattern well by now. If he stopped to pursue her, she would continue to hide, moving more like an Alzari assassin than one of the high priestesses of Ilumni she claimed to be. Why would a Devout venture this far into Ostania? The thought was just one of many troubling him about the woman. He couldn't remember ever seeing one with such high rank as she without their silver uniform or their full retinue of guards. He considered hiding himself, but at eight feet tall, conventional methods of concealment presented dilemmas. In this case, drawing on the essences within the elements of Mater to mask his presence wasn't an option.

He took another quick look behind. He'd opened up more distance, but she still followed, as dogged as a hound. Again, he resisted the nagging temptation to go after her. But he couldn't let her just roam free could he? Not with Kahkon's safety at stake. Choice and consequence continued to pry at him.

He made up his mind.

"You wish for me to join you to chase her down?" Sakari's smooth voice broke in, the words more a suggestion than a question.

Ryne's forehead wrinkled. *When did I link with him.* "No. I only intend to lead her away," he answered in a level voice. He used the link with Sakari to gaze through the man's eyes. Sakari, accompanied by four hunters, worked their way through the forest several miles east of Ryne's location. "Continue to follow the tracks until they lead you to the beast's lair and Kahkon."

"If you hold back, you will not capture her," Sakari responded, as if he heard nothing Ryne said.

"I said I have no intention of chasing her right now. Besides, if I don't hold back, I'd have to kill her." Ryne's mouth curled with distaste at the thought. He shook his head.

"Not if you allow me to help."

Ryne's forehead wrinkled at the sudden urge to ask for his companion's assistance. Could he trust himself with his earlier loss of control? He hardened his tone, "No, you stay with the others. Find the boy. I promised his mother. He mustn't end up the same as those corpses we found, and we can't allow him to disappear like the others. I'll do what I can about Mariel." Not wishing to second–guess his decision, he broke the link before Sakari could reply.

When he swept his gaze behind him once more, Mariel was a mere speck. At that moment, the hunter's horn sounded in a long, undulating bray to announce the others had located their quarry. Swearing, Ryne chased Mariel from his thoughts and dashed off toward the sound.

As Ryne drew near, the ever–present lump in the back of his mind that told of Sakari's presence grew in size. Feet flew by like inches and miles fled like yards as he followed his connection to Sakari along a path the hunters had hewn through dense undergrowth. The smells from fruits and orchid blooms and the twitter of birds hurtled by with each stride. One with the woods, Ryne avoided any branches and vines the men had missed. Within minutes, he reached the horn's origin.

An abrupt silence greeted him.

Lenka, gray–haired and wiry, stood with horn in hand behind a large mahogany tree. Its thick branches drooped from the weight of its leaves and the lantum vines snaking among them. The canopy in this part of the Fretian Woods grew in a tighter knit than elsewhere. If one didn't know the time of day, the murky light could easily be mistaken for dusk instead of late afternoon.

Sakari and the other four hunters, all in scaled leather armor with short swords at their hips, melded with the tree trunks within the area until all were one and the same. Not a sound or motion gave away their positions.

A familiar smell akin to spoiled meat assaulted Ryne's nostrils. He stared in the direction of the scent and Lenka's crooked arm and forefinger. The stand of trees the man pointed out was darker still, deep night to the rest of the area's dusk. Ryne watched and waited as Lenka joined the other five men.

From deep within the knits of vine and sapling leaves, a guttural sound reverberated similar to a man's death rattle as he choked on his own blood. *Except no man makes that sound.*

Branches snapped and heavy footfalls thudded as if whatever approached walked on stone instead of the leafy rug that covered the forest floor. Ryne kept his gaze trained, his body tense, and his hand hovering over his sword hilt. The earlier tingle returned, but this time it built into the familiar thrill of his battle energy.

Where the other six men hid appeared as nothing more

than shadowed trunks and foliage. The footfalls grew closer until they became thunder in the silent forest. Each step played a rhythmic beat to match Ryne's own heart.

The sound silenced. Not just the noise from the footfalls, but all nearby sounds. Leaves rained to the ground as branches whipped back and forth among the saplings directly across from Ryne. The black greenery parted.

Snarls and grunts ensued. Two golden embers for eyes appeared. A wide muzzle and a head bigger than a massive bull followed.

Once again, Ryne observed the unusual amounts of shade that clung to the lapra's aura. *Could it just be the rot?*

The lapra stopped before its body became exposed. Shrouded in the darkness, Ryne didn't need to see the grotesque red and black flesh dripping with decaying meat. From the near suffocating stench that clawed at him, he could picture the beast.

Another face, this one human, appeared not far from the lapra's. The man's aura, also tinted by more shade than normal, wavered in patterns Ryne recognized but couldn't quite place. Paint covered the man's face, blending with the leaves and shadow.

Ryne's breath quickened. *An Alzari mercenary? Here? Did Mariel already inform the Tribunal of my presence? Have they hired these assassins to hunt me down again?*

A cry rang out in Kahkon's unmistakable high pitch before Ryne could think of answers. Immediately, the lapra's head and the Alzari's face retreated among the trees. Sakari gave the signal and the hunters moved, all sprinting toward the stand.

From the corner of his eye, Ryne caught a flash of long golden hair and an unfamiliar feminine form just as it fled behind a trunk. An aura with a peculiar mix of light, shade, and earth essences emanated from the stranger. *Who is that?*

Heart thudding in his chest, his battle energy crawling across his skin in static charges, Ryne brought his hand down to his greatsword's hilt and eased from his hiding place. But there was no sign of the stranger or her golden tresses. Her aura had also vanished.

Crashes and shouts abounded as the hunters from Carnas engaged the lapra and its master. The creature's roars joined the men's voices. A yell cut off with an abrupt cry. Howls changed to snarling whines. The lapra's thunderous rumbles continued to echo.

Ryne raced to his friends, his brow drawn together in a lumpy frown. How could an aura he identified disappear as if it never existed?

The lapra's roars continued, occasionally interrupted by a whine or a snarl. The clang of metal meeting metal also rose.

Ryne passed through the shadowy trees into an unexpected sight. Carnas' five hunters had the grotesque ten—foot beast surrounded. From varied directions, they thrust, sliced, and feinted. Multiple wounds littered the lapra's moldy fur. Its head dipped from side to side as it attempted to defend all attack points. Skin sloughed in places, and its blood dripped viscous and black.

But that was not what surprised Ryne. The shock was in seeing Sakari battle not one but two dual—dagger wielding Alzari.

Clad in dark leather matching the color of the forest, their faces covered in war paint, they circled Sakari. As one, the assassins attacked him from opposite flanks, darting in faster than any other of their clan Ryne had ever faced.

The three men twisted and turned. Their steps synchronized as if they danced to a tune only they could hear.

Sakari was ever on the defensive, dodging and parrying stroke after stroke. His face remained impassive even when the Alzari's black blades scoured his armor and licked at his flesh. Bright red trickles decorated his armor from his many cuts.

With a snarl, Ryne joined the fray, his battle energy surging to a torrent.

The closest Alzari twisted away to meet Ryne's attack. Silversteel swished through empty air where the assassin once stood.

Unlike his partner, Ryne's opponent dodged his strikes instead of making any attempt to parry. Ryne attacked with the basics as he tested the man's defenses. The Alzari ducked, dodged, leaped, and spun, his movements an elusive glide.

Sweat marred the assassin's painted face. His eyes narrowed as Ryne's attack paused. In that lull, the Alzari struck.

His daggers spun in his palms. A complicated pattern of slices followed. The attack flew up, down, left, right, into circular motions then to feints and lunges.

Ryne recognized the Style at once—Amuni's Hand, the God's Way—but the assassin's speed was so surprising he couldn't dodge every strike as the leafy carpet under his feet caused him to move slower than he would have preferred. Nor could he raise his greatsword in time to parry despite its feathery weight. His armor parted with a soft hiss at the shoulder and chest followed by his own pained grunt. A burning sensation followed as did a trickle of warm blood. Ryne frowned. No normal steel could cut through his leathers. The Alzari's weapons were imbued. *Where could these men have found divya?*

Ryne's Scripts roiled across his body and armor. The voices surged into his head. They begged him to release his bloodlust, but he gritted his teeth against the feeling.

With Ryne's recognition of the Styles came understanding. He considered each Stance the man would use before attacking with a Style. After parrying a few blows, Ryne adjusted to compensate for speed, a smile playing across his face. The Alzari's brow puckered in concentration as he continued his onslaught.

Ryne faced Earthtouch—the Alzari shifting his feet, daggers pointed down, then bending slightly forward to dig deeper and connect with the Forms of the earth—with Voidwalk. In the Stance, Ryne became many times lighter, like a wisp upon the wind. Not even the dry leaves below him showed any effect from his great size. Ryne waited, relying on his Stance's weightless air essences to counter whatever Styles the Alzari attempted when he attacked with the strength of earth essences behind his blows.

As if part of the rock and soil, the assassin sank knee deep into the earth and flew forward, leaves and dirt spurting into the air with the path he made. His blades sliced at Ryne's lower extremities before they rose up, and the man soared from the hole he'd created. Ryne sprung backward in a massive leap, floating on currents of air to avoid the strikes. Face drowned in sweat, the assassin's feet touched the ground, feather soft, before he rushed forward, his breathing labored as he strived to reach Ryne.

A sense of calm passed over Ryne. He already knew the man's next attack. Almost every enemy he ever faced overestimated his size and strength and underestimated his speed and agility. This assassin was no different.

As the Alzari swept forward and up, his blades stabbing one above the other in a Style called Climbing the Mountain, Ryne leaned back into Bending with the Wind—his body folding back on itself with effortless grace until the back of his head almost touched his thighs. Ryne kept his sword held out from his chest as his body curved away, the assassin's daggers striking nothing but air where Ryne's stomach had been. In the same motion, Ryne pulled himself straight, knocked the blades to one side, drew his hand back, and stabbed.

He used the momentum from his lean to whip forward with Lightstrike—a direct lunge.

The Alzari managed a grunt when Ryne's greatsword tore through leather, cloth, flesh and scraped past bone as it exploded from the assassin's back with a shower of blood and viscera.

Ryne drew his sword back and flicked it to one side to rid it of the blood. He spun, ready to help Sakari, but the fighting was already over.

A few feet away lay the other Alzari, his daggers still gripped in his lifeless hands. His only wounds were two precise slices, one across his stomach and the other across his neck. Blood pooled below his body, leaving the grass and fallen leaves slick.

Several cuts in Sakari's armor revealed his tan skin. He gave Ryne a reassuring nod.

Sightless eyes staring into the sky, the dead lapra lay between the hunters. Deep rents marred its fur in several places, and even dead, the monstrous body, black with blood, appeared too big for the beast's six skinny legs. Putrid fluid leaked, the stench overpowering the smell from the rotten flesh.

Denton, the youngest of the five hunters who had left from Carnas, nursed claw wounds to his chests and arms. His torso heaved and his pale cheeks labored with each ragged breath. Lenka limped severely, his armor ripped from waist to knee. Torn muscle exposed white bone through the holes where blood trailed down and painted his leather red. The other hunters bore no injuries.

"Since when could Alzari tame these things?" Dren nodded toward the giant lapra's corpse.

"Since when the beasts be leaving the Rot be a better question," Keevo added. The grizzle–faced man kicked at the lapra's mutilated leg.

Dren's square jaw tightened as he regarded the Alzari assassin then Ryne. He nodded toward the corpse. "I thought the Tribunal had given up on you."

"So did I." Ryne shrugged. His chest and arm throbbed.

Dren continued, "Now, we find two Alzari mercenaries here. With the bodies we've found the last few weeks, this makes for a strange coincidence. But I guess now we know who killed those men in the kinai orchards."

"Alzari weren't responsible for those deaths," Ryne said.

"Really?" Dren bent to take a closer look at the Alzari's corpse. "How're you so sure?" He poked at the war paint on the assassin's face before he straightened.

"They always leave a ritual dagger as proof of their work. Plus, no weapon of theirs could have made the wounds on those men." Ryne's gaze shifted to the infected lapra. He stroked the scars on his face as he eyed the elongated claws and teeth. No lapra could leave the gashes on those bodies either. He decided to keep that to himself.

"Do you really believe this beast could've killed them?" Keevo's scarred face puckered with doubt. "It was so infected with rot, it moved like mud. Amuni's balls, the tamer ones on the plains could have taken this." He spat at the remains.

"If the Alzari accompanied it, then maybe," Ryne said. "Alone, I'm not sure. But who knows what can happen when you underestimate what you face." He cast a sidelong glance toward the wounded men.

"Malka." Ryne gestured toward the man.

Malka turned to regard Ryne. His nose and eyes peeked out from the brown bush that covered his face.

"Gather some kinai and help Sakari tend to the others." Ryne nodded to the sweet, red fruit growing in thick clusters within the stand. "Keevo and Dren, check for signs of the boy. Shout if you see a woman with golden hair or that so called Devout, Mariel." The men nodded and hurried off to do as he bid.

As Ryne surveyed the clearing, he removed the paste the sisters had given him and applied some to his wounds. The mixture had a sweet smell, but it stung enough to make him wince. Droppings from the lapra indicated the creature had used this particular area for some time. Bits of bone and carrion from the beast's previous feasts littered the ground. Besides their footprints and the Alzari's, there were no other human tracks. Ryne's brow furrowed. *If the creature dragged Kahkon here, why not kill the boy once it reached its lair? For* that *matter, why didn't the assassins finish the job?* He still pondered the question when Keevo and Dren returned.

"There be a blood trail and the animal's tracks from the direction you came." Keevo pointed south to an area with disturbed undergrowth. He shook his head, clearly baffled. "Why not return to the Rot or go farther north toward Alzari territory?"

"I think something worse must have forced the lapra out here. The assassins were trying to fight back." Ryne lifted his chin toward broken branches and brush dragged across the stand's easternmost side. "There's wards carved into those tree trunks to hide a path there. I've only ever seen those symbols used by the Alzari clans when protecting their territory. Whatever it was, they didn't want it to follow, and the lapra was too afraid to return to its home."

"Burning shades," Keevo hissed. "Do you think it could be Amuni's Children—"

"No," Ryne snapped. "Things are worrisome enough without you dredging them up. There's enough fear in Carnas already. Besides, none of the wards I placed in the Rotted Forest have been disturbed. Even the Children aren't strong enough to bypass those."

"If not them, then what else?" Keevo's face relaxed visibly, but he still glanced out toward the blockage to the east.

"I don't know yet, but it's best not to start any rumors. Extra scouts will need to be posted when we return," Ryne said.

Footsteps behind them announced Sakari's arrival with the other men in tow. The wounded hunters both chewed on kinai. Paste from the fruit dyed their bandages a brighter red, but the mixture appeared to be doing its work. Denton no longer gasped, although he did wince with each breath, and his color appeared close to its normal tan. Lenka, his leg now wrapped in bandages, moved with a less pronounced limp. For Ryne, his cuts had subsided to a dull ache.

"What about this person with golden hair?" Dren asked.

"None of you saw her?" Ryne asked in disbelief.

The hunters gave him blank looks.

"I did," Sakari said. He tilted his head to the hunters. His green pupils expanded ever so slightly while the silver flecks crowding his eyeballs flickered.

The men looked away from Sakari's stare. Ryne wasn't surprised by his companion's answer, but the villagers' response troubled him. They were all experienced hunters. It would take a person with considerable skill to avoid detection from every one of them.

"Master Waldron, no offense, but you sure it wasn't Mariel again? Maybe the light in the woods played tricks with her hair." Lenka peered out into the woods.

"Or maybe an Alzari woman?" Dren added.

"No," Ryne said, "this person is taller than Mariel with a more muscled build. And an Alzari with golden hair? Listen, you five head home. Lenka and especially Denton need to be seen by the menders. Me and Sakari will find Kahkon."

The men protested, but Ryne shushed them with a wave. They gave in with curt nods.

After a few moments of preparation, they parted ways. Malka and Dren assisted the two wounded while Keevo scouted ahead. Ryne watched the men leave before he and Sakari headed south to follow Kahkon's bloody trail.

"Why not send one of them to help Lenka and Denton and have the other two come with us?"

"Whoever was in the forest," Ryne said, "She managed to elude their tracking ability. And she escaped me even after I read her aura. In the seventy years since I've woken, that's never happened. One moment she was there, and the next she didn't exist. My ability to see auras is unique among my people, how could someone—." Ryne's mouth dropped open at his last sentence.

Never before had I thought of any skill in reference to my people. Who are my people?

"Has a memory surfaced?" Sakari cocked his head sideways.

Ryne attempted to connect his words with an image of his people, but as usual his efforts were met by a thick fog.

He pushed deep into the white mist clouding his mind until he encountered a red wall. There, he stopped. He wanted to will himself to go further, but his brief trips past the wall rose fresh in his mind. The excruciating pain and dread he experienced when he became lost within its glare became palpable. The faces of slaughtered innocents and him poised over them with his sword in hand swirled about him. Sakari's touch had rescued him from insanity back then. He couldn't afford such again, not now, maybe not ever. Ryne withdrew, his eyes focusing on Sakari.

"Well?"

"No, there were no memories, just a stray thought," Ryne answered. "As for the stranger I saw, Keevo and the others would be no help if she proves to be an enemy."

"Sometimes a distraction is needed to complete a task."

Ryne scowled. "I won't put them at any more risk than I already have. A person who can avoid my power? That's unheard of. We need to move with care. My presence has already cost Carnas and its people too much. They're as much a part of me as you are. I will not see them harmed."

Sakari's head dipped briefly. "As you wish."

They continued their search in silence with Sakari gliding ahead. Occasionally, they discovered torn strips of cloth left along the wayside as the tracks changed course.

Ryne resisted the temptation to open his senses and gain a better awareness of what lay ahead. Luring another lapra or worse would only serve to hinder the boy's chances at survival. *Dear Ilumni, I beg of you, keep the boy safe.* Dizziness swept through Ryne. His jaw grinding with the effort, he fought the feeling off and concentrated on their search.

Almost a mile farther, they found Kahkon. The boy lay curled between two large tree roots. His right leg was a jagged stump and his shirt no more than tattered cloth covered in dry blood. Hair that should have been a healthy dark color now contained several white streaks.

Ryne rushed to the boy's side, resisting the urge to cry out. He removed the pouch of kinai paste and passed it to Sakari. "Here, the sisters had Taeria prepare this before I left Carnas. It should be potent enough to help."

Sakari took the pouch and inspected the contents as Ryne bent and eased Kahkon over onto his back. Ryne sucked in a gasp at what he saw. A gash ran down the left side of Kahkon's chest all the way to his stomach. How the boy had lived, much less dragged himself this far was beyond Ryne. Rage and grief warred within Ryne at the sight.

Kahkon's chest heaved, each breath a gurgle, and his brown skin was a pale shadow of itself. His eyes snapped open and stared sightlessly before they focused for a moment then widened with terror.

"Ma...Master W...Waldron h–help me," Kahkon said in a hoarse whisper. "Sh–shade"

The boy's words, combined with the itch that often nagged at his mind whenever someone watched him, brought uneasiness creeping down Ryne's back. A decayed odor wafted through the air as he took in his surroundings. It was the same stench as at Miss Corten's but multiplied tenfold. His gaze immediately picked out an aura of shade among a nearby copse. It took him a moment to realize the aura emanated from the trees themselves. The branches and leaves were as black as a moonless night.

"Take care of him," Ryne ordered Sakari as he lay Kahkon's head down and stood.

Ryne eased his way through the undergrowth, his hand on his sword. The brush ended well short of the copse of rosewood and teak. Tangled vines, roots, leaves, and creepers spread across the forest floor in an advanced state of decomposition. He squelched through the decay, the brown of his boots becoming black.

Careful not to touch the trunks, he slipped through an open space between the trees. The putrid smell of decay and moldy fur as if he stood inside a mismanaged dog kennel grew to choking proportions. As he entered, a lapra howled from Sakari's direction. Ryne turned to go back when the sight of what lay in the middle of the area caught his eye. His hands coiled into fists.

The eight missing villagers, their bodies black and purple, lay among festering roots and rotten kinai fruit. Fleshy tendrils connected them all together in a mass that vibrated with a beating heart's rhythm. The men and women's chests rose and fell slowly.

Beside them were four beasts joined in the same fashion.

The creatures appeared to have been lapras at one time, but their snouts were now more elongated like a wolf's. Their mouths lolled, revealing rows of sharp teeth. The middle legs were almost fully withdrawn into their torsos. They were each at least seven feet in length. Muscles rippled beneath ebony skin and fur.

Memories of similar creatures before and during the War of Remnants surfaced within Ryne. *Wraithwolves?* He frowned even as the thought brought a chill crawling along his back. *Is someone or something attempting to create the beasts? But that's supposed to be impossible in this realm. They must be what's left of the host from the war. If so, how did they cross the Rotted Forest without triggering my wards?*

Ryne sucked in a breath at the auras around the shadelings. They were the same as the one he saw around the Alzari. He remembered where he saw them before.

Amuni's Children.

The realization led to several conclusions. These particular Alzari must have given themselves to the shade. They had to be protecting these shadelings for Amuni's Children not fleeing as he first thought. Which meant the Children had indeed breached his wards, crossed the Rot from the lands beyond, and were somewhere within Ostania.

Ryne drew his sword.

"Use our power," hissed the deep voice. *"It's the only way to be sure."*

The other, opposing sentience remained silent.

Ryne's Scripts thrummed to life, and Mater surged through him. His bloodlust triggered, and he didn't subdue the feeling.

CHAPTER 6

Irmina hunkered down among the branches and leaves, staring slack–jawed. Below her, the fight between the giant's bodyguard and the lapras raged. These particular ones were normal in size, only about three feet across. They'd attacked as soon as the giant disappeared among the strange black trees.

Silvereyes danced among the lapras, always keeping himself between the closest one and Kahkon. The man's movements were a blur of inhuman speed.

At first, the creatures had tried to dart in and snatch at the boys legs, but once they realized those efforts were futile, they resorted to attacking the Ostanian. Jaws dripping, lapras snapped and snarled as they pounced, their dark fur made darker by the waning light. Each one that sprang in fell to the ground. Wounded animals struggled to their feet to limp back among the trees. Yet, the creatures continued to pour from the forest's dark recesses.

The bodyguard moved like a snake, his arm flickering as if he and his sword were one. Not once did he harm any beast more than to maim it with a precise slice to render it harmless. Numerous wounds scoured his armor from slashing claws and snapping teeth, tallying up with the other older scratches and nicks to leave his leathers a bloody mess. But not one lapra passed him. If she was not seeing it with her own eyes, Irmina wouldn't have believed one person could hold off this many beasts.

With the back of her hand, Irmina flicked the salty sting

of sweat from her eyes. Frowning, she stared from the wetness on her hand to Silvereyes. Where she was covered in perspiration from the day's heat, no such sheen reflected from his face. The man didn't appear fatigued, much less bothered by his injuries. Who or better yet, what was he?

Irmina winced each time his sword met flesh and at the yelps and plaintive cries that followed. She hadn't meant for this to happen. When she tamed the leader of one of the lapra packs, she'd only intended on keeping the giant man off her. Somehow, the animal had broken from her control while calling to other packs and everything went terribly wrong. She'd tried in vain to touch the beast's mind again, but it was as if a dark cloud hung within the creature's head, preventing her from making any connection. Her efforts were met with the same intense resistance as when she attempted to force the infected lapra off Kahkon.

The only other time she failed to tame a beast was when she attempted to control Charra. The daggerpaw's mind was a vise she couldn't touch much less pry open. Thinking about Charra made thoughts of Ancel bloom fresh in her mind. She suppressed the memories and the longing they brought and focused on the events below.

Gradually, the beasts' attacks lessened until they stalked around the boy and Silvereyes in a wide circle. The bodyguard's armor, dark with his and lapra blood, hung in tatters in some places, but he still appeared unaffected by his wounds. Not even his chest rose and fell with the heavy breaths of exertion. He cocked his head to one side as if listening.

Hair rose at the back of Irmina's neck, her shoulders tensed, and a prickle eased up her spine.

Silvereyes whirled to face the copse of trees into which the giant had disappeared.

Blistering waves like an open furnace struck Irmina. The blast of scalding air snapped her head around and forced her to hold her face away from the heated backwash. Snatching frantically at a branch, she just managed to prevent herself from falling headfirst.

A bellow echoed in a voice to challenge thunder.

When she was finally able to face the copse, Irmina stared, her jaw unhinged. Flames licked out from amongst the blackened woods. Branches snapping, the great trees yawed, then toppled to the ground. Luminescence as blinding as the noonday sun forced her to snap her eyes shut. Bright spots still dancing before her eyes, she pried her eyes open to gaze at what was left of the stand and gasped.

Distorted by heated waves, a giant form stood swathed in white light and surrounded by fire.

A voice cried out.

Irmina's head whipped around toward the sound.

Silvereyes swayed before he dropped to one knee, his hands gripping his head as violent throes wracked his body. He fell face first, his head at an angle where she could still see his eyes.

A mind touched hers—a mind with a similar feel as when she communed with beasts. She locked gazes with Silvereyes.

For the first time, she saw his eyes in detail. Silver flecks dominated where there should have been white, and his irises glowed green. As she watched, they changed, becoming deep pools of obsidian like ink dropped on a pristine, white canvas. A feeling as if she would drown in their depths sucked at her. She thought she saw the man's lips twitch before he crawled onto his knees.

Breaths coming hard and fast, her chest heaving, she clawed her gaze away and forced back the touch probing her mind. She noticed then the lapras had scattered to parts unknown and what little remained of the black cluster of trees.

From what was now a clearing within the woods, strode the giant, fires petering out behind him. When he reached his bodyguard, he hauled him to his feet. A few words passed between them.

Something about the smaller man seemed off, but she couldn't quite place it. Sifting through jumbled thoughts, she scoured the recollection of the fight before she sucked in her breath, her hand covering her mouth.

Silvereyes' armor was not only whole and seamless once more, but he no longer bore so much as a scratch.

Irmina shimmied down the trunk as fast as she could and sneaked away to put more distance between her and them as the men set about cutting down a few branches. When she felt more secure, she stopped to watch.

They'd constructed a litter. The giant picked up

Kahkon, laid him gingerly on its surface, then stepped away. The bodyguard took his place. He rubbed something over the boy's wounds causing the youth to shudder.

Irmina continued to follow their movements while they worked on the boy. Time passed and clouds scudded across the heavens as the deep oranges and purples of the twilight sky dwindled to a slate blanket. Seemingly finished, the two men waited a few moments, peering into the undergrowth at the sounds of rustles and crashing branches. A lamp sparked to life in Ryne's hand. After a final look in her direction, they picked up Kahkon and made their way through the forest.

Ryne kept an eye on Kahkon. With each of the boy's whimpers and ragged breaths, Ryne's fist clenched tighter where he held the makeshift litter carrying Kahkon's broken and bruised body. Moans escaped Kahkon's lips followed by painful gasps and cries as they worked their way through a particularly rough part of the woods. A moment later, the boy fell into a feverish bout filled with coughs and unintelligible mutters, bloody spittle bubbling from his lips.

"Tend to him, Sakari," Ryne ordered, working hard not to let his voice quaver. He paused as they set the litter down. "Be extra careful with his leg and his stomach. Please."

As much as he wanted to comfort Kahkon, Ryne stepped away instead. Stroking the boy's face and whispering reassuring words would only serve to encourage the anger smoldering deep inside. Waiting to one side as Sakari administered the kinai mixture again and changed the boy's saturated poultices, Ryne let out his breath in a deep whoosh.

Denestia's twin moons had risen and now lay hidden behind a mass of clouds made sluggish from the windless night. The day's heat that normally lifted at sunfall, sat like a woven quilt, heavy and thick, and added a palpable quality to the darkness of the surrounding woods. Ryne had the feeling that without its glass container, the lone flame from the lamp he held wouldn't have flickered. Not even the shadows cast by its light wavered.

Insects chirped, owls hooted and foragers rummaged

about in the undergrowth before they ran off, scared away by the guttural snarls of beasts drawn to the pungent aroma of Kahkon's blood. On occasion, Ryne caught the occasional glimmer of movement or shining eyes among the silhouettes of trees. Off to one side, branches shook, but he made no attempt to be quiet, knowing only the most dangerous creatures would attack.

However, the beasts didn't bother him as much as the knowledge that Mariel still stalked them while Kahkon lay helpless. And that in itself was a rockslide compared to the avalanche he'd discovered in the forest. *Was the golden haired stranger responsible for the creatures? Could they have been an attempt to create wraithwolves? If so, how?* From all his research, such an undertaking should only be possible in Hydae. And Hydae was sealed away from Denestia.

What was the Tribunal's stake in all this? Could those among them who engineered his capture and torture so many years ago be involved in whatever plot was afoot? The old scars on his back ached with the thought, and he shuddered. He shut away the memory before it enveloped him.

Sakari raised his head from the boy's body and peered off into the dark trees, silver eyes aglow.

"Is she still following?" Ryne asked, wishing for a different answer than what he knew would come.

"Yes," Sakari answered from where he hovered over Kahkon. "She is staying quite a bit farther back than usual."

The corner of Ryne's lips curled, and he grunted his irritation. Kahkon whimpered, and Ryne's back tightened at the sound. One tentative foot rose before he stopped himself, focusing instead on the rustles and furtive sounds among the trees.

"What are your plans for her now?" Sakari asked, poultices sopping with blood as he worked on Kahkon. Yips of a lapra sounded nearby followed by an answering growl.

"I don't know. What I want to do is proving to be an unwise path to take. Carnas would only suffer," Ryne confessed. He held the lamp up to peer among the trees in time to see dark fur and dog–like shapes disappear among the trees.

"If she is who she says she is, restraining yourself only serves to delay the inevitable."

Ryne squeezed his eyes shut against the tightness in his chest as if mere sight could will away the truth behind Sakari's words. If indeed Mariel was a Devout in the Tribunal's employ, eventually one of the messages she sent every morning would include his description. If one had not already as the presence of the Alzari assassins seemed to suggest. If everything stayed true to his past, more assassins or worse, a cohort, would be dispatched to take him. Either way, his time in hiding was at an end.

Frustrated by his lack of options, Ryne growled. There was no telling which faction within the Tribunal Mariel represented. And he couldn't simply ask. Added to that, using his power to capture her was not a viable option with his recent waning control. Drawing on his Scripts to destroy the shade's abominations in the woods had brought him to the brink. Luckily, the killings had been enough to appease his power's hunger.

"He's safe for now," Sakari said.

Ryne took in Kahkon's pallid face. The boy writhed, but at least he seemed a deal calmer, his aura steady. With a relieved sigh, Ryne picked up his end of the litter, and they set out again, shadows cast by the lamplight chasing them.

"I do not believe the Tribunal sent those assassins for you. I think it was mere chance,"

"You know what I think of chance," Ryne retorted.

"They failed too many times before. The Alzari have never seemed the type to risk men foolishly. If they indeed came for you, they would not send two assassins. And a cohort would require the Tribunal to seek permission of the Ostanian Kingdoms, no?"

"Yes," Ryne agreed. Although he'd yet to find a connection, he still found himself wondering if Sakari's knack for mirroring his thoughts had anything to do with their link. "But when has that ever stopped them? Besides, the negotiations would only give us but so much time."

"Time enough to escape," Sakari said.

Ryne's mouth twisted with distaste. "And leave the villagers at Tribunal's mercy? Abandon them to the Alzari or Amuni's Children and the shade?"

"And if this is all Mariel's doing?"

"Then she dies," Ryne answered, leaves crunching underfoot like the crackle of a fire.

"The end result would be the same," Sakari said.

Kahkon moaned and began another set of fitful mutters. Padded feet pattered among the trees followed by a whine that whispered through the still air. Ryne held the lamp out again. A svelte forest lapra slunk away from the light, its three–foot lichen–covered body fading into the undergrowth. Several similar forms slipped by at the edge of the lamp's range followed by more low whimpers and snarls.

Ryne eyed Kahkon for a moment until the pain etched on the boy's face eased, and he settled down once more. "I'll convince them to move to the Nevermore Heights or southeast to Bana land."

"If you say so," Sakari said.

Even as he'd said it, Ryne knew the villagers would never flee. They were refugees from the territorial feuds that plagued Ostania through the years, and many had faced their own bloody trials during the War of Remnants. They would stand, fight…and die.

"I'm surprised you're concerned for them. You never were before," Ryne said, eyeing Sakari askance.

"I am not," Sakari replied. "Alive. Dead." He shrugged. "They matter not to me. You are my sole concern, and it seems you have forgotten your summons by the Svenzar is due. Your choice to protect Carnas will be even more difficult."

"I haven't forgotten. You know as well as I do that if the summons comes, I will have to answer." Ryne's fist clenched on the litter as he sifted through his meager choices. "Being bound to their gods' wills is not something to be ignored. Besides, in the thirty years doing as they bid, I've made greater strides to control my fate than I ever have since I awoke. Seventy years, Sakari. Seventy, since I woke to your face with only the knowledge of my name and how to use these Scripts. I don't see myself giving up the chance to discover who I am, why I exist, and why this craving still smolders within me."

"Not even if it means Carnas will have to do without your protection?"

"When the answers could provide me with the chance to save the village? Yes. Maybe I'm growing old, but the suffering I've caused weighs on me a little more every day. I would rather stay here and live my days in peace than to spread death as I have in the past. If the Sevnzar have the answers to such a path as they promised, then I'll ask the questions and pay whatever price is necessary." Ryne waved the lamp around to his left as the slinking noises of the lapras drew nearer before they dwindled under the light.

"Sometimes the cost is more than a person can bear," Sakari said.

Kahkon coughed and spat up blood. They stopped and set down the litter. Ryne stood guard with the lamp held out as Sakari bent to tend to the boy. Around them came the crunching tread of paws on fallen branches and leaves, the snap of small twigs, the swish of leaves brushing against fur. The sounds were nothing more than a soft susurrus. But they numbered in the hundreds. Ryne picked out as many as twenty svelte forms slinking through the woods and brush. Could Mariel really be in control of these beasts?

A slight breeze swirled just then. With it rose the rank smell of lapras. The lamp's flame flickered, causing the shadows to bob and caper.

Sakari straightened until he stood as silent as their surroundings that was suddenly vacant of the night time noises of its normal denizens. His eyes glinted like polished silversteel as he peered around them. "How far until the Fretian ends?"

"A few thousand feet."

The forest lapras began the low crooning they used when they called to other packs. The hair at the back of Ryne's neck stood on end. Wails answered in several directions, some ahead along the dark path. By Ryne's count, there had to be at least five packs, which meant more than thirty lapras.

"Sakari, do you think you could—"

"I've already tried. These beasts are not responding to me. Fresh blood has driven them past the point of control."

"So it's not her doing?" Ryne turned quickly to follow the sound of padded footsteps. The brush rustled nearby before settling.

"No. She could not control this many creatures, no matter what anyone claimed they saw." Sakari gripped his scabbard. "Take the boy. I have tied off the wounds so they should not bleed much, if at all." Sakari looked up through the branches above them. "When the clouds clear the moons…" He drew his sword.

Ryne nodded and set down the lamp. He bent and gathered Kahkon's ragged form in the crook of his left arm, tucking him against his side.

The rustles among the brush grew more purposeful. The lamplight played along the ground with its own life, elongating the shadows into looming black creatures that attempted to swallow the already dim radiance. Among those shadows, the forest lapras flitted back and forth.

The clouds began to drift by the moons.

Sakari snatched the lamp up and fled down the path. With his sudden movement came yowls and snarls.

Ryne followed, not looking back to see what the noises meant. The lamp's luminescent pool bobbed and dipped as they bolted for the forest's edge. Ryne kept Kahkon hugged close to minimize the effect of their movements as Sakari weaved his way ahead.

Silhouettes of the beasts trailed them on either side, eyes glinting. When they crossed clear patches in the canopy, the moonlight painted a clear picture. The woods crawled with lapras, mottled fur black to match the night, the lichen on their bodies near impossible to tell apart from the shadowy undergrowth.

Ryne and Sakari sped toward an opening ahead that revealed the moonlit Orchid Plains beyond. Agitated barks and growls revealed lapras snapping at each other in their eagerness to attack.

Sakari stopped short. "I will hold them here."

Offering no protest, Ryne stretched to a long lope as he passed Sakari. Within moments, he left the whines and wails echoing behind him. He increased his speed to a dead sprint, his heart thumping in his chest, the familiar thrill of his battle energy resonating within him.

Ryne burst from the woods into the dense fescue and grass of the plains. Four shadowy forms emerged before him. Cradling the boy against his body, he reached for his sword.

"Master Waldron, stop, it be us," Keevo's panicked voice rang out.

Ryne drew up short and eased his hand away from his weapon.

Behind Keevo stood three dartans with Dren perched upon one aiming his bow at the woods.

"We hoped you would take the same path back when you found Kahkon. The mayor and a few elders voted against us coming, but we did anyway." Keevo's teeth showed in a wide grin before his face puckered with concern at the sound of fighting within the forest. "Where be Sakari?"

"He's holding them off until I—" Ryne cut off, movement along the plains drawing his attention. He passed Kahkon's prone form to Keevo.

A thousand feet or more from where they stood, the grass swayed, disturbed by something other than the wind. The entire expanse bent and shifted as if the pasture itself advanced toward them.

"What—" Keevo began. He turned and his face drained of color.

Small–bodied plains lapras by the score trotted out from the underbrush.

Ryne leaped into the saddle of the closest dartan. "Pass him to me!" he yelled.

Keevo lifted Kahkon up above his head as Ryne drew close.

Almost all at once, Ryne snatched the boy and tugged the chain reins to force the mount around to face the lights of Carnas shining in the distance. "Ride!" he commanded. "Ride like you never have before!"

The breeze that had kicked up earlier now blew stronger. Carried by the eddies were the howls and pained yelps from Sakari's battle.

The plains lapra packs swept across the field in silence.

Ryne whipped his reins as he fled toward Carnas. He didn't look back.

CHAPTER 7

Alys Valdeen's nails scratched under Ancel's chin and down his neck. Each stroke soothed the itch from the short black hairs sprouting through his skin. He closed his eyes and sighed as he contemplated shaving off his beard soon. How other men in Eldanhill managed the itching, he couldn't fathom. They must have stone for skin. Maybe that was why most who grew facial hair were miners. All that quarrying and mining must have made them extra tough. Either way, his days growing a beard to impress the women were done.

"Do you really have to leave now?" Alys' voice purred. Her long fingers, each with a matching silver ring, traced slow lines down Ancel's muscled chest and stomach.

Ancel squeezed his eyes shut for a moment and forced himself to stop her hand. The last thing he needed right now was to be caught up in another session, no matter how much he enjoyed her naked curves and the intoxicating scent of her sweet perfume. "Yes, I have to go." He brought his hand up and brushed her delicate, sunset orange and red strands from her face. "If I let myself go with you again, I'll miss the chance to pick the kinai at its ripest."

She rolled over and pulled him on top of her. "You and those damned fruit. They can wait. I want you," she implored, her green eyes shining with need.

"If I miss this chance, I'll have to hear my father's wrath tomorrow." Ancel stroked her hair. "You know how important Soltide is this year. Inspectors are coming from the capital, and the Council expects the best product from my father's winery. I—"

She acted as if she didn't hear a single word he said and curled a leg over his. Without thought, he stroked her thigh, his tan hand offsetting her pale skin. Her soft, supple body called to him, and her hand reached down below his waist as the warmth between her thighs pressed against him. A groan escaped Ancel's lips. Almost on its own accord, his back arched with pleasure. He looked down to see Alys staring into his face, her eyes reminding him of his own emerald ones, except his had a slight shade of blue.

In an attempt to resist the ecstatic tingle easing through his body, he pictured his parents' scathing tongues and the off chance he may miss class if he indulged himself once more. His Teachers' berating would be just as bad. Another demotion would loom over his head. What did it matter? Surely, he could… No. Mirza had been right. He needed to focus on his training. As the thought crossed his mind, Alys' hands tugged on him with slow sure strokes. He shuddered. *I guess I'll have to miss my studies.* How much could that hurt? Unbidden, his hands reached for her breasts.

"Ancel!" Mirza's voice rang out. A fist pounded on the bedroom door. "It's time, man. You don't want to hear Stefan's voice today, do you? And the Clan Council's. And Teacher Calestis's." Another thump sounded on the heavy oak door. "Alys, don't drain the man. He has work to do, classes to attend." A cackle followed.

Her face reddening, Alys jumped up and pushed Ancel off her with a squeak. "You really need to tell your friends not to interrupt when you have company."

Ancel rolled over on the soft bed and groaned. He'd forgotten about the bet. His best friend never could resist the chance to play a part in something he found funny, or what he saw as a decent wager. "I'll be right there, Mirz. Give me a few minutes," Ancel called.

Mirza snickered. "You have five minutes. If you're not out by then, I'll come back with your father." Footsteps receded down the hall.

Ancel swung his legs over the edge of the bed and sat

up. Running his hands through his hair, he heaved a great sigh and gathered himself. He stood, walked to where his light green silk shirt and matching linen pants lay in a pile on the polished wood floor, and picked them up.

"Gods, I love your ass." Alys' sultry voice trembled.

Turning to her, Ancel grinned. "You probably like this more."

Alys' green–eyed gaze roved down his naked body, past his waist and she giggled. She eased from under the satin covers and squirmed in the bed, the red silk sheets beneath her setting off her smooth white flesh. "Are you coming back when you're finished?" Her voice purred once more.

He shook his head. "I have to train when I return, but you're welcome to come watch." He picked up his longsword, still in its white scabbard, from the floor.

Alys' face reddened again, and her eyes flashed angrily. "I'm not one of those tramps. I'm not going to ogle you while you practice."

With a shrug Ancel turned and headed for the oak door, grabbing a towel from a wooden rack. "It didn't seem to bother you yesterday. Either way, I'll be enjoying myself later tonight. It's your choice if you want to be a part of it."

The sound of a frantic shuffle and the clink of metal on glass made Ancel duck. A vase flew over his head. Water droplets sprinkled across his back as the vase crashed into the door, pretty, blue bellflowers spilling onto the floor and the thick, mountain cat fur rug. The head of the beast still attached, its great jaws leered at Ancel. He looked over his shoulder.

Alys stood with the silk sheets gripped in one trembling hand. Her eyes were glistening pinpricks of loathing. "You said I was special. I bet if Irmina was here you wouldn't treat her this way."

Ancel's blood boiled. *How dare she mention* that *woman?* He opened his mouth to speak but snapped it shut, his lips pressed tight against the hurtful words he might utter. Turning back to the door, he yanked it open and slammed it behind him.

Not long after, the Streamean temple looming ahead,

Ancel and Mirza sat atop their dartans as they trotted along the Eldan Road past the neat stone edifices of the now closed Mystera. Dusk lay across the town like the gray cloaks they wore, matching the clouds that roiled above the Kelvore Mountains to the north. Arcane lamps heralding the Soltide Festival hung from almost every building in the town and across the quiet streets, their glow reflecting from the windows, tinting the granite and sandstone buildings like cobalt lightning. Charra loped next to the young men, his bone hackles sighing in soft swishes, and his padded paws near inaudible.

As they rode by the Streamean temple and its tall clock tower wreathed in blue light, Ancel dipped his head in prayer. Their mounts carried two long wooden racks, each nailed to the bottom of the animals' humped shells. Thick leather straps slung over the dartans' backs helped to hold the carriers in place. Empty sacks were tied in even spaces on each rack, one hanging to either side of each of the beasts' six legs. The dartans mewled to each other, snake–like necks swinging from side to side.

Other than Ancel, Mirza, and the occasional town watch, no one else traveled this part of Eldanhill. Most had retired after a long day filled with Soltide preparations. In another four weeks, the festivities would begin in earnest, and these same streets would overflow with revelers. Eldanhill's celebrations and its kinai juices and wines were well renowned, bringing people from all across Granadia even from as far south as Ishtar and its port cities. Each year Ancel looked forward to the festival more than the year before. The revelry often helped him to forget Irmina. He pushed the thought of her away before it set him to brooding.

"Which patch do you want to go to first? The glen?" Mirza asked.

Ancel tied his shoulder length hair into a ponytail with a leather cord and shook his head. "Let's go through the Greenleaf first, see if we can't find a wolf or two for Charra to have some fun. Then we head to the glen." He flapped his reins. "I fed these boys fresh beef this afternoon. They're ready for a good run. I'll race you back home when we're done." A grin tugging at his face, he added, "If you're up to it that is."

Mirza chuckled and shifted his position in the saddle carved into his mount's shell. "It won't be a race. You know, you've already lost one bet today. Best not to make another.

Dartans may be more suited for the work we're about to do, but if you think that's your advantage, then you're mistaken. Dartan, horse, hmmm…" Red eyebrows raised, his head bobbing to the left and right, he weighed the choices. "It makes no difference."

Ancel smiled at the opportunity to win back his coin. "If you feel so good about it, I'll hold onto your coin until we get back here. Double the bet?"

Mirza looked down at his yellow shirt and dozens of frills that covered the sleeves. "I could use a new shirt anyway. I've been putting on weight, I think." He flexed a skinny arm. "You're on."

"Weight?" Ancel shook his head and chuckled. "Is that what that is?" He glanced at the frills. "Fooled me."

Mirza waved him off, his tone becoming serious. "How hard is she taking it?"

Ancel shrugged. "She'll get over it. They always do. If she doesn't—its Soltide. There'll be plenty new women to dance with this year. I heard the princess herself is coming from Randane." His lips twitched. "Ilumni knows, I love this time of year."

Mirza's voice rose in a brief cackle, mirth dancing in his eyes. "You have as much chance of bedding the princess as you have of bedding a High Ashishin." Mirza appeared thoughtful for a moment. "No, you've a better chance bedding the princess if it came down to it. Hydae's flames, you've a better chance bedding the Queen than a High Ashishin." He shook his head slowly and smirked. "My good sir," Mirza's tone became mocking and aloof in imitation of a lordling, "I admit I envy your luck with women, but the princess is above even you."

"Ha. Luck? Never luck. It's all in the tongue."

Mirza grunted. "Spare me the details. They'll wise up when that ass of yours becomes old news." He burst out in another cackle and flapped his reins before Ancel could reply. His dartan bounded forward in four great, yet feathery, leaps before breaking into a gallop. Mirza's cloak streamed behind him.

With a loud, throaty bark, Charra chased after Mirza. Laughing, Ancel whipped his own reins. His dartan's six thick legs stretched as it sped along with a silent grace that easily outstripped a good horse's gallop without the uncomfortable jounce. They headed north toward the Greenleaf Forest and the black sentinels of the Kelvore Mountains' shadowy forms looming beyond.

Just over an hour later, sweet smells from fist–sized kinai drifting upon the breeze, they rode along the trail to their secret glen hidden among the sandstone hills at the edge of the Kelvore Mountains. The ripe fruit filled the sacks on Ancel's mount. They'd kept Mirza's sacks empty so as not to mix the two crops. Charra had run off to scout the way ahead.

Their hunt for wolves had not gone as well. Ancel wrinkled his brow with the thought. Every wolf trap they visited had already been triggered, paw prints in various sizes covering the ground, yet they saw no wolves. The missing wolves and Charra's disconcerting whines had put Ancel on edge. The promise of a storm from the charcoal clouds gathered above the mountains did little to help.

However, neither his mood nor dusk's dim light could hide the beauty around them. Enhanced further by the dying sun's orange hues, low foothills lush with long needle grass, and yellow and blue bellflowers rose about them. An occasional copse grew along the slopes, the young pine and cedar often thinning out until just one or two trees grew between each thicket strung together like jewels on a necklace.

Ancel frowned. Not a hint of song from the usual evening birds drifted on the stiff breeze that was blowing. He slid his hand to the reassuring feel of his longsword's pommel.

Loud, incessant barks burst from Charra, startling Ancel and Mirza. The dartans mewled to each other, eyes rolling back in their heads, their necks swinging.

"You smell that?" Ancel scrunched up his face at an earthy, rotten odor.

Mirza gazed at the narrow entrance between the hills where the daggerpaw stood. "Yes. It smells like spoiled kinai."

Bone hackles forming a ridge of hardened, knife–sharp edges, body straining forward, Charra stared down into the glen. The daggerpaw's tail whipped back and forth, and a spiky bone appendage slid in and out from its tip.

The young men pushed their skittish dartans into a

gallop and topped the rise at the glen's slim opening. Ancel's breath caught at the sight beyond the daggerpaw. Mirza gasped.

Fungus crawled over decaying kinai fruit trees, hanging in thick dark ropes. Some of the head high trees bowed to the earth under the weight, dark worshippers at pray before a forsaken god. Branches still visible under the fungus were black rather than brown or green. The rotten stench choked the air as the sickly growths strangled the orchard. Bloated, decaying kinai covered the ground in clusters, their fluff spread like thick, red spider webs. The buzzing of thousands of flies gorging themselves rose with a chill breeze as the insects swarmed over the crop, their wings glinting with blackness.

Cold, clammy fingers trailed down Ancel's spine. "What, in Amuni's name, could've done this?" he whispered, his voice shaky.

"I—I don't know," Mirza uttered, his often flushed face now a pallid mask.

Ancel reached a tentative hand down next to his saddle and retrieved his bow. He slung it over his back. Steeling himself against the dread running through him, he said, "I need a closer look." He dismounted and double–checked on his longsword at his hip.

"Y–You sure about this?" Mirza dismounted next to him with a spear in his bony hands.

"Yes. We need to find out what did this and report it to my father." Ancel's voice trembled, but he fought down the urge to mount and ride home.

"We're only in training, Ancel. Remember that." Mirza looked up at him, gray eyes radiating fear, his hands shaking. "I'm with you though."

Ancel glanced at his daggerpaw. "Charra can protect us."

Mirza nodded, but his knuckle–white grip failed to keep his weapon steady.

As they eased forward, Ancel found himself wishing he'd continued this training, that he could Forge the essences within Mater like an Ashishin. He would have used the waning light and heat to make a fire, ready to hurl at any threat, or dried the decaying mulch beneath their feet. Better yet, he would have Forged the Forms in the earth to make a solid pathway or a shield of stone. The lack of ability made him grip his sword hilt that much tighter.

They squished their way through the decayed fruit toward the small stream feeding the glen. Disturbed flies buzzed about before they settled once again among the squashed kinai that stained the youth's leather boots and Charra's paws, a somber red. A reek similar to moldy unwashed fur mixed with shit underlay the odor from the kinai. The stench reminded Ancel of Master Javed's disgusting dog kennels and grew to near unbearable levels as they approached the stream. Charra whined.

"Oh Ilumni…" Mirza pointed as the stream's muddy banks became visible.

Black clumps of shit littered the water's edge, and some floated in the stream. Ancel turned back to the kinai field. Black mounds lay among the trees, half hidden by the fluff. Huge paw prints, similar to a humongous wolf's or a mountain cat's, but twice as big, trailed from the muddy banks. He couldn't tell if the other tracks he saw were manmade.

"We have to leave this place. Now." Ancel's gaze swept across the glen for signs of movement, but he saw none.

Mirza needed no prodding. They both sprinted for their dartans, their cloaks flapping around them.

"Home, Charra!" Ancel shouted.

At the command, Charra bounded ahead, growling the entire time. Ancel and Mirza mounted and dashed from the glen down the long trail.

With Charra leading the way, they galloped from the sandstone foothills. Not once did they look back as they crossed a field of long, swaying grasses, oak trees, and gooseberry vines. A wind blew with tangy gooseberry smells upon it, but it carried no warmth. Ancel took a deep breath, grateful to be rid of the stench from the glen.

Insects chirped and lightflies flitted among the grass and trees. Twilight's glow had disappeared from the sky, replaced by the brilliant twin moons. Still, the celestial bodies did little to brighten the Greenleaf Forest when they entered past looming pines and oaks that stood sentinel. Ancel didn't need a lightstone to guide them through the dark woods, but he used one anyway. Uneasiness tickling the hairs at his nape, he and Mirza wound their way through the trees.

Resinbuds with their yellow, purple, and white blooms

blinked on and off among the trees—the light within the flowers attracting numerous insects. Several times, he thought he saw movement from the corner of his eye, but when he tried to glimpse the source, he saw nothing but shadowy trunks and brush.

Charra stayed next to them this time with his ears pricked up and a low rumble in his throat. The daggerpaw's hackles remained upraised. Ancel scratched at his itching neck in an attempt to shake the uneasy feeling, but it stayed. Mirza must have sensed the same thing because his wary gaze swept around them often.

Even with the usual hooting wood owls, buzzing insects, and other noises from foraging night creatures, the feeling not only persisted, it grew. So did Charra's rumbling growl. Ancel fidgeted with his bow and made sure he could reach it with ease.

They pushed the dartans harder through snarls of gooseberry vine snaking through the bushes in their path. Branches like reaching fingers snagged at their cloaks. Once, Ancel was almost yanked from his mount as his cloak caught then tore free. Breaths coming hard and fast at the close call, Ancel pulled what remained of his cloak tight around him.

Charra's rumble increased to a sharp snarl that could challenge a mountain cat's growl. The wind picked up, carrying with it the same fetid stench from the glen. A chill slithered through Ancel's gut.

They urged their mounts on, but the foul odor grew stronger. Cold sweat trickling down his brow, Ancel flicked a hand across his eyes to clear his vision and snatched a look behind.

Shadows flitted between the trees, and branches crashed and snapped. Resinbuds, that moments before had added light, blinked out in an advancing trail ahead of the shadows, racing toward Ancel and Mirza as if the dying glows chased them.

Ancel whipped his reins harder.

The dartans crashed through small branches and brush, oblivious to the rake of broken wood and scratch of thorns. They warbled in short spurts, and their breaths came fast and heavy. The wind swirled through the trees around Ancel and Mirza, the rotten smell chasing them, riding the breeze.

Ancel's heart pounded in tune with his dartan's stride. He pushed his mount until they burst from the Greenleaf Forest.

The tingle within him had grown into the familiar feel of energy he gained when he sparred. Wind whipping at his face, his cloak billowing behind him, he glanced over his shoulder and abruptly drew rein. Mirza followed suit.

Charra had stopped and was standing prone, eyes fixed on the dark forest. Growls issued from his throat in a steady rhythm. Tail whipping back and forth, he made to bound forward to the woods several times. Each time he did, the daggerpaw's growls ended in a sharp, barking howl.

"Hold, Charra," Ancel yelled.

The daggerpaw obeyed, backing down into a snarl, but his hackles didn't recede. His tail, with its spiked appendage, thrashed furiously from side to side.

The shadows melded with the darkness of the forest as the last of the resinbuds winked out. Then all was deathly still. Ancel sucked in a breath at the sight within the trees.

Two giant wolf silhouettes, Charra's size, with glowing, green orbs where the moon reflected in their unnatural eyes, appeared among the trees. The eyes burned into Ancel's own as if they stared only at him. Silence reigned.

Ancel's heart thumped. Calling on his training, he sunk into the quiet place within him. As his heart calmed, he snatched his bow from his back and nocked an arrow. In the back of his mind, he heard Charra growl. Ancel ignored him, not allowing his gaze to waver from the creatures' dark outlines or those eyes.

He drew the bow, fletching to ear…and blinked.

The shadowed forms and the eyes had disappeared. The night sounds resumed once more.

With his focus on where the beasts once stood, Ancel backed his mount away from the forest. His gaze went to the surrounding trees but saw nothing. Wiping away salty sweat that stung his eyes, he retreated several feet without seeing the creatures again.

"Let's go, Ancel. Now!" Mirza shouted sending his dartan rushing toward Eldanhill.

Ancel turned and galloped toward the distant town's blue lights.

Charra's growls started again behind them. From the woods, a howling screech sounded. Charra's barks became a roar.

CHAPTER 8

Purple and black bruises marred Kahkon's skin from his shoulders down to where bandages swathed his ruined leg. The parts of his body not swollen or slick with blood and bile bore a pallid, corpselike color. Tight lines pulled at the edges of his open eyes, and dark circles hung below them. Moans escaped his throat, and spittle leaked from his lips, his sunken chest barely moving with each labored breath.

Ryne studied the flesh where the massive wound once ran down Kahkon's chest. Taeria, Carnas' most experienced mender, had managed to sew up the gash. She'd used a complex Materforge, blending water to help with blood, the boy's own tissue, as well as a thick mixture of herbs, and sela essences—which were life and death combined—to mend the damage, leaving a thin line where once there was only pulpy, red meat. The woman fussed over the boy, her withered arms and legs moving with an efficiency that belied her leathery skin and protruding bones.

Fluids leaked and clotted around the catgut and poultices the mender used. Ryne's fist clenched as he thought back to Mariel and the golden-haired stranger. *If those women are responsible for this, I'll show them no mercy.*

Inside Taeria's small home, lit by numerous lamps along the walls, Ryne kept his head and back bent so he wouldn't hit the ceiling. The boy rested on a table surrounded by four chairs and a wooden bench. A smaller table held the mender's instruments—

bottles with fluids, several sharp knives, needles, and clean bandages. Shelves with various herbs and other items of her craft decorated the white walls around the room. Blood stained the floor a dark, somber red as if the wood had quenched its thirst on Kahkon's life fluids.

Taeria waddled from one side of the boy to the other. Every so often, she brushed back patches of stark white, wispy hair from her splotchy forehead. Sweat ran down her face, sticking some of the errant strands to her face. Her aura glowed in multiple hues as she worked, colors waxing and waning around her each time she applied the poultices dipped in a concoction made from kinai, pink, sour fleshberries and other herbs.

Ryne remembered his own experience with the potion. The potent mending mixture was only effective with the person still conscious. Kahkon's body shuddered each time a poultice pressed against his wound. Ryne wished he could take the boy's pain and make it his own.

A coughing fit wracked Kahkon's body, and Taeria cradled a hand behind his head for support. The boy's finger rose an inch from the table. She leaned down, her white hair almost touching the table, and brought her ear close to his mouth.

Kahkon's words were a dry whisper.

"He wishes for a story about the shade's defeat." Taeria said as she straightened as much as she could. "He would prefer my sweet voice." She regarded Ryne, her milky white eyes standing out in her wrinkled face. "But he will settle for your braying today since I am busy." Her lips spread in a toothless smile.

Kahkon coughed again. His mouth twisted into a rictus that might have been an attempt at a grin. Spit flew from his lips.

Ryne wanted to return the sentiment, but he couldn't. Instead, he thought about which story from *When the Gods Walked Among Us* Kahkon liked best. His gaze met the boy's watery blue eyes and he began.

"The moment before the Eztezian Guardians pulled him from his home in Hydae and trapped him in the Nether with the other gods, Amuni, the Lord of shade, made one last effort to cross the Planes to our world. He wished to break the seals the Eztezians were building. Once, he would have relied on his brother Ilumni for help, but no more. The two were foes now.

"Instead, using a skill called the Bloodline Affinity, he

scoured Hydae for humans and beasts who could touch Mater. Once he found enough subjects, Amuni, weakened the Kassite—the great barrier between the Planes—and was able to open a rift into the Nether and capture several thousand netherlings. He then taught his most powerful followers, the Skadwaz, how to create monsters to do their bidding. Using a great Materforging, they combined the netherlings with the people and beasts they collected to create a new breed of creature—shadelings. The Skadwaz ravaged the worlds for all manner of unique creatures on which to use this transformation. When their army was strong enough, they attacked Denestia.

"But the Eztezians had a great power on their side. A power akin to the gods.

"The netherlings, who hated Amuni and many of the other gods for the experiments they often used on their kind, had imbued their power into the Eztezians. A power said to be stronger than the essences we see around us. Using that power, and led by Eztezian Damal Adelfried, the Denestian forces defended against the shade's hordes in battle after battle. Oceans boiled and swirled into maelstroms or became deserts, mountains crumbled, forests died, becoming barren lands..."

Ryne told the story just as the book did. Some of his earlier tension eased from his body as Kahkon's eyes took on an added spark. The telling continued for over an hour before Taeria was finished, and Kahkon fell asleep.

A knock sounded on the mender's door. The old woman wiped sweat from her forehead and away from her weary eyes, and shuffled to the door. A few words passed between her and her visitor before she returned to Ryne.

"Mayor Bertram wishes to meet with you at Hagan's," Taeria said.

Ryne nodded. His eyes remained on the boy. From the youth's aura, he still struggled, but his chances at survival had increased tenfold. "Thank you for all you've done, Taeria. I'm sorry I brought this upon Carnas."

"Foolishness," Taeria said, "We knew what you were when we accepted you here among us. Besides, living in the Ostania's wilds was never meant to be safe. Go now before Bertram and Hagan kill each other."

Ryne smiled at that last, opened the door, and ducked

outside.

Although night had fallen, the day's heat lingered in the air and wispy clouds scudded across the dark sky. Denestia's twin moons shone silvery blue, their hue glimmering in deviate highlights over anything the lamps and torches in Carnas didn't touch.

Striding down Carnas' main road, Ryne barely noticed the villagers who greeted him, many hailing him for saving Kahkon. Lara shuffled for a place by his side. She too showered him with thanks as she matched his long strides by running in short bursts. Ryne acknowledged her with a distracted smile and a nod while peering over the throng gathered near Hagan's Inn.

The few older children out this late ran beside him, their laughter haunting him, every face familiar. They all came to his home to hear his stories, to learn. Feet pattered next to him for a while longer until his long strides left them all behind. Still, he couldn't escape the occasional frown or weighted gazes from other village folk on his path. Neither could he shut out the occasional caustic tone when they mentioned his name in whispers at the edge of his hearing.

The day he woke over seventy years ago came to him as he relived it. Dazed and confused, he'd opened his eyes to a strange place filled with the most exotic life one could imagine, overflowing with primordial forces of Mater that flooded him. Sakari stood over him, expressionless as always. An Entosis, Sakari would later tell him, is where he awoke. A place hidden from the rest of the world only those with a gift like his could see much less enter. On that day, he rose with no memory of his past. All he knew was his name, his skill with his sword, how to utilize his Scripts, and to his shame, harness his power to murder.

Through the years, he'd tried so hard to disappear, to hide himself away from the many wrongs he'd committed since then, to find the answers the Svenzar said he must seek. His many names spilled through his head.

Ryne the Shadeslayer, Ryne the Lightbringer, Ryne the Deathbringer, Ryne the Lost Battleguard. That last made him spit. He remembered the fools who worshipped him back then as if he really was some god's Battleguard. Yet, over time, his name became lost. It dwindled to a whisper, a myth, something told by mothers to scare their children. Sakari would return with stories from cities he'd visited where people believed Ryne never did exist or was dead, and finally he thought he found peace. Until now.

Ryne seethed. This woman, Mariel, this priestess of Ilumni, changed all that. She tracked him as if she knew his identity, and since her appearance, the deaths had begun. And now, not only had Alzari assassins once again appeared, but Kahkon's life hung in the balance. As if all of that wasn't enough, one of the greatest threats Denestia had known during the War of Remnants and the Shadowbearer War had reappeared.

He didn't believe in coincidence. Things would get worse. Maybe he should've killed her when she first appeared, but that little voice in his mind, the one that reminded him of his past, the one he often listened to the last few years convinced him to stop. Maybe this time the voice was wrong.

Without so much as a nod to the two guards outside Hagan's Inn, he jerked the door open and entered. "Hello, Hagan," Ryne said, his quiet voice carrying through the room. "Bertram." He nodded in the general direction of the ebony–skinned mayor. "I'm tempted to go after Mariel again."

Double chin jiggling, Hagan's head snapped around from giving instructions to his serving women. Vana and Vera went off to do his bidding.

"Please, don't do anything rash," begged Hagan, his heavy brow furrowed as he took in Ryne's scowl. The innkeeper sat at an oak table, his stubby sausage fingers dwarfing his pipe.

A few feet away, Mayor Bertram sat, the expression on his face perking up at Ryne's statement.

"Rash would've been to kill her the day she showed." Ryne strode to the table, the stained wooden floor creaking beneath his weight. He slung the leather strap connected to his scabbard over his head, placed his sheathed greatsword on the table, and eased into the only chair in Hagan's Inn made to accommodate his eight–foot frame.

On any other night, the establishment would already be crowded with villagers, even more so with the unusually dry weather the past few days. There would be singing and dancing with many taking turns on the small stage to recite poetry while Miss Lara would play her ivory flute. Not now. Tonight, the pall and gloom of the day's events dimmed even the lamps that hung from braziers and cast their flickering light about the serving hall, and made the moonlight filtering through curtains inconsequential. The tables and chairs spread throughout the room and set against the inn's sandstone walls were empty. The guards at the inn's entrance made sure they stayed that way. No glasses clinked, no laughter roared, and there was no buzz of conversations. The silence whispered ill tidings.

"You could've saved some lives if you killed Mariel that first day. The boy wouldn't be hurt right now." Single eye glinting, the mayor's scarred face puckered with the accusation. "How's he doing?"

"He may yet live," Ryne answered. He continued as Bertram muttered a thankful prayer, "And to be honest, Bertram. I think we've saved more lives by not killing her."

The mayor grunted his disagreement. "I'm telling you, those murders, and now this. She's responsible."

The innkeeper's potbelly threatened to burst from his sweat–stained shirt as he leaned forward. "For all we know, them bodies could be the work of lapras. Or this other golden–haired woman Ryne saw. Or the Alzari mercenaries. They be more ruthless than any." Holding up his pipe to the lamp, he used the meaty thumb on his other hand to knead giana leaves into the bowl.

"Or they could be her work," Bertram retorted. "You shouldn't be so willing to rule her out."

"And you shouldn't be so willing to condemn her," Hagan admonished. "Not without proof." Lighting a tinder stick in the oil lamp on the table with one over–sized hand, he stuck his pipe into the corner of his mouth with the other.

"Because what Forian said isn't proof enough?" Bertram's eyebrow arched.

"You put him up to that nonsense," Hagan scoffed, touching the tinder stick to the giana leaves and puffing.

"I may have done many things, but that wasn't one of them. People do have a mind of their own. Her preaching that Streamean puke doesn't help much. How many of them worship Ilumni's light will always be tainted by those who sacrifice bawling babes and animals to appease Amuni's black heart. I wonder how many within their own Tribunal partake in that blasphemy."

"There you go again." Hagan rolled his eyes. "It be shit

like that makes our people act the way they do. You say what you want and refuse to think of the consequences. What if it is that golden–haired woman and not Mariel?"

Bertram grunted. "The golden–haired woman that no one besides Ryne and Sakari have seen?"

"It sounds like you be saying Ryne didn't see what he saw." Lips curled into a tight smile, but his watery eyes deadly serious, Hagan puffed on his pipe once more. When he exhaled, perfumed giana smoke spilled into the air.

Bertram fidgeted when he eyed Ryne. "I'm not saying that, but it wouldn't be the first time someone had visions deep in the woods."

Ryne shrugged. "She was real enough. I have Sakari keeping an eye out for her and Mariel."

"All I'm saying is there's been six corpses since Mariel showed up," Bertram argued, "And eight of our own have went missing. I would think that's enough proof. Been what? Six years since the last killing in Carnas?"

"Could just be coincidence that an infected lapra decided to hunt in these parts," Hagan said.

Bertram gave Hagan a sidelong glance. "Not even you believe that. And I would bet if we allowed your regulars in, they'd agree with me. The old prophecies say—"

"Yes, yes." Hagan waved his hand dismissively. "I know what they say. What I believe be something different."

Ryne let their argument wash over him. "No lapra could shred bodies in such a way. If you bothered to look at Kahkon's wounds, you would know what attacked him didn't kill those strangers we found. Neither did the Alzari."

"See," Bertram began, as if Ryne's words confirmed his suspicions about the woman. "That means she—"

"I found the missing eight."

The two men gaped. Smiles began before they turned into frowns at Ryne's grim expression.

"They're dead, aren't they?" Bertram asked, his voice soft.

"I was forced to kill them." Ryne's shoulders slumped, and he closed his eyes for a brief moment. The memories of what the villagers looked like when he found them swept through him. *You freed them from their suffering. Death is a better place than what life they did have*. When he opened his eyes, both men's faces had their horrified thoughts written all over them.

"Why?" Bertram finally managed to whisper.

"Someone was feeding them to wraithwolves. Amuni's Children have crossed the Rotted Forest."

Hagan snorted. "Foolishness. The remnants of Amuni's Children be gone. Dead. Dust. Over twenty–five years." Despite the apparent confidence in his voice, sweat bloomed on Hagan's forehead, and his pipe hung limp in the corner of his mouth.

Ryne's expression remained impassive.

"Are you sure?" Hagan asked, his eyes round and fearful.

"As sure as the sun rises and falls."

"But how?" Bertram's question was a mousy squeak. "How could they pass your wards? How could our scouts miss them? I don't believe it."

"I don't know," Ryne answered. "You can believe what you will, but extra scouts will need to be posted. I suggest you abandon Carnas. Make your way to—"

"I'm not abandoning all we've built here. We fought them once, we can fight them again," Bertram said, a stubborn set creeping further into his jaw and chasing the color back into his face.

Removing his pipe, Hagan turned to the mayor. "We fought them, but at what cost. Bertram, don't—"

"Don't speak to me of costs." Bertram's eyes glittered. "I paid my price several times over." He wagged his stump for an arm and shifted his head so he could show his ruined face and eye on the same side. "They cost me these and my family. I told you all we should've killed this Mariel. This can only be her precious Tribunal's doing as it was then."

"You always forget this same Tribunal saved you," Ryne said. He glared at Bertram. "And you're quick to talk of costs. Our people have paid quite a price already. When will it be enough?"

Bertram met Ryne's angry eyes for a moment before he looked away. After a moment more of tense silence, the mayor asked, "How many shadelings did you find?"

"Four."

Hagan expelled a sigh of relief and tucked his pipe back into his mouth.

"As I expected." Bertram's tone was triumphant. "No more than a handful of the beasts could have survived."

"Maybe," Hagan said, "But what of Amuni's Children?"

Bertram waved his gnarled hand in dismissal. "They are but men. They can die as easily as any other. With there being so few shadelings, we should be able to muster enough *divya* between the elders to defend ourselves."

Hagan shook his head. "We should do as Ryne says and leave."

"You would think like that," Bertram snickered.

"This be about the safety of all," Hagan said. "Not just your personal vengeance."

Bertram began to reply, but stopped as Vana and Vera brought three cups and two flagons to the table. One flagon contained wine and the other juice, both drinks made from kinai. Ryne acknowledged the sisters' fond expressions with a nod and a smile of his own. After quick bows, the women returned to arranging the furniture around the room with practiced efficiency.

With a sigh, Ryne reached for the kinai juice, chair creaking under his weight. "Listen. As much as I despise the Tribunal for my own reasons, not all of them are bad or intend harm. However, if you hurt Mariel in any way, no good will come of it. And as for fighting against Amuni's Children." He waited impassively for Bertram's one–eyed gaze to meet his. "Not everyone in Carnas fought in the wars, Bertram. You have women and children here. Don't let your hate continue to blind you. You may be willing to cross the doorway to death, but plenty others here still want and deserve to cling to life." He filled a cup and took a sip. A tingling sensation followed, quickly spreading from his gullet through his body. "To be safe, head south to Berin, it's the fastest and the safest path. The Bana won't turn you away. You might want to consider sending some scouts to cross the Black Reaches and take word to Castere too."

A thoughtful expression crossed Hagan's face as he puffed on his pipe a little more than usual. Smoke roiled into the air once more.

Mayor Bertram massaged his stump. "Fine. Let's convene the elders to see what we should do. In the meantime, we should take Mariel. Question her properly about who she is. Find out what part she plays in what's happened."

Ryne grunted. "You forget she won't let me or Sakari get close to her, which in itself is part of my concern."

"Be her fleeing from you two such a danger?" Hagan chewed on his pipe. "I'd run too if I saw a giant with a face like yours carrying that monster you call a sword." He gestured with his head toward Ryne's five–foot greatsword.

Ryne smirked, fingers creeping up to touch the scars that striped the left side of his face. "I don't think my appearance scares her much, if at all."

"Oh?"

"When you're afraid of a person, you don't stalk them," Ryne said. The initial energy burst from the kinai juice wore off, so he emptied his cup. He never quite grasped the need for the wine. Kinai juice or the fruit itself bore enough energetic properties all on its own. Why anyone would want to dull the feeling by impairing their faculties was beyond him.

"Maybe, she be how we were when we first met you. Scared but curious. It's not like you be the most normal looking fellow," Hagan said.

Ryne glanced at the Scripts drawn on his arms. They matched those covering his entire body and his armor up to his chin. Each displayed scenes more detailed than epic tapestries. If he stared at them long enough, they appeared lifelike, almost as if he could reach out and touch the leaves upon the trees, or the water within the lakes and waterfalls, or smell the battlefields etched into his skin.

Still, neither who Mariel represented and how she trailed him meant well. Only creatures on the hunt moved as she did, appearing and vanishing in the bat of an eyelid but leaving the feeling she hid close enough to pounce.

When faced by the unknown, cut out its heart before it can take yours. An old teaching he and Sakari had used countless times. *And how has that worked for you in the past? Thousands of innocents slaughtered is how.* Either he or Sakari needed to find another way to get rid of Mariel without harming Carnas.

Thoughts of his friend made Ryne become acutely aware of the lump at the back of his mind. Right now, it felt distant, but as Sakari moved closer, the feeling grew more solid. Ryne sensed his companion somewhere to the east. Did he manage to find out anything new about Mariel?

With that thought, Ryne's link to Sakari bloomed. He saw through Sakari's eyes as if he walked in his boots. The man stood at the edge of the Fretian Woods watching Mariel's distant figure.

"She has not allowed me to come close once," Sakari said, his tone empty. "She moves every time I do."

"That's fine. Just keep an eye on her," Ryne said before breaking the link.

The sight through Sakari dissolved. Ryne saw only his surroundings within the inn once more. He noted Hagan's knitted eyebrows and Bertram's fidgeting.

"You feeling well? Should I send for Taeria?" Hagan asked.

Ryne shook his head. "I'm fine."

"Well, you were just staring off into the air and talking to yourself," Bertram said, but avoided Ryne's eyes.

"Just thinking aloud." Ryne ignored the men's skeptical glances. "What were you saying before I became caught up with my thoughts?"

"I be telling Bertram when I seen her, she spoke every bit like a priestess or a Granadian noble. You know the sort. They expect to be heard and obeyed," the innkeeper said. He pursed his lips while looking at the mayor from the corner of his eyes. "He still wants us to run her off or worse."

"We all know running her off won't work," Ryne said.

"Which leaves the worse," Hagan concluded. "Do you really want to do something that might make them dispatch soldiers looking for her? If she be who she says she be, what will the Granadian Tribunal think if them eagles she sends every morning stop delivering messages?"

"And what if it isn't Granadia she's delivering messages to? What then?" Bertram shifted his head so the ruined side of his face turned to Hagan then Ryne.

"We know your opinion of the Devout. But suggesting she be sending messages to Amuni's Children, wherever they are, be foolish. And blasphemous."

Ryne almost told Hagan it could be a possibility. But Bertram would only feed on such a suggestion.

"In Humelen's name, Hagan," Bertram said, his already black skin growing so black it shone with his rage as his aura gave an almost imperceptible quaver. "Open your eyes. The Tribunal has always wanted to conquer Ostania. Ever since Nerian rebelled, and they lost their hold on us. I tell you, the War of Remnants was their doing. It was their way to get a toehold back into Ostania."

Hagan chuckled. "You and your plots. I know the reason you wish to harm her. We all do. Maybe you have the right of it, but—"

"You're damned right I do," Bertram blurted out.

"Bertram, your son's death be—"

"You think this is just about my son?" Bertram's face twisted with the question. "I forgave Ryne long ago for my son's death. It wasn't by his hand. The Alzari assassins hired by your precious Tribunal were the ones responsible. The same Tribunal that's responsible for everything else me and the rest of Ostania has suffered. I'll be damned if I let someone else get hurt or grovel at their feet. I'm sick of it."

Ryne kept silent. He'd apologized many times for the loss of the mayor's last family member. Sometimes, he felt as if he had never been in Carnas the boy would be alive today. However, if he'd not been here, the village would have fallen to raiders years ago. That had never made him feel any better about what the Alzari had done to the boy. He knew no words to console Bertram.

"This be foolishness," Hagan said, his lip curled in disgust. "Blame the Tribunal for sending them Alzari back then, fine. But harm Mariel for the sake of vengeance, and the Tribunal's attention will turn on us. You wish to condemn us all? Killing their assassins be one thing, but to kill a Devout?"

"A Devout? Ha," Bertram scoffed, the angry scar from his burn twitching, "If you're so blind as to believe she's just out here to teach us 'savages' about the purity of the Lord of light, then you're more fool than I thought, Hagan. Ilumni...Amuni, they're all Streamean in case you forgot. The Tribunal use the Devout to preach justice and spiritual harmony and meanwhile conquer all who don't convert. Same shit, different chamber pot. Next, you'll tell me you believe she's really interested in how we survive, and why we risk settling this far into the wilds. Tell me this, since you do believe she's *just* a Devout. Would you be satisfied with the offer she has made to take those who wish to follow her to Granadia?"

Hagan poured himself a cup of wine. "Of course not, but if they no longer wish to be here, who be we to stop them?"

"We're a free people, that's who. Beholden to no one. Free to worship which gods we please, when we please. Free to fight whoever threatens us. Free to live out here away from the grip and poison of other peoples."

"Funny thing this freedom of yours be," Hagan said, knocking the contents of his pipe into an ashtray. "It seems to ignore our choice to come and go as we please." When Bertram only glowered in response Hagan added, "That be what I thought," and took a sip from his cup.

Bertram snatched up the flagon of wine. His jaw clenched while he filled the last remaining cup, and the flesh from his burn scar tugged at his lips as he muttered to himself. With another glare at Hagan, who raised his own cup as a toast, Bertram downed the drink. He glanced at Ryne and took a deep breath. "We may be doomed anyway. If those Alzari in the woods were sent for you then the Tribunal knows you're still alive. And that means Mariel already sent word."

Ryne scowled. He'd known this was coming. "And yet I haven't killed her or suggested you do. Concern yourself with your people, Bertram. Convene your elders as you will. I've had my say. Tell them what I found. Then decide what's best." He stood, picked up his sword, and headed toward the door.

"Where will you be? It may be best if you tell them yourself." Hagan's voice pleaded for Ryne to accept the offer.

Pulling the door open, Ryne paused and turned to meet Hagan's gaze. "I have a summons to prepare for. It cannot be avoided if I'm to help you regardless of what decision the elders make." He stepped out into the night.

CHAPTER 9

Irmina's hand fidgeted close to her sword. Cloudless, dark skies sprinkled with stars stretched as far as she could see beyond Silvereyes. Sweat beaded her forehead, and her shirt clung to her back as she fixed her gaze on the Ostanian who was watching her from atop a small slope, not making any attempt to hide himself.

Rolling her shoulders, she stretched her neck to one side to work out the tightness from maintaining her vigilance. The throbbing pain along her shoulders eased ever so slightly, but the unbidden urge to nod off gnawed at her. Occasionally, she pricked herself with her Devout pin, the carving of the moons and sun etched into its shiny surface reflecting what little light existed.

She needed to stay awake. The one moment since coming to Carnas that she'd allowed her attention to lapse, she'd almost paid the price. That time, Silvereyes snuck close in the minutes her concentration wavered, and forced her to use every trick she knew to escape him. Since then, she made certain to keep her campsites out in the open on the Orchid Plains. The events in the woods when he'd touched her mind, changed his eye color, and somehow repaired his armor without the use of any materials, only made her more wary.

The humid night stoked her anxiety. Shadows stretched across the sparse trees and layered fescue, making Silvereyes become little more than a silhouette. A flash of memory brought those obsidian eyes screaming back, and she shivered. She touched her sword hilt for its reassuring comfort. Even home in Eldanhill, she'd kept her sword close at all times. Ancel used to say her sword received more love than he did. She squeezed the hilt with the thought.

From the corner of her eye, she saw the commotion still bubbling within Carnas. They must be in an uproar over the boy. She blew out a breath, still wishing she could have helped Kahkon. But at least the giant man had found him. Whatever he had done, she knew he used Mater. She hadn't needed to open herself to her Matersense to be able to tell. The sheer power he used resonated to her core. A feeling she'd never experienced before. Not even in her master's presence.

Jerem's words and his grave expression returned to her.

"Irmina," Jerem said. *"This man is the deadliest person you will ever meet. If he discovers you are a Matus, he will become hostile. If he learns you are a Matus powerful enough to be an Ashishin, he will most certainly kill you without hesitation. Until you learn a way to approach him, you must maintain a distance where he cannot read your aura. Under no circumstances must you use Mater in his presence."*

"My aura?"

"Yes." Jerem stroked his wispy beard. *"His kind has a unique ability to see essences around any living thing without engaging their Matersense."*

"What is his kind? And what is he called? His name? I'd like to know what or who I'm facing."

"Knowing that part would make no difference. He's had too many names to count. What he calls himself now," he shrugged, *"I have no idea. Suffice it to say, if he doesn't wish to accompany you then you will not be able to force him."*

"So how am I to bring him back with me?" she asked.

"That, dear one, is a problem for which you must find a solution. One thing is certain. You must not fail," High Ashishin Jerem said, his raspy voice harder and more grave than she had ever heard.

A quick movement from Silvereyes broke Irmina from her memories. He darted away toward Carnas.

Irmina's stomach writhed. She didn't wish to follow, but what other choices were there? If she needed this to complete her training, to secure her revenge, then so be it. Hand on her sword hilt, she jogged after Silvereyes.

Ancel stumbled through the side door of his parents' winery with Mirza and Charra on his heels. "Da! Ma!" He rushed down the hall past hanging paintings and startled servants toward the study. He banged the door open.

Ancel's father looked up from poring over his books, his black hair streaked with white spilling about his face. Stefan's expression darkened as he straightened in his chair. "What's all this fuss about? Shouldn't you two be out picking kinai?"

Ancel and Mirza's words tumbled over each other at the same time, their recount of the night's events spilling out in a jumble.

His father's hard slap rang off the tabletop. "One at a time."

"Stefan, sir," Mirza began, wringing his hands.

Stefan stroked his pointed beard and arched an eyebrow at him.

"S–sorry," Mirza stammered, his cheeks flushing red, "I mean, Master Dorn. Sir, we were just chased by…by…"

"Spit it out, boy."

The heavy oak door creaked open. Ancel's mother peeked in, her gray hair wrapped in a bun. Her steady, silvery blue eyes took in both their disheveled appearances before she stepped inside and closed the door behind her. "Why do you two look as if you were dragged through a field? And what's this mess you brought in with you?" She pointed at the red trail their boots and Charra's paws left on the carpet. Her nose wrinkled "And what's that awful smell?" She leaned back outside the door and called for one of the servants, barking instructions before turning her gaze back to the boys. "Well?"

Their replies burst forth again, a jumbled roll of both voices at once.

"Both of you calm down," his mother ordered, her voice a melodic chime that still carried authority. "Take a seat." She pointed to the soft, cushioned armchairs as she glided across the room. Her dark blue dress brought out her eyes as it flowed around her. "Give yourselves a few moments to breathe and then begin again. From the start this time." She nodded to Stefan and then to the large room's opposite side.

Stefan pushed back his chair from the table and stood. His white silk shirt and biege trousers showed stains from his last meal. Muttering under his breath, he strode past the many bookcases to the second entrance into the room, peered outside, then pulled the door shut.

Ancel and Mirza made their way to the chairs near the table and sat. Books littered the oak surface, many of them open or containing a marker. Charra trotted over and stretched on the rug next to them.

The thick rug under his feet soothed Ancel as he suddenly realized that his legs were watery weak. Taking a deep breath, he stretched them out, savoring the smell of old books and the flowery scented oil his mother favored in the lamps along the walls. This was the only room in the house without a window, and the lamplight played across the wall hangings depicting the history of the Ostanian tribes. Considering how his father often boasted about their ancestors' bravery, Ancel wondered what they would have thought about how he fled the Greenleaf.

"Well, which one of you is ready?" His father once again took his seat at the table. Mother stood next to him and rested her hand on his shoulder.

"I am," Ancel answered. He sucked in a great breath and relayed all that had happened, from the missing wolves to the rotten kinai in their secret glen, to the two wolf–like creatures that had followed them.

His father's brow rose and lowered with the telling until his eyes became slits when Ancel mentioned the two beasts. His mother's face remained impassive until he mentioned the kinai. A slight hiss escaped her lips then.

"Have you told this to anyone?" Stefan's stern expression took in both Mirza and Ancel.

"No, Da."

"No, Master Dorn."

"Good. Keep it that way until I say otherwise." A thoughtful look crossed his father's face.

"I know that look, Stefan Dorn," Mother said. "Don't think of running off and doing anything foolish."

"I'm not, Thania, dear, but this needs to be investigated."

"Tell the Council. Let them have this task for once."

His father sighed. "I wish it were that simple."

"It's always simple," Mother said dryly. "Some clans have come down from the mountains with wild mountain wolves to use in one of their feuds. As usual you decide it's your matter to settle." She shook her head and huffed.

Stefan appeared taken aback, and his eyebrows climbed his forehead as he turned his head up to gaze at her. "You know better," he said, his voice somewhere between scolding and a quiet reminder. "If it were only ruined kinai I would pass this over, but the smell he described and the green eyes…" His voice trailed off as Mother rolled her eyes. Stefan glanced around at Mirza and Ancel.

"As if they could cross the Vallum of Light," his mother retorted under her breath. In a more even–tempered voice she said, "Take some extra men with you if you must be the one, but only a soldier or two. There's no need to scare the boys any more than they already are. We wouldn't want their imagination to get the better of them." She eyed them as if waiting for either of them to say something different, but they both remained quiet.

"You're right as usual." Stefan bowed apologetically. "I let the old days come creeping through when I heard their story." He gave a strained chuckle. "I'll see which mountain clans are fighting and inform the Council. You boys…"

The rest of his father's words washed over Ancel in a disquieting wave. He answered Mirza's raised brow with a bewildered expression of his own. Ancel mulled over the descriptions in his head; wolf–like beasts with green, glowing eyes, a smell like old, unwashed fur mixed with death. Coupled with his mother's mention of the Vallum of Light it clicked like a key in a lock.

Wraithwolves? No it couldn't be. They couldn't cross the Vallum of Light and its Bastions. Besides, in the books, shadelings often walked like men. What he and Mirza saw did not. *So what were they?* He turned to Mirza to see the same realization dawn on his friend's face.

"Da," Ancel broke in on whatever his father was saying. "Do you really think those were wraith—"

"I never said such a thing," his father snapped, his voice hardening into steel. "And don't you repeat that in front of

anyone. Rumors are the last thing we need. Do.You.Understand?"
He punctuated his words by pointing his finger from Ancel to
Mirza.

Ancel recognized this as a time that he wouldn't get
around his father, and that the instructions weren't negotiable.
He nodded, seeing Mirza's head bob slowly beside him.

"Answer me. Both of you. I want to hear you say it."

"Yes, Da."

"Yes, Master Dorn."

"Good. Now—"

A knock sounded on the door. Mother glided over and
opened it.

Mensa, an elderly servant with a bent back, bowed to her
before she ushered him into the room. He carried an iron skillet
in one hand, liquid sloshing around its insides. In the other hand,
he held a leather satchel.

Mother pointed to Ancel and Mirza. "Start with their
boots and Charra's paws. Then clean the floor."

Mensa nodded and shuffled over to Ancel and Mirza
as they bent to take off their boots. When they finished, Mensa
reached into the satchel and removed two identical pairs of boots.
He put one next to each of them and took theirs in return.

Ancel frowned but said nothing. He and Mirza slipped
into their new footwear.

Charra growled when Mensa bent to take one of his
paws.

"Stop it, boy," Ancel murmured.

Charra quieted, but he stared at Mensa as the old man
soaked a cloth with the clear liquid in the bucket and took his
time cleaning each paw. When Mensa finished, Charra cooed.
Mensa took the same cloth, got down on his knees, and wiped
the trail they had left on the rugs and carpet. When he finished,
he bowed and left.

Stefan looked over to Ancel and Mirza. "Now, off with
you two. We have things to discuss. Mirza, I'll be out soon to
escort you home."

"Thank you, Master Dorn," Mirza said.

"I'll go with him to the front," Ancel said.

His mother nodded and they turned and left. With

Charra padding behind them, they headed out into the foyer, leaving his parents to their talk.

"Do you think those animals could've been…I mean, with the cleaning…" Mirza peered around, anxiety radiating from him.

"I don't know, but I'll do as my father says, at least until he takes some men out to the glen." Ancel did his best to hide his own doubts. "Da's right. We shouldn't talk about this."

"And if it's true?" Mirza whispered. "I mean, you know what they say about those things in the books, about who and what they hunt. We live in a town full of Matii. If they're, you know…"

"All the shadelings in our world were destroyed during the War of Remnants. The only place shadelings can be created is in Hydae," Ancel quoted with great conviction. "And Hydae is sealed away." The statement brought him some semblance of calm. *All the books and reports couldn't be wrong, could they?* "Whatever they were, the Council will handle it. None of it has anything to do with us, be it a feud or something else." Ancel nodded to one of the servants as they walked through the foyer and out onto the porch.

From where they stood, Eldanhill's lights shone a few miles below them in hazy waves of blue. Charra trotted across the porch and onto the stairs.

"Tomorrow at school, we're going to act like none of this happened," Ancel said. "Hopefully, it's like my mother said. Just the mountain clans infighting again."

"Hopefully," Mirza repeated, his tone distant.

Ancel watched as servants and workers bustled about the estate. Those returning from last minute efforts to finish harvesting kinai trudged along, while others whipped at mules or bulls pulling drays laden with the crop toward the brick buildings that housed the fermenting equipment and the wine press. He wished everything would remain as calm and serene as it appeared, but for some reason his mind told him otherwise. The thought of wraithwolves marauding through the woods and hunting down anyone who used Mater brought a chill to his bones. He drew his ripped cloak around him.

CHAPTER 10

Ryne took one more look out to Mariel's campfire before he decided to head home. He'd spent the last couple hours waiting outside Hagan's Inn while the elders met. They still had not come to a decision. When Sakari joined him, Ryne said a quick goodnight to the guards. Together, they made their way past row upon row of mostly dark homes toward Carnas' western outskirts.

The reek from clogged drains made Ryne eye the cloudless skies. Two weeks between thunderstorms was a rare event. If the weather continued, they would be forced to remove the levies from the tributary of the Fretian River that flowed close by. The still air felt as if a great creature inhaled and now held its breath. His skin prickled with the thought of that breath's release.

Ryne's mind was still on the weather when they arrived at his over-sized house, lamplight pooling from several windows. Wispy smoke swirled from the brick chimney, and spicy food smells filtered from within. Before he could reach the wide front door, it opened, and light flooded the road.

Vera's buxom silhouette stood in the doorway. "We hoped you would be back in time to eat."

"And we hoped we would get to dance for you tonight," said Vana from somewhere in the room.

Ryne grinned as he stepped inside and embraced both

women at the same time, one in each arm. "I thought you two would be going back to Hagan's?"

"Master Hagan knows better than to ask us to work late with you out and about," Vana said. "We overheard you say you had a summons to attend to." She flicked her long dark tresses to one side.

Vera chimed in, "Who else would feed you before you left?" She tossed her head the opposite way from her sister, her hair falling past her shoulders.

Leaning into his hug, their heads barely reached his abdomen. They still looked as beautiful as the night he saved them from a slaver's brutal whips. Maybe tonight he wouldn't act shy when their bodies, which still bore the scars from their abuse, swayed as they danced the Temtesa for him. Ryne still couldn't decide what to do about their affections, or which to choose, or even if he should. 'A nice dilemma to have,' Hagan often said.

While the sisters fussed over Ryne, Sakari disappeared down a lamp–lit hall toward one of the two rooms in the rear. Ryne couldn't help the twitch of his lips. He'd tried many times, but Sakari insisted on keeping to himself.

Finished with their playful banter, the sisters vanished in the direction of kitchen. Ryne shed his boots in a corner near the front door, strode across the large room, and eased himself into a chair at the dining table with a heavy sigh. It felt good to be home.

After a moment, he stood and strolled over to one of the many bookshelves lining one wall opposite the kitchen door. Close to the shelves, a huge padded chair sat below a window looking out onto the plains and the Nevermore Heights outlined to the north. The hidden slopes brought anticipation trembling through his body and made him glance at his books. He'd received several there.

Most of the books on the shelves were detailed studies and theory on Mater from great professors of the topic like Shin Henden and Exalted Calestis. Many of them detailed different Forges, how to use essences within different elements to combine to make another element. They made it seem so complicated. He recalled his first attempt, taking water from the element of Flows and cold from the element of Streams, to make ice which was a part of the Forms but still bore properties of the other two. Soon after, he'd been required to kill, not only to replenish that which he had lost, but to appease the voices in his head. He cringed with the thought.

To him, it was all so simple. Liquid plus energy to make a solid. Solid plus energy to make a liquid. Most, if not all things, required the energy of the Streams. Take that away and it broke down to its baser components. Forging worked best on something already in existence with a source to draw upon, like pulling heat from a flame to create a fireball. Or the charge from a storm for a lightning strike. Sure, some of it could be stored, but when the essences were readily available around you, the Forging was that much more powerful. It wasn't as if most of the elements weren't already incorporated into each other. He remembered when he used to doubt whether the elements existed in everything, but wherever he looked in the world he saw where different essences combined for the tiniest of creations.

Other books dealt with military strategy and instruction on the Disciplines of Soldiering. Those included fighting styles, relaying stories of warriors who could summon massive Constructs to do battle for them or lose themselves, battle–bonded within the clarity of the Shunyata, undefeatable. Some contained myths and legends of peoples and creatures long lost—the Eztezians, the Erastonians, the Chroniclers, the netherlings and many more. But within every myth there was some semblance of truth to be found. Others gave detailed recounts of Denestia's split into Ostania to the east and Granadia to the west. He always believed if you had to read, then make certain you gained practical knowledge.

Ryne took off his sword and leaned the white scabbard with its gold rune embossing next to the bookshelf. A series of white glyphs were etched into the guard and long golden hilt. He straightened to see Vera bring him a plate piled with venison stew. The peppery smell from the meat and the scent from the baked bread in her other hand made his stomach grumble.

"You know you can't eat with those on, right?" Vera pointed to his leather armor. "Well, not that you can't eat," she corrected herself, "But we won't serve you until you remove it and show us you didn't get hurt earlier today."

"Sometimes I forget myself, Miss Vera." Her raised brow at his lie brought a smile to his lips.

The two–piece armor always felt loose at first, but once he pulled them on, they melded to his body, as if tailored just for him. If he didn't know the power of the Scripts drawn on each piece he would have wondered how such flimsy looking, fitted armor could protect a man. The leather itself was harder than any metal he knew and more pliant than the finest cloth weaves. The multicolored Scripts were an exact replica of those covering his body up to his chin.

Vera's green eyes studied him the entire time as he peeled the armor off. Her gaze didn't drift even when she placed the plate on the table. Her sister soon joined her, carrying a pitcher of sweet kinai juice and a glass. They giggled as he laid his armor over his chair.

He stood before them in tight undergarments made from fine cotton, crafted so they wouldn't hamper his ability to put on his armor. Giving them both a ghost of a smile, he said, "Well, you ladies had your fun, and have done your inspection. You see I'm not hurt. May I eat now?"

"Yes, you may, my Lord," they both answered.

He strode to the table, sat, and dug in with zest.

Hours later, after another night with little sleep, a long, whistling wail penetrated Ryne's skull—the summons he anticipated.

The calling was more a feeling than a sound. Ryne's head resonated with it like one of his many headaches. He fought off the familiar dizziness swirling through his mind as the euphoria from the kinai juice he drank earlier battled the whirling sensation. After a few moments, the lightheadedness dwindled. With the dwindling came an irresistible pull like a maggot to a corpse.

He stared off through his window toward the cloud–shrouded Nevermore Heights. The summons pulled him there. He knew the place well.

Smirking, Ryne put down the ancient leather–bound tome he'd been reading. The title leered at him—*The Principles and Tenets of Mater by Exalted Thanairen.* After twenty years reading the book, every single word within it remained etched in his mind. One part came to mind as he took in the gloomy light of dawn peeking through the clouds. *Dawn and dusk—The Spellforge hours— the times when light and shade were the most balanced—a period for great power.*

Ryne stood and the two young women at his feet stirred. Vana and Vera had swayed and gyrated in the Temtesa until they grew tired. Then they sat and listened to him read from the book until they fell asleep. He waited a few minutes to make sure they were sound asleep once more. Satisfied with their slumber, he gathered his armor and his sword and slipped from the room.

In the adjoining room, Ryne donned his armor. Tightening the laces, he savored the feel of the leather molding itself to his flesh until the Scripts on the armor and those on his body became seamless. He tossed the strap for his scabbard over his head and his greatsword came to rest at his waist, the pommel slanted across his stomach.

With one last look at the sisters, he strode through the living room. Sakari detached himself from the wall following like Ryne's own shadow. For a moment, Ryne thought about leaving a note, but he changed his mind. The women were used to him leaving for extended periods. Hopefully, they wouldn't worry too much this time. When he returned, he would let them know it didn't matter they were once bed warmers. He cared for them regardless. Sighing, he opened the door and stepped outside.

As usual the air was thick and humid. Dawn pricked the eastern horizon, the shaded gloom of thunderclouds blanketing the sky. *Good, we'll finally get some rain today. Gods know we need it.*

Ryne spoke to Sakari without looking at him. "I didn't think you would've felt that summons."

"My affinity to what you feel has increased of late. I am sure you feel it too. Do you really think they will have the answers you seek?"

Ryne pondered the question for a moment. "They haven't failed me so far. What have I got to lose?"

"Our freedom."

"What sense is there in being free if I don't know who I am? What my purpose is? Why this craving to kill thrives within me? My mind itself is a prison. Regardless, like you said, things are changing. I can feel it." Ryne peered at the storm clouds. "The inconsistent weather, these mysterious women, the change in our link, the reappearance of Amuni's Children and the wraithwolves. Maybe, answering the Svenzar's summons is a part of this change."

"What about the villagers?"

"Bertram and Hagan will know what to do should things worsen. I believe the elders will come to the right decision and at least have the women and children head to safety. Besides, with the way my power has acted recently, I hope the Svenzar can help bring me better control. I'll need it to help Carnas. For their sakes and mine, I have little choice but to answer the calling."

Face betraying no emotion, Sakari bowed, his silver–flecked, green pinpricks for eyes staring calmly back. Sometimes, Ryne still found himself wondering if the man had any insides.

"Come, let's go," Ryne said. "We'll take the most direct path through the Mondros Forest." He would have preferred to ride, but the trees in the deep rainforest and the treacherous Heights would hinder any mounts.

Without another word, Sakari started out across the Orchid Plains at a slow jog with Ryne trailing after him. Halfway across the plains, Ryne glanced over his shoulder.

A small figure moved away from Mariel's camp in the distance behind them. For the first time, Ryne realized this trip provided him with a great opportunity to be rid of the woman.

Lightning flashed and highlighted Mariel's form as she headed in their direction. Heartbeats later, thunder rumbled its defiant response and rain began to patter to the ground. The long awaited storm arrived.

CHAPTER 11

A ncel marveled at the ebb and flow of the battle between the two men in the distant city. *Dear Ilumni, I beg you, let your light bring victory.* As the prayer crossed his mind, he licked his suddenly dry lips, before taking a quick glance around him. *Calm down man, stop jumping at shadows.* Yet, here in Hydae where the shade held sway he couldn't help the fluttering in his stomach.

At that precise moment, citrine and emerald lightning skittered across the banks of char–colored clouds drawn to the conflict raging in the city. The flashes made Ancel's gut lurch, and he gritted his teeth at the sky. Why was he here on this forsaken ledge exposed to the angry elements?

Ancel's loose–fitting clothes flapped about him as the winds howled and swirled like a crowd decrying some terrible act before a revolt. Eddies snatched at his cloak in an effort to fling him from his rocky perch high above the vast black plains and forests. He took a slow breath and forced his stomach to near silence.

Elemental power continued to roil across the sky as if the gods of Streams and Flows battled for supremacy. Ancel could imagine them and their fear inspiring visages clad in the finest armors, only their sparkling eyes showing through slits in their helms.

On one side, there would be Ilumni and Amuni wielding light and shade representing the elements of Streams. Ilumni's power resonated in the lightning flashes and in the wan afternoon sun. Amuni's taint bubbled everywhere, from the foliage below, infected and decaying with his shade, to the darkness choking the air. Even the sun appeared diminished in Hydae.

On the opposite side, Ancel pictured the twin gods of Flows lashing out together; their power sending prickles across his skin as if he stood naked on the ledge. Aeoli commanded the void, using the air itself to form the storm winds. Hyzenki paired with his sister in the fight, breaking the thunderheads to make water join the fray. Black rain pelted down before howling winds whipped the drops sideways like arrows shot from a million bows.

A loud, piercing chime echoed from the city like steel screeching against stone. Something metallic flew into the air, Mater shooting from it in sparkling glows. The winds, rains, and clouds swirled into a gigantic maelstrom above the city—.

A sharp tap on Ancel's head knocked him from his daydream.

"Ancel!" shouted Teacher Calestis, drawing her slim staff back.

Ancel shook his head as his eyes focused on his surroundings. The expectant gazes from the Teacher and several students of varied ages, from youthful like himself to wizened and bent–backed like Calestis, greeted him. Mirza leered at him from his bench across from Ancel, his gray eyes a reflection of his expression. Besides the benches filled with students and the Teacher's chair and table, the only other furniture in the room were a few bookshelves. Two windows in the yellow brick walls looked out onto Eldanhill's cobbled streets.

Teacher Calestis rapped her staff into the floor with a dull wood on wood crack. "If Nerian the Shadowbearer was a Devout—a priest bonded in heart and soul to Ilumni—why did he forsake the Lord of light and answer the shade's call? Why did he turn to Amuni?" Several students raised their hands, but Calestis ignored them all. "Ancel," she said, pointing a gnarled finger and scowling, "This question is yours. Since the Teachings bore you so much, you must know all the answers."

"He was misled into believing his people were betrayed and massacred at the Tribunal's command. He convinced himself the Skadwaz had somehow crossed from Hydae and delivered Amuni's power to him. Blinded by rage, he sought revenge, resorting to the use of shadelings," Ancel answered without hesitation.

Galiana's golden eyes twinkled. "And how did he persuade the remainder of those loyal to the light to follow his lead."

"By the sword. However, a few did support his cause willingly, convinced of their retribution. Those who resisted were forced to fight or die. Once many saw Nerian could stamp his name in history as the first to reunite the world and return Ostania to its former glory, they accepted his rule. They ignored that he now wielded shade and all its horrors to do his bidding."

Calestis gave him a small smile. "Well done."

As soon as Calestis's attention shifted elsewhere, Ancel allowed his thoughts to drift back to his daydream. Why did he keep having these images of a land that existed only in the stories? What city was that with its sparkling spires and streets lined with colonnades and fountains? His dreams the night before had also included the green–eyed beasts and the kinai rotting in their glen. What were those creatures? Could they really have been wraithwolves? He'd thought about approaching Teacher Calestis, but his father's warning prevented him from doing so. Ancel sighed. He wished he had someone he could confide in. Ever since Irmina left Eldanhill, he dreamed more often than before. Without her to talk to, little made sense.

Thoughts about Irmina made his gaze drift to Alys Valdeen in time to catch her soft eyes regarding him. Her hair shone in as deep an orange as a brilliant sunset. Her eyes glittered, and she sniffed, turning away from his gaze.

"Thinking about Irmina again?" Mirza's voice broke Ancel from his thoughts.

Ancel glanced around at his friend and saw Teacher Calestis had dismissed the class. Students headed to the doors, laughing and chatting amongst themselves, most happy to see the end of another day of learning.

"Something like that," Ancel finally replied. "I wonder what she's doing now. Did she complete her training? Did she pass the test? If she would at least write—"

"You would go running off to wherever she is," Mirza quipped. "Or try to. Even if she was somewhere across the sea in Ostania."

Ancel shrugged and stood.

"You know, you piss me off sometimes." Mirza shook his head, his unkempt hair, the color of dirty red bricks, spilling about his shoulders. "I mean, you've been blessed to be with two of the prettiest girls in all Eldanhill and you moon over Irmina. The girl was as rough as any soldier. Me? I prefer them soft and supple like Alys." Mirza's gaze followed the girl who was now just leaving with a few friends.

Ancel's lips twitched. "And here I was thinking you had no preference at all. We both know even one of the old apothecaries or retired Shin like Teacher Calestis would please you, wrinkles, warts, and all."

Mirza stared at him, aghast. "I know Irmina addled your brains, but I didn't think you lost all your senses. Here, let me run call Alys for you, maybe she can make you feel better some." He made to run after the girls.

Ancel snatched at the arm of Mirza's beige coat. "Don't you dare."

Mirza grinned. "That's what I thought."

They were the last to leave the building used as the Mystera's main study hall. Bright afternoon sunlight greeted them accompanied by a breeze from the snow-capped Kelvore Mountains. The mountain range stretched as far as the eye could see to the north in this part of Granadia. No sooner had they stepped outside when ham-sized hands snatched Mirza at the door and twirled him as if he was a dancer at a ball. A body built like a draught horse, deep and broad of chest with legs that could be two of Ancel's came into sight as Mirza tottered away in the opposite direction. Ancel burst out laughing.

"I hope you're ready to spin the girls and dangle them on your knees." Danvir Bemelle slapped his big hand on his thigh as Mirza stumbled to a stop. "We're leaving this evening to deliver the kinai wine."

"What?" Ancel's eyebrows rose and his lips curved into a smile.

"Yes, my Da convinced yours he should let you go. He said it was best for your nineteenth naming day not to coddle you anymore." Danvir tilted his head as he regarded Ancel with eyes of burnished copper, the one feature that might make a person overlook his bulbous nose. "Although, I'm not so sure. You still behave as if you're pining away to me."

"Wooo," Mirza said, finally regaining his breath. "Taverns, wine, women, and song." He rubbed his hands together. "Here we come. Oh, and yes, he's still mooning over Irmina. As usual, he was lost in class."

Danvir grunted, and rubbed at his oversized ears. "Did the old bag clip him on the head again?" He straightened his coat back into position, running his hands down the sleeves and nodded with satisfaction.

"You know it." Mirza chuckled. "Then somehow he managed to answer a question about Nerian the Shadowbearer without missing a beat."

Danvir let out an exasperated breath while combing his well–oiled, blond hair back until it fell neatly at his shoulders. "That nonsense again? I still don't understand why we need to study history anyways. What does it all have to do with becoming a Matus."

"Well," Mirza began, "you know what Calestis always says—"

The three youths looked at each other and grinned. "Becoming a Matus is not just about touching the elements of Mater that reside in the world around us," they recited in their best all–knowing imitations of their Teacher. "Becoming a Matus is to learn from the Ashishin before us who have wielded Mater unto their own demise like the Skadwaz. After all, Mater is more than just the elemental force that resides in everything and drives our world. It drives all worlds. Just as present action dictates our future, so does history dictate our present." They all burst into laughter afterward, Mirza's gaunt face going red, and Danvir's guffaws making a rumble in his broad chest. Tears streamed from Ancel's eyes.

"At least the seats you took up in my class have not been a total waste of space."

Ancel jumped at Teacher Calestis's voice, his laughter coming to an abrupt end. His two friends gave the bent old woman wide–eyed stares. Calestis drew herself up straight, her golden eyes stern, and tapped her staff on the cobbles. The youths all began stumbling over themselves with apologies.

"Nonsense," Teacher Calestis said, waving a dismissive hand, "I do tend to ramble on, but you three have remembered an important piece of your training. So, I will let you have your moment." They all breathed easier. "However," she continued, "Should I have any issues from you in class at any time, your parents will be informed about you making fun of the Teachers. A disrespect well worthy of a chore penance I'm sure. Now off with you."

Given a reprieve, they didn't wait to have it withdrawn. They scampered away, heads held down.

Ancel glanced over his shoulder once to see Calestis shambling off in the opposite direction. He was tempted to run after her and tell her about the creatures and what he suspected. Coming to a swift decision, he turned. Before he could take a step, a hand grabbed his arm. He looked around to see Mirza.

Mirza shook his head. Ancel had wondered how his friend could act all day as if nothing happened. Now he saw the truth. Mirza's slate–colored eyes bore the same concern as his, but somehow he did a better job of hiding it. Ancel nodded, and they followed Danvir who was in the process of righting his clothes again after the short run.

They travelled along Learner's Row, and its multitude of buildings, practice areas, and side streets packed tightly together where Teachers held classes and lectures for a variety of arts. The dense gathering of structures often made the Mystera appear to be a miniature village within Eldanhill. Ancel often wondered if the other Mysteras in other towns and cities were similarly built.

Weaponmasters, bearing the Lightstorm insignia on their breast, drilled soldiers in enclosed spaces between the buildings, each practice area large enough to hold two hundred men. In other sections, Teachers practiced Materforgings with students, teaching them how to grasp the essences and direct earth, fire or light in various applications from lighting a torch to opening a pit in the ground. Yet others taught more mundane tasks like cooking to more advanced like apothecary and alchemy.

The students walking ahead through the Mystera were mostly dressed in earthy yellow or beige uniforms, the men in tunics and pants, and the women in dresses that stopped below the knees. Among them soldiers stood with their chests puffed out in their deep blue garb, golden shield and sword pins shiny upon their breasts. Ancel's eyes shone with admiration as he watched them strut among the students. The Teachers kept to the other side of the Row, most striding with a purposeful gait in their pristine white robes.

Ancel noted the vast majority of students still bore the book and pen insignia stitched or pinned onto their breast or shoulder denoting them as novices. Remembering when he once displayed the same, he smiled and fingered the silver sword on his lapel, puffing himself up with thoughts of his promotion to trainee. With the memory, a longing for Irmina flashed through his mind. He touched his breast pocket.

A step away from a Matus. One more step. Then I'll earn the right to petition a Weaponmaster to be trained as a Dagodin. He smiled inwardly with the thought as his dreams swept away to a more ambitious status. *A Dagodin so I can graduate from the Mystera and study either in Calisto or at the Iluminus to become an Ashishin. Then I'll join the Pathfinders. No one will be able to stop me from finding her then.* His smile grew wider.

"You know, I would hope that look meant you're eyeing some new girl," Mirza said, his lips pursed. "But knowing you the way I do, that'd just be wishful thinking on my part." He sighed as Ancel offered no reply. "Hey Dan, who's escorting us with the delivery?"

Danvir's eyes twinkled and his mouth twisted into a slow grin. "Headspeaker Valdeen."

Mirza cackled. A groan escaped Ancel's lips. The last thing he needed was to be in the company of Alys' father especially after what happened the evening before.

"There'll be several guards coming with us to help protect this year's delivery because of the recent feuding between us and Doster. Maybe—"

"You know, Dan," Mirza interrupted. "You always say us when you speak about Sendeth, but—"

"Yes, yes, I know," Danvir retorted. "I swear you listen to your father too much about how they treat us. We pay taxes and tribute to King Emory regardless. And the whole of Whitewater Falls belongs to him, Eldanhill included. Whether we're far north and behind the King's back as people like to say, it doesn't matter. We pay all the same. Think on it." Danvir gave Ancel a sidelong glance, his annoyed expression changing to a grin. "Anyway, as I was saying, maybe Ancel can huddle with the soldiers so Master Valdeen doesn't get to questioning him about his plans for his daughter."

"My chances of avoiding that man are about the same as us running into Dosteri raiders," Ancel grumbled. "Slim to none."

"Well, I'd suggest you make nice with Alys before we leave then," Mirza said, making a humping motion.

Danvir chuckled, clapping Mirza on the shoulder hard enought to make him stumble.

Ancel ignored his friends, staring off toward where the girl rounded the corner off Learner's Row onto Henden Lane on her way home. The end of the Row split into several streets that meandered through this side of Eldanhill before they met the Eldan Road. Houses great and small, all sandstone or brick with tiled roofs, painted in white shades or dull yellows lined the roads. The citizens of Eldanhill bustled about the streets, busy with their preparations for the upcoming harvest celebrations. For a moment, he thought about hurrying after her before he changed his mind.

"He has more women on his mind than he knows what to do with," Mirza's distant voice said.

Ancel stopped walking. His friends stood a few feet behind him both acting as if they did not see him.

"Happens to the best of us," Danvir quipped, "or so my Da says."

"Does this mean we're better than him?" Mirza nodded toward Ancel.

Danvir rubbed at his clean–shaven chin, his face feigning seriousness. "I don't know, maybe he just needs a class in how to love them and leave them. Let them do the chasing. Maybe, you and I…"

Ancel couldn't take anymore. Yelling, he chased after his friends as they ran off laughing.

CHAPTER 12

Ancel and his friends spent the better part of the next hour startling numerous merchants and townsfolk along the cobbled streets. Most were lost in preparation for the Soltide festival or busy hawking their wares.

Those who recognized them swore to tell their parents or chased them with brooms and switches. Their fun and nuisance making finally stopped after the town watch became involved. When they saw the gray uniforms advancing down Market Row onto Thanairen Square, they snuck off through one of the many back alleys crisscrossing Eldanhill. A short while later, they parted ways, and Ancel headed home.

As they did every year for Soltide, his parents had chosen to stay at their four–story townhouse in Eldanhill rather than their sprawling estate at the winery farther north. His father preferred to be close to his business dealings this time of year. Not that Ancel minded. He enjoyed being in town for Soltide rather than among the kinai orchards or watching his father instruct the workers in the correct methods of kinai juice distillation.

Ancel skipped down Damal Way past matching houses with their oval, stained glass windows, sloping, tiled roofs, and double doors that appeared as if the architects modeled every home after the first one built. Flowers in full bloom among the well–tended gardens added splashes of color to the otherwise bland white paint of the brick edifices.

Old man Finkel stood outside his home, tending his roses. When he saw Ancel, the man's eyes narrowed.

"Hello, Master Finkel," Ancel said.

"Don't hello me, boy. The only thing I want to hear from you is that you're going to leave my daughter alone. If you don't..." Finkel's voice trailed off as he stabbed his shovel into the soft dirt.

Ancel nodded and hurried by the front yard before the man actually decided to use the shovel.

Not long after, he passed by the Jungs. Their daughter Shari was outside, playing with their black and white hound dog.

"Hi, Ance," she called, her eyes glinting mischievously.

"Hi, Shari." Ancel moved close to the wrought iron fence.

Shari came down to meet him, her hips swaying as she moved. "When will you take me dancing again?"

"Tomorr—" A gooseberry slapped the ground next to Ancel, the yellow fruit splattering onto his boots. Ancel looked up. Shari's older brother threw another gooseberry.

"Stop it, Caron," Shari yelled, whirling to face the youth.

Caron threw another gooseberry. "You know Da doesn't want him around. Do you want me to go call him?"

"Look, Shari,' Ancel said. "I don't want any trouble. I'll head on home. Maybe we can speak during school tomorrow."

"I'd like that," Shari replied as she walked away smiling, her hips swaying once more.

Ancel glared at Caron before he walked away, continuing on home. More familiar faces greeted him along the street. There was Miss Jillian Flaina, Irmina's aunt, in one of her usual extravagant dresses, green silk with yellow Calvarish lace ruffles along the hem and bunched at the sleeves. Next to her strode old Rohan Lankon, his hat perched on his head in such a way that a slight wind might blow it off. They were involved in some heated discussion, and Jillian looked none too pleased. Ancel graced them with a bow, to which he received an icy stare from Jillian. What her issue was, he had no clue.

Ancel quickly forgot them as he saw Mirza's father, Devan Faber, and Danvir's old man, Guthrie Bemelle, across the other side of the street. To see the two of them together made him smile. Devan was as hard as the rocks he quarried, and Guthrie as soft as the gooseberry pudding his Inn was famous for. He shouted a greeting, but the men only gave him a half—

hearted acknowledgement. They were both too engrossed in conversation to notice him. He wondered if they'd just all come from a meeting at his house. His father had a tendency to call these councils whenever he came to town, but usually they held them at Guthrie's Whitewater Inn.

They must have been discussing what we saw in the Greenleaf. Spurred on by the thought, Ancel picked up his pace and took a left onto Tezian Lane. As he reached the stairs to his house, a loud sound somewhere between a rumbling grunt and a dog's bark issued behind him. Ancel turned to the sound as a mountain of shaggy, white fur crashed into him. He pivoted while snagging fur by the fistful.

Hot breath filled with stale smells greeted Ancel. He'd avoided being knocked to the ground, but he couldn't escape the hearty licking he received.

"Charra!" Ancel wheezed. Laughter poured out from him as his daggerpaw's rough tongue continued to bathe his face. "Stop it, boy." The licking continued unabated. "Sit," Ancel commanded. "Let me take a look at you."

The daggerpaw cooed and sat back on his haunches, his jaws spread in a toothy grin. Ancel stood and brushed himself off. Charra nuzzled into Ancel's chest, his soft hackles swishing with the move that felt more like a stiff head butt than a playful nudge. Ancel lost his balance momentarily before using Charra for support once more.

"Well, you're as fine as ever." Ancel brushed at a red stain on Charra's lower jaw. "And I see you've been in the kinai again. Naughty boy."

Charra whined.

Ancel chuckled. "It's fine, boy. Come." Without waiting Ancel walked up the stairs to the double doors.

Charra's low, rumbling growl stopped Ancel in his track. The daggerpaw stood stiff as a frozen board where Ancel left him, his eyes riveted on something down the empty street.

Frowning, Ancel followed Charra's gaze. Memories from the encounter in the Greenleaf Forest rose fresh in his mind. But all he saw were the eight houses, four per side, the gardens, and the empty road. People passed by his street and the one that intersected another lane further on. Nothing appeared out of sorts that would make Charra act as he did. Not that the daggerpaw needed any excuse for his moods, but the creatures in the Greenleaf whatever they were, had only made Charra's temperament worse.

"Charra."

Nose quivering, the daggerpaw cocked his head for a brief moment, but his attention remained on Tezian Lane.

A prick nagged at the edge of Ancel's consciousness like an annoying splinter in his finger. Eldanhill's noises played a muted buzz in the background. Somewhere on an adjoining street came muffled barks.

Ancel's brow knitted. *Where were the neighbors' dogs?* Normally, they would be in the gardens barking and howling at Charra from behind the safety of their fences. Now, they were nowhere to be seen. Ancel raised his foot to step down the stairs when Charra turned to him with a low coo.

The dog across the street started barking. Moments later, it came dashing through the hedges, jumping at the fence and snarling at Charra. The daggerpaw padded up the steps to the doors as if nothing happened. The chill and tension eased from Ancel's back as the other neighborhood dogs soon joined in a yelping chorus.

Ancel let out a breath, took one last look down the street, and pulled open the front door. Sweet smells of cooking wafted out to him. His mouth watered, and he found himself licking his lips as he paused for a moment to allow Charra to push past him as usual. Instead, the daggerpaw faced the street, stretched, and lay on the landing.

"Have it your way," Ancel said with a shake of his head. He stepped inside and closed the door behind him.

"About time." His father's resonant voice echoed down the long hallway as Ancel wiped his feet on the mat. "Your mother's cooked up a quick meal. She was becoming worried you were off playing the fool with your friends again."

"No, Da." Ancel shed his short cloak and hung it on the stand with the others. "I hurried home as fast as I could."

Stefan waited for him down the hall. When Ancel reached his father, the older man gave his school uniform a quick inspection, allowing only his penetrating emerald eyes to move. His father paused at the stains on Ancel's trousers where some merchant's plums had found their mark. A ghost of a smile touched his father's lips before he tilted his head to meet Ancel's eyes. Ancel swallowed.

"I suppose those two told you about the trip to Randane?"

Unable to hold his father's knowing gaze any longer, Ancel dipped his head, his face flushing with embarrassment. "Yes, they did."

"Good. You must be on your best behavior this trip. Headspeaker Valdeen will be presenting the kinai to the King's tasters this year, so you'll be taking the horses. Social status and all that. Impressions, my son," his father added in response to Ancel's raised brows as he led the way through the study.

Ancel gawked. "Da, then you should—"

"Oh?" Stefan clasped his hands behind his back. "First you lie, and now you're telling me what I must do?"

The words stung, and Ancel hung his head. He kept his attention on the bookcases lining the walls, then let his gaze rove across the long, polished table, and the soft chairs within the room. The plush carpet below their feet made for an uncomfortable silence. Finally, Ancel spoke up, "No, Da. It's just that this trip is so important. I don't want to ruin anything."

His father's voice softened. "You'll be fine, I'm sure. Besides, I'm unable to make the journey this year. I have another meeting to attend."

Ancel pursed his lips. "What could be more important than the King of Sendeth?"

"As much or more rides on my meeting as this year's Soltide offerings to King Emory."

"But, Da, without the King's agreement the Council won't be allowed to expand Eldanhill into a city as the Council wishes."

Stefan placed a hand on Ancel's shoulder and gave it a reassuring squeeze. "Sometimes, son, one must sacrifice for the bigger picture."

Pondering those words, Ancel was so lost in his thoughts it took a moment before he noticed his father's sword. "Da."

"Yes?"

"Is something wrong?"

They crossed into the large living room with its neat, cushioned benches and multicolored rugs. The aroma from the food grew stronger.

His father tilted his head slightly, his dark hair with its white streaks falling to one side. "What makes you ask?"

"Well, that for one," Ancel replied, dropping his gaze to the sword at his father's hip.

His father's hand brushed against the weapon's hilt. "And?"

"Charra's been acting strange the last few days even before we saw those creatures in the Greenleaf."

His father snorted. "There's no accounting for Charra's moods. He's worse than a woman." Stefan leaned his head toward the kitchen and dining room. "Don't tell your mother I said that," he added under his breath.

Ancel smiled. "And your sword?"

"We went to check this glen of yours and backtrack to where you said the beasts chased you. All the signs pointed to the creatures being mountain wolves or daggerpaws accompanied by hunters from the Seifer clan."

"But Da, mountain wolves don't have green eyes, neither do daggerpaws."

"The eyes were the resinbuds playing tricks on you two. From the markings they left on the trees, I'm sure it was the Seifer. Looks like they're feuding with the Nema again. Probably poisoned that secret kinai crop of yours because they figured it must be the Nema's. You two boys were actually lucky. If you weren't on dartans, I may now be in the Kelvore bargaining for your freedom. For now, stay away from those parts until I know this feud is over."

Ancel nodded, but the way his father fingered his sword as he talked about the wolves wasn't convincing.

His father continued, "As for my meeting. King Emory is sending a noble here. Some trumped up lordling who'll meet with a Dosteri embassy to discuss the recent troubles. The King's advisors suggested we get used to dressing the part of active Dagodin once more." Stefan shrugged. "I assume they wish to impress the Dosteri with pomp and ceremony. As if that wasn't enough, a Tribunal member is coming to mediate."

Ancel faltered at the prospect of a High Ashishin's visit. His father had said it all with as much interest as if this meeting was as common as the winter storms that blew down from the Kelvore Mountains every year. "Things have become that serious?"

"Serious?" His father's voice rose a notch. "Not at all. The Dosteri have taken affront to the smallest occurrences of late. I assume the King would rather not have anything happen they could construe as an insult. That's all but reassured with a High Ashishin's presence." Stefan paused, his thumb stroking his lip. "At any rate, this is nothing for you to concern yourself with, not at this moment anyway." His hand dropped and began caressing his pointed beard.

Ancel's brows drew together for a moment. His father often stroked his beard when he lied or only told part of a story. *What's he keeping from me?* "Da, are you—"

"Ah, here's your mother," Stefan said as they entered the dining room. "Thania, love, you've outdone yourself."

Ancel snapped his mouth shut as he noticed the dining table for the first time. Porcelain dishes filled with food were set out in neat lines around the marble centerpiece—a sculpture depicting Ilumni. His mother placed a plate filled with slabs of steak on the table. There were potatoes, cabbage, carrots, sweet peas, and sliced quail breast. Several bowls contained creamy sauces. Mouthwatering aromas rose from them that made Ancel want to rush to the table and dig in. Grapes, gooseberries, and sliced bananas adorned several platters next to a basket of freshly baked bread. A pitcher containing crimson colored kinai wine and another with kinai juice, its color paler than the liquor, sat next to each other.

"Mother," Ancel exclaimed, "you did all this without the servants?"

His mother smiled. "I see my son has forgotten his mother's ability to cook with the best."

"I didn't forget," Ancel said in a half–hearted, embarrassed protest. "It's just been so long."

Mother looked thoughtful for a moment. "It has, hasn't it?"

Ancel nodded. Remembering his mother's cooking set his mouth to watering once more.

"Well, stop standing around drooling," she said. "Go wash your hands and hurry back."

Ancel didn't wait to be told twice. Leaving his parents

to their small talk, he hurried through the dining room and into the adjoining kitchen. He skirted the big oak table with its pots and cooking utensils, passed the large stone oven and hearth and stopped at the kitchen sink. With food on his mind, he quickly washed his hands and rushed back to the dining room. His parents stood at their customary positions at the head of the table. Ancel took his place and bowed.

"Ancel, seeing that this is all for you," Stefan said, "Today, you'll lead us with the prayer."

Ancel nodded, closed his eyes, and began in the most reverent voice he could muster, "Dear Ilumni, thank you for the meal you've provided for us today. I pray you bless this food and this family. I thank you for allowing me to enjoy this meal with my parents this day. I beg your Battleguard keep me safe on my trip so we can enjoy many more days together. Blessed in your light, we pray."

A sudden tightness eased up Ancel's chest. Multiple shades of color bloomed around his parents. His head spun for a moment, and his vision blurred. The sensation was as if he spun himself in a circle repeatedly then stood outside his body watching himself fall. He grabbed at the chair.

"Ancel! Son!" His parents' shouts sounded far away.

Ancel struggled not to topple over as his father's hand appeared on his shoulder for support. Ancel's body shuddered. He shook his head in an effort to clear the dizziness while his father helped him into the chair. His mother hovered over him, her hand dabbing at his forehead with a cool cloth.

"What happened?" his father asked.

Slowly, the room came back into focus around Ancel. "I–I don't know. One moment I was praying and the next I felt dizzy and saw these colors."

"Did you have lunch today?" Mother's concerned voice overshadowed her stern expression as she leaned over him.

"No, no, I forgot," Ancel answered before he could think.

"In Ilumni's name, boy. I've told you time and again you need to eat properly," Stefan scolded. "Your body must be fed as well as your mind for both to work in concert. Have you learned nothing of the Disciplines?"

"Stefan," his mother said in the soft voice she used when

she was angry, "Be a dear and take your seat."

His father grumbled under his breath, but he complied.

Her hands shaking, Mother picked up a plate from the table and proceeded to heap food onto it. "Eat up before you faint again. And your father's right, so don't think I'm taking your side." She paused for a moment her eyes distant, then said under her breath, "Maybe we ought to send you to the menders, but that wouldn't cure what ails you, would it?" She finished preparing his meal then went to the opposite side of the table and took her seat.

By this time, Ancel's head had fully cleared. "I'm sorry," he muttered.

Mother waved him off. "No need to apologize. We've been meaning to have a talk with you," She prepared a plate for herself and gestured toward Stefan with a slight tilt of her head.

His father regarded him without the irritation he'd shown earlier. "We've both heard the stories of all these girls you bed. We don't approve." Ancel opened his mouth to speak but his father overrode him. "You need to control your emotions as you've been taught. That's not to say I didn't have my day when I was a young man like yourself. But it's not what you're doing that bothers me as much as the why. Ever since Irmina left, it's been as if a dark cloud has hung over you. You've even neglected your studies, resorting to brandishing your sword to impress the skirts. Treating women as you have will neither bring her back nor make you feel better about her or yourself. If you want to bed them, do so. But don't do it out of spite or lead them on in hopes they will feel the pain you do."

"What your father means to say is to respect women as you would me. If you wish to experience the many flavors of female companionship, I cannot and will not stop you even if it bothers me. But take caution with what you promise. We've had quite a few complaints the last few days. The worse of which has been Headspeaker Valdeen—"

"I grow weary of the man," his father interrupted.

"As do many on the Council," Mother said.

Ancel pushed a slab of quail into his mouth, hardly tasting it as he chewed. Knowing the Headspeaker had complained to his parents made him even more reluctant to go to Randane.

"Well, that's part of the reason we're allowing you to go," his mother said.

Ancel frowned. *Did I say that aloud?*

"Smooth things over with the Headspeaker. In turn, we'll talk to whichever fathers have taken issue with your relations with their daughters," his mother said.

His father nodded. "And when you return, resume your training in earnest. Take the same emotions that confuse you now and feed them into your quest to learn. Bind them to your will. Remember, control is everything if you wish to surpass me as a Dagodin." His features spread into a wide smile as he spoke. "Teacher Calestis stopped by today and said you could be the best student she has again if you would only apply yourself."

Ancel held his breath, waiting for the outburst that would come if Teacher Calestis had told of the day's earlier events. But none came.

Instead, his father said, "I learned, as you must, that a man is only as good as his honor. Life is what you make it, son, and in turn, life shapes you. It's up to you to work that shape into something positive. Yes, you'll make mistakes along the way. But, remember, mistakes are lessons. Positive moments are gold. Collect both with the right person and you'll be wiser and have a treasure of happiness for the rest of your days." He smiled at Mother and in return, she blushed.

"Thank you, Mother, Da." Relief washed through Ancel like a cool breeze. The dirty looks he'd begun to receive from fathers and brothers of the many women he bedded had begun to weigh on him. He knew it was only his parents' status that prevented them from doing more than mutter veiled threats.

"Now, enough of that talk," Stefan said, still smiling. "The reason your mother did all this is because you won't be here for your nineteenth naming day." He poured three glasses of kinai wine and passed them around. "This is to your nineteenth, son. You're a man in every sense of the word now. You should be enjoying this time in your life." Stefan raised his glass. "Here's to you, son. We're both proud of you."

Ancel beamed and took a long drink. Warmth flooded his body.

"Oh," his mother exclaimed, putting her glass down. "I have a gift for you." She fidgeted in the folds of her dress for a moment before she produced something golden. Ancel attempted to see, but she kept it hidden as she stood and crossed to him. "Wear this always," she said, her voice almost a whisper as she positioned herself behind him. "Promise me."

A thin chain dropped around Ancel's neck to rest on his chest. From it hung a pendant. He took it in his hand. An exact likeness of his mother's face, intricately wrought in silversteel down to the shining gray blue gems for her eyes, stared back at him. Ancel gawked, but the only words he could find were, "I promise." Tears welled up in his eyes.

"Thank you for being a wonderful son," his mother said before she squeezed his shoulder and returned to her seat.

Still dumbfounded, the small talk that followed about his day at school and the preparations for the trip washed over Ancel. Several times, he touched the charm before he glanced at his mother. She graced him with a serene smile every time.

"Oh, I forgot to mention," Stefan said. "You will be taking Charra with you."

Ancel's eyes widened. In the past, his father had banned Charra from leaving the Whitewater Falls area. *Now he wants me to bring him to Randane?*

"Don't ask why," his father said before Ancel could utter a word, "Take him. Oh, and should you wish to partake in some of the entertainment Randane has to offer, please remember we Dorns have a family name to maintain. In fact, I would suggest you take a peek at The Dancing Lady. I doubt anyone would recognize you there." His father shrugged at Mother's stern look before they both resumed eating.

Thoughts swirled through Ancel's mind. His father's sword, Charra's recent behavior, his mother's gift, strange beasts in the Greenleaf Forest and the mountain clans' feud were foremost. This was compounded by the upcoming meeting with the Dosteri, his trip to Randane, and his father's command to take the daggerpaw. Calestis' words in Discipline class came back to him.

When several separate events occur at an opportune or inopportune time, people call it coincidence. Coincidence, my students, is nothing more than the birth child of intricate planning.

Ancel lost himself in his ponderings hardly tasting the food.

CHAPTER 13

Evening had come by the time they sat at Eldanhill's southern outskirts. The day had raced by in a whirlwind of preparations, and Ancel and his friends were allowed to skip their studies as they gathered the necessary supplies. Danvir spent most of his time at the tailor making sure he obtained quite a few outfits for their planned revelry. Both he and Mirza attempted to convince Ancel to take clothes other than the black he favored recently. He'd settled on a sky blue coat, a matching shirt, a tan cloak, and tan pants. All his other clothes were either dark gray or black.

Ancel's horse whickered in response to Charra's impatient coos and pawing at the ground. Charra stared off behind him, but Ancel's attention remained on Eldanhill as he played with the charm around his neck. Far north, beyond the town, the last vestiges of sunlight swathed the Kelvore Mountains in purple and orange hues. Ancel hadn't found the time to say goodbye to any of his other friends, but the worst part was that not having the chance didn't bother him. Doubts crept into him about how much he would miss his home. Charra cooed once more.

"Gods, I'm glad they let us ride these beauties this time," Danvir said, patting his white mare. The horse's coat shone with the waning evening sunlight.

Ancel smirked. "I'd much rather if we were on dartans."

"I'm sure you would," Danvir replied. "But there's nothing more beautiful than a well-groomed horse. Why else would they be the status symbol for nobles all across Granadia? Seriously, if you want to tout your beloved dartans so much, then move to Ostania. I'm sure the savages over there would encourage your love for those massive beasts."

"I don't see why you insist on saying Ostanians are savages. Not when some of our own folk were descended from them," Mirza said. "Who knows, maybe you are too."

Danvir's mouth upturned with loathing and his large ears reddened. "I doubt that very much. At least those of Ostanian heritage here don't eat horseflesh or feed horses to dartans like their ancestors." With each word, his face matched his ears, becoming as red as his jacket. Since he'd lost a few of his stock to a raid from one of the mountain tribes, he often became enraged when discussing his beloved animals. "If they did, I'd move to a more civilized town or even Randane itself."

Ancel shook his head. "You really need to calm down. I never said I didn't like horses. None of us did. And I'm not one of the Seifer or Nema, nor am I Ostanian. But for all a horse's grace and beauty, dartans are faster, offer a smoother ride, and when fed well, they can gallop for hours and hours nonstop."

"Because they're fat on fucking horses," Danvir snapped, teeth showing.

"Come on, stop it," Mirza interrupted before Ancel flashed a response. "And that's not fair, Dan. None of our own has ever done that. Especially not Ancel. You know the Dorns keep some of the best horses in Eldanhill. Burning shades, man, he gave you a few ponies from his best stock just months ago."

Danvir's face softened, as much as a rugged cliff miner's face could. "You're right. I'm sorry, Ancel. You know I get beside myself when we talk about horses." He rubbed his mare's neck.

Ancel waved him off. "That's an understatement if I ever heard one. You go berserk. Anyway, you'll need to change your attitude when you become a Dagodin."

"I know," Danvir said, crestfallen. "Then I'll be surrounded by the beasts." Muttering under his breath, he shook his head, his face twisting into a disgusted mask.

Still annoyed, Ancel kicked the stirrups of his bay and

walked to where he could get a better look at Eldanhill. His hand itched to reach inside to his pocket and remove Irmina's letter. Resisting the urge, he pictured her and the smell of her flowery perfume. The letter's words came unbidden.

My dearest Ancel,

There's no easy way for me to put this, but there is another.

Whatever you felt for me cannot be. Being with you would only become a distraction, so I'm forced to cut you free. The time has come for me to move on. You must forget about me and live your life. My duty may not see me back in Eldanhill for years to come if at all. By then, who knows where my heart, or yours, will be.

Life and love are brutal teachers. Learn, adjust, and survive. Or die. Those are your choices. I choose life.

One day, after you complete your studies and pass the trials, your time will come. Then, you'll understand.

Your ruffian, Irmina.

She left a red lip imprint using the paint he loved to see her wear. The mark was a mere smudge now, but he didn't care. He kissed those lips at least once every day.

Charra's low growl jolted him out of his reverie, making him aware of the slow clip clop of hooves on the dusty Eldan Road. With Danvir and Mirza on their mounts a few feet away, Ancel knew who the rider approaching from behind had to be. He didn't bother to face him. Instead, he prepared himself for what was to come. At least the Headspeaker hadn't waited until they were well on their way.

"What's troubling you?" Edwin Valdeen asked.

"Nothing really."

"Really?" Edwin raised a bushy eyebrow. The Headspeaker's abundant facial hair contrasted with his shiny, bald head. "I would think that much is on your mind. After all," he gestured behind them, "The caravan is already moving down the road, yet here you are staring home. And those two," he nodded to where Danvir and Mirza waited, their horses stamping and tossing their heads, "look about as impatient as suckling babes."

"It's nothing much, Master Valdeen," Ancel said with a little more confidence. The last thing he needed right now was to let Alys' father know he was thinking about another woman.

"Missing Irmina again, aren't you?"

Ancel deflated. Had his feelings become that obvious to

everyone?

"I can tell you a thing or three about women, young man," Edwin said as if he had not seen Ancel's expression. "They can never make up their minds about what they want. You can never please them. But love them the right way, and they'll give you their all."

"Or snatch your heart from your chest," Ancel replied in a glum tone, mouth downturned.

"There is that. I've been with my share of women. Alys' mother was not my true love, but she's the one I ended up with. She stood by me when I needed a hand and someone to lean on. She's been with me ever since. In the end, that's what matters. I've heard stories about your, shall we say, appetite?" Edwin's voice hardened. "I won't have my Alys mistreated by anyone, not even you. I would've thought your father would teach you better." He gave his beard a quick stoke. "Then again he himself has been known to lead a merry chase or three."

Ancel did not meet Edwin's piercing eyes, instead choosing to focus on Eldanhill once more. The town's lamps winked on one by one along the streets and lanes that carved paths like branches flowing from the Kelvore River to Eldanhill's east. "I'm not trying to mistreat Alys. I do care for her. But…" He didn't quite know how to say the next part to the Headspeaker in a way that wouldn't make the man furious.

"But?" Edwin repeated.

Ancel steeled himself and turned to meet Edwin's eyes. "I still love Irmina. I think about her daily. At the same time, I've promised to never allow myself to be hurt that way again. To be honest, Master Valdeen, the women, they soothe me. They keep my mind from thinking about what could've been. They keep me from charging off to go find her. Alys plays a big part, but I cannot tell you what future there may be between us."

The Headspeaker's face had reddened with each sentence, and his jaw worked. He gave a few nods and caressed his beard again, his hand tightening at the end of each stroke. Finally, he said, "I'm glad you're honest with me, boy. I can understand this foolishness in a way. I've promised Alys not to interfere, but one way or another, you'll need to make a choice. I won't stand for my daughter crying the way she does since she fell for you. You have until the Soltide Festival." The warning in Edwin's words was clear.

Ancel opened his mouth to reassure the Headspeaker, but his words fled him. He couldn't bring himself to promise more than he could offer. Edwin gave him one last sharp look before wheeling his horse to follow the caravan.

"That could've been worse," Danvir said as he and Mirza rejoined Ancel.

"I think it went bad enough," Ancel said.

"Think on it like this," Mirza chimed in. "He could've threatened to bring the question of his daughter's honor before the Council."

Ancel groaned. Another complaint like the ones already leveled against him wouldn't go over well. Not even his father's position could save him then. He could see it now. His father having to pay great debts to make good to the parents who said Ancel had sullied their daughter's reputations and chances to land a good dowry. "Well, it's not as if I didn't make it clear what my interests were," Ancel grumbled. "Most of those girls had their petals plucked long before me anyway."

"Further sullying their names will gain you much sympathy." Danvir shook his head.

"Now I know why the courtesans make such good business," Ancel said, "No complaints, no attachments, maybe—"

"If you think your father's upset now, imagine if you took to them. Although," Mirza gave a mischievous grin, "What he doesn't know couldn't hurt."

Danvir smiled, but the prospects didn't lighten Ancel's mood. Nothing thrilled him more than the chase and well, the working women didn't offer much for sport.

"Just promise us one thing," Mirza said. "Promise to wipe Irmina from your mind for this trip. It's going to be your naming day. Start fresh."

"I promise," Ancel answered. The lie came rather easily. He was sick of everyone's advice.

A breeze swept past them, carrying with it the chill from the Kelvore Mountains. Charra growled and fixed his gaze on the Greenleaf Forest and its darkened contents to the west. The daggerpaw stood stock–still. His bone hackles flexed before rising upright into hardened, knife–like protrusions. Each row swished into position and clicked. His golden eyes glowed.

"What's his issue?" Danvir followed Charra's massive head.

"I don't know. He's been this way lately. Restless and snarling at the slightest things." Ancel attempted to act as confused as Mirza. His bay pranced a bit, and he snapped his reins and used his legs to keep it under control.

"Well, something has him spooked good." Danvir peered in the same direction as everyone else, his brow furrowed.

"You think it could be…them?" Mirza asked.

Ancel stared at him. Danvir's raised eyebrows and his eyes shifting from Mirza to him spoke for themselves. Ancel sighed. Their friend wouldn't give up until he felt they no longer hid anything from him.

"I'm sorry," Mirza said, his expression meek.

"So out with it then," Danvir said.

Ancel told him what happened in the Greenleaf Forest. Danvir's eyes grew round with the telling. By the time Ancel mentioned what his father had begun to say about wraithwolves, Danvir's eyes nearly popped out of his head.

"Gods be good. What do you think they were?" Danvir asked in a low voice.

"My Da says the tracks they found belonged to mountain wolves and daggerpaws."

Mirza gave Ancel a dubious look. "What about the green eyes?"

Ancel shrugged. "He says it was the resinbuds playing tricks on our sight."

"You never mentioned resinbuds," Danvir chortled. "Those damned flowers do have a way of changing colors." Relief washed across his face. "Think on it, if it were wraith—" he glanced around, "Two of you would be dead with your hearts torn out."

"I guess you're right." Ancel gave a weak smile.

Mirza's doubtful expression hadn't changed. "Well, whatever they were, I'm not sitting around here if they're what Charra is sensing now. I think it's past time for us to catch up to the others." With that, Mirza shook his reins and sent his horse trotting after the dwindling caravan.

Ancel felt the same way as Mirza. He'd seen Charra kill wolves before. His daggerpaw's slobbering jaws and the glint in his eyes spoke not only of an intent to kill but of fear. Ancel could think of nothing Charra feared.

Ancel rode after the others, Charra loping next to him, his gaze focused on the Greenleaf Forest.

CHAPTER 14

Shin Galiana Calestis leaned on her staff after each step up the wide stairs to the Dorn's townhouse. She used the white balustrade and its pillars to help her climb.

Stefan stood on the landing above her dressed in the crimson uniform of a Dagodin. The five gold knots of his Knight Commander rank stood out on his right breast. Above them shone a pendant depicting a sun with lightning bolts striking in front of it—The Lightstorm insignia. It had been a long time since she last saw the emblem. Stefan's dark cloak ruffled in the chilly breeze that reached down from the Kelvore Mountains. The sword on his hip fit him like a soft, fox fur glove. Years had passed since she last saw him wearing a weapon. Lines creased his forehead as he gazed toward the Eldan Road and Eldanhill's southern exit.

She couldn't help but think how much of a young Stefan lived on in Ancel. If not for the slight difference in height, the white streaks in Stefan's hair, and his pointed beard, it would be difficult to tell them apart.

"I see you have taken well to wearing your uniform once more," she said as she gained the landing. She shuffled over to stand next to the older Dorn and took in the great Streamean temple, its clock tower, and the blue lights reflecting from the town's streets and buildings.

"It suits me as well as yours does you," Stefan replied with a nod toward her own red dress with its white–striped silver sleeve.

Galiana chuckled. "I have so become used to my role as Teacher, I forgot this is what I once was."

Stefan gave her a wry look. "No one can forget being an Ashishin, Galiana. The world won't let you."

Nodding at his statement, she asked, "How did Ancel handle the news of the trip?"

"He's happy enough. How could he not be?" Stefan shrugged. The breeze died down. His cloak came to rest above his calf high, brown leather boots. "He's with his friends. He has his parents' blessing. And he will be able to skip classes for a few weeks while chasing women." A hint of bitterness carried in his soft–spoken yet firm voice.

Across from them the same blue lamps of Soltide that lit up the town adorned the few homes on Tezian Lane. A dog barked from one of the gardens.

"You would do well to worry less," Galiana said.

Stefan turned to regard her. The festive lights at the front of his home and the three pillars lining each side of the stairs enhanced his emerald eyes. His gaze reminded her of the breeze, biting and cold. "How can I? His power manifested yesterday."

Stomach churning, Galiana kept her face a blank mask. "And what happened?"

"Thania suppressed it. Then I stressed to him to remember his training and to control his emotions."

"Good."

"Good?" Stefan's face darkened with anger. "How so? He needs supervision. You said yourself he's lost his focus. Yet you asked to allow him to go to Randane. To be away from those who can train him. To be away from those who can show him the path he needs to take. Away from those who can protect him." The tight lines about Stefan's jaw eased, and his eyes shone wetly. "I'll not lose a second family, Galiana."

"Sometimes, the best course of action is inaction. Sometimes, the best way to guide is not to guide."

Somewhere in Eldanhill, a smith's hammer clanged. Someone had stayed up late to finish their work.

"Quotes from the Disciplines?" Stefan snorted. "I'm no longer your student."

Galiana smiled. Stefan had always been stubborn. "You will always be my student."

"I doubt you understand."

"Oh?"

The cold breeze picked up, rattling a wind vane. Galiana pulled her cloak tighter, huddling into its comforting folds. "I watch my son every day." Stefan stared off at nothing. "The way he mopes around. His apparent disinterest when I teach him the sword. His mood swings that are sometimes worse than Charra's. I see it all. He's not been the same since Irmina left. Or should I say since you and Jerem sent Irmina away. You need to bring her back. She gave my boy a stability he now lacks."

"Some would say the same about me with this." Galiana straightened with ease and raised her staff. "He will manage without her. Besides, her current mission is unavoidable and too important."

Stefan shook his head. "You've always been one to deceive with appearances, but I know what I see in him. He needs her."

"He does, I admit. But not in the way you think. If she fails her task, Ancel's stability will no longer be in question. His life will be forfeit."

"And if she succeeds?"

"Then he stands a chance when the time comes."

"And if harm should befall him on this trip, none of these plans will be of consequence." Stefan paced to the other side of the landing, his broad back to her. "You should've let me accompany him."

"No," Galiana said firmly, "Another has been tasked to protect him. Besides, do you really want Valdeen to be the one the Dosteri meet?"

"You don't trust him with the meeting, but you trust him with my son?" Jaw clenching, Stefan graced her with an incredulous stare.

"The negotiations with the Dosteri are a delicate matter."

"And my son isn't?" Stefan's voice had become soft, almost inaudible, a dangerous undertone lurking beneath his words.

Galiana bit back the scathing words on her tongue. "You know better. The meeting is not suited for the Headspeaker."

After a moment's contemplation, she added, "Unless you are willing to risk his recent attitude and his lack of foresight during the proceedings. Not to mention the risk that the High Ashishin the Tribunal dispatches may sense Ancel's growing power. Would you rather he was here if they decided to send a Pathfinder?"

Stefan hesitated. "No, but still—"

"He may have acted irresponsibly the last few months, but give your son some credit," Galiana said. "He can take care of himself. Not that we would leave his safety only to himself or Valdeen, mind you. We have commissioned someone who is more than capable."

Stefan's sudden whirl to face her almost forced Galiana back a step. Hand clenching on her cane, she held herself steady. He took two purposeful strides toward her until he stood so close she could smell the soap he bathed with and see the mist rising from his mouth and nose. His towering frame blotted out the sight of Eldanhill.

"Who?" The corner of Stefan's mouth edged up as he spoke softly, a little louder than a whisper, but with a blade sharp edge. "Who did you entrust with my son's life?"

She raised an eyebrow. Stefan's shoulders slumped as he turned away and let out a deep breath.

"I can assure you between his guard and Charra, Ancel will be fine," Galiana said. "You have been particularly testy since he and Mirza returned from the Greenleaf. What did you find?"

"Nothing."

Galiana frowned.

"There were plenty signs kinai once grew in their glen, but there were no trees covered in rot as they claimed." Stefan paced across the landing. "The crop appeared to have been thoroughly cultivated. The trees stood bare as if it were the dead of winter. I've never seen anything like it."

"The tracks and the droppings, were they—"

"They were the same as made by wild mountain wolves or daggerpaws, nothing more. The other tracks were human. Markings on the trees identified them as the Seifer clan."

"And the shade within the area?"

Stefan stopped pacing. He looked out toward the Greenleaf Forest. "No more than usual." His brows drew together. "In some ways, the essences seemed too perfect."

"Do you think the boys could have imagined what they saw?" Galiana asked.

Stefan stroked his beard. "Stranger things have happened, but no. Not both of them. When they came home that night, Charra's paws and their boots left enough stains to support their claim. Not to mention the stench they brought with them."

"Wraithwolf?"

"Similar in many ways, but as I said, the tracks sang a different song."

Galiana nodded. The thought Stefan couldn't tell what type of creatures followed the boys chilled her. Sending Ancel away became a better idea by the moment. "Well, we must be careful, nonetheless. Post extra guards. I will instruct a few Dagodin to keep an eye on the Greenleaf."

"Risky if you don't wish for the Tribunal to begin an inquiry," Stefan said.

"I have not lost my wisdom with my youth, Stefan. These men will all be loyal to our cause. And even if they should send a Pathfinder, Ancel will be safe in Randane."

Stefan grunted, and he gave a quick nod. "What of your wards?"

Galiana couldn't help pursing her lips. "None have been disturbed." That fact had been her only reassurance Ancel hadn't encountered wraithwolves since she received Stefan's report about the glen.

Stefan stroked his beard once more. "What do you suggest we tell the Clan Council?"

She gazed out to the Kelvore Mountains and the twin moons shining high above. "We tell them nothing for now. At least not until we can be certain of what the boys saw. If Amuni's Children have somehow crossed the Vallum of Light, there must be no doubt."

"Not that I would doubt you, but—" Stefan began.

"No you would not, would you?" This time Galiana didn't hide her smile.

Stefan looked at her from the corner of his eyes. "Not even the Shadowbearer could cross the Vallum. Why do you believe that which hasn't been breached in a thousand years could be breached now?"

"The Chronicles have never been wrong, Stefan," she

said simply.

Stefan smirked. "The same Chronicles you followed back then? That cost so many lives? Lest you forget, Galiana, the last hundred years have not been kind to our clan. And—"

"Yes, I know," Galiana huffed, not attempting to hide her annoyance, "You lay the blame for their misfortune at my feet."

"Am I wrong in doing so?"

Galiana took in Eldanhill's blue–lit streets once more. *So tranquil. There's a peace here I refuse to lose.* "No. You are not wrong. It was my fault for trusting Nerian, yes." She let out a deep breath, her back bowed, and she leaned on her staff once more. "But our people live."

"If languishing at the Tribunal's hands can be said to be living. If spread across the corners of Denestia, families shattered, can be said to be living. If suffering without knowing their homes or the truth of their heritage can be said to be living, then yes you're right." Stefan's words cut deep.

Galiana fought against the hollow that grew in her chest with each sentence. "We live and breathe. As long as we have that, we shall prevail." Her sigh matched the cold breeze. "After all these years, you still dredge this up."

"How can I not?" Stefan said, the bitterness in his tone unmistakable. "We're not only the last of our clan, but maybe the last of the Setian."

"And I have apologized and repented time and again." Galiana fought not to raise her voice. "No, it will not bring back the dead, but it is a burden I bear. Believe me, it weighs on my shoulder more than you can imagine." Her head throbbed, and her back ached. "If time were mine to command I would change what happened."

"But it isn't, and you cannot," Stefan whispered, that lost expression in his eyes again.

"We can do this for the hundredth time. Or you can trust me as you once have. The time draws near. Ancel must complete his training."

"And yet you send him away."

"Your stubbornness borders on being idiotic," she snapped, her temper past boiling. "Your lapse in respect has become more than bothersome. Demand respect, but first show respect. Demand discipline by showing mastery of self. The first and the last Disciplines that you seem to have forgotten. I am beginning to wonder if I should not have Valdeen represent us instead of you after all."

Either her tone or her words struck a chord. The lines creasing Stefan's forehead grew until his eyebrows almost touched. He bowed to her. "I, I'm sorry, Shin Galiana. I forgot myself. You're right. I should carry myself better. Lead by example as the Disciplines say. I'm glad you quoted them. I've been so worried by the boy's erratic behavior. Then with everything else happening, I've been of two minds where my duty lies. I know it's here. Ancel is well past the age where he should need to rely on my guidance."

Galiana smiled and stared out to the south. Stefan would never admit it, but he was forever her student, and she knew how to manipulate him when he needed it most.

Chilly gusts buffeted them, flinging strands of Galiana's silver hair about her face. She drew her cloak tighter. "The Dosteri are moving. Ostania stirs. There have been reports the Svenzar have appeared in the Red Ridge Mountains. Old feuds rise anew. Threats of war sweep the land. The elements have become unstable. It is as the Chronicles say. The shade is rising."

CHAPTER 15

Two weeks into the journey, Ryne still fought his urges to harm the woman. His bloodlust continued to hover below the surface—a caged animal mewling for release.

Mariel now trailed them along a sun–blasted ridge deep into Ostania's Nevermore Heights where mist–shrouded peaks poked into the clouds as if the heavens stood upon their rocky shoulders. *Had the killings stopped since she left Carnas? What does she want? Better yet, why should I care what she wants? She followed me from home to here; I should just let my sword ask the questions.* Teeth clenched till his jaw ached, and knowing his feelings were a mix of his unstable control of late and his frustration at her ability to elude him, he kept his breathing as even as possible.

For all her tracking, Mariel still hadn't made a threatening move. Even with this landscape, where if he looked back, he could see behind and below him for miles, she remained careful. The one time she almost wandered within range, he recognized her dark hair and the yellow shirt and trousers she often wore. A dark–colored veil or scarf covered her face. He assumed it served two purposes—hiding her and protection against the blustery wind.

The day was another muggy one, thick and heavy, the air itself pushing down upon them. Despite the mountainous altitude and the wind, there was little solace from the heat. Glancing down the long trail behind him at his mysterious follower's tiny figure, Ryne wondered how she was handling the sun. Even his sandalwood skin color had tanned a bit. As if on cue, thunder rumbled, and a shadow crept across the land.

Ryne studied the skies, stroking a hand down the thin lines of scar tissue striping the left side of his face. They ran diagonally from forehead to chin and felt as if some beast had clawed his face several times. Maybe something did. He frowned, sifting and straining to find a fragment, anything, of memory. As always, none came.

Thunderheads boiled above them and blotted out the noonday sun. The air was laden with the scent of rain yet to fall. Ryne would welcome the storms if they arrived today. Two weeks had passed since the last one, much longer, and the next could be dangerous, bringing lightning in sheets, several feet of pelting rain, and winds that would snap trees like twigs.

Up ahead, a Harnan herder watched a flock of yellow, long–necked slainen. The six–legged creatures nipped at kinai trees along slopes dotted by medium–sized evergreen saplings. Fluff from the kinai littered the slopes in bunches. A few slainen uncoiled their snouts, reached up among the lowest branches, and picked pink fleshberries from entwining vines.

Ryne bit into the kinai fruit in his hand before he offered it to Sakari, knowing his friend would refuse. He smiled when Sakari did as expected. *One day, I will see you eat, my friend.* He still remembered the shock he felt when he'd asked Sakari why he never ate. The man's response had been as cryptic as his persona.

"Because you do not see a thing does not mean it does not happen," Sakari had said. "Do you see when the plants feed? No? Consider me as one of them. My sustenance comes from Mater itself."

Ryne had found the statement hard to fathom until Sakari had him open his Matersense at dusk to watch the kinai trees. The leaves and bark spouted tiny feelers. They waved in the air and along the ground, drawing multiple essences as they did so. With the feeding, the fruit themselves blossomed a brighter, riper red.

Ryne popped the kinai into his mouth once more and savored the sweet taste and the brief euphoric feeling. Consuming enough kinai made him feel as if he could accomplish anything. He wondered if the trees felt the same.

"You wish for me to speak with him?" Sakari nodded toward the herder.

"By all means," Ryne answered.

They climbed off the dirt trail and worked their way among grasses and small shrubs. Birds glided among the flora, twittering as they flew. Insects buzzed between triangular shaped abida flowers and white and purple mixta blossoms, the perfumes from the blooms lighting up the air.

Farther down the mountain, past gentle inclines, trees spanned into rainforests. From the mountain's base, it would look like clouds topped those forests instead of mists. Harnans named them the Cloud Forests. Miles below and beyond the Clouds sprouted the Mondros with its multiple shades of green canopy. Wide meandering rivers, sparkling lakes, and the mirror–like glint from towns and cities dotted Ostania's vast landscape.

Somewhere to the far east, close to the Rotted Forest, rose a pillar of black smoke. Ryne's forehead wrinkled and for a moment, he wondered what could be the cause of the billowing mass before he returned his attention to his immediate surroundings.

The pale–haired Harnan man made a hooting noise, placing a hand on his sword hilt when Sakari came within thirty paces. Sakari's strides did not falter or change once, continuing to convey a sense that not a muscle was wasted.

A rockhound, distant cousin to the lapra, trotted from behind a lone mahogany tree. The earthen beast appeared a mottled green rather than its natural grayish color due to growths of moss upon its body. Measuring six feet in length and sporting massive square shoulders, the hound grumbled at Ryne, its thick tail whipping back and forth. Stone chips rained against the tree trunk as the beast shook like a large dog waking from a doze. Golden–eyed gaze still fixed on Ryne, it lowered onto its stomach.

Inclining his head to the hound, Ryne slowed his approach in an attempt to appear as non–threatening as possible. The herder's gaze locked on him. With each step Ryne took, the herder's eyes tightened.

Ryne blew out a breath and gave a slow, resigned headshake. The herder's wariness toward him alone was not surprising. Sakari always appeared as a native wherever they traveled, even down to his clothes. Sakari now stood a few inches shorter than the Harnan herder with a similar slight build, identical tanned skin, and pale, almost white hair. From a distance,

Sakari could easily be mistaken for the herder's relative.

On the other hand, I'm an eight-foot sculpture with tapestries painted upon it. Ryne's greatsword, added to his size, ruined any chance of a casual appearance.

The rockhound's rumble increased to a cracked howl at Ryne's continued approach, so he stopped long before he reached within fifty feet of the Harnan. Sakari sauntered toward the herder with no such reaction from the beast.

As was customary of late, a familiar itch between Ryne's shoulders made him look for Mariel. The woman crouched on the trail above with her veil no longer covering her face.

"How are you, herder?" Sakari asked in Ostanian with a Harnan accent.

"Warm day, traveler," the herder replied.

Frowning at another uncalled link to Sakari, Ryne turned his attention to the two men. The unbidden link was not the only strange occurrence that concerned Ryne. He repeated the herder's tone in his head. Harnan accents bore a slight difference from typical Ostanian lilt. They stressed the end of their words and dragged them out. This Harnan herder did not; his accent was smoother, more musical.

"The Clouds grow well." Sakari gestured beyond the slopes.

"Does that one follow you?" The herder nodded toward Ryne.

"Yes. He is the reason I am here."

The man squinted at Ryne. "Strange tattoos he has. They live on him. It's rumored Amuni himself sent his children to seek such as he some thirty years or more ago."

Sakari shrugged. "So he has been told."

"He doesn't fear the children of the god of shades?"

"My master fears no one."

The Harnan's eyes widened, the whites making his black irises mere specks. "Not even the gods?"

"He respects the gods. Fear them? No. Why should he fear that which does not walk among us? Besides, he serves Ilumni. Why should he fear the brother of his god?"

"Dangerous words should the gods hear, traveler. All the gods should be feared. Anger one and our world ends."

The herder licked his lips, and peered around as if he expected something to jump from the air itself. Ryne chuckled inwardly at the man's superstitions. When nothing happened, the herder let out a relieved breath.

Sakari gestured to the adjoining mountain. "Last time we were within the Clouds, we sought and found the Svenzar on those slopes. This time they are not there."

"Yes. Rumor says when they could not find your master, Amuni's Children unleashed death upon the Svenzar." The herder's jaw hardened as he spoke. "The Svenzar fled and called all the Sven back to the safety of Stone."

The air about the herder shifted for a brief moment. His aura wavered before it became solid again. In that second, the man appeared different to Ryne. The herder's body bore dirt and stone in place of his flesh.

"He's a Sven," Ryne said. He strode toward the man, ignoring the sudden rumble from the rockhound.

"My master will speak to you now," Sakari said. "You should call off your pet. My master knows what you are."

Sweat ran down the herder's forehead. The liquid left a trail like water trickling over parched earth. He reached for his sword.

"That is not a wise choice, Sven." Sakari's tone never changed.

The Sven hooted to the rockhound.

With a snarl, the beast lurched into a hunched position, forepaws forward, back up, and tail rigid. Not once did Ryne look in the hound's direction as he continued toward the Sven.

"I shall save you from yourself and my master. You will thank me one day." Sakari turned to the rockhound.

Several hoots issued from Sakari in perfect imitation of the Sven. The hound whined and looked confused. It stared at Ryne for a moment more, then the beast stalked down the slope, slipping through grass and brush toward the evergreen tree line.

The Sven opened his mouth, and his hand touched his sword. Before he could unsheathe the weapon, Sakari's foot thudded against the herder's temple. The man dropped to the ground.

"I told you I would save you," Sakari said in the same flat voice.

Ryne stood over the Sven. In the Sven's own language, which was more musical rumbles than speech, he said, "I can see your Form, as you can see the elements within me. Drop the disguise and the pretenses. Take me to the Svenzar. They summoned me."

The man's aura wavered again. This time when the shift happened, his real form remained.

A creature of gray, hewn stone, with small cracks filled with soil, lay on the ground among the grass. It looked as if a stonemason had put together a life–like statue carved from myriad pieces of rock using dirt for mortar. Strong, wet earth smells drifted up from the Sven.

"How is it you speak my tongue, man of many swirls?" The Sven's voice was a deep rumble of rhythmic thunder.

Ryne shrugged, answering in Sven. "I speak every tongue. Whether a gift or a curse, I can't say."

The Sven righted himself. It was not so much that he stood, as the ground writhed about his feet and under his body, until he shifted upright and like some great pillar, he grew from the earth.

"Sakari." Ryne turned his body so he could see Mariel on the trail above.

"Yes?"

Ryne gave a subtle nod to where the woman now crouched even closer. She'd inched near enough for him to read her. Light sparkled from her aura in varying, dancing patterns. He would always remember her now. "I don't wish for her to see any more than necessary. Send the hound after her."

Sakari bowed and hooted several times.

The rockhound bounded out from the trees and sprang toward the woman, dirt and grass flying into the air as its powerful legs and claws propelled the beast forward. In long, leaping strides, the hound covered half the distance to Mariel before she reacted.

When she did, it was with astounding speed. Her head snapped toward the hound, and she snatched at her sword, sprinting to her left and up the hill. But the hound closed in faster still, its huge body a brown and green blur that matched the surroundings. There was no way she could escape.

Just as the beast stretched within a few feet of the fleeing woman, she turned abruptly to face it, skidding through dirt and shale, her arms windmilling with the movement. Before Mariel's body came to a full stop, the beast pounced, its jaws stretched wide, rows of white fangs closing quickly. In the middle of her slide, Mariel pushed up, somersaulting into the air and over the onrushing rockhound. Unable to stop its momentum, it crashed to the ground with a solid stone on stone thump, kicking up dust in its wake. Mariel landed, sprinted down the hill, and disappeared below a dip in the land. With a growl, the rockhound gathered itself, shook its body, and lurched after her.

Ryne could only arch an eyebrow at the display.

A basso musical laugh echoed from the Sven who now stood nine feet tall. The stoneform grabbed his stomach in his mirth, vibrations passing through him with every rumbling peal, dirt and rock chips falling from his body. The Sven's eyes were smiling red pits, and his mouth nothing more than a curved slit. He had no nose or ears. His entire countenance now resembled cracked marble, shiny in some places and dull in others.

"She runs well for one so small," the Sven said between breaths.

Ryne smiled. "Come. Take me to the Svenzar."

The Sven nodded, and his laughter subsided. As he climbed the slope, his feet trampled grass and brush in their way. The foliage sprouted upright soon after each passing step.

They followed the twisting trail for several miles, past glens and running springs. A few times, they passed roaring waterfalls that cascaded from some unseen height. Overhead, ominous thunderheads still threatened. The white cliff they soon reached soared up into the dark blanket above. Vines and moss climbed the walls, and flowers in rainbow–like colors grew in erratic patterns all along its surface. A slit showed in the cliff face.

"Pass through here. The Svenzar will meet you on the other side." With that, the Sven touched the cliff, melting into it as if he walked through a curtain of rock.

Ryne glanced at Sakari, who shrugged. After a deep breath, Ryne stepped into the slit.

All sense of balance and direction fled him, and he felt as if he fell a great distance in the dark. The bottom of his stomach dropped.

A few moments later, they stood in water up to their

ankles within an area enclosed by four cliff walls. Small pebbles and rocks lined the ground. Of the slit, no sign remained.

Ryne's eyes widened at the sight around him. Sakari stood beside him, his face passive. Moss, lichen, and flowers carpeted the cliff faces. Birds with brilliant plumages sang and soared from wall to wall, and large insects flitted and buzzed. Thousands of feet above, waterfalls dropped from each precipice with a muffled rumble, their foamy waters ending in midair, but somehow light mist still brushed Ryne's face.

More shocking than the sight though was what he felt. Even without his Matersense he could feel the elements buffeting around him. He knew of only two other Entoses. Never did he expect to find one here in the Nevermore Heights. How many more were there in the world?

As the thought raced through his mind, the essences grew more violent. They crashed around him in a pull so strong he almost reached out to them. In response, his lust rose in a red–hot wave and attempted to surge to the surface to greet the primordial forces. He battered the rush until it calmed into a gentle flow lapping against a distant shore. A shudder passed through him as the heat subsided.

Sakari's hand tapping Ryne's arm brought his focus back to what lay before them. From the opposite wall grew a gigantic granite creature. Easily three times Ryne's height, its carved body of sharp planes stretched half as wide as it was tall and its feet disappeared beneath the waters of a calm pond, pristine white lilies floating undisturbed upon the water's surface.

"Welcome, Ryne Waldron," said a soft masculine voice in Sven.

The giant's mouth seemed big enough to swallow a wagon. Its voice tinkled in musical tones. After it spoke, a light breeze carrying an earthy odor reached Ryne and sent ripples across the pond's surface. The creature's body remained set into the cliff.

"Halvor?" Ryne gaped at the giant. "Um, you've grown a bit since we last met. I thought you said you would be full grown when you reach a millennium. You were…nine hundred then?"

"Yes. And I am a millennium now."

The breeze reached Ryne again. "But that was only thirty years ago."

Halvor chuckled and the walls vibrated. Stone and earth broke away and dropped into the water with a splash. "Our years are not your years."

"Evidently. Halvor, I must speak to your masters."

"I am a master now. I am a Svenzar." Halvor's breath came a little harder this time.

Ryne frowned. Last time he saw Halvor, the creature was a Sven, only as big as the one that led them here. "How?"

"Soon after you visited, Amuni's Children arrived, hunting you. When they could not find you, they took several of our leaders." Halvor's girth seemed to shrink. "A dark time for us. Dark indeed."

Ryne's eyes narrowed. "How could they take them?"

"There were those among them who bested my masters."

"Here?" Ryne's concentration on holding his lust at bay while not succumbing to the Mater around him faltered with his surprise. He wrenched his will back into control, keeping his face smooth so as not to reveal his struggle. "They bested you here where the elements of Forms are strongest? Where the earth, stone, and forests of the mountains themselves answer to your power?" Ryne tilted his head toward Sakari, but his friend showed no reaction to the news.

Halvor's arm swept away from him in a wide gesture. Boulders tore from around him, fell, and sent up a great showering roar of water and debris when they impacted around his feet. His tinkling voice penetrated the din, "Yes. Look to the lands. The shade advances. They are more powerful than any thought."

His eyebrows knitting with doubt, Ryne asked, "I've seen a few, but surely they could be no real threat? Not after the destruction they suffered at the hands of the combined Denestian armies."

"You invite defeat by underestimating your enemy," Halvor said.

"What did they do with your leaders?"

"We do not know, but those who resisted were killed and their children with them. The remaining masters did not want to risk them discovering Stone and all our people living there so they gave of themselves."

"I'm sorry, Halvor."

The Svenzar waved a massive hand. "It is Humelen's will."

With that wave, the Svenzar's stoneform changed. His great size reduced until he stood the same height as the Sven. His feet splashed through the water, sending up a shower of lilies as he strode to them. The lilies landed back onto the roiling surface of the pond in impossibly perfect order, bobbing as if they'd never been disturbed. Ryne took an inadvertent step backwards before he forced himself to stand his ground.

"Seeing as you accepted the summons, it means you have answers to what the masters asked of you, and questions for me." Halvor stopped just before he reached them.

"Who am I? Why am I here?" Ryne asked before he stopped to think.

Halvor smiled, and stone chips fell from his face like crumbling earth kicked off a precipice. "You ask questions without providing answers. That is no way to bargain."

Ryne exhaled. Halvor tried his patience during his last visit as well. Ryne knew better than to get angry as he did then, so he answered, "Light to balance shade. Light to show honor. Honor to show mercy." *Light's Tenet.* "Why do you require this from me anyway?"

The Svenzar's face smoothed in quiet contemplation, his gaze fixed on Ryne. When Ryne said nothing more, Halvor's face brightened. "You're a warrior."

Ryne gritted his teeth. "That's it? The answer to my first question? So many years waiting and you tell me something I already know?" His tenuous control waned with his frustration.

"I told you. You already have the answers, yet you still seek them. Now you must complete the ceremony."

"And if I don't?" Ryne countered.

Halvor's lips turned downward. "Again, you already know this." He locked gazes with Ryne. "You stay here forever, lashed to Humelen's and Liganen's wills."

Ryne knew the Svenzar spoke the truth, and he could do nothing about it. If he did not finish this, he would remain trapped by the gods of Forms.

"The elements of Mater must exist in harmony," Ryne said. *The first Principle of Mater.*

Halvor gestured to Ryne's body. "And that which covers

you? Your Scripts?"

Ryne grimaced. He sought answers, and instead, he faced questions. Ryne pointed to the intricate, lifelike artwork of his Scripts. "A representation of Mater—the core of all creation and the elements and their essences that exist within it. The solids of the Forms, the liquids of the Flows, and the energy of the Streams."

The Svenzar's stone face crinkled as he beamed. "You have learned well that which you already know."

"I'm not here for the games and riddles." Ryne scowled. "If I already knew as you say, I wouldn't be here." The red wave began to roil once more.

Halvor's voice changed to a monotone. "We may smile and laugh, but the Svenzar never play. And I have told you no riddles, just the truth."

"Then tell me why you required this of me."

"Because, in the past you abused all the Tenets and Principles when using your Scripts. You were as a child with no parent to guide you."

Or a man drunk from his own power. "And now?" Ryne asked.

"Now, you are still a child, but one who has shown a degree of maturity. Remember, the most important Discipline is control. Without it, you are nothing."

Ryne balled his hands into fists. "I didn't come here for a lecture. Just tell me what my purpose is in this world?" The primal elements outside beat at him as his bloodlust rose to a boil. He wanted to strike out, while another part of him struggled for some semblance of control. It would be pointless, not to mention fatal, to lose himself within the Svenzar's home. Something about the lily pond and its impeccable flowers drew Ryne's attention, tickling a memory.

As if he sensed Ryne's impending rage, and Sakari's small shift to attention, Halvor slowly melted into the floor. His body became one with the stones in the water.

"What's my purpose?" Ryne shouted, the boiling within him surging with increased violence. Instead of forcing back the feeling, he embraced it and guided it deep inside himself until it seemed to float like the lilies on the pond's surface.

"To battle."

"Is that all I am? Death, destruction and suffering?" Ryne yelled as the Svenzar faded. *There must be more. Dear Ilumni, make it so there is more to me than this.*

And just like that, he found tranquility. A moment later, his eyes blurred as a dizzy spell snatched at him.

Halvor's voice tinkled all around. "You are what you choose to be."

An emptiness filled Ryne. What was the point of coming all this way if he would end up with the same issue as before. "What if I don't wish to make these choices anymore? What if I no longer wish for battle? What if I just wish to be left alone?" With his bloodlust gone, the Mater within the Entosis settled evenly about him.

Halvor reappeared in the wall. "That time has passed. Your enemies know you're here. They will seek you out. Your days of rest are done."

Ryne opened his mouth.

"A way to your answers has been provided for you. A way to make things right. If you seek it."

"What way?" Ryne asked.

"You'll know him when he is ready." Halvor paused and cocked his head to one side. "Be careful what you pray for. The gods march."

Ryne fell, his mind spinning as if he spiraled into cavernous depths. Darkness engulfed him.

CHAPTER 16

Dimly aware of her eagles following high above, blood thundering in her ears as she fled for all she was worth, Irmina crashed through brush and branch, flower and fauna, vine and leaf, her breaths a burning rasp in her chest. Sweat drenched her shirt, causing it to cling to her back and chest and trickle down into her crotch. Behind her the rockhound's heavy footsteps pounded, and more than once she heard the splintering crash of wood as it sheared through another tree trunk, head first, not bothering to skirt them in its pursuit.

She'd barely managed to reach the Nevermore Heights' Cloud Forests ahead of the beast, having to rely on a headlong plunge off a precipice to gain her some distance. A glance over her shoulder after she landed and rolled, showed the mottled girth of the stoneform creature pacing at the cliff's edge. Smiling, she relaxed. That had been her first mistake. The loud thud of the beast landing behind her sent her scampering away once more. Her second mistake was thinking the undergrowth and thick boles within the forest would win her a big advantage. They certainly did slow the rockhound, but it was inevitably catching up.

Thighs numb from the constant pumping of her legs, Irmina continued to flee. Through the brush, another mottled form sped adjacent to her. A second hound. Her heart thumped louder, and she drove her legs harder. The one pursuing her roared, the sound reverberating through the air as it announced its territorial claim. A whine issued from the new hound, and it drew to a halt, its gaze still fixed on her before the beast passed from the edge of her vision.

Irmina sucked in a deep breath, her heart rate soothing just a touch. Until another roar from her pursuer echoed. This time closer. At least within twenty feet if her judgment was correct. She dared not look back. Not that she needed to; the crashes of a massive body through brush, the crunch of stone paws on broken branches, the guttural snarls of the beast told a story all of their own.

She'd be lucky to make it another hundred feet.

Whipping her head from side to side, she desperately sought something, anything, that might ensure her safety. But the forest was the same wherever she looked. Gigantic trees stretched a hundred feet or more into the air, trunks smooth, sometimes covered in moss that made climbing near impossible. The smaller trees proved to be even less ideal. The rockhound's penchant for charging through the trunks as if they were paper and not wood made that point abundantly clear.

Irmina's fists clenched against the urge to look back, to see just how close the rockhound was. Instead, she focused ahead, her mind racing. Like lightning on a dark day, it struck her. How had the beast decided to chase her after appearing so intent on the giant? Silvereyes must have…

But could she risk trying? So far, her control of Ostania's creatures had proved tenuous at best. There was no time to doubt. If she continued running, she was dead. If her taming failed, she was dead. Somehow, she needed to put a little more distance between her and her assailant to make an attempt. Dread lumped in her throat with the thought.

Seventy feet, maybe.

She veered toward the biggest tree she could find: a giant redwood whose upper branches disappeared in gloom among dense canopy broken by pale slivers of sunlight. Branches from saplings snagging at her clothing, vines attempting to trip her, she darted forward, her chest a living firebrand as she pushed herself.

Fifty feet.

The hound's paws thundered closer. She could hear its snarling breaths now.

Thirty feet.

Now the footfalls were directly behind her. She imagined

stony claws tearing through decomposing vegetation, crushing worms and any other slow moving creatures that called the leafy mass home. A blood–chilling growl made her skin crawl.

She reached the tree. Two nimble outstretched leaps from her sore legs up onto buttress roots brought a grimace to her face. Then she was around the massive trunk and sprinting away. She called to her two eagles, and they answered with high–pitched cries.

Behind her came a snarl, abruptly followed by a resounding crash. Irmina's heartbeats slowed to mere increments as she stopped and turned to face the beast.

Splinters exploded from the giant redwood. Through the shower of wood chips flew the rockhound, leaving a gaping hole in the center of the tree trunk. The tree leaned listlessly and began to topple, the roar of branch tearing against branch rumbling through the air.

Eagles screamed in defiance. Giant, living arrows of feather, beak, and claw shot down through the canopy.

Sunlight streamed through the space that slowly cleared as the tree continued to lean to one side before stopping, supported by its neighbors, their branches snapping under the weight. The hound's chipped rock surface glinted when it landed in that patch of radiance with a thud, its bestial, golden eyes shining with violent intent. The creature roared, its maw lined with white, stony teeth, its tail sweeping back and forth.

The sound of beating wings played a slow rhythm as the first eagle swooped onto the hound's head, claws clicking as they gouged into flesh and left bloody furrows. The hound howled, swiping a huge paw through the area where the eagle had already vacated. Before the stoneform beast could draw back, the second eagle alighted on its back, beak stabbing, claws tearing. The hound bounded to one side, lost its balance, and crashed to the ground, its massive frame leaving indentations in the earth before it sprang upright once more.

As the creature gained its feet, the eagles screeching and circling to attack in sudden bursts, a transformation began. Its body, previously stone–like but covered in parts by mottled green moss, rippled. The lichen receded beneath hard skin etched with fissures like some eroded stone formation. The rockhound became stone in truth, a carapace of what could pass for grey feldspar covering its body. When the change completed, the hound ignored the now harmless attacks of the eagles, focusing on Irmina instead.

Their gazes locked. The rockhound bounded forward, its long strides eating up the remaining distance between them.

Heart racing, Irmina sucked in a deep breath and pushed the lump of fear crawling through her chest down into her gut. She stretched her mind out, similar to reaching out to pet the animal, to soothe its rage. Her touch sped along the eye contact and pierced the beast's psyche. And slammed into a wall. The lump threatened to come crawling back up her gut, but Irmina drew her brows together in concentration.

The hound snarled, the sound a heart–stopping rumble, and leaped the last ten feet. Its maw opened wide, a slimy rain of slobber flying from its jaws.

Seconds seemed to stretch into minutes. Irmina pushed against the wall with all her willpower. It gave a little before rebounding back at her with near insurmountable force. Staggering from the recoil, she clung to her link as dogged as the hound itself. She could see the golden irises of the beast now, locked on her, murderous intent clear.

"No! Damn you! No!" Irmina yelled, her heart a thump that drowned out all else. "You're. Mine!" With those words, she snatched her mind back like a bullwhip and snapped it forward into the resistance.

But it was too late. There would be no way to avoid the impact now or those fangs. Was she left to die like this? Eaten? Without fulfilling her revenge, or completing her training, without revealing who and what the Dorns really were? Never seeing Ancel's emerald eyes and long dark hair again?

No. No. NO!

Irmina screamed, the sound piercing her head, echoing through the forest, chasing away birds. With the last strength she could muster, she battered at the barrier.

The wall crumbled.

Practically stopping in mid air, the hound crashed to the ground with a resounding thump. It writhed for a few seconds before going still, then struggled to its feet once more.

Pushed to the limit by the taming, Irmina felt the pressure as the hound struggled to regain control. She wouldn't be able to keep the eagles and the beast. She needed all her focus, so she sent a command to the birds to return to Jerem. With wild screeches, they flew off. The pressure subsided to a distant throb at the back of her mind.

Chest laboring from her exertion, Irmina strode over to her new pet. The hound's eyes shone defiantly and it growled.

"It's fine, boy," Irmina said, her voice a soft coo. She reached out and touched its stony skin, and her pet whined. "It's fine. I mean you no harm." She sent pictures of her intent, of her love for animals, her bond with them across her link. When she reached out again, the hound gave a plaintive growl, and its stone carapace retracted. Irmina stroked its neck, and the hound crooned.

"Come, let's go." A scowl twisted Irmina's features at the thought of Silvereyes sending the creature after. She gazed back up toward the mountainous slopes. "We hunt." Her pet followed.

CHAPTER 17

In a corner of the Dancing Lady tavern that smelled of sweat, liquor and giana smoke, Ancel Dorn sipped from a wine glass so thick its surface appeared frosted. A slight tingling crept along his body and his head buzzed in a jumbled susurrus.

Through the peeling paint on the window next to him, he spied the occasional passerby, often with their heads bowed, hurrying in the direction of Randane's temples. A prayer bell tolled. Ancel couldn't help his smirk. He could picture Randane's palace and its spires alongside the pristine pillars of the Streamean temples. At this moment, patrons would be crowded beneath the massive statues of Ilumni and the smaller ones depicting Rituni and Bragni at his sides. *If only the gods knew the debauchery I have planned.* He took another drink.

I wonder what you'd think if you saw me now, my dear Irmina. After all, I'm doing what you asked. What a life I'm living. This time, he took a long gulp. Warmth coursed down his gullet, and the buzz increased.

Sweet kinai wine could have such an effect on anyone. The drink crept up a little bit at a time until it kicked you in the head like a wild stallion. The kicking had not started yet, but he intended to get to that point soon enough. He swilled the red liquid around in his glass. It did not taste as refined as what his family made back home in Eldanhill, but it would do.

He should have left for home days ago in order to make it in time for this year's big Soltide Festival. Or to resume his training. He shrugged both ideas off, the buzz from the liquor feeling better by the moment. He might regret drinking himself into a stupor in the morning, but he would worry about that in the godsforsaken morning. First things first was to find himself a woman.

Mirza and Danvir sat opposite him at the round table, both nursing their own drinks. Unlike him, they were garbed in eye–catching silk shirts and trousers. Tonight, he wore black. They'd chided him for it all the way to the Dancing Lady. Their attempts to convince him to return to their inn and change into something more celebratory for his nineteenth naming day went ignored.

Tonight, Danvir's hair, so blond it appeared almost white, was oiled and brushed until it hung above his wide shoulders. Mirza had cut his hair short and used some scented plant from Torandil to make it spiky. He claimed it was a new style among the Dosteri. His hair drew many an ill look from Sendethi along the streets, and almost caused a few fights. Ancel kept his dark hair in a simple ponytail tied with a leather cord.

They ended up picking this place for a few reasons. The first, his father had suggested The Dancing Lady, second, its famed dancing girls, third, it was one of the few establishments in Randane where they could still find a decent seat.

Patrons filled all the other more reputable places to the brim. A usual occurrence whenever Ancel delivered his family's kinai wine to the other taverns. Not that he couldn't have forced the issue at any one of the numerous inns to find him accommodations, but he'd promised his father not to ruin the Dorn name. Another reason they had agreed on this place. The Dorns earned a pretty penny off their drink, and he intended to spend his portion with glee.

The Dancing Lady, however, did not buy the Dorns' kinai wine. The owner preferred to try copy the product. Ancel did not mind one bit. The more who failed to find that special taste, the more fame the Dorns' winery earned. Ancel smiled. This seedy place with its windows painted with dancing girls and dim, smoky interior would do just fine.

Ancel's favorite serving girl swayed across floors sticky with mud and spilled drink. He figured the ability to move that way on such a surface required great skill and practice. Her pretty face soon hovered before him as she delivered another round. A smack rang out as Mirza slapped her on her rump when she turned to leave. An upturned nose and a headshake greeted Mirza's wayward touch quickly followed by the smile she shot Ancel's way. Yes, he was definitely going to bed her tonight. Ancel held up his glass toward her in appreciation of her slim figure and dark curls. The gesture earned him an almost sinuous sway of her hips.

The jumbled conversations and laughter subsided when the music started again. Oil lamps around the small stage flared until their light highlighted a seated, grizzled man playing a takuatin. The instrument always reminded Ancel of a long, skinny lute, but instead of fifteen strings, the takuatin had thirty–two, said to represent the thirty–two winds. Stories had it that like people caught in the fateful winds, the most brilliant players could get lost in their instrument's rhythms, eventually going insane, lost to the world forever.

The musician kept his head down and eyes closed as he played, his head nodding to the timing. He strummed the instrument in a slow tune, his finger work sure and steady. The tune's speed gradually increased into a wonderful takuatin rhythm, and he began to sing.

Now, Ancel was always one for a fine piece of music, after all, it tended to lighten the mood and often made it easier for him when he was on the prowl. But someone needed to tell the player he croaked. Every time the man hit a high note, Ancel looked to his glass to see if it cracked. Nevertheless, the patrons clapped and sang along to *The Peasant Thread the Needle:* a vulgar little number about a peasant who has his way with a nobleman's wife and lives to tell the tale.

Both his friends clapped right along and sung. Danvir's deep rumble and Mirza's girlish tone made for quite a contrast. Ancel soon joined in.

> *He pounced when she bounced,*
> *He bang when she rang,*
> *When the peasant thread the needle.*
> *He slipped and he slid,*
> *In and out he sure did,*
> *When the peasant thread the needle!*

On and on the song went, with men and women laughing

and clapping. Drinks flowed like water, and the music lowered as one of the dancing girls strutted onto the small stage next to the takuatin player. The music changed to a soft, flowing tune like clear water trickling down a spring.

Ancel recognized the song—Damal's Sacrifice—but he pushed it to the back of his mind, and it was quickly forgotten as he drank in the sight of the performer. He'd seen dancing girls before but none to match her. Mirza sucked in a breath. Danvir whooped.

The musician kept his rhythm going, and she began to sway. No, that didn't properly describe what she did. Her hips, waist, and buttocks moved in circular motions as if they were separate from the rest of her body like some sinuous creature that was half woman, half snake. The movement accentuated her curves and the shine of her coppery skin. Her waist–length, honey–colored hair hung behind her and her sheer, lace garb teased with the promises her body offered.

Ancel stared, his mouth agape. It wasn't just her exquisite beauty that held him enraptured, nor her movements. Color her hair black, lighten her skin tone, and she would be Irmina. The fact Irmina had danced in a similar fashion for him did little to help.

The music sped up, and her gyrations increased to match. The rhythm slowed again, and she coiled with mesmerizing seductiveness. Ancel couldn't tear his eyes from her even if he wanted to. Then, the music stopped, and she retreated behind the curtains.

A deafening roar exploded from the patrons. Smokers set down their giana pipes and yelled, some coughing as they did so. Men and women whooped and hollered. Everyone clapped. People cried for more. Glasses tinkled. Bottles broke. Knives flashing, two men fought, and the big guards dragged them out by their ears.

"Close your mouth, Ancel." Mirza guffawed, placing a hand ungraciously under Ancel's chin and pushing.

"You should see the look on your face," Danvir roared, his voice carrying a slight slur. He did not hold his liquor well.

Ancel shook his head slowly. "I don't know what you two are on about. I've seen women dance like that before."

"Yeah, sure." Mirza laughed again. "Where?"

Danvir leaned forward, his glassy eyes shining. "Do tell."

Ancel opened his mouth and shut it again. He'd seen Irmina move that way a few times. Well, not quite like that, but close. Something she said her mother showed her as a child. Once, when his father saw her do it, he scolded her. However, his father did brag another day when filled with drink, that Irmina couldn't dance as well as Ancel's mother. Ancel's face flushed with the memory. However, he did not intend to tell his friends about Irmina's skill. Besides, she was part of the reason he avoided leaving with Valdeen. No matter how hard he tried to forget, he still missed her soft touch. His hand strayed to his breast pocket where he kept her letter. Having to answer what he intended with Alys wouldn't have made for good conversation.

Mirza slapped Ancel's hand down. "Remember, you promised if she wasn't back in a year you'd burn that thing. Well, today is the day. A bloody year. We're here to celebrate, so don't you dare whip that out." He somehow managed to say it all without slurring once. His ability to hold drink seemed uncanny to Ancel. He often wondered if Mirza had a hole in his stomach.

Danvir passed Ancel a new drink. "Here, have another."

Ancel took the glass. "Thanks."

Again, I find myself thinking you're right, Mirz. Ancel didn't dare share the thought with his friends. The fun they would have at his expense would make him miserable. He needed to forget about Irmina, but seeing that Ostanian dancer had served to rekindle those memories. Shoving them aside now would not be easy. Drinking usually helped, so he took a sip. He'd taken to bedding many women over the last eight months. Being deep in some pretty lady's flesh also helped him to forget Irmina. Yet, both sex and drink often proved fleeting distractions as the memories came crashing back soon after. *Yes, both of you are right. I'll put her behind me starting tonight.*

"You know they say she's Ostanian." Mirza stared off toward the stage. "They say it's near impossible for a Granadian to bed one of them. At least not without paying."

Ancel almost groaned, finding the temptation to wager that he could bed her almost unbearable.

Danvir snorted. "Really?"

"Well, that's the word going around. And she sure isn't local."

"Speaking of Ostania," Ancel chimed in. "Have you heard the recent talk?" He needed some way to change the subject.

"About that so called army?" Danvir scoffed. "Peddlers' tales."

"I'm not so sure." Ancel lowered his vice. "I mean, I heard it myself when I delivered the kinai to the palace. Someone sent word to a Herald at the Vallum, and they passed it on to the cities. We may be going to war."

"I'd look forward to that," Mirza said. "To see the rest of the world and be a Dagodin just like my Da once was."

Hearing such words from Mirza was strange. Ever since Mirza's mother died and his father turned to drink, he and his son argued most of the times Ancel saw them. Mirza once complained he believed all his father's old stories about the wars and battles were all lies. He'd turned to hunting and working with Ancel at the winery ever since, instead of mining and quarrying with his father.

Ancel sighed. "I'm not so sure I'd be ready. I've skipped Mater training the last few months."

Mirza gaped. "I knew about the sword classes, but I never expected... Did u give that up because of her?" Mirza's eyes studied Ancel for a moment.

The warmth of embarrassment bloomed across Ancel's face. "It just doesn't feel the same without her there. Before we left home, I had thoughts about beginning again. This report from the palace has me thinking it would be for the best. Completing my training would give me a chance to get away from Eldanhill."

"I agree," Mirza said. "Ancel." Mirza's voice became softer, almost pleading, but at the same time serious. "Promise me you'll complete your Mater training." He scratched his head. "I mean, I'd hate for you to lose control and—. Never mind."

Ancel frowned, but Mirza clapped him on his shoulder. "Listen. If she loved you like you loved her she wouldn't have left you the way she did. Besides, at the rate you're going, both me and Dan will surpass you in school. And if you think your Da's upset now, can you imagine how he would be if you're no longer top of the class?"

Danvir sloshed his wine around and said with a snort, "Um, he hasn't been top of the class for a few months now."

"Maybe, you're right," Ancel confessed as he thought about his father's recent displeasure. Only his mother's words had saved him from Stefan's wrath.

Mirza smirked. "Of course I am, you fool. When am I ever wrong?"

Danvir snorted again. "You almost always are."

Mirza's red brows bunched, and his head turned from side to side like a sparrow.

A smile touched Ancel's lips at Mirza's cluelessness. "Speaking of being wrong. Dan hasn't cursed. You owe me coin, Mirz."

"That's not fair," Mirza cried. "You need to give me more time."

"You said three drinks." Ancel pointed to Danvir's drink. "That's his fourth. Now pay up, I'll need the coin for your little Ostanian dancer."

Mirza chuckled. "In that case." He reached into his pocket and took out four gold coins with a bird imprinted on each. "There you, go. Four hawks."

"You bet four hawks on me cursing?" Danvir slurred. "Amuni's balls. You're as stupid as they say when it comes to wagers."

Mirza closed his hand over the coins. "There, he just did it."

"Oh no, you don't. You bet three drinks. You already lost."

Mirza gritted his teeth and handed over the coins.

"Thank you. Nice doing business with you, my good sir."

The music started up again, this time a slower song. Another girl came out and danced. A black–haired girl, wide as a bull, with ear lobes pierced in multiple places in the typical Dosteri fashion. Her dancing paled in comparison to the Ostanian, but the patrons showed their appreciation all the same. War did not matter to the Sendethi men when it came to enjoying a woman's pleasures.

The honey haired dancer now visited tables. Ancel tried and failed to watch subtly, and instead, openly stared.

Mirza signaled for more drinks. "So, do you really believe what you heard at the palace?"

Ancel's shoulders rose, eyes still riveted on the dancer. "Why not? I'd bet there's a lot of truth to the story." Ancel didn't quite know why he felt that way, but something in his gut told him he was right.

"I'd take that bet." Mirza grinned and held his hand out.

"Me too," Danvir slurred.

Ancel wagged his finger. "Now you know I'm not making that wager."

"How about another then?" Mirza's eyebrow arched.

"I'm listening."

"You and the Ostanian."

Ancel suppressed the need to draw in a breath.

"Don't tell me you're scared," Mirza chortled. "Not good old Ancel who can charm scales off a fish."

"Fine, fine," Ancel said. He wasn't about to be outdone by Mirz. "Let's say five hawks. Each."

Mirza pursed his lips and stroked the stubble on his chin before nodding. "As long as you don't pay for her services. Charm the dress, well, underwear off her."

"I'll only use what coin it takes to get her to the table."

Danvir and Mirza glanced at each other. "You're on," they said together.

The serving girl returned with their drinks. She winked at Ancel and smacked Mirza's hand before he could slap her ass again.

Ancel did not really want to, but he would have to disappoint this serving girl. He scratched his head. What was he saying? He wanted to disappoint her, especially since it meant chasing after the Ostanian dancer. That was indeed half of the intrigue—the chase. This serving girl offered no challenge; he could have her any time. Now the dancer, she was special. Several men were after her, and she'd already refused quite a few. He needed something unique to stand out.

Ancel flicked a gold hawk to the girl. "Tell the Ostanian I want a word with her. There's another hawk in it for you and four for her."

Danvir spit out his drink. "Did you get knocked over your head? That's fifty silver owls you just offered to go with the ten you gave her. Enough to buy drinks for everyone in here twice over." Danvir slurred so hard now he sputtered.

Ancel shrugged. "It's just coin."

Danvir grumbled under his breath about wasting good coin and put his drink back to his mouth. Mirza had one of those leers of his written across his face. The girl's eyes widened at the coin, before they narrowed when she grasped what Ancel asked her to do. She gave him a look that said he didn't know what he was missing.

"I guess this means it's you and I threading the needle," Mirza sang and flicked her another hawk. "There's more where that came from."

The girl caught the coin despite the tray she carried, and now she graced Mirza with a smile. She saved a pout for Ancel and strutted away.

Mirza rubbed his hands together. "This, I can't wait to see."

A few moments later, the honey–haired dancer arrived at their table. Up close, she was even more breathtaking. Her slim curves reminded Ancel of Irmina again, but he pushed the thought from his mind. A thin mouth and a dainty nose highlighted her smooth face. Looking into her deep, lemon–colored eyes made him feel as if he could drown in them. Perfume drifted from her carrying the spicy scent of bellflowers.

"Well, are you going to say something or just stare all night?" She asked in a thick, singsong accent.

"Oh, um, hullo." Ancel said, fidgeting with his hands. *Direct, like Irmina too.* He almost pinched himself.

Mirza chortled. "Why I never thought I'd see the day when some woman made your silky tongue stick to the roof of your mouth."

Ancel glared at his friend before turning back to the dancer. "Would you mind taking a seat?" Under the table, he kicked Danvir's chair.

The big man pulled his face from the mouth of his glass. "Hmmm? Why're you kicking my chair?"

The Ostanian shook her head. Ancel rolled his eyes. He stood, walked around to the other side of the table, and pulled out a chair for her.

"Why, thank you," she said in a sweet tone, but her eyes spoke in volumes of ice.

A smile tugged at the corner of Ancel's mouth. Without the use of coin, this conquest appeared more difficult than he expected. A refreshing thought. He'd noticed how standoffish she was earlier when she patronized other tables. The men in this place were so lost in their drink they either did not notice or did not care. Music started up again.

Ancel took a chair next to her and met her defiant gaze with a smile. "I'm Ancel. May I have the pleasure of knowing your name?"

"Iris." She still wore the same cold look in her eyes.

"That's a very old Granadian name for an Ostanian woman."

Her expression changed, and she leaned forward slightly. "What do you know about Ostanian names?"

"I know," he said as he took out a silver flask from the inside pocket of his velvet jacket. "That Ostanians love good kinai." He took a swig and nodded to the flask. "I also know you say your names and eyes are windows to your soul as—"

"Your words are doorways to the heart," she finished in a soft voice.

"So, should I ask again?"

"Kachien."

"Ah, a flowing wind. It suits you." Ancel passed her the drink.

Kachien sniffed at it, and her eyes widened. "You know our sayings. You understand our language. And you have distilled kinai. Who are you?"

"Miss, I was about to ask the same thing myself," Mirza said, his gaze fixed on Ancel. He stood, flipped on his hat, and left a gold eagle on the table. "I think I'll retire now. Dan?"

Danvir grumbled and stumbled to his feet.

"One moment," Ancel said to Kachien.

Ancel stood and helped Mirza get Danvir's big arm over his gaunt friend's neck. His gaze followed them as they stumbled out. At the door, Mirza paused and tipped his hat to Ancel, who smiled in return.

"Now, back to me." Ancel savored the tone of her tanned skin as he sat. "My parents are famous for their kinai wine. My father always brags about his travels, saying Eastern Ostania was the most cultured place he ever stayed in. They lived there for many years before moving here and brought the art of kinai making with them. I used to drink in all his stories about Ostania. Not that I had much choice. He always talked about the place."

She studied him for a moment, her eyes narrowing slightly into a dubious expression. "Did he also tell you that many of the women from that part of Ostania are hard and not easily impressed by boasts or flattery?"

"Indeed. But more than most, you have an undying love for song and poetry."

"We do?"

"Yes. If you let my father tell it, many of our songs were taken from old Ostanian lore. He even claims the best musicians lived in your side of the world, and much of their music was steeped in truth."

Eyes keen, Kachien leaned forward even more.

"Take the song you danced to for example. Damal's Sacrifice. A strange song to dance the Temtesa to."

"Why?"

"Well as the legend goes, Damal was one of the last Eztezians. A great Teacher. Supposedly, in a desperate attempt to save Denestia, he ventured into Hydae in order to battle a Skadwaz overlord. The battle took place at the once great city of Jenoah with its gleaming spires and famous fountains. Having found out he was betrayed by the Exalted Ashishin—something I don't believe—Damal sacrificed himself to trigger some great Forging. One that would make the Kassite impassable, sealing the Planes of Existence, not only imprisoning the gods in the Nether, but locking away Denestia from Hydae's threat."

Kachien sat staring into his face, her eyes wide with wonder. Ancel smiled. When her lips curled with the same warm expression, this feeling came over him. Not the heat of his loins or the racing heart that often began when he knew he'd made some headway. This was different, seeing her smile. It was sunshine glowing through dark clouds to spark a rainbow over freezing waters. Whatever coldness he harbored toward women, somehow fled, chased away by Kachien's radiance.

She broke into a mischievous grin and took a sip from his flask. For an instant, a flash of hunger filled her eyes. "So was your curiosity what made you call on me?" She set the flask down, her thumb playing around the rim.

Ancel blushed, but he didn't waver. He knew he had her now. Drinking from his flask meant her interest was assured. "No."

She cocked an eyebrow at him. "Oh?"

"By the way, your Temtesa…it was…exhilarating."

This time, she blushed. So far, his father's words proved true. Ancel shrugged. *Why not?* "Kachien, I came here tonight to seek pleasure and hope to forget about some things in my life. I've decided. I will forget about them with you."

Her slim fingers brushed against his. They sent a tingle up his spine.

"I thought you would never ask," she said in a breathy voice. "Come." She stood and swayed toward the door leading upstairs.

Did all these women go to a school to learn to walk that way? Ancel picked up his flask, firmness pushing against the fabric of his trousers when he stood. As he placed his drink container into his jacket pocket, he felt Irmina's letter there. He took the letter out and dropped it into his glass. Red kinai soaked into the paper. A thin tinder stick the smokers used to light their giana pipes rested on a stand next to him. Picking it up, he lit it in an oil lamp, and touched it to the paper in the glass.

Irmina's letter burst into flames.

With that flare—up, the kinai took hold and another kind of blaze soared through his loins, enveloping his mind as he stared at Kachien's swaying form. *Yes, tonight marks a new beginning. And I'll start by threading your honey—haired needle.* He strode after the woman with a smile on his face.

CHAPTER 18

A week later, Ancel strolled alongside Kachien through a field outside Randane. They had left behind the fifty–foot wall, the cobbled and flagstoned streets, the King's castle and its spires and parapets, the Streamean temples and their shining pillars, the network of canals, and the din of the crowds.

Lilies, roses, and bellflowers around them adorned the air with their sweet perfumes. Still, none were as aromatic as the smell wafting from her. He'd grown to love the powders and paints she used to make herself even more beautiful, but those paled in comparison to her scents. She'd explained each. Today, her fragrance of choice was jasmine and lavender mixed with a hint of mint.

The time spent with Kachien had flown by like a dream. An unforgettable kinai induced fantasy filled with passionate lovemaking. Most days they listened to music while he lost himself in the sway of her body as she danced the Temtesa. Other days they sampled fine foods from different taverns around town. There were tender delicacies such as river crab legs, eel in a gooseberry sauce, and lamb served with creamed potatoes. Kachien always made sure to dress in the most enticing and revealing clothing, many of which Ancel chose. Their conversation often involved sharing stories of their homes while they strolled in each other's company.

At night, that would change when Kachien needed to work. He tried to convince her several times to give up her profession, but she refused. Glancing at Kachien, Ancel heaved a sigh.

He longed to touch her hand, kiss her lips, and feel his body against hers, but he resisted the temptation. There would be time enough for that later. Instead, he enjoyed the day's warmth while admiring the way the sun played through her honey hair, giving it a golden sheen. He had no wish to break the hypnotic pull of her beauty, so he studied her curves in silence.

Ever vigilant, Charra loped through the short grass a few feet from them. He'd not taken to Kachien on the first day he met her, and more often than not, he growled when she touched Ancel in any form. However, his reaction then was nothing compared to how he acted if Ancel attempted to keep him out of the bedroom or sneak away with Kachien. Charra resorted to uncontrollable howling fits then. Ancel had resigned himself to taking the daggerpaw wherever he traveled.

"So what will we do today, my dark haired Granadian lover?" Kachien asked, her tone light and playful, a lazy smile playing across her face. "Shall I teach you some new positions?"

Ancel gaped. He had difficulty dealing with her openness about sex. He used to think of himself as bold and experienced, some said cocky, but he was a mere candlelight next to Kachien's flame. "Out here? For anyone passing to see?"

She giggled, her ample chest heaving. The tight bodice of her yellow dress amplified the movement. "Why not? Maybe the lover who gave you the charm you will not part with will pass by." She indicated the replica of his mother with a nod of her head.

"I told you several times, my mother gave it to me for my naming day."

"Oh, yes. You are a man now or so they say. But what man has never made love in the open?"

"I've had plenty women. None have ever complained. I don't see what's so special about outside."

Kachien's eyes twinkled. "Ah, my dear, you have not experienced true love–making until you feel the wind caress your body as the heat takes you. Your people have strange beliefs about passion. The gods made us naked. Why hide behind all this?" She pointed at her clothing. "In most parts of Ostanian, it becomes too hot to wear this much clothes. Come, let us go down to the stream so I can show you what I mean." With those words, she hiked up her dress by its flared ruffles and took off running.

With a chuckle, Ancel chased after her. Charra bounded beside him, growling all the way.

Kachien led them through the flowers and past budding oaks and cedars until the ground slanted down toward a stream. At the water's edge, she paused long enough to remove her dress with a speed Ancel refused to believe. Garbed only in her diaphanous shift, she waded into the stream.

Ancel paced along the rock–strewn riverbank, pebbles crunching underfoot, as Charra ran back and forth cooing and growling at Kachien. Almost out in the middle of the stream, she turned toward him and waved for him to join her. Peering around to make sure no one watched, Ancel shed his clothes. He took a running leap into the cool water. Within moments, he was frolicking beside Kachien while Charra sat and whined.

"I think today I will teach you how easy it is to float." Kachien's mouth curled into a mischievous grin.

Before he moved, she gripped his arm and drew him closer. He attempted to pull away playfully, but she kept her hold firm. Vaulting onto him, she wrapped her legs around his waist.

When he felt the warmth of her body against his, coupled with her scents and her eyes that almost matched her hair as she stared into his, he gave in. Or rather, all his inhibitions fled. Not that he needed much more convincing. His hardness sang its own song.

He cupped her ass, her shift already having slid up her body. Closing her eyes, Kachien leaned away from him with her neck arched, exposing her chest. Her nipples stood hard and proud, darker still than the already tanned beauty of her skin.

No other invitation was needed. Ancel raised her ever so slightly and suckled on the curves of her neck. Her pulse became a fluttering bird beneath his tongue. His lips slid down until he took one nipple in his mouth. A moan escaped her throat.

The warmth of their bodies built to a transcendent heat as he nibbled her succulent flesh, his nips increasing to bites, and her moans growing louder and more breathless. She arched her back and neck until he could no longer feel her heavy breaths against his ears. Her eyes opened, glazed in ecstasy. Their gazes locked, and she smiled warmly. She drew his head to her, and they kissed long and deep, their tongues playing against each other. The feeling was sweeter than cold water on a blazing day.

Her hands slid down his body, below his waist. Ancel arched his back. When their flesh entwined, his world exploded.

Their lovemaking became a blur of gyrating hips, moans, gasps, and digging fingernails. In the water, his strokes became effortless. When he climaxed, it was as if he saw the world through a new light.

He opened his eyes, and a ragged moan tore from his throat. Colors bloomed all around him. Everything appeared more alive than ever before. Reds were deeper, blues darker, pinks brighter. On and on the hues swirled about him across every living surface.

Whites, grays, and browns wavered around Kachien herself.

Ancel gasped as another release shuddered through his body. His eyes snapped closed against his new sight. When he opened them, all was normal.

Kachien's hand stroked his face. "Are you well? You look like you saw a spirit."

Ancel nodded. He was so caught up in the throes of what just occurred words refused to rise to his lips.

"I told you, I would teach you how easy it is to float," Kachien gloated, flashing him a naughty smile again.

"That you did," he finally managed, his voice hoarse.

"Come, let us go to the field and sun ourselves." She unwrapped herself and waded toward the shore.

Ancel closed his eyes once more and drew in a deep breath. Usually, after lovemaking, he would be spent. But not this time. He felt rejuvenated as if he could run a hundred miles without pause. He swam after Kachien.

She reached the shore and rose from the water, her shift clinging to her curves. The material was so thin it made her appear naked. He visualized every nuance of her body beneath his touch and hardened again. With a great effort, he willed away the picture, and his arousal subsided.

When he left the water, she had already picked up her dress and was heading up the hill in her swaying walk. Her hair fell behind her in wet tresses, dark gold in the sunlight. Despite its thickness and length, it did little to hide the myriad thin white scars across her back.

Ancel watched her for a moment more before he grabbed his clothes and followed. Charra padded after him.

At the hill's crest, Kachien flattened a patch of grass big enough for both of them. She placed her dress down and stretched out on her back like a tan and gold fox basking in the sun. Ancel joined her.

"Something happened out there," Ancel said, as he stared at the wispy clouds littering the cerulean sky.

"You think?" Kachien said with mock offense as she played with the charm around his neck.

Ancel turned his head to find her peering into his face. "Seriously. I saw something unusual. It's happened before, but I never thought of it until now."

Kachien frowned. "What did you see besides my nakedness?"

"It was as if every living creature shone with color. Too many colors to count. In my Mater training—" He cut off at Kachien's gasp.

"You can touch Mater?" Kachien stopped twiddling his pendant and sat up, her eyes wary.

Ancel paused for a moment. He had not intended to let his Teaching slip. But near Kachien, he didn't feel the need to keep secrets. "No. Not yet. I can sense it around me when I open myself. The world comes alive when I do. This was like touching my Matersense but different."

Kachien hugged her knees. "When I lived in Ostania, my people, the Alzari, could do these things with Mater. They were among the first killed by the shade in the War of Remnants." A shudder passed though her body. "There are many among us born with this curse."

"It's not a curse," Ancel protested. But the pain etched on Kachien's face spoke on its own. She'd spoken about losing everyone she knew before, but she'd never been this specific. "Matii help the keep the world safe. It's a great honor in Granadia to become one. It's them who saved Ostania during the same war you speak of."

"I know this. It is why I choose to live here, despite how some of your people look at me. But still, we were taught to touch this Mater was a curse. The idea was whipped into us. It is a hard thing to make myself think otherwise."

Ancel brushed his hand down her face and shoulder then down her back. Her scars were smooth stripes below his fingers. Kachien's eyes closed. She shivered at his touch.

"Was that where you received these?" he whispered.

"Yes."

"Why? Why whip you like this?"

"So we would not forget. My people believe your feelings bring out your power. Our Formist gods were said to feel the turnings of the world through their emotions. It is only through their control that kept the world from tearing apart or so our priests say. Those among us cursed to touch Mater had to show the same control. Everyone had to take the trials, and they included beatings in order to bring forth the most primal emotions. If you could touch Mater, it rose in you then." A tear trickled down Kachien's face.

Speechless, Ancel wiped the tear away. In her eyes, he saw the truth of Kachien's pain, and in her voice he'd felt a touch of sorrow the depths of which he couldn't begin to comprehend.

"I should have asked you if you were one such before I touched you in the ways I have," Kachien said, her voice apologetic.

"No. You didn't need to. I wanted you more than anything else I've felt in a long time."

Kachien shook her head. "It is you who do not understand. We were taught only those who could control their emotions would be allowed to wield Mater. They were given no choice but to complete their training." Although she sat beside him, her eyes said she was a thousand miles away. "If they failed in this, they were killed before the madness took them. Our histories show those who escaped the culling. The suffering they later brought has become legend. They killed and destroyed without care, forever a slave to the power burning within them. They were called the Deathbringers."

"How did Materforging drive them mad?"

"We believe there are three things necessary to make one a Matus. First, your body and mind had to be like...a...a... No, that is not the right word." Kachien's shaped brows drew together.

"A conduit?" Ancel offered.

"What is that?"

"It is a pipe or channel allowing something to pass."

"Yes. A condooeet to your sela so Mater on the outside could touch within." She frowned at Ancel's smile to her pronunciation. "Then, you had to be able to store enough essences. A man who couldn't store any but could still sense the elements would become a warrior fighting with *divya*. A Binder, similar to your Dagodin."

Ancel nodded to show he understood. What Kachien was saying was not much different from what Teacher Galiana taught.

"The second requirement is there must be enough emotions within you to Forge as you people say. Without the emotions, nothing happens. Sela, your soul, and your feelings are all connected. The easiest way to tap into your sela and touch the Mater without is through your feelings. The more powerful the emotions, the more you can do. But your ability also depends on what you can store. Once spent, time is needed to regain enough essences to Forge. If you use up your sela, you die."

"And the third requirement?"

"Control. You have to control your emotions in order to command Mater. Within yourself, your sela rests in a calmness called the Shunyata. That is where you must thrust all you feel, and call upon those emotions only when you wish."

"We call the same thing the Eye of the Storm. I use it in sword training," Ancel said.

Kachien's lips pursed before she continued. "My people believe the essences are living things. They seek lives. If you lose dominance of your emotions and give in to your power's whispers, you will kill and feed them. Once you have chosen to appease the essences with a life, there is no return. You are lost forever like those caught in the thirty–two winds, doomed to kill and kill until the power drives you insane, shrivels your soul and you die."

"Deathbringers," Ancel whispered.

Kachien nodded. "In the books of our Formist worship, it is said this is what happened to the Eztezain Guardians of old. They then broke the world. A man or woman who could store, touch, wield Mater and above all force the power to succumb to their will through control can become a Matus. One who cannot is considered born dead. To prevent another culling of the world as is foretold, my people kill any who lack control."

The thought of such a ruthless way of thinking made Ancel cringe. "But if the essences are alive, and you use Mater to kill, how would you not feed them?"

"You place the whispers from the power and your emotions into the Shunyata. Once trapped there, the essences cannot feed off your kills. This is what some call battle bonding. However, the essences do feed off your sela so you can only hold them trapped for so long before you are forced to release them. If they have fed enough in the Shunyata, you will no longer feel the lust to kill. This is a delicate balance."

There were subtle differences between what he learned and Kachien's explanation, but Ancel understood. He tried to reassure her with a smile and squeeze of her hand. "You don't have to worry about me. Or about someone killing me. We have our own tests, but nothing as brutal as your people. No one is taught how to touch Mater without passing the trials for control."

"What about those who fail?"

"They become Dagodin. The chance of their power surfacing is sealed away."

"And those who touch Mater on their own accord without control?"

"There aren't any such people among us." Even as he said those words, Ancel's brow knitted. Surely, there were those who touched Mater without the use of the Mysteras. Those who never had any training of any kind. Why hadn't he ever considered the possibility? Although being born with an affinity to Mater was a rare event, how was each person located?

"I see even to you, this does not make sense."

"No, it doesn't. Kachien, if you cannot sense Mater, why'd they put you through the trials?"

Her eyes became slits. "As I said before. All were forced to take the Trials of Sight. It was the only way to be sure of who was born with the power. Any who tried to leave without taking them were executed. I do not doubt if in secret something similar happens among your people."

Ancel opened his mouth to argue, but he couldn't find the words. There were too many questions spinning through his head to which he had no answers.

"Please, Ancel." Kachien gave his hand a squeeze. "Promise me you will complete whatever training you have undertaken. You have made a special place in my heart. I do not think I can stand another loss."

Ancel found no ways to resist her pleas even if he wanted to. "I promise."

"Good," Kachien said, her entire face brightening. "Now, let us speak of more pleasurable things. Where do you intend to take me today?"

Ancel smiled. "I've plans for a tavern with the best Granadian food you've ever tasted. There'll be curried goat, roast piglet, fish basted with a sauce that is both sweet and spicy all at once—"

"Will there be music?"

"Yes. I hired a harper."

Kachien's eyes widened. Ancel's smile broke into a grin. She'd shared how much she enjoyed the music of the harp.

"Come, then," Kachien said, jumping to her feet. "Let us get dressed and go. This way I can spend much time listening and kissing you while he plays before I return to work tonight."

Ancel froze in the middle of rising to his feet. His chest tightened with the idea of her work. The idea of other men touching her body.

"Oh, Ancel," Kachien whispered near his ear. "It is only a job. No one can make me feel as you do."

Despite her soothing words, a lump of jealousy remained as they made their way to Randane.

CHAPTER 19

Pain pounded in Ryne's head like an incessant hammer slamming onto an anvil. His eyes fought his attempt to open them. With great effort and a groan, he managed to will the pounding into a dull throb.

Soft leaves cushioned one cheek. What felt like a damp rug stretched under him, and sweltering air greeted him with both fresh and moldy smells. Jungle sounds clamored all around him. From the scratching of some forager, to the rustling branches caused by animals traversing trees, to the howl of a hunting forest lapra, all conspiring to increase the throbbing in his head once more.

He reached a tentative hand to his shoulder. The leather belt for his scabbard was gone. Not that he needed confirmation—the sword was near enough he could still feel it. His eyes fluttered open. He was not surprised when his vision showed he was no longer in the mountains. Great evergreens with smooth trunks and widespread canopies towered over a hundred feet into the air. An occasional beam of morning sun broke through the covering. *The Mondros Forest, then.*

Ryne sat up among a smattering of leaves. Undergrowth starved for sunlight bunched around him in a tangled, multicolored mass of flowers and choking lantum vines with heart shaped leaves.

Sakari sat on a gigantic root a few feet from him. He now appeared as a typical Western Ostanian with black hair and sunburned skin, his face all sharp angles and planes. He'd resumed a more powerful build with broad shoulders and thick arms, and his faded trousers and cotton shirt matched the trees and forest. What remained of a long dead fire nestled where the trunk and roots met.

"How long did I sleep this time?" Ryne asked.

"You have been in and out for a week."

Ryne shook his head and shrugged. He'd become accustomed to the unexplained loss of consciousness over the last few years. Whenever he woke, he would have vague memories of dreams during his stupor. Yet, try as he might, he could never grasp those dreams beyond the sight of him shrouded in light.

"You can finish the drink I fed you during your sleep." Sakari gestured toward a waterskin near the coals. "And I roasted a rabbit." The animal rested on a smooth stone still spitted.

"Did you eat any?" Ryne smiled at Sakari's impassive face. When he saw no answer was forthcoming, he stood. The leafy carpet sunk under his feet as he walked over and picked up the waterskin and took a sip. Pleased to see Sakari had kept some kinai juice, he took an even longer drink. He wasted no time in tearing the spongy flesh from the rabbit limb by limb.

When he finished eating, Ryne removed the leather cord from his ebony hair, brushed back loose strands, and retied the string. A quick look at a rustling brush revealed a slim forest lapra with leaves growing from parts of its body, no doubt drawn by the food scents. The lapra dipped its head to one side and slunk among the shrubbery.

"How deep in the Mondros are we?" Ryne asked.

"A few miles. Something about the Nevermore Heights made me uneasy."

Ryne raised one eyebrow and the corner of his mouth twitched. "You...had a feeling?" The blank stare he received from Sakari in response almost made him burst into laughter. He shook his head at Sakari's lack of humor and picked up his sword. A sense of calm passed through him with the feel of the glyphs etched into the hilt. "Is Mariel still following us?"

"No. Not since I set the rockhound after her. Maybe it caught her." Despite the change in Sakari's appearance, the same flat monotone laced his words

"Unlikely. She's been too cautious for an animal so simple." Ryne unsheathed his greatsword and inspected the blade before placing it back in its scabbard and slinging the leather strap over his shoulder.

"Time to head home?" Sakari asked.

Ryne nodded. With a smooth leap, Sakari hit the ground and took the lead. The ease with which Sakari moved made it appear as if he followed a path carved ahead of them. They avoided the vines and bush, never having to hack their way through.

Questions about Halvor's words rose within Ryne's mind. *What is it I already know? If I knew who I was, I wouldn't still be searching. How could the gods march? They were all trapped in the Nether, locked away for millennia by their own power according to the legends. Who is this person who will show me the answers I seek? Could it be Mariel? No, Halvor said, he.* His thoughts drifted to the Svenzar's defeat. Who or what among Amuni's Children could have been strong enough to defeat the Svenzar?

Ryne shook his head in an effort to clear his thoughts, but they continued to swirl through his mind in a never–ending cycle. His pondering only made his head throb more. Too many years with too few answers weighed on him.

Almost two hours in, Sakari raised his hand. Ryne stopped. Around them, the forest noises dwindled into silence. A branch snapped.

Sakari took off toward the noise. Brown and green darted among the trees ahead of him. Ryne followed.

The colors resolved into a man who slipped among the trees with uncanny speed. His aura matched the forest, pure and clear.

Ryne kept to the path Sakari wove, tree trunks and vines flashing by as they pursued. A forest lapra flanked them with its nose pointed toward the man who fled.

Battle energy surged through Ryne with the chase, and his heart beat faster. His headache faded with the rush. He allowed himself to feel the trees around him. Every obstacle became clear, and he bypassed them all, gaining on the silent man. Something about the man's movements bothered Ryne, but try as he might he couldn't discern the source of his discomfort.

The chase continued for a few minutes before Ryne realized they no longer gained. In fact, the man stayed just out of reach the entire time. A face, covered in dark green and yellow paint, flickered back at them.

Another Alzari? This far into the Mondros?

Ryne glanced to the side again. Two lapras now loped along their flanks, focused on the Alzari. *Seeking easier prey then, or what'll remain when we're done.* Ryne smiled with the thought.

The assassin's body twisted and his hand flung out toward Sakari. Before his hand retracted, he faced forward again without losing any momentum to his flight.

Sakari rolled his shoulders and slipped to one side. Three daggers flew past where he was moments ago.

Sunlight glinted from the blades now flying toward Ryne. Unable to duck, he leaped to one side without stopping. The daggers stuck into a tree trunk somewhere behind him with near simultaneous thuds.

Ryne reached through his Scripts for Mater around him. At that moment, what bothered him became clear. He stopped himself from touching the elements. Still in pursuit, he frowned.

The Alzari were Matii who could Forge the element of Forms and its essences. Why didn't this one do so and make himself one with the trees? Why did he make the mistake of breaking a branch, but now ran without touching a single leaf?

Ryne skidded to a halt, his heart racing. "Sakari. Cease."

Sakari glanced back at Ryne, and then he too stopped. His smooth gait returned him to Ryne within moments. The Alzari still ran without a sound.

"Is all well?" Sakari showed no signs of exertion.

Ryne's breathing slowed to normal. "Alzari assassins aren't allowed on their own until they perfect their craft. If he intended to try to kill one of us, we wouldn't hear him coming. And this one doesn't have the aura of Amuni's Children."

Sakari's face remained blank.

"Either he wanted us to hear him and lead us into a trap, or he's protecting something. Think. When we came within range, he slowed for us. He never used Mater to escape as they often do. Why's that?"

Sakari shrugged. "Let us return and see."

Winding their way back, they stopped to check several

possible hiding spots. Behind them, lapras howled. The earlier beasts had drummed up the courage to attack the Alzari after all, Ryne thought with a smirk. The fight wouldn't end well for the animals.

They continued to search until they stood close to where the chase began. A slight movement drew Ryne's attention. His gaze crossed an area that did not quite fit within the leaves and brush. An aura bloomed with light in patterns he recognized, but he pretended not to see.

"Mariel's returned," Sakari said.

"Yes. I meant to ask you on the mountain. Have you ever seen an aura like hers?"

"Besides yours? No."

Ryne's eyes narrowed at Sakari's answer. He was about to speak when an unusual sound fluttered behind them. The noises of the forest ceased. Moments later, the sound repeated from behind the roots of one of the biggest trees.

A soft whimper.

They looked at each other and turned away from Mariel's aura. The noise issued again, followed by shushing sounds. Ryne and Sakari split apart and crept closer.

A figure leaped from behind the roots, hands flashing. Several daggers flew through the air.

Sakari rolled to one side, three blades cutting the air where he once stood.

Three other daggers sped toward Ryne. He swung his sword swung up, batted them away with loud pings, and sheathed the weapon in the same motion.

Hands gripping two matching, wide–bladed knives, an Alzari woman stood before them, her hair shorn short like all the others of her clan. War paint hid her face. Keeping her elbows squared with her arms extended in front of her, one above the other, she held the knives flush against her forearms. The foot–long serrated blades pointed outwards, steel glinting as she swayed from side to side. Blood stained the right shoulder of her tight green shirt. Reddish–brown crusted her forearm. Her lithe body trembled, and dark circles rimmed her wild eyes, her gaze shifting from Ryne to Sakari.

Several dozen feet behind the woman, three new lapras crept through the trees. Whimpers rose from the roots in the animals' path. Before the sounds subsided, she attacked.

The woman flowed toward the closest threat, Sakari. He extended his arm with his unsheathed sword held by the middle, chest–high, between him and the assassin. Her blades spun upright in her hands as she swept in.

The woman's hands flickered with lightning speed. She attacked low, her blades slicing at Sakari's thighs. With a subtle shift of his body, he dodged. In the same motion, her knives swept up toward his face. Sakari leaned away from the strokes, and they swished through empty space.

The assassin's blades flashed again, hurtling down at Sakari's now exposed midsection. He sucked in his stomach and chest, the weapons missing flesh by a breath and slicing his shirt instead.

The Alzari woman continued her attack, her hands in perpetual motion. She spun and sliced, up and down, left to right. Her feet took tiny steps through the damp leaves as if she danced.

Dodging every attack, Sakari danced with her. Not once did he unsheathe his sword.

The woman's brow furrowed, and she growled. Her attacks sped faster and faster. A storm of movement.

Yet, for all her attacks, she didn't use the Stances like the other Alzari they encountered. Her attacks were basic, and only once or twice did Ryne notice a Style. Not one blow touched Sakari's flesh.

Under her marred war paint, Ryne could see her jaws clench. Now she grunted with each missed attack, her breaths laboring. Fresh blood showed through the shoulder of her shirt.

The blows slowed, and there was a brief respite as the woman paused. She no longer held her weakened arm in a fully poised position. Instead, she tried to hide that she cradled it with the other. Sweat flowed freely down her face. Her good hand edged up until she wiped her forehead.

In that instant, Sakari darted in.

Still sheathed, his sword rammed into her stomach. She gasped, the air knocked out of her. With the same motion, he landed a spinning kick to her head. As his leg swung down from the kick, his fist shot out and slammed into her bloodied shoulder.

She staggered, her knives falling from limp hands. Sakari caught her before she hit the ground and eased her onto the leaves.

Whispers upon the wind were Ryne's only warning. He dodged three small daggers that split the air within an inch of him.

The Alzari assassin from earlier sprinted among the trees toward him. Two blades spun up into his hands.

The whimpers from behind the roots increased. They became a full-throated baby's bawling.

Ryne reached for his sword and ran toward the roots.

The Alzari woman screamed.

CHAPTER 20

Ryne landed behind the tree roots, sheathed sword in hand. Below him, against a corner where two large roots met, huddled two children. One was a young boy, no older than three or four, and the other, a crying baby, both dirty and disheveled. The boy's eyes bulged from their sockets, staring past him.

Spinning away from the children, Ryne unsheathed his greatsword and swung up. The blade took the first lapra's head with one blow while the second creature was dashing in, dripping jaws agape. Ryne's sword flashed down as part of the first motion and another head fell. Green, foul smelling blood spurted into the air in viscous jets. The third lapra turned tail and fled.

The Alzari jumped over the roots behind Ryne. Blades bared, he placed himself between Ryne and the crying children.

Ryne turned to face the man with his palm upraised. "I mean you and yours no harm." With a flick of his wrist, he shed the blood from the sword before returning it to its scabbard.

Short for an Ostanian, but like any other Alzari, rife with languid muscles and sinew rippling beneath his fitted clothes, the assassin swayed from side to side. Eyes like burnished gold stared out from behind the war paint. His daggers remained raised, but he kept silent, gaze flickering from side to side.

"Sakari, let her up," Ryne commanded.

Sakari lifted his foot from the woman and stepped back. She crawled to her feet, her right arm limp as she bent and picked up her knives, sliding them into sheaths at her hips. Hands on her stomach, she limped over to the roots.

The Alzari male's eyes shifted from Ryne to her. Flinging a leg up onto the root, she attempted to crawl over, her body leaning precariously to one side. The man's hands flashed, and his knives dropped into hidden sheaths along his forearm. Before the woman fell to the ground, he caught her and set her down next to the crying children.

"Why are you out here?" Ryne asked in a level voice. "This is well outside your territory. Why are children with you?"

Groaning, the woman propped herself up beside the infants, cradling the baby in her arms as the young boy stumbled over and hugged her. Their sobs dwindled to whimpers. The Alzari male kept himself between the woman and Ryne, his gaze flashing to Sakari for a moment before his attention returned to Ryne.

"He won't hurt you," Ryne said reassuringly. "Neither of us will. Why'd you attack us?"

Eyes hardening, the man crossed his arms. "You chased me. I had to protect my family." His voice was smooth and soft.

"You wanted us to chase you, and we did. Throwing the daggers was something else entirely." Ryne tilted his head toward Sakari. "My friend only defended himself against your mistress."

The Alzari's lips pursed. "Melina thought you were going to kill us. Try to claim our heads for bounty. Your reputation precedes you among our clan, bounty hunter. You're Ryne the Shadeslayer or for some, the Deathbringer." He nodded toward Sakari. "And he's Sakari the Stone. Together you're unbeatable."

"And yet, we didn't wound either of you once," Ryne countered.

The assassin nodded and uncrossed his arms. "I'm Jaecar. Our little boy is Kass. Our baby girl is Blas. Thank you for saving their lives. We're forever indebted to you." He bowed to Ryne.

Lines creased Ryne's brow. *He revealed their names.* He knew the truth of such a revelation. A sign of trust. Ryne's gaze followed Kass' to the animals' remains. Already, tiny foragers, worms, and many–legged insects gorged on the dead animals. The boy glanced wonderingly at Ryne while his sister quieted and played with her mother's face.

Finally, Ryne spoke, "It's nothing. I did what any man

with honor would do."

Jaecar's lips twitched. "It's strange hearing such from you."

"And that means?"

"I've watched you kill from afar for many years. Like the storms, you didn't separate the young from the old or woman from man when you killed. Now you speak of honor and spare our lives." Jaecar gestured to himself and his family.

The pain of memory burned in Ryne's chest. Another time, another life. He shrugged. "Maybe today the gods shine on you."

"Then I shall remember to praise Humelen," Jaecar whispered.

Overhead, thunder rumbled. The forest already no brighter than early dawn, darkened. Seen through gaps in the canopy, gray clouds blanketed the sky in rolling waves. Lightning illuminated the thunderheads and the leaves and vines a mild blue. Through the same gaps, rain fell. Jaecar's aura appeared to give off a subtle shift and grow darker, but the next instant, it was whole and perfectly normal again. Ryne squinted, but there was no change, so he dismissed it as the effects of the storm.

"Come," Jaecar said. "We have a shelter not far from here."

Jaecar helped Melina to her feet before picking up Kass. Without a backward glance, he made his way deeper into the forest. Ryne nodded to Sakari, and they followed.

Rain smattered harder and harder as they trekked through the evergreens, the water a welcome respite in the baking forest. Breathing in deep, Ryne savored the rich earthy smells the downpour imparted.

"There's a woman following you," Jaecar stated without looking behind.

"I know." Ryne gazed out into the dim forest where Mariel's light aura hovered at the edge of his range. "I'm surprised you haven't killed her."

Jaecar chuckled. "I would say the same about you. For me, it wasn't from a lack of effort." He raised his shoulders. "She has a rockhound with her. It's what has the lapras so upset."

Ryne frowned and glanced as Sakari. "It was chasing her?"

"No. Not at all. This woman speaks to the beast. It attacked a few lapras that threatened her. They couldn't take her, so I guess they thought me and mine would be easier."

"Hmmm," Ryne said, masking his surprise. What Forian had said was true after all. Mariel could tame animals. The confirmation brought his suspicions roaring to the surface. He bit back on the sudden anger before it bloomed into something much worse.

"We're here," Jaecar announced.

They arrived at an ancient rosewood that dwarfed any others close by. The trunk spanned twenty paces across and leaned slightly to one side, its massive buttress roots stretching across the ground in rounded humps. Jaecar passed Kass to his mother and strode to the side the tree tilted toward where small branches and vines hung in a thick mass. After dragging the foliage away, he revealed a hollow, the size of a tiny room, carved into the trunk. Inspecting it briefly, he ushered Melina inside.

The small room contained piled dry leaves, several blankets, an iron bucket filled with water, and two saddlebags. Two swords leaned against the dark brown bark. Melina eased into a corner and laid the baby down with care. Blas' eyes were closed in a contented sleep. Kass snuggled next to his sister.

Ryne's hand made an involuntary clench at the sight of the enclosure. A memory blossomed of him locked in a cell just as small by the Tribunal's command. Pain from long healed lashes tore across his back and sides as if he suffered the whipping right there and then. Stepping away from the trunk, he closed his eyes, and allowed the pattering rain to fall on him.

"You still haven't told me why you're out here," Ryne asked as he calmed.

Jaecar watched his family for a moment more before he turned to Ryne. "Our clanhold was destroyed."

"What?" Ryne brushed water from his eyes and returned under the trunk's shelter.

"I don't know how many survived or if any others did. We were lucky to escape."

"Your entire clanhold? How?" Ryne found it difficult to picture anyone destroying an Alzari clanhold. Even the artisans among them fought with enough skill to be worth three soldiers in any other army.

Jaecar's eyes shone wetly as he spoke. "They came in the dead of night. I had started Kass on his survival training, so we were in the woods. I smelled the smoke and heard the fighting. Melina, she always comes with me, hates to be alone. Even when she was pregnant she helped on missions. I sent her away with the children to one of our secret places like this one, and I went to see what was happening. When I reached the clanhold, it crawled with soldiers. Our clansmen had no chance. These invaders were dressed in all black armor I've never seen before. They didn't fight as well as we, but they were too many. For every clan member, there must have been five to ten men. At first, I thought we had a chance to beat them back. But then I noticed they were not all men."

"What do you mean?"

"My clansmen tried to hack their way through. But our weapons had little effect unless they took a head or a leg."

Ryne's body stiffened. "Are you sure?"

"Yes. I would never forget such. No one who took part in the War of the Remnants could."

Ryne agreed with an absentminded nod. Could this be the reason for Halvor's warning? One slipping by he could understand, but how could an entire army bypass his wards. *How did they survive where I almost died?*

"If it had been men alone," Jaecar continued, voice steeped in melancholy, "most of our people would have fled and used their skills to hide. Indeed some tried. Those were among the first caught. I watched from among the tree branches as clansmen used the Forms to hide themselves. Horns sounded and wraithwolves appeared by the hundreds. The shadelings tracked each and every use of Mater and revealed those who hid. Against such a force, not even the Eztezian warriors of legend could have held." Jaecar's lips trembled.

Ryne almost asked if the assassin could be mistaken, but he knew better. The look on Jaecar's face spoke for itself. Even if he hadn't seen the beasts when he found the missing villagers, he would've believed the man. He exhaled deeply, his hand folding into a fist.

Jaecar sighed and hunched into himself. "At that point I fled among the trees making sure not to use the Forms. It's why when you chased I didn't use them to hide. I dreaded drawing the creatures here."

"Why didn't you go warn the other clanholds?" Ryne asked.

"I thought about it, but first I used the lantums to scale a great tree." Jaecar gestured to the large vines entwined around the trunks and branches. "There was smoke coming from the other holds within the Scattered Hills. Farther south, I saw more smoke, toward the Fretian Woods. I decided the safest way was here. So, I took my family and ran and have been doing so ever since. I'm going to the Vallum of Light and beyond if I have to."

Ryne's thoughts whirled. Jaecar's revelation explained the smoke he saw from Nevermore. Still, for all six clanholds to be defeated, the numbers required to accomplish such a feat would have to be staggering. "Do you think some among your people knew they were coming?"

Golden eyes becoming glittering beads, Jaecar took a step back. "You're suggesting we were betrayed by our own. No, I refuse to believe it. Why would you ask such a thing?"

"There were two Alzari deep within the Fretian. They bore the mark of Amuni's Children. They were also accompanied by an infected lapra."

"I know nothing of this. The taming of infected lapra is an old thing. Some say they were once used to fight the shade."

Ryne allowed himself to ponder what the man said, staring off into the forest. Something about his words nagged at Ryne like a gnat. The flash thunderstorm finished spitting its torrent, and water runoff played a distant staccato as it pattered to the ground from leaves.

Then it clicked. "You said you saw more smoke, south, near the Fretian? How long ago?" Ryne asked.

"A week gone now. It's why I didn't try to reach the other towns and cities in that direction. The shade's armies are headed that way."

Ryne's hands made an involuntary clench as a chill crept through him. "Are you sure?"

"Beyond a doubt."

Ryne pictured the terrain. Carnas' position on the Orchid Plains, a few miles southwest of the Fretian Woods, was not in the direct path of the advancing army but still close. If the invaders stayed on the path Jaecar mentioned, they could well reach Ryne's home in another day.

"Sakari, come. We have to go. I'm sorry to leave you like this, Jaecar. May Ilumni guide you and keep you and yours safe."

"Is all well?" Jaecar asked.

Closing his eyes, Ryne inhaled deeply. "No. My home in Carnas..." He couldn't finish the statement.

The corners of Jaecar's mouth turned down. "May Humelen lend you the strength of the Forms."

As Jaecar turned away and entered the shadowy interior of the small hollow with his wife, his aura wavered once more. Ryne studied the man's back for a moment, frowning at the strange occurrence.

Sakari shook him. "Come. We must go now."

Without further thought, Ryne followed his shorter companion's lead through the trees. From time to time, Ryne surged ahead, fighting a constant battle not to let his fears get the better of him. The earlier rain had not caused many floods so they made good time, skirting the muddiest sections as best they could. A few hours of hard running later, the forest thinned, and they arrived at a small, grassy plain with stunted trees. Sakari scouted ahead while Ryne remained in the woods.

All's well within Carnas. It must be. Ryne pictured successful hunts and afternoon meals. Children played, their laughter tinkling through the village. Babies suckled at their mothers' teats, and the able–bodied women would now be finishing up dinner preparations. Hagan would be bustling about the inn, preparing for another night of drink. Maybe he'd finally secured a singer or dancer as he often promised. Mayor Bertram would have everyone ready to leave at a moment's notice should something be amiss with Hagan hovering over him offering his input, never cowed by Bertram's brash exterior.

Images of Vana and Vera before he left swirled fresh in his mind. Their laughter and teasing when his face heated from the Temtesa's swaying gyrations made him smile. Since meeting them, he'd given up his penchant for visiting the brothels in Astocan towns. For years, he fought the need within his loins whenever the twins were around. With his many enemies, avoiding any attachment had become a necessity. Of late, he felt his resolve wane, and he often looked forward to the sisters' company at his home. When he returned to Carnas he would choose one of the sisters, maybe both. They would be pleased.

"We can cross now." Sakari's words snapped him from his reverie.

With Sakari in the lead once more, they sprinted across the plain and entered the Fretian Woods. They kept close to the forest's edge so they could see any threat that may come their way. The closer they came to Carnas, the more tension built within Ryne until his shoulders ached. Eventually, he pushed hard for home, often outpacing Sakari. Twilight's ethereal fingers pricked the clouds on the horizon in bruised purple hues as they reached the Orchid Plains.

A mile out from Carnas they found the first body. It was Hagan. Something had torn his body in half.

CHAPTER 21

Ryne snarled at the sight of Hagan's body. Around the corpse, dried blood, the color of rust covered the earth and crushed grass in a congealed mass of entrails. Yellow and brown stained the crotch of Hagan's pants. Urine and the choking stench from offal drowned out the scent from the man's spilled fluids; the reek increased by the day's lingering heat.

From the evidence in the area, Hagan had died without a fight. Jagged wounds along his torso looked as if giant claws had shorn through his body, similar in many ways to those found on the bodies discovered the last few weeks, but the damage was too great to be sure. A lump formed in Ryne's throat. *Oh, Ilumni... Carnas.*

Dying sunlight glinted from the village's thatch and wood roofs poking out just above a dip in the plains. Fingers clenched around his sword, heat swelling within him, Ryne took a step toward Carnas. Sakari's iron grip on his arm stopped him.

"This is not like you, acting with your emotions rather than your head," Sakari said with more than a hint of nonchalance.

Snatching his arm away, Ryne pointed at Hagan. When he found his voice, it came out as a strained hiss. "That's someone we knew. A man I considered a friend. In that village are the only people I held dear since the day I woke. We've known them for years, and you act as if all is well. Do you feel nothing?"

"No." Sakari's eyes were dead pits of silver and green.

Ryne quivered, his hands balling into fists against the sudden urge to stab Sakari. It would be pointless. Sakari acted no different now than the first day Ryne woke to his unflappable and expressionless face. Whether during the wars or the many killings they were party to over the years, the man had never showed a single emotion. *Why should I expect anything different?* With a great whoosh of breath, Ryne let his half–drawn great sword slide back into the scabbard.

"Look around you. And not with only your eyes," Sakari said.

Ryne reached out to his Scripts.

"No. You do not need those or Mater right now. Think. What if there are as many wraithwolves as Jaecar said? What if they are still close by?"

He's right. How could I let myself become so overwrought that *I almost made such a mistake?* Relying instead on his innate talent to see the auras around Carnas, Ryne studied his surroundings. Blue and red orchid blooms covered the plains in clusters, their stalks swaying to the warm southerly wind. Unnoticed before, but now prevalent, was a faint whiff of char. The occasional tree and large thorn brush broke up the expanse of flowers on the rolling landscape all the way to the foothills in the distance, their shadows beginning to elongate with the rising twilight. As Sakari had said, Mariel no longer followed them, but something else was not quite right. Ryne couldn't grasp it, but it hung like a dark shroud at the edge of his consciousness. His eyes narrowed.

"Do you see now?" Sakari whispered.

Ryne nodded. "There aren't any animals. No plains lapras, no brown–furred holehogs, no stray dogs. No pheasants or other game birds. I don't even sense the vermin. Worst of all there aren't any crows and ravens. At least they would keep the dead company."

Ryne's gaze drifted across the land, but he saw no aura that could be a wraithwolf. Sure he was safe from detection, he finally opened his Matersense.

Immediately, his bloodlust surged within him, burning with intense fire, screaming for release. The feeling threatened to overthrow his dominance. Arms trembling with effort, teeth grinding, he forced the emotion and the voices down into his gut until they became nothing more than a whimper. As he grasped control, his sight expanded.

Everything around him intensified. Colors became deeper, auras more vivid, and the very air felt as if he could mold it to his will. Yet, the Mater close to him was all wrong. Usually the elements felt and looked as if they were etched into the air with razor–sharp edges. Now, those lines appeared dulled like an artist's drawing with smudged borders. Ryne shook off the distorted image, focusing on Hagan's corpse. A low gasp escaped his lips.

Shade's taint boiled within the innkeeper's body akin to a roiling black ant's nest. The black and gray hues of the essence poured from his open mouth, nose, and ears. It riddled the massive wounds on his body. Recoiling at what he saw next, Ryne lost his hold on his Matersense.

"He has no life force—no sela." Ryne's mouth hung open, his voice becoming a barely audible whisper. "Even in death the essence should be there."

"Exactly," Sakari confirmed. "Life and death cannot be separated. Something ate Hagan in more ways than one."

"A daemon?" Ryne's forehead wrinkled.

Sakari shrugged. "Perhaps. If there were as many shadelings as Jaecar mentioned, then we should consider that a possibility. We must be cautious."

"But that would mean there has to be a Skadwaz to unleash and control the creature." Ryne's hand slid to his sword, wary gaze flitting to the shadowy areas on the plains.

Sakari nodded.

Ryne shook his head in disbelief. "How's that possible if they were trapped in Hydae a thousand years ago?"

"If we listened to every legend then you are dead or just a myth. And shadelings and daemons too. Yet, we know they exist, as we know you live. Unless someone else has learned how to harness daemons, we must assume the worst."

Ryne closed his eyes and allowed his friend's words to sink in. Events were rapidly spiraling beyond anything he imagined. When he opened them again, he unsheathed his sword. A quick stroke removed Hagan's head.

Amuni's Children, shadelings, and now daemons and the Skadwaz. He could see how the Svenzar could have been defeated. But it still begged the question. If the Children ran with daemons during the Remnants, if a Skadwaz worked behind the scenes, why wait until now? Why not unleash their power with the Setian people during the Shadowbearer War? Nothing the Children had done made sense to him. No matter how he viewed the puzzle, the answer eluded him.

He motioned for Sakari to lead, and they eased away from the corpse, staying low, moving from bush to rough grass. Along the way, they encountered several other bodies. These too lacked signs of a defensive fight, and all were scouts they recognized. Every corpse was mangled, and each one crawled with shade and had its sela essence drained. Ryne cut off their heads.

They continued toward the village, first crouching, then dropping flat on their stomachs and crawling through short grass until they lay below a small dip in the land behind some thick fescue. Using the brush for cover, they studied the village.

The wooden wall surrounding Carnas was broken in several places. Squat buildings huddled together along the main road with a few roofs hanging at precarious angles or caved in altogether, burnt timbers and broken beams unable to support them. Those buildings not burned were left in shambles.

"I shall venture for a closer look and make sure the way is safe," Sakari said.

Before Ryne could reply, the man was sliding into the surrounding brush. With a shake of his head, Ryne watched. He didn't need his friend's protection, but Sakari insisted. Long ago, Ryne had abandoned his attempts to tell the man he was not his personal bodyguard.

While he waited, Ryne immersed himself in the sights treasured by many who lived on the Orchid Plains. Distended gray clouds reflected the setting sun's tenuous glow in purple and orange, the light brushing the plains like an artful masterpiece. To the south, out of sight at the end of the plains' thousand mile stretch sat the Misted Cliffs and beyond, the Sea of Clouds. He once promised to take the children and the sisters to visit the sea. The trip might never happen now.

Sakari returned before the clouds crossed more than a few feet across the sky. "The village is clear."

"Have you seen anyone alive? Kahkon, Taeria, Vana, Vera?"

Sakari shook his head.

"Corpses?" Even as he asked the question, a lump crawled into Ryne's chest.

"Yes, a few to the east and south. All the same way as the others we found, but none were those you asked about."

A sliver of hope eased through Ryne. Maybe Bertram had managed to get the others away.

"The scouts and hunters I found all died before they could react," Sakari said.

The words drew prickles across Ryne's skin as he remembered the golden-haired woman had moved without any of the others seeing her. After scanning his surroundings with utmost care, he motioned for Sakari to lead the way.

They stood and trotted toward Carnas. Ever vigilant, searching for the slightest movements that might signify life, Ryne fingered his sword. They found nothing but the dead. Two more corpses they passed were blackened by flames, but Ryne recognized them still—Dren and Keevo. Both bodies contained no sela. Saying a brief prayer to Ilumni, he also took their heads.

After circling the village, they approached Ryne's home first. The structure had been razed, so they continued moving. They headed toward Taeria's home next. Along the way, any buildings still intact displayed broken doorframes or windows with doors and shutters hanging askew, creaking in the wind. Inside the mender's house, they found dried blood, old bandages, and the ransacked contents of the healing room. Of Taeria and Kahkon, there was no sign.

Nothing living moved within the village. No dogs barked, no chickens pecked, no ducks waddled, and not even the abundant tame pheasants clucked along the streets. Deserted roads and burnt homes continued to taunt them, their windows and entrances dark gaping holes like the eyes and mouths of blackened corpses. They found more charred bodies in a few homes. Other houses stood empty. A hint of moldy fur, of decayed flesh, threaded the air within the homes not burnt.

They came upon Vana and Vera's house. No flames scarred it, but the door hung off the hinges. A black cloud of flies buzzed in and out of the open doorway. Taking a few apprehensive steps, Ryne entered. The unmistakable reek of rotting flesh hit him.

The sisters lay splayed on the floor with their feet and

hands nailed to the wood. Their faces were sickly, black and red messes, battered in such a way they did not resemble themselves. Bile rising in his throat, Ryne squeezed his eyes shut against the sight of their naked bodies. Before he could think, he was stumbling back outside, retching. His arms trembled, fists clenching and unclenching repeatedly, and his eyes filmed over as if a red sheet covered them. He dared not touch his sword. He bent over, his hands against the wall, and sucked in several drawn out breaths until he managed a seething calm.

Eyes lifeless sockets, Sakari just watched him, saying nothing. They moved on.

At Carnas' southwest end, they found Lenka, Malka, and Denton, bodies riddled with gashes. Trampled grass spread for miles—signs of an armies' entrance into the village. How had this army reached here so fast and coming from the southwest instead of farther northeast? And if they had shadelings, where were the creatures now?

With each new body, a pattern became clear to Ryne. The wounds bore too many similarities to those found on the murdered men from weeks ago. Whatever weapons or power used to kill those men near the kinai patches had been used to kill Carnas' inhabitants. Now he knew this army had been scouting Carnas for some time. And neither he nor Sakari had known of their presence.

Hope diminishing with the increasing death count, Ryne trudged on. The chance of finding a single survivor became a fleeting wish whispering on the wind. Outside the homes without bodies, they found dark, russet splotches and streaks that signified a dragged body. There, the malodorous odor of unwashed dog fur and rot were strongest. Every spot they found like this pointed toward the village square.

With night upon them, and storm clouds brewing overhead, Ryne gave in. "Let's head to the green."

They followed the main road toward the middle of the village. The dried blood splatter and drag furrows increased, scuffmarks and gouges pointing their way towards the village square in trails of dust and dirt. A faint smell grew stronger as they ventured nearer. With the wind blowing the opposite direction, they had not smelled it before. After a few more feet, the odor clung to the air with a stench similar to what they encountered within the sisters' home multiplied a hundredfold.

Ryne strained against the urge to run to the plaza. Along with the smell, there came a sound. A buzzing as if a thousand bees flew close by. The corpses became visible before he entered the square.

"No. No," he whispered. "Dear gods, no." Ryne ran.

The distended bodies looked no different to logs or firewood stacked on top of each other. They littered the area by the thousands. Men, women, and children. Not one was spared.

Large, black corpse flies swarmed the bodies. Not a single body contained any sela essence. Whatever ate the other villagers had gorged itself here. Congealed blood covered the ground as if a river of blood once flowed from the green. Bile bubbled unbidden within Ryne's mouth.

Ryne attempted to approach the corpses, but Sakari held him back. "No, master. There is nothing you can do to help. Going too close to so many consumed by the shade may taint you."

Shuddering, Ryne slapped Sakari's hand from his shoulder, the control he realized he'd found in the Nevermore Heights splintering. He opened his mouth to speak, but he could find no words, and the scream he tried to release came out as a hoarse croak. He collapsed to his knees before sitting, eyes staring sightlessly.

Everything he cared for had been ripped from him. Pain stabbed his heart like an Alzari's blade. The malevolent voice whispered delightful revenge, beseeching him to reach for the Mater around him. The second voice muttered and moaned while his bloodlust attempted to soar up from the pits where he'd thrust it. Drops of blood pattered to the ground from his hands which were curled into vise–like fists. Like a drowning man clutching at a floating log, he clung on, knowing if he surrendered, there would be no controlling the craze to kill when it rose.

Ryne's vision grew bleary. Wetness trickled down his cheeks and before he could stop himself, he was sobbing uncontrollably, his face contorting with grief. He'd clung to hope for so long that this eventuality overwhelmed him.

He didn't know how long he sat there with his eyes closed. When he opened them, night had fully come. The colossal twin moons stood high to the east, lighting everything in silvery–

blue, dark clouds steadily encroaching on them.

Ryne stood and was surprised to find his legs steady as he strode to the large shed close to the square that held the firewood the villagers had collected. One by one, he took wood and stacked it in the square around the bodies. Each log bore bloodstains from the small punctures his fingernails had inflicted in his palms. He could care less if he somehow became tainted. These were his people, and they needed to be sent off to the gods in the proper fashion. They deserved at least that much. Numb to the occasional splinters digging into his skin, and the weight on his shoulder, he labored on.

Every trip to the green brought different feelings bubbling to the surface. At times, his eyes filmed red, and he burned inside. Other moments, his shoulders slumped. A chill crept through his body as he imagined what they must have felt in their dying moments.

He couldn't help heaping the blame for the massacre on himself. Maybe if he lived a different life before he settled in Carnas this wouldn't have happened. Maybe if he hadn't answered the summons he could've saved them. Maybe the souls of all the people who died at his hands had cursed him. Did he commit some other great atrocities in his past life—the life he couldn't remember—which warranted such punishment from the gods?

His thoughts shifted, and he laid the blame at the feet of Amuni's Children and whatever shadelings committed these terrible acts. *They will pay for this in blood.* And if he found out Mariel or the golden–haired woman were involved, they too would pay. His ponderings went on for hours before he stopped and studied the firewood piled around the bodies and decided he had collected enough.

Searching among the homes still intact, he collected oil in several buckets and lined them up around the pyre. Grief gnawing at his heart, tears running down his cheeks, he poured the fuel onto the wood stacks and the villagers' remains. Black corpse flies were buzzing angrily at his interference before they settled to gorge themselves once again. Oblivious to the stench, he stood before the bodies and lit several torches. Ignoring the shadows that danced across their now grotesque forms, he pictured the villagers as they once were, alive and filled with promise.

Hagan, you and your pipe, always generous and willing to help those in need, among the first to accept me. One–eyed Mayor Bertram, you loved to argue, but you placed yourself before the village too many times to count. Vana and Vera, thank you for taking care of when I was hurt. I will miss your Temtesa. Lara, you always cooked the best meals. Kahkon, your thirst for learning I've never seen in anyone before.

On and on the faces swept through him. He etched each into his mind.

"May the gods find a place for your souls and may their Battleguards keep you safe." Ryne threw the torches onto the wood.

The logs burst into flames with a whoosh, heated waves from the pyre forcing Ryne to take a step back. He stared into the roaring blaze. Black smoke billowed into the air in greasy plumes, and the acrid smell from the burning flesh filled the air.

Ryne whispered another prayer, then a torch and the remainder of the oil in hand, he strode to Vana and Vera's home. He didn't go inside. He wanted to remember them as they were the night he left. He doused their home with oil and set it ablaze.

As he watched the conflagration, Ryne lost himself in thought. To have taken the six clanholds, and keep moving the way they did, the advancing army must number over a hundred thousand or more. *How many of those are shadelings or worse? Halvor said my enemies sought me. Well now, I'll seek them. If my purpose is to battle, then I'll once again embrace my bloodlust. They will know fucking fear.*

A withering heat filled Ryne as if he and the inferno were one. "We'll need to behead and burn the other bodies. Afterward, we have cities to warn. We need to find Thumper. He should be at his favorite clearing in the Fretian."

After destroying the other bodies and setting more homes on fire, they strode from Carnas, heading to the southeast. There, they found signs of blood mixed with the tracks left by the army leaving the village.

"Have you realized we did not find Kahkon, Bertram, or Taeria and the other menders?" Sakari asked.

"Yes," Ryne answered, but he offered nothing more as he pushed the chance for survivors from his mind. If any did live, they were as good as dead.

They jogged across the plains, and Ryne took one last look back at Carnas. The village itself was now a huge pyre with a black pall darker than the night rising into the air to meet the dark clouds rolling across the sky.

He turned away, his face as hard as silversteel, and his heart ice.

CHAPTER 22

Irmina Nagel gestured to the rockhound, sending an image of what she wanted along her link with the creature. The beast padded behind her to guard her back.

Undergrowth wreathed in darkness and silhouetted tree trunks that wore their leaves and branches as black mantles surrounded her. They provided easy cover for the short Ostanian man with the painted face to remain hidden while making his many surprise attacks. Ever since the giant and his companion left, this had become his pattern. After graduating Eldanhill's Mystera and attending the Iluminus, she had placed at the top of her class when it came to scouting and using her surroundings to mask her presence. Yet her stealth was a pale shadow of this man's.

Painted Face had gradually moved toward the outskirts of the Mondros Forest as evening drew to night and clouds moved in to obscure the twin moons. Not once did he allow her to come close to his family.

The multiple howls and screeches within the woods spoke of creatures much deadlier than any Irmina saw during the day. Once, when she heard nearby thrashings from one such animal, she allowed her innate sense for living beasts to reach among the trees. The animal repulsed her touch as if she were some paltry annoyance.

Through her link, she sensed the rockhound react to a feathery landing on sodden leaves. Luckily, the beast did not rely on its nose to track Painted Face. He'd hidden his scent well using mud, and the fresh smells from the earlier rain only served to help him. Still, his precautions didn't matter. Any touch he made that connected to the earth gave him away.

The rockhound's growl warned Irmina of the impending attack. She spun, but the hound pounced into position to guard her, ducking its head, its stoneskin hardening.

The short man's daggers bounced off harmlessly, falling to the ground. Irmina met the man's eyes for the briefest moment to see them flash with frustration before he slid among the undergrowth once more. She knew it made no sense to chase, not if she wanted to stay alive.

Hours playing this game had proved fruitless. She needed some way to force Painted Face to speak to her. Watching him meet with the giant convinced her this Ostanian and his family held the key she needed to approach her target. How else could he have convinced the giant and his bodyguard not to kill him? There must be another way to get through to this man.

She surveyed the land through the trees, casting her gaze out onto the road meandering next to the forest. Something about the lay of the land, the short hills, and the rolling plain beyond tickled her memory. Lights peeked back across the dark terrain like lightflies at play. Could it be? She weaved her way to the road. Sure enough, in the distance was the farm where she left her mount before making her way to Carnas. She couldn't suppress her smile.

She sent an image across her link to the rockhound to track the man. The animal snorted and bounded away. Irmina cut across the road and jogged toward the farm.

An hour later, Irmina returned to the Mondros with her dartan, Misty, and two other mounts in tow. She trilled twice to Misty—a sound similar to what the dartans made. In response, Misty swung her long snake–like neck out, cocking her head to one side at the sounds within the forest and shifted closer to the other mounts. Like all dartans, she was taller and wider than a horse, but her bulky form belied her grace. The green hump of her shell was slick from the light drizzle falling, and Irmina hunkered down in the saddle carved into it. Beside her, the other two larger dartans mewled nervously, tails flicking back and forth. The farmers had been ready to give the extra mounts to her at no charge, but she'd shushed them and offered payment.

A smile on her face at the intimidating effect of her Devout uniform, she dismounted and carried herself with her head held high and back straight. The lamp she carried lit her path as she entered the forest. Leaves and twigs crunching underfoot, she followed her link to the rockhound.

This time, the man and his family were no more than twenty feet in. Both he and his wife stood with blades bared toward the rumbling hound.

When they saw Irmina's silver uniform, the trousers and tunic bearing the stripes of her station, they gaped. She held up her lamp to make sure they could see the insignia of the sun encased in a halo on her breast. The symbol of Ilumni's Devout glittered with its own light. Weapons lowered, and the two Ostanians bowed from the waist.

"I'm Devout Mariel Nagella. In the name of Ilumni and Granadia's Tribunal, you will both come with me." She indicated the other two mounts, one with extra saddles carved into its shell to carry the children.

Painted Face cocked his head to her then looked at his woman. He said something in Ostanian. Irmina knew the language by sound. Outside of a few names, she didn't understand the language, nor did she care to.

The man stepped forward. "I, Jaecar," he pointed to the woman, "this Melina, wife." He said something else in garbled Granadian Irmina couldn't quite grasp but took to mean they would follow her.

Irmina dropped the reins of the extra mounts and waited for the Ostanians to gather their belongings.

Flickers of lightning illuminated the leaden clouds shrouding the twin moons. Moments later, thunder offered its response in continuous growls. Irmina didn't bother to wipe the rainwater running from her hair. Instead, she allowed it to caress her forehead and cheeks as she held her face to the sky and smiled at the clouds that leaked the light drizzle. Next to her rode Jaecar, his wife Melina, and their two children. Jaecar's odd looks and cold eyes made her regret releasing the rockhound before they left the forest.

Thinking about the hound made her consider the men who set it on her. Why did her master send her after this stranger? And on the other side of the world no less, where a Granadian uniform representing the Tribunal proved to be one of the few things these Ostanians respected or feared. Well, at least now she could make some progress in securing the giant, or so she hoped. If not, she would return to Carnas after helping this family reach a town where she could be sure of their safety and where she might find someone who could translate. Jaecar and Melina could take care of themselves, but the children would be at the mercy of the wilds if either faltered. What could've driven them to risk travel not only in the Mondros, but at night? Irmina wished she'd taken her language lessons more seriously.

Ahead of Irmina, Melina rode in the front–most saddle position, the long, chain reins in her good hand, and her children strapped in behind her. The boy, Kass and his sister Blas, had gone from wide–eyed expressions and whimpers when placed upon the dartans, to comfortable sleep within an hour. Melina often glanced over her shoulder at her children. Without the vile–looking paint covering her or her husband's face, the worry creasing her features was plain to see.

They rode on a much–traveled road lined by low foothills, small pastures and the occasional copse, having left the Mondros behind to their southeast and the Nevermore Heights in the opposite direction. Jaecar urged them on until the drizzle, as it increased, whipped by them. Combined with the cooling wind, it was a refreshing respite after the hot forests.

"We stop soon. Town come," Jaecar shouted.

At the man's insistence, they'd skipped every village and farmstead along the way. From the man's frantic gestures and mispronounced words, he wanted his family as far away from the Mondros as possible. Irmina nodded, glad she could understand that much. Almost as if he could read Irmina's thoughts, Jaecar grinned at his wife and said something in his language. Melina smiled at him—the first time Irmina had seen a pleased expression from the woman. They rode the rest of the way in silence.

The rain ended a short time later, and they rounded a corner out of the foothills. Lights sparkled in a wide, square shape below. A twenty–foot stone wall, with towers spaced at matching intervals, encircled the town.

Jaecar pointed. "Ranoda." Flapping his reins, he raced down the hill.

Ilumni works in mysterious ways, Irmina thought, her lips twitching into a brief smile. She'd secured a place in Ranoda on her way to Carnas. At first she hadn't recognized the town as it appeared a lot different at night. Here, she would be able to get all she needed.

They reined in before a closed, wide gate. Large oil lamps inlaid into the walls and several torches hanging from braces threw yellow light across the area and glinted off the helms of soldiers who manned the bulwark. A guard called a challenge from a window slit in one of the two towers on either side of the gate. Movement on both towers and between the crenels of the wall resolved into more guards armed with crossbows.

Jaecar raised his hands to show he was unarmed. He then pointed to his wife and said a few words. Irmina remained silent, allowing her uniform to speak for itself.

The wait seemed to last forever. The dartans mewled to each other, and their necks swung from side to side. Restless murmurs came from the walls above them.

"Devout Irmina," called a familiar voice with a hint of surprise.

Instructions bellowed from the same voice in Ostanian. A sally gate swung open, and they entered in single file with Irmina in the lead. A bleary–eyed, scarlet uniformed Dagodin, Knight Caden, stood with his hands on his hips a few steps inside the wall.

"I apologize, holy one. We didn't expect you back so soon from your inspections, and coming from this direction, no less. Why—"

"Is that your excuse for having me sit outside and wait?" Irmina pursed her lips as she studied the short, square man.

"No, Devout Irmina." Caden's eyes flashed for the briefest moment before he dropped his gaze from hers. "Discipline must be maintained as by Tribunal law. No one is allowed into a Granadian occupied town without the officer in charge confirming their identity. It—"

"Thank you, Knight Caden. You do not need to quote

the law any further. It's good for you to maintain discipline even this far from Granadia's borders. My superiors will be pleased to see this in my report." *That should keep up appearances nicely. Let the fool man mull over my perceived intentions.*

Knight Caden blinked and smiled.

"Send Knight Ormand to me at my office. I'm in need of his services." Her stomach growled. "And send up some food." Without waiting for Caden's response, she inclined her head for Jaecar and Melina to follow and rode toward the barracks.

They trotted down a wide cobbled main road intersected by winding, narrow streets and alleys at haphazard intervals. Occasionally, the murmur of conversations between passing townsfolk interrupted the sound of the dartan's padded feet thudding softly on the cobbles. Music tinkled through the air in muted tones, often interrupted by distant laughter or cheers. Irmina flicked her thumb across her nose at the noxious fumes of piss and refuse spilling from the overflowing drains that the earlier rain had did little to help unclog. Ever since she'd come to Ostania, she found herself longing for the nightly sanitation practiced by large Granadian towns and cities.

Breaking glass sounded over the music drifting from the many taverns along a nearby side street. Irmina turned her head to the noise.

Three tall Ostanian men stumbled out onto the main road, throwing bottles, singing raucous songs and cursing. Within moments, men garbed in tawny town watch uniforms confronted them and a brief scuffle ensued. When it was over, the watch dragged the now unconscious men down the street toward the holding cells. They would release them after they slept off their drink. Irmina shook her head and continued to the barracks.

The small, drab building stood only two stories tall. Some superstition to do with the Ostanians who resided here preferring to stay closer to the earth and its Forms. Like Jaecar, many gave their praises to Humelen or one of the other gods of Forms instead of Ilumni. Grimacing with the thought of the backward Formist religion, Irmina led them toward the open gate in the wooden fence surrounding the structure.

Two guards in burnished armor stood at attention before the gate, each with a lance twice their height. They kept their eyes forward under bowl–shaped helmets as Irmina and her charges rode through.

An old man with a bent back, accompanied by two other handlers, hurried out from the adjoining stables and pens and bowed to Irmina several times. She dismounted and passed Misty's reins to the old fellow. The other men waited on the Ostanians.

When they finished, Irmina led the way through the wide training yard and into the building. Inside the barracks, Irmina ignored the hallways to the left and right, leading them straight ahead to a set of stairs that creaked as they ascended.

Upstairs was just as bare as the floor below. Irmina guided them to the large corner room she used as both bedroom and office. A simple oak table and four chairs, one of them cushioned, sat on the large center rug, and a bed hugged one wall. Several lamps hung on the walls at even intervals between the room's windows, already lit for her arrival.

A painting of Ilumni and his Battleguard standing before a rift to the Nether hung on the wall above her table. Depicted as a gigantic, faceless man swathed in white light, the god and his Battleguard, a darker man holding a massive sword, stood back to back in defensive stances. The light from both men held an encroaching darkness surrounding them at bay.

Bowing to the painting, Irmina issued a prayer. When she finished, she turned to Jaecar. "You can rest the children on the bed."

Jaecar nodded and spoke to his wife. Her shoulders relaxed, and she eased over to the wide bed with its thick mattress and lay Blas upon the covers. Jaecar rested Kass next to her. Both children were sound asleep.

Irmina flopped down onto her cushioned chair and closed her eyes, the effects of the long, trying day settling on her. When she opened them, both Jaecar and Melina stood next to the bed studying her. Irmina gestured to the chairs. "Take a seat." The couple complied.

A few moments later, a knock sounded on the door.

"Come in," Irmina said.

Knight Ormand, a heavyset man with a thick mustache and beard entered. His forehead furrowed until his bushy eyebrows almost touched as he took in Jaecar and Melina. Behind him came a Cadet pushing a cart laden with food. The door swung shut behind him, ushering a spicy whiff from the dishes into the room.

Ormand bowed to her with a fist placed over the crossed, double bronze swords pinned to the lapel of his scarlet jacket. "Devout Irmina, praise Ilumni for your safe return."

"Only the light can save us from the shade," Irmina responded.

"I see you have company, holy one." His eyes drifted to the children on the bed, and then back to the two Ostanians.

"They're the reason I asked for you. I need you to translate. Sit, Ormand."

"Ah. Thank you." Ormand tipped his head to Jaecar and his wife when he sat, and they responded in kind.

After much bowing and scraping to her, the Cadet laid out dishes and trays on the table. Scents from roasted pheasant, stewed mutton, several types of spiced rice, and sweet potatoes mingled in the air creating a mouthwatering brew. After dried rabbit and fish, Irmina's stomach growled, and she licked her lips. The Cadet topped off the dishes with several flagons of wine and yellow gooseberry juice.

Irmina smiled wryly at the two Ostanians as their eyes lit up with each dish. They gave her an inquiring look and she indicated they could eat. She didn't need to make the gesture twice. Soon, the two were tearing at mutton while swallowing down wine in deep gulps. So much for the Formist belief that eating meat was to give one's self into the impurities of the flesh, which weakened the body and was thus forbidden. Irmina shook her head and nodded her thanks to the Cadet.

As she studied the two strangers, Irmina took her time eating her fill. She even gave in to the temptation of licking her fingers. When she finished she poured herself a glass of wine. The liquor was not as good as the Dorns', but she still found it refreshing. "By the way, Ormand," she said between sips, "did you find out anything concerning the man I inquired after?"

"Very little," Ormand replied, his voice muffled by his chewing before he swallowed. "He's revered as a great warrior among the Ostanians. His name is Ryne Waldron. Most became silent whenever I mentioned a giant man with tattoos or his name. It was...strange." Ormand paused, his face reddening. "Wish I could have gotten more, holy one, a–apologies." The man's hands drifted to his neck, and he loosened the collar of his high–buttoned jacket. An unusual amount of sweat cast a bright sheen on his forehead.

Irmina's brow creased at the sight of the man's concern. Failing High Shin Jerem's requests often came with unpleasant consequences, but their master had nothing but praise for the Knight Ormand. "No need to apologize. At least I have a full name to add to the face now. You've done better than I have and found out more than I could. It's not like our master gave me much to go on when he sent me here. Well, the good news is this man here seems to know Ryne personally." She indicated Jaecar with a dip of her head.

Ormand gave her a weak smile at her compliment and dabbed at his forehead with a handkerchief he produced from inside his jacket. "Where did you meet them?"

Jaecar eye's followed their mouths whenever they spoke. His face wore a frown.

"In the Mondros Forest. They had a fight of some kind with this man, Ryne, and his bodyguard. During the fight Ryne saved their children from several forest lapras. After they spoke Ryne ran off with his bodyguard."

"The Mondros Forest? Most stay away from the place. Too wild. And they were there with children? You said they fought, your holiness. Where are their weapons?" Ormand leaned forward, his eyes intent on the Ostanians.

"I had them leave their knives and daggers on the dartans." Why was Ormand curious about their weapons?

"Knives and daggers?" Ormand's eyes narrowed. "Did they have their faces painted, holy one?"

"Yes."

Ormand's body stiffened, and his pudgy hand drifted toward his sword. Jaecar made a great show of placing his hands with his fingers spread wide onto the table. His eyes became slits as he watched the Dagodin.

"Cease, Ormand," Irmina commanded. "I invited them here." She looked at Jaecar. "You, stop."

"B–But, Devout, they're Alzari," Ormand blurted out.

Irmina shrugged. "And that means what to me?"

"They're wanted mercenaries who fight in the territorial battles among the cities here, and—"

"Are they considered enemies to the Tribunal?" Irmina asked in a soft voice as she slid her hand closer to her sword's hilt below the tabletop.

"No, your holiness."

"Ostania's internal squabbles are not a concern of ours, Ormand. Please, remember we have a task. Or would you rather disappoint High Shin Jerem in pursuit of some bounty?" Irmina's eyebrow rose.

Face paling, Ormand said, "No, Devout Irmina."

"Good. Now, ask them who Ryne is, and why were they in the forest." Irmina focused on the Alzari.

Ormand turned his attention to Jaecar and began to question him. With each answer, Jaecar gestured several times with his hands. Neither his golden eyes and or his facial expression changed.

"He says Ryne is a hunter. A hired killer to be exact. He's surprised we don't know him. Claims Ryne fought for the Tribunal in the War of the Remnants."

Memory followed by pain flared at the war's mention. Irmina took a breath and forced the feeling down. Why would High Shin Jerem need an assassin? That was her job. Unless he wanted to use someone who couldn't be traced to him. *But why send me to fetch him? Did Jerem also send the strange golden–haired woman?* No, she doubted it. Jerem knew she worked alone. He was obsessive about maintaining comfort for those who served him.

Jaecar continued talking. With each word, Ormand leaned closer.

"He says he hid his family in the Mondros because their clanhold was destroyed."

Irmina almost waved Ormand off. *No.* The best way to find information sometimes was to feign concern for the plight of those she questioned. She put on her most sympathetic face. "How? What happened?"

The conversation between Ormand and Jaecar resumed. A change came over Jaecar's face. His eyes flickered in fear, and his pitch increased and sometimes grew soft. Tears ran down Melina's cheeks. Ormand's mouth hung open.

"What is it, Knight Ormand?"

"All their clanholds were destroyed, not just one," Ormand whispered.

So some force had defeated these warriors. Irmina shrugged. Their plight was not her concern.

Ormand continued, "You've seen them fight, your holiness. They had six clanholds. Each occupied by eight to ten thousand warriors, each fighter as capable as these two, if not better. He says everyone in his clanhold died or was captured within an hour. He says the invaders used shadelings. He claims the army was led by Amuni's Children."

"Impossible," Irmina whispered.

Her haunted memories flashed again. Word of her parents' death to shadelings in the War of the Remnants felt as if she just heard it. That night her life had shattered, and remained in shambles even after the Dorns took her in. Somehow, she'd managed to patch herself together with the love they showed her. Through it all, she'd fallen in love with Ancel. Then came her last Ashishin trial when she'd discovered who the Dorns were, the part they played in the War of Remnants and the Shadowbearer War before it. The part they played in her parents' deaths, in the demise of much of her family.

"Devout Irmina?"

Irmina looked down. She was standing with her unsheathed sword in her trembling hands. "I–I'm fine." She took a deep breath.

She hadn't noticed the heat flowing through her. The same heat Jerem taught her to control when she touched Mater. The same heat that brought a craving to kill. She forced the feeling into the coldest part of her mind until it dwindled to nothing.

Neither Jaecar nor Melina had moved, but a still air hung in the room. Irmina met their gaze and slid her sword into its scabbard. Jaecar's lips parted before he gave a simple nod. Ormand sweated profusely, and he wrung his hands several times.

"Continue your questioning." Irmina paced across the room.

With a nervous nod, Ormand turned to Jaecar, and their conversation resumed. If Jaecar was telling the truth, an army possibly several hundred thousand strong was sweeping across Ostania. Those numbers must be an exaggeration. Yet, she needed to consider the worst. She would get word to High Shin Jerem and the Tribunal regardless.

"Ormand, did he say which way they were headed?"

"Yes. Southwest, toward the larger cities beyond the Orchid Plains. It's why he came this way. He's trying to reach the Vallum of Light to warn our armies there, and to get his family to safety."

Irmina pondered the news. If indeed the invading army headed across the Orchid, it would only be a matter of time before it reached the Vallum itself anyway. She needed to get a warning across as soon as possible. She stopped pacing. "Where are the closest Envoys or Heralds?"

Ormand shook his head, reading her thoughts. "There are none before the Vallum of Light."

Striding to a window, Irmina stared out at the twin moons and another set of thunderclouds. She would have to do it herself then. Misty would have to run like she never ran before. Granadia's fate may well depend on it.

"Ormand, gather the men," Irmina commanded. "Let them know what was said. Also dispatch several eagles with messages of these tidings. Tell Jaecar he can leave with me if he chooses, but I won't be staying with them. I'll push to the Vallum to warn the army and pass word to the Heralds for the Tribunal."

"Devout Irmina," Ormand said, his tone a plea. "I mean no offense but, it's one thing to speak to us with your authority as a Devout, your holiness, but the laws prevent you from commanding any military into action. Knight Caden is most… particular about the laws."

Irmina's mouth curled into a devilish smile. She strode to her desk, reached down, and clicked a hidden lever. An extra draw slid open. She removed a rather skimpy crimson uniform and two pins, one in the shape of crossed lightning bolts and the other of the Lightstorm.

Ormand gaped, his eyes shifting from the clothes to Irmina. Her gaze met the man's as his recognition of a Raijin's uniform changed his eyes from those of reverence into fear. As the elite assassins among the Ashishin, Raijin could command anyone at anytime and their rank fell just below a High Ashishin. Irmina had not noticed a reaction to her real name from Jaecar earlier, but the Raijin garb brought a gasp from him and a hiss from his wife. Both dropped to the floor with their heads down.

Snapping to attention, Ormand rose to his feet. This

time when he bowed, it was from the waist, and his eyes never left the floor. "I shall inform them, Shin Irmina."

Outside, lightning flickered and thunder rumbled. A scream sounded. Then another. A trumpet wailed.

Irmina swung her head around toward the window. Instead of Ranoda's lights or the dark curtain of clouds crossing the moon, blackness greeted her in a raspy whisper.

CHAPTER 23

Hands sticky with blood, Ryne moved with practiced efficiency. Cut, contour, split, pull, followed by a wet tearing sound. Fluids dribbled to the ground like viscous red wine as skin and hide parted from flesh. He raised his head from the work, tossed the useless fur to one side, and dropped another lapra's hindquarter onto the pile of meat near the fire.

Gray lined the skies, a remnant of the storm the night before, and mist crept through the forest as if the clouds had descended among the trees surrounding the glen. A nearby stream gurgled its soft song.

Cocking his head, Ryne listened to the thrashing within the undergrowth for an imminent attack, but none came. Growls and snarls announced predators stalking within the woods drawn by his work's pungent aroma, their eyes often glowing among the trees. However, none of the animals had attacked since he and Sakari slaughtered the first few. The beasts now resorted to challenging each other.

The night before, Ryne and Sakari had found Thumper alive and well at the glen. The dartan lay next to a stream, his extremities retracted into his shell, his olive carapace a giant, rounded rock. Scattered remains, mostly from plains lapras that had hunted Thumper, littered the ground. Among them lay a few of their bigger forest lapra cousins. To cause such devastation there must have been at least four forest lapra packs defending their territory. Although, a few carcasses did the show the results of Thumper's enormous fangs.

Thumper hadn't moved since Ryne and Sakari found him with his claws protruding at the six openings for his legs, his head tucked where only the carapace on its crown showed, and his tail curled snug under his shell. He could remain this way for days when he felt threatened.

"Do you think you have enough for him now?" Sakari asked as he dragged a fourth carcass over through the muddy leaves.

Ryne studied the meat next to him. "Yes. He won't be able to resist this. Skin the last one for me to roast. I'll go feed him."

Sakari nodded and dropped the remains next to the fire. A knife appeared in his hand, he sat cross-legged on the ground, pulled the lapra by a leg, and began cutting.

Ryne dragged the meat to where Thumper lay, leaving a bloody trail through soggy leaves. Calling Thumper's name in situations like this never worked, so with a great heave, he sent the chunks tumbling under the dartan's head. The meat struck the shell with soft thuds.

After a few moments, Thumper's shell rocked back and forth. Legs eased out, revealing mottled, blue-green skin. When the claws touched the ground, all movement halted. The dartan remained motionless for a moment before his legs eased farther down and pushed up until he stood twenty-four hands from the ground to the rounded top of his shell—the same height as Ryne. The dartan's tail uncoiled at the same time that his head stretched forward. Thumper mewled when he saw Ryne.

Ryne stepped up under his dartan's head, a smile on his face. "Good boy. You missed me? I knew you wouldn't be able to resist a good meal."

Thumper's neck curled down, and he rubbed his head against Ryne's arm. Rows of sharp teeth clicked against each other in a face too small for the dartan's girth. As he sniffed at Ryne's hand, Thumper's tongue flicked out and licked the blood. His bulbous eyes rolled, and his gaze shifted to the meat.

"Go ahead, enjoy," Ryne said. "Wish I could've found you some kinai to go with that, but this will do for now."

The dartan rocked from side to side and turned to the carcasses. He tore into the meat and swallowed in loud, gleeful slurps.

Ryne ran his hands down Thumper's neck and along his sides and underbelly where the carapace was softest, searching for any wounds. Finding none, he reached up along the base of the shell where his bags hung and retrieved his reins. They were still in good shape.

He checked the two deep saddle grooves cut into the spine of the shell a few feet apart, one behind the other. Over a month had passed since he last rode the dartan, and left alone, the saddles tended to grow back in, but so far, Thumper's had not. A good sign, Ryne thought, considering how he allowed Thumper to roam in the wilds. When he finished, Ryne inspected the small hand and footholds carved on either side of the shell. Satisfied, he washed his hands at the stream and rejoined his friend.

Sakari finished skinning and skewered the meat onto a few sticks Ryne had prepared earlier. Soon, the succulent flesh hung roasting over the fire, juices dripping and sizzling when they touched the flames. The sweet smell made Ryne's stomach grumble.

"After we're done eating, we'll make for Astoca," Ryne said. "Thumper should be strong enough from the meat to run for a good eight hours nonstop. We'll see if we can find some kinai fruit patches on the way to give him a real filling. If we can keep him stocked, we should reach the capital in a week."

"You're not going to warn the other towns between?"

"There's not enough time," Ryne said. "Besides, those towns can't be helped if this army attacks them. Their only salvation rests with the Astocans. They can field the largest legions of the Ostanaian kingdoms, and we're more likely to find an Envoy in Castere than any of the other capitals. Once forewarned, they should be able to muster a large enough force to repel the invaders. At least until the Envoy gets word to the Tribunal and they send the Dagodin legions."

Sakari shook his head. "It will take more than Dagodin Matii to stop what Jaecar mentioned and the daemon we suspect. They will need at least an entire legion of Ashishin."

"I still don't understand how they reached Carnas so fast, and from the southwest." Ryne frowned. "Something just doesn't make sense. But you're right, with the numbers Jaecar reported and what we saw at Carnas, it'll take more than Dagodin to stop them." Did the Tribunal have that many Ashishin to spare? And if they did would they risk sending them? Maybe, the best course of action was to warn the King, then head to the Vallum himself. If Varick still commanded there, he'd listen. Maybe, he could convince Varick to influence the Tribunal should they not think this a credible threat. "At any rate, we must eat before we go." Ryne took in Sakari's expressionless face. "I must eat before we go," he corrected himself with a rueful smile.

Breakfast passed in silence. While Sakari practiced the sword, Ryne plotted the route they would take to Astoca, revising the trip several times in an effort to shut out the thoughts of Carnas' dead and those who were captured, but their faces crept in. *Hagan, you and your pipe, One-eyed Mayor Bertram, Vana and Vera, Kahkon, Lara, Taeria…*On and on the memories swirled. As Sakari's sword work whistled in the background, Ryne prayed they'd found quick and merciful deaths, but he could no more rid himself of his morbid thoughts than he could forget the lives he took in the past. Such thoughts could consume a soul, he knew.

The song from Sakari's sword drew Ryne, its tone crooning a soothing rhythm he knew too well. He stood.

Sakari stopped mid strike, sheathed his sword, and strode to the fire in his gliding gait. With an exaggerated bow, Sakari indicated the open space within the clearing.

Ryne strode to the center of the area where a light breeze prickled the hairs on his arms. He unsheathed his sword, the Scripts etched into the hilt pressing against his palm as he lifted the weapon in front his face in a salute to the gods. His movements came slow and easy. Strange and sweet at the same time. He'd disciplined himself to practice daily but hadn't done so since the Nevermore Heights, and this felt as if he'd been locked in a windowless room for months until one day someone let him out into the open air.

He flowed through the basics, repeating every parry, cut and strike like a lost lover's kiss. The swish from the slick carpet of mud and leaves under his feet became a part of him, and he glided through it unhindered.

Speed increasing as he progressed into Stances and eventually into Styles, his blade became a whirlwind in his hand, lighter than thistledown. Ryne's swordplay built into a soothing melody that played within his head. In his mind, he poised upon a pond covered in floating lilies, his steps never disturbing its smooth surface. The melody built into an orchestra played at a ball, but strain as he might, the music remained at the edge of his hearing, barely discernible.

As he often did, he strove to reach the music, and as usual, it remained beyond his reach. He settled to listening to the faint notes, allowing his body to move in accordance to the tune. He danced, his feet drawing a trail through the ground in the patterns his mind wove. Nothing else existed, but the distant melody and his sword.

When Ryne sheathed his sword for the final time, two hours had passed, and the sun had burnt off the early morning mist. He strode toward Sakari and the now smoking embers, his thoughts clear. Sakari acknowledged Ryne with a nod. Without a word, they climbed onto Thumper's back and left the glen. They stayed to edge of the Fretian Woods before cutting clear across the Orchid Plains.

The first two days were uneventful, filled with pushing Thumper and only stopping for six hours a day to rest, hunt, eat, and for Ryne to practice the sword. Ryne chose a circuitous path to avoid any towns, usually staying close to the Tantua River, whose meandering path flowed out from the Mondros Forest to the northeast. Along the way, they saw no smoke from burning structures. Good news for the settlements, but it bothered Ryne. Where was this army? He'd made sure to bypass any areas where one could hide such a large force, but to be able to hide any sign at all should have proved impossible.

On the third day, they reached the first kinai farm in a fertile stretch a hundred miles before the Astocan border. Fields of wheat, corn, cabbage heads sprouting like green–white balls, and the bushy sprigs from carrots spread in small patches before them. Beyond those fields stood large kinai orchards, the rounded, leafy trees growing in neat rows.

"Strange," Ryne said when no one came to greet them as they crossed up onto the road leading to the farm.

The fields were empty at a time when harvest should be bountiful, and the farm filled with the bustle of working folk, trundling wheels, and the cries from laboring pack animals. From his vantage point, the farmhouse, the barn, and the storage sheds appeared deserted. Guard dogs that should have barked their challenges slunk away instead. Several yellowbeaks sang a mournful chorus.

"Do you think they finished their harvest and all left for market?" Sakari asked.

Ryne noticed what Sakari meant. Where there should have been red kinai clusters, only green leaves showed. "I'm not sure." The pink fluff from the harvested fruit carpeted the ground, often shifting with the breeze. A trace of the kinai's sweet smell still caressed the air. "Maybe they prefer not to have anyone here after harvest in case raiders strike." Ryne doubted the words even as they left his mouth.

"Should we stop?"

"No. Something here doesn't feel quite right," Ryne said. Maybe, the sensation came from the yellowbeaks' keening. Whatever it was, he did not wish to stop. "Let's move on."

The next farm they reached was the same. At the third such farm, Ryne stopped at the orchard's edge. "Maybe one farm I could begin to understand, but three? All abandoned?" He shook his head. "This goes beyond just being odd."

Sakari shrugged. "Raiders?"

"I thought so too at first," Ryne pointed to the orchards, "But the crops have been harvested too cleanly at every farm. And they've taken every farm animal and any stores." He glanced around, examining the field cautiously, then dropped from Thumper's back. "This isn't natural. And we've seen no signs of a struggle. Up here, almost every farm employs mercenaries at this time of year. It would be near impossible for the small bands raiders prefer to do all this." Ryne motioned for Thumper to stay and he and Sakari strode deeper into the orchard.

No more than fifty feet in, Ryne found the patterns he sought. There were too many footprints in the fluff and soil. Too many for farmers and the extra hands they hired for harvest. Too many for raiders who generally hunted in squads of fifteen men or less. There were enough tracks for a small army.

"You think these are from the same forces that attacked Carnas and the clanholds?"

"Maybe. If they decided to split into smaller compliments

for this work." A sudden stillness prickled against Ryne's skin, igniting uneasiness. "Do you feel that?"

"The disturbance in the air? Yes."

Ryne opened his Matersense. The world blossomed as if he viewed it through a magnifying tube tacticians often used to survey a battle. Smells sharpened. At the corner of his vision, he saw the same distortion as he did in Carnas. The razor sharp edges of the elements of Mater he was accustomed to were now smudged. Hidden among the perfumed scents from the harvested kinai wafted a slight decayed aroma mixed with what he could only describe as a wet dog's stench. The same scent from Miss Corten's, the strange woods with the half–formed wraithwolves and from within Carnas. Ryne released his Matersense.

"The air is the same as Carnas," Sakari said before Ryne could utter a word.

Ryne nodded as he surveyed the field before them. Six murdered men at the kinai patches around Carnas, the clanholds destroyed, his entire town slaughtered, and now these farms, devoid of people and kinai. Yes, this army advanced, but what did it all mean? Sooner or late, he would find his answers. He hoped it would be sooner.

They left the fields, collected Thumper, and headed to the buildings. Each one was as empty as the orchards. Within the farmhouse, the furniture was intact, children's and adults' beds made up and boots still at the front door. Rotting food sat on the kitchen table with a pot of tea and a pitcher of juice. Maggots crawled across what might have been venison and a baked chicken. The food's rancid smell filled the air. They found no corpses.

By the time they left, night had come. Ryne had no wish to camp close to the farm, so he pushed them for a few miles until they found a copse of trees he preferred. There, they built a small fire within a hollow and cooked lapra meat Ryne had preserved with salts the day before. While Ryne ate, Sakari went off to keep watch.

When he finished his meal, Ryne resorted to sword practice once more. The farms joined Carnas foremost on his mind. *Hagan, you and your pipe...* As Ryne remembered each of his friends, the action soothed him. Sometime later, he completed his practice, and found sleep's solace.

Ryne woke abruptly from his slumber. The fire was nothing more than glowing embers, its smoke a faded scent. Thumper's humped form was a mere silhouette in the night. Overhead, a cloudy veil occluded the twin moons and the stars, the resulting darkness enveloping the copse. He felt them coming before Thumper's plaintive mewl or before he sensed Sakari through the trees.

He leaped to his feet and sprinted to Thumper. The dartan did not need much encouragement and stood ready, his neck swinging from side to side. Heart racing, Ryne snatched up the reins and leapt onto Thumper's back.

Moments later, Sakari burst through the brush and sprang into the saddle behind him. "There are at least twenty of them."

"Twenty–six," Ryne corrected. His Matersense revealed all before him. He extended his sight and smell well beyond their normal range by using the air and its endless void as part of the element of Flows. Within this sight, the dark became late evening.

The black auras he depicted with this increased range engulfed the night itself. They shone with their blackness, making the night appear as nothing more than a gray shadow.

At the head of the interlopers bounded eight wraithwolves. From time to time, they sprang up on two legs like men, sniffing the air before dropping onto to all fours to leap again and again. Elongated muzzles adorned their faces, and thick hair covered arms and bodies, muscles pumping with each movement. The fetid stench of wet dog's fur mixed with decayed flesh rolled from the beasts in waves. As one, the wraithwolves stopped and lifted their snouts toward the copse. Green eyes glowed.

A chill prickled Ryne's skin at the things that followed behind the wolves.

At first, he thought they were humans, but as his sight touched them, he knew differently. These creatures glided instead of running, similar to Sakari, but where Sakari's feet touched the ground, these men did not. They also possessed no solid forms. They appeared as mist or smoke in the shape of men. Wherever they passed, the elements around them distorted from sharpness into dulled edges. They easily kept pace with the wraithwolves.

"Darkwraiths," Ryne whispered. As he turned to whip Thumper's reins to send him running, bloodcurdling howls echoed into the night. He glanced over his shoulder.

The wraithwolves no longer ran. Instead, they swelled, and he sensed more than he saw the shade they pulled within themselves. Then they vanished. They reappeared from the shadows themselves some twenty feet closer.

Ryne dismounted. "The wraithwolves just Blurred," he said without looking up at Sakari. The thrill for impending battle fluted across his skin. "There is but one place we can find safety. Take Thumper there, I'll meet you." He held up the reins as Sakari leaped into the forward saddle.

"As you wish." Sakari flapped the chains and sent Thumper speeding through the copse.

The darkwraiths screeched a keening wail. Ryne focused on them. They too Blurred, using the shade to leap from shadow to shadow.

Ryne calmed his battle energy and reached through his Scripts to the elements of Mater stored there. The celestial bodies etched into his skin came alive with his touch. Their light filtered from among the Streams.

The heat he had ignored when he first embraced his Matersense raced through Ryne's body like wildfire on dry tinder. His toes curled, and he leaned his head back. A morbid grin twisted his features. He no longer needed to hold his bloodlust at bay. He no longer needed to calm himself. The voices called, and he embraced them, allowing the Scripts to work. Above him, the clouds parted to reveal the moons.

Hagan, you and your pipe, your body ripped in ways that *shouldn't be possible. Vana and Vera, impaled on the floor and ravaged. Kahkon, bloody and torn. Lara, your throat ripped out. None of you deserved to die in such a way.* The fire within Ryne burned brighter.

He painted a mental picture of himself as a fleeting luminescence, and his Scripts took over, adding the moons' light to theirs. The two Forged together. An ethereal glow bathed Ryne's body.

The shadelings drew closer, eyes burning embers among the shadows.

White flames flared within Ryne as his bloodlust burst forth with the Forging. He threw his head back, a smile twisting his lips, the thirst to kill filling him in a wave. Ryne's battle energy and lust intertwined as one, long lost lovers in a wanton embrace.

Greedily, his Scripts gobbled up the coupled energy and emotions mixing them with the Mater within him. The glow from the essences subsided, absorbed by his Scripts and body.

Using that power, Ryne Shimmered from one moonbeam to the next, appearing thirty feet from where he once stood.

Behind him, the shadelings howled and wailed.

CHAPTER 24

Irmina teetered in the saddle. Her eyes snapped open, and she lurched upright for what felt like the hundredth time. *I must stay awake...cannot allow myself to fall asleep now.* Shadowy cobwebs clouded her vision, and fatigue weighed on her body. She shook her head. If there was a time she wished sleep would abandon her, it would be now, but slumber clung to her like a needy baby.

Pain lanced across her stomach and back. With each laborious step Misty took, Irmina's legs and ass chafed and burned more, the normally soft padding used on her saddle having long outlived its usefulness. If she dismounted now, she would find her skin bloody and raw. Her wounds felt as if someone stuck a red–hot poker into her flesh before trailing the metal tip down her skin. *But his weapon hadn't been a poker had it? Had he used a dagger?* At times, she was unsure.

Humid air adding to her need to close her eyes if only for a moment, she swayed again. She could, couldn't she? Shut her eyes and rest? When next she leaned to one side, her eyes fluttered then drooped shut before she forced them apart again by sheer force of will. Or was it the sweat from her brow now burning her eyes that made them open?

Teeth gritted in determination, she forced herself to an upright position. A fog–shrouded hand rose to her face and slapped her. It took her a few slaps and stinging cheeks before she realized the hand was her own. Her stupor cleared enough to take in her surroundings. Night hung heavy, and the surrounding foothills evoked a feeling of something watching her. Shivering despite the hot, heavy air, she glanced down. Her bloody uniform, what was left of it, clung to her in tattered silver and red rags.

At least Misty's holding up well. As if Amuni heard her thought, the dartan chose that moment to stumble to four legs before pushing herself back up onto six. *How long has she run this time?* Irmina would've trilled a command to rest if she could have, but her mouth was dry as brittle clay.

A painful mewl resonated a few feet from Irmina. She looked toward the sound. Ormand's black dartan followed not too far away, but from its unsteady gait, the animal wouldn't last much longer without rest. Languishing behind Ormand were two more Dagodin Knights atop mounts. All that remained of Ranoda's cohort. Three left out of over four hundred. Her chest heaved with the thought. With every step, the distance between her and the men increased.

She knew she needed to do something, but what she couldn't truly say. Her mind tried to function, but mired in a stupor as it was, her rational thoughts found ways to delve into a nightmare. *This is a nightmare, isn't it?*

She shook her head again and slapped her face a few more times. Some nagging in the back of her mind insisted she avoid the areas engulfed in the shadows cast by the hills. She tried her best to comply. But when she trotted deep into one such passage where even the moons were hidden from view by several rock outcrops and hardy trees, memories of what occurred in her office rushed into her mind in disjointed dregs.

A black nightmare seeped through her window, blotting out all light from outside. The thing congealed until the blackness resolved into a manlike shape made from shadows. Red eyes appeared and froze her where she stood, while howls rose in a chorus outside.

The many books she'd studied about the Shadowbearer War flashed through her head. Shadelings in the form of smoke or mist bearing black blades had swept down on many cities then, slaughtering all before them. She'd etched the pictures of the darkwraiths in those books into her mind.

Even as she recognized the creature, her body refused to respond. Heart aflutter, she screamed at her trembling limbs to move as the shadeling's sword rose inexorably in billowing, black hands.

With a crash, the door caved in to reveal Knight Caden and several other Dagodin. That singular act broke her from the fear riveting her in place. Her sword left its sheath with the speed of thought and turned aside the incoming blade.

Black metal met glinting silversteel in a caress of sparks that showered in a cascading arc.

A sharp pain scoured her back. Twisting away from the agony, she came face to face with Jaecar, a dagger in his hand, and the young Cadet who served the food clinging desperately to his back. She threw herself away from the Alzari, his next slice passing a hair's breadth from her chest. As she hit the carpet she rolled and bounced to her feet facing the darkwraith.

From pure instinct, her left hand rose, and she Forged Mater. Flames roared out from her palm in a scorching wave to meet the shadeling. The creature wailed just as a concussion rocked the room, knocking it back through the window with a shower of glass and throwing Irmina off her feet. Heat washed into her face from the blast and matched a similar rush thrumming within her. Before she could crawl back to her feet, Jaecar was on her again like a miniature whirlwind.

The Cadet lay to the side, his bowels spilled, blood pooling under him.

As Irmina attempted to parry the Alzari's high slice, he changed direction and caught her across the stomach. Her uniform parted like silk. Warmth gushed down her abdomen to her loins.

Snarls and spittle flying from his lips, Jaecar yelled in a language she didn't recognize. He swept in again, but she was never given a chance to defend herself as Knight Caden and his men intercepted the Alzari and drove him toward the window.

Irmina's chest rose and fell in shudders as she sucked in deep breaths. A hand snatched at hers. Deep in the heat of battle, a craving to kill rose with her Forging. She almost took the arm attached to the hand until she looked up to see Ormand. She sought the harmony deep within her mind to abate the Streams' thirst for life in return for its gift.

"Raijin Irmina," Ormand implored as she hesitated, "Run! There's nothing you can do here but die." He pulled her toward the door.

She hesitated for a moment as she considered unleashing the power building within her on Jaecar and Melina, but the soldiers blocked her path.

It was enough time to see Kass, his infantile face twisted into a grotesque mask, make an inhuman leap from the bed with a blade in hand onto the back of some unsuspecting Dagodin.

The child buried the knife to the hilt in the soldier's back. The man screamed, clutching futilely at the dagger. Kass cackled.

Irmina dashed after Ormand.

In the barracks' halls, men in dark armor with black tattoos across their faces squared off against several clusters of bloody, disheveled Dagodin. Irmina wasted no time. She fed the Streams. Light and heat from the lamps around the walls answered her calling. When she Forged, a firebolt spewed forth toward the men.

Hair crackled, paint peeled, metal buckled with a screech, skin melted and the aroma of roasting flesh filled the air. The dark armored men barely had time to scream.

With their deaths, Irmina's craving abated. The Dagodin who recognized what she did dropped to their knees in supplication for a brief moment. She heard multiple murmurs of Ashishin in awed voices. The moment passed, and soon they were rushing down the stairs.

Outside, Ranoda was ablaze. Screams pierced the air, and smoke and ash billowed skyward. Mouth agape, Irmina swore she had entered a scene from one of her many nightmares of what her parents must have experienced.

The Tribunal's soldiers fought men and beasts alike. Black-furred wolfish creatures with green eyes walked like men, ran like wolves, and ripped the throats from whomever they encountered, all the while lifting their bloody muzzles to the sky and howling.

Green-eyed gazes turned to Irmina's group. Without hesitation, she reached for the light essences of the twin moons and the many fires as well as the energy from the flame's heat. She unleashed her fury with a cold, calculating certainty, scouring all before her, creature and man alike. If Dagodin died then so be it, these abominations needed to feel the power a servant of Ilumni wielded.

The surge of the Streams through her clamored to be fed. So she obliged.

Again and again, she struck, death flying from her in fire and light. Men screamed, wraithwolves wailed and darkwraiths shrieked as she cleared a path to the stables. Her wounds, suffered by Jaecar's blade, were a dull throb lost in her mind.

Forming a wall, the Dagodin followed Ormand's commands to protect her from shadelings and men alike. But it was not enough. A few creatures still managed to claw through, and she suffered several gashes from long claws or from the edge of wild spear swings.

Strength ebbing, she somehow managed to climb onto Misty's back. She hadn't realized when the soldiers managed to free the mounts from the stables. Nor did she care. Her bloodlust felt like an all-consuming flame within her. Somehow, she recognized the danger. She'd used too much Mater. The Streams always had to have their due. She would pay it either with her life or someone else's.

With the last of her power, she blew a hole through the fence. She didn't remember how they escaped the town. All she could remember were snatching claws, swinging spears, trampling man and beast and almost falling from Misty's saddle several times. All else was a blur.

"Raijin Irmina. Raijin Irmina." Ormand's urgent voice sounded so far away. A hand shook her.

Irmina looked up at the stars above. *When did I lay on the ground?* She attempted to lean up onto her elbow. *Did I fall asleep?*

"No, Raijin Irmina. You need rest. We all do. We must reach the Vallum. Running the beasts any more ragged than they are won't help. Here, sip this," Ormand implored.

Throat dry and burning, she took what he offered. She slurped and kinai wine flowed down her throat. "Thank you," she managed, choking back a cough, the drink sputtering from her lips.

"Take your time. It's all that's left, blessed one."

Warmth swam down her gullet and into the pit of her stomach, and an energetic feeling ensued. She managed to prop herself up. Several dark mounds marked what must have been the dartan's at rest. Drained as she was, she couldn't sense Misty.

"How are you feeling?" Ormand asked, his tired and bloodied face a mask of concern. "Your wounds haven't healed much. We need to get you to a mender."

"I, I had a dream," Irmina said. "In it, Ranoda was attacked by shadelings and—"

"It was no dream. It happened."

Her eyes were too heavy to register the shock she felt. A nightmare came alive in her head again. It was black and it seeped in through her office window.

CHAPTER 25

Rain played a constant drumbeat on the roof. The rhythmic pounding made Ancel think about the days spent with Kachien. Her perfume lingered in the air from earlier, mingling with the slight scent of their lovemaking still on the sheets he sat on. Small bumps rose on Ancel's bare back from the chill easing through the room despite the closed windows.

"So," Mirza said with a leer painted on his face, "Did you learn anything new today?"

Ancel pursed his lips. "I really don't feel like talking about that right now."

Spiky red hair standing on end, Mirza sat in a cushioned armchair near one of the many ornate lamps around the room. "You know, we came here for a good time. Here you are having all the fun, and you still find time to be in a worse mood than this weather."

"What do you want me to say?" Ancel shot back with a scowl. "I like the woman. Yes, she's a whore, but she's taught me more in the last few days than I've learned in my short lifetime. In many ways I feel for her." Stories of the sufferings among the Ostanians, their trials and the vicious cycle of their territorial battles and political games played through his mind as if Kachien told them anew. Atop it all rode the truth of her scars.

Mirza snorted. "Feel for her is an understatement. It's as if you're falling for her. A whore, Ancel. Think on it. You didn't come here for that. I mean, you came here for women, yes, but not to fall for some whore. To make things worse, you get angry when she's doing her job. Like tonight. Burning shades, it's what she does for a living."

Shoulders a taut rope, Ancel stood. He glanced at Charra. Colorful swirls rose around the daggerpaw. Ancel squeezed his eyes shut. When he reopened them, the swirls were gone. Seeking the calm he used when he practiced the sword, he welcomed the reassuring feel of his mother's charm against his neck and the rug under his feet as he trudged over to the wardrobe close to Mirza. He refused the urge to glance at his friend for the moment. If he did, there was no telling what he would say.

Charra's head rose before he set it down on his forepaws again. Since the night they came to the Dancing Lady, Charra had refused to allow Ancel to go anywhere without him. Ancel had to pay double before the innkeeper allowed him to bring the daggerpaw upstairs. Whatever bothered Charra set him on edge, and more often than not, Ancel found himself looking over his shoulder when he walked Randane's streets.

When Ancel reached his wardrobe, he finally felt calm enough to speak. "You don't need to remind me. I'm fond of her, but I'm not falling for her." Even as he said the words, he knew them to be lies. Whenever Kachien left the drinking room with another man, he felt a burning jealousy he struggled to control. The feeling overcame him with the thought.

"See, there it is," Mirza said, pointing and giving his head a slight shake, his hair not moving an inch. "Anytime you start talking about what she does, this look comes across your face."

"What look," Ancel said, trying not to sound defensive while choosing a plain black shirt. The color felt even more right the last few days. He slipped into the clothing and buttoned it to the neck.

"That look." Mirza pointed at his face. "The one that says you're ready to murder some merchant who can afford Kachien's services."

Trying to ignore Mirza, Ancel chose dark gray trousers and pulled them on. Satisfied with the fit, he closed the wardrobe's door and inspected himself in the mirror, passing his hands through his black hair to make sure it was still oiled enough to lay the way he preferred. He poked at the dark rings under his emerald eyes and gave himself the most appealing smile he could.

"Listen, you didn't come here to forget about Irmina then get attached to some other woman. Especially not some Ostanian whore. You came here to be free. Where's the ruthless, cocky womanizer I know? Can you find him for me? Please?" Mirza's gray eyes pleaded as much as his words.

"He's about to go down to the drinking room and join Danvir if you don't stop," Ancel retorted as he turned from the mirror to glare at his friend.

"All I'm trying to do is—"

"Give over already, Mirza, I won't lie to myself. I like Kachien. Do I love her? I don't think so. It's all a bit confusing where my feelings are, but I'll sort them out. I still have Alys to think about, and only the gods know how many more women will be waiting back in Eldanhill at Soltide. So, no I haven't lost myself. Let me enjoy what I have here with Kachien for now. She's helped me past Irmina. Soon enough, we'll leave, and I'll put her behind me too."

"If you say so."

"I say so."

Mirza sighed. "Well, while you've been up here I found out more about the fighting in Ostania. Something to do with one of the old clans. Rumors are spreading that the Tribunal won't involve themselves, but I'm not so sure. The Herald who sent the message received word from an Envoy in some city named Castere."

Ancel whistled. "That's in Astoca, it's the largest Ostanian city. We trade more with them than any other place."

"The warning came from the King himself. People are starting to grumble that if the Tribunal chooses to do nothing, there could be trouble."

"The Tribunal can't afford to let this affect trade. They'll act. The question is when," Ancel said.

"Normally, I'd agree." Mirza gave a pensive frown before continuing, "But the issues between Sendeth and Doster have taken a turn for the worse."

"What're you talking about?" Ancel asked.

Lines creased Mirza's forehead. "I know you've heard the stories in the drinking room about the recent killings?"

"To be honest, I haven't paid much attention. I figured it was just the usual brawls, or some footpads robbing merchants."

Mirza shook his head. "Dan did say you haven't been listening to much anyone says. Especially when Kachien is around—"

"Don't start."

"I'm not," Mirza said, "but the killings have not been brawls or footpads. You're right about one thing. The victims have all been merchants. Almost every one of them came up from Ishtar after bringing their goods over from Ostania. Every one was Sendethi."

Ancel's eyebrows knitted. "They think it's a Dosteri doing the killing?"

"Yes, that's the word on the street. And the regiment's been on the watch for a golden–haired Dosteri man."

"Why?"

"The last any of these merchants' bodyguards remember were their masters meeting with this golden–haired Dosteri," Mirza said.

"Well then the guards can identify him, no?"

"That's the strange part. None can remember exactly what he looked like. They just know he had golden hair."

Ancel's frown grew deeper. "What would make them so sure this man's Dosteri then?"

"The message he leaves next to each body written in ancient Dosteri…" Mirza hesitated, a reluctant expression crossing his face.

"Well, are you going to tell me?"

Mirza's normally light voice shifted to a somber tone, and he began to recite.

"From Ostania's ashes and Erastonian blood, the Dosteri rise,
Granadia will fall,
Devout and all,
As it was before
So shall it be again
World without end
War without end
When comes the appointed hour,
Under the rule of the one with Etchings of Power,
Stone will crumble,
The void shall rumble,

Clouds will grow,
Water shall flow,
Light and shade as one,
Fire and ice as one,
Denestia shall bend to its knee,
Until the elements exist in harmony."

Ancel gasped. The words were said to be an ancient Dosteri mantra their soldiers chanted during battle long before the Shadowbearer War when Doster warred with much of Granadia. The first time he and Mirza learned those words were when they read their father's old Chronicle—the Chronicle of Undeath—they found hidden in the attic. The tome spoke of a day when the dead would not remain dead, but walk Denestia in service of the shade. He never forgot the beating they received that day for going into his father's things. The glint in Mirza's eyes said he remembered also.

"We've been through this before," Ancel said. "None of it makes sense. The Erastonians are dead, wiped out by Nerian himself before he turned to the shade. Not even the last bit that refers to the first Principle is any more sound. The elements already exist in harmony."

"I've been thinking about that." Mirza bit his lip as he spoke. "What if the elements don't? What if it means even within each element?"

Ancel's brows rose. "What?"

"Think on it. Mater is made up of the three elements, right? Streams, Flows, and Forms."

Ancel nodded as he paced to the window. The rain fell in sheets as if a god released a waterfall from the heavens.

"And," Mirza continued, "In each element are their essences. What if this refers to the essences within each element? Shade and light fight, they're opposites. So does heat and cold. All within the element of Streams."

Ancel stopped his pacing. "Yes, but if you remember from class, Streamean worship encourages the acceptance of all religions as one harmony and the essences as such. Look at those from the Forms and the Flows. They work in concert."

"Exactly my point," Mirza said, his eyes lighting up. "What if it's just the Streams that need to find the same peace to exist in harmony?"

"Maybe you're right. We can ask Teacher Galiana—"

"We can't ask anyone, Ancel. Remember, we're not supposed to know about the Chronicle of Undeath."

Ancel smiled. "We don't need to refer to the tome. We have the note left by this killer to use. It's more than enough to start with and—"

Charra snarled. From outside, a blood freezing scream pierced the air.

"What in Amuni's name…" Mirza swore as he rose to his feet and rushed to the door.

The scream changed to incessant shrieks.

Driven by the urgency of the wails, Ancel ignored his boots, snatched up his sword, and followed Mirza. He took the stairs by twos and threes, his bare feet slapping on the wood whenever he landed.

Mirza crashed out the back door to the Dancing Lady a few steps ahead of him. Ancel skidded to a stop in water, mud, and filth in the alley with Charra splashing at his heels. The daggerpaw focused down the lane, a warning rumble deep in his throat. Glass lamps at the front and rear of the inn and the adjoining buildings provided dim light that did little to dispel the alley's deeper shadows. Wiping rain from his eyes, Ancel followed what drew Charra's attention.

A person in what appeared to be wet, red silks lay on the ground. Someone wearing a dark cloak crouched over the body. Blood streamed away from the prone form.

The squatting person in the cloak glanced up. Their eyes widened.

Ancel caught a glimpse of honey colored hair and a smooth face more like a young boy's than a man's. In his hands, the youth held two weapons, no longer than short swords, but they reflected no light. It was as if the weapons drank the illumination from the lamps along the walls in the alley.

A yell echoed behind them from the alley's entrance.

Ancel snatched a look over his shoulder. Several dark liveried men with swords brandished were running down the alley pointing toward them. He turned to see gold hair fleeing into the dark. Charra bounded after the youth.

"Wait," Mirza shouted when Ancel made to follow his daggerpaw. "We shouldn't follow him, not in the dark. Let's not add ourselves to his list. Charra can handle himself. Besides," he gestured toward the body on the ground, "his bodyguards are already here and the regiment should be here soon too."

Ancel shivered as he peered down the alley, his clothes so soaked they stuck to his body. Charra's gray–white form, obscured by the deluge, disappeared among the shadows. He knew his friend was right. To follow would be folly if not fatal.

Within moments, booted feet were thumping and splashing toward them. Six merchant's guards in chain mail with boiled leather peeking from under the metal sleeves, the Charging Boar of their blue and green surcoats wetly plastered to their armor, surrounded the young men. Eyes glared from inside hooded cloaks. An old guard with a potato for a nose and a pitted face pulled his hood back and stepped forward with his sword raised.

"No, these two had nothing to do with this," said Innkeeper Callan who stepped out from the back door. The pear–shaped man shouldered his way through the guards. "They were upstairs when the screams began." His eyes shifted when he looked at the body on the ground, and he wrung his hands before wiping them on his soiled apron.

The pit–faced guard strode by Ancel and Mirza, water swirling around his boots. He sheathed his sword and signaled to another soldier. Together, they flipped the merchant's body over.

Ancel shivered more from the sight than the cold rain beating down on him. He'd never seen such terrible wounds before. Entrails hung out, and steam rose from the corpse. The man's face was an unrecognizable mess. Not even Charra could do such damage.

"Seize those young men," the old guard ordered, his voice drowning out the rain.

Rough hands snatched Ancel from behind. He twisted, and a fist as hard as a brick struck him on the side of his face, and his sword clattered onto the cobbles. Stars danced in his vision coupled with the ground rushing to meet him. Before he could muster a coherent thought, he found himself struggling to catch his breath as a boot mashed his back and kept his face pinned into a rancid puddle among the broken cobbles. His eyes stung from the bilge. Sputtering to catch a breath served to fill his nostrils and mouth with the foul smelling and even worse tasting runoff.

A loud growl echoed in the alley.

From somewhere in his stupor, Ancel heard the frantic cries of the guardsmen. He thought he recognized Danvir's deep bellow. Was that the sound of steel clashing against steel?

As Ancel regained his senses, the man above him cursed. The weight of the boot against Ancel's back lifted. Retching up the filthy water, he crawled to his knees. Sure enough, the metal clang of swords and the shouts and grunts of exertion sounded all around him. Mixed in were moans, plaintive cries and Charra's snarls and growls.

Head down, eyes still stinging, Ancel could just make out armored legs stumbling about. He reached out blindly along the ground until he felt his sword hilt, then he struggled to his feet. Lightning flickered, brightening his surroundings. Thunder rumbled and drowned out the noise of the rain drumming against the slate roofs and pattering on the cobbles.

Danvir and Mirza, swords in hand, stood over the bodies of two dead guardsmen. Charra cooed next to two others, their armor pierced in over a dozen places by his bone hackles, their blood pouring like the deluge.

The daggerpaw's gaze was locked on a slim figure dressed in clinging gray pants and a shirt. A black cloak hung limp as the person inspected the corpses of the other soldiers. Honey colored hair spilled down the figure's shoulder and back. There was no mistaking the dual short swords that seemed to drink the light from the alley's lamps.

The bells of the Streamean temples tolled.

Lightning skittered across the sky once more, casting the alley into daylight for several heartbeats. The killer turned to them.

Sword held out before him, Ancel edged closer to Charra. *How didn't I recognize those eyes earlier?*

"Come," Kachien said, sheathing her black weapons. "We have to leave now if you wish to live."

CHAPTER 26

Ryne Shimmered across the field.

Decades had passed since he last used this ability. So much so that he'd almost forgotten the rush it brought. Every time he Shimmered, it felt as if he stood at the edge of a precipice and flung himself into the depths. His stomach clutched with the sudden falling sensation. The light beam where he would land pulled until it swallowed him, and they became one. To a person without the power to see, he would vanish and reappear at the location he targeted. To those who could see, he simply moved at blinding speed.

"Go! Kill, tear, maim, destroy. The world is at your fingertips. Take them, they deserve death. They killed yours. You kill theirs. One good turn…" On and on the deep voice droned whenever his Scripts drew in more Mater, the energy caressing his ears with vengeful whispers.

His head filled to the brim with the words as his body embraced the need to kill. The voice built into song. A chaotic opera with blaring instruments playing a rousing rhythm. Sakari had named it his kill craze, and rightly so. Ryne cackled with the thought. A maniacal sound he didn't recognize as his own voice.

The second voice attempted to find purchase, but this time it gibbered. *"No. Calm yourself. Harmony. Seek it. Calm. Kill only if you must. Draw back, peel away. Subdue the power of the Scripts."*

Ryne sneered. He slammed his thoughts shut against the second voice's pleas.

Heat exploded from him like the mouth of a volcano, an insane cackle erupting from him once again.

A grin splitting his features, he reached the middle of the field and spun to face his pursuers. He'd yet to meet man or beast who could hold onto Mater longer than he could without losing their sanity or dying from the pressure on their mind and body. The languishing shadelings proved no different.

Across the myriad copses, rutted trails and open fields, the shadelings now ran instead of Blurring. As expected, with their long leaps and bounds, the wraithwolves had separated themselves from the darkwraiths in the long chase. They continued to open the distance, so lost in their own murderous frenzy they no longer ran as a pack.

The first beast leaped across the trail to Ryne's field. Ryne Shimmered to the wraithwolf before it landed in the knee–high grass.

He drew his sword with his right hand. The Scripts triggered. Light raced down the blade as if a fire chased fuel, and the sword rose in a backhanded slice to meet the leaping wolf.

Green eyes winked out as the creature's head parted from its shoulders. Before the slice reached the highest point, Ryne was already drawing the weapon down and sheathing it. The wraithwolf's flesh dissipated like ash blowing on the wind, the powdery substance never reaching the ground, the smell of roasted meat filling the air.

The next wolf gained the field. Ryne repeated the same attack. With each kill, the pressure from his kill craze eased a miniscule amount. Clouds scudded across the sky as the sixth wraithwolf managed to land among the grass while Ryne was finishing off the fifth.

Black fur ruffling with the wind, the shadeling bounded through the grass, muscular arms and legs pumping, its eyes ablaze, snarls issuing from its gaping jaws. Ryne relaxed as the beast drew shade, Blurred, and emerged within reach of him. Hot breath and froth from the shadeling's maw brushed Ryne as its jaws snapped. Long, poisonous claws slashed.

Ryne stepped around the attack, and within the same motion, he called on the Scripts of the twin moons. His arm flashed up in a circular motion and back down, the move mimicking the shape of the moons. The wraithwolf's left arm went flying into the night followed by a pained scream from the monster. Ryne sheathed his greatsword.

The shadeling retreated, circling him tentatively. Ryne dropped his sword arm, inviting it in, and the wraithwolf took the bait. It Blurred once again, swiping and snarling at his right side.

This time, Ryne pictured dust swirls carried on the wind and moved with his Scripts. He spun beyond the slashing claws in a full rotation. His sword came out and up. The strike lopped off the creature's right arm. The wraithwolf mewled in terror with the loss of two limbs as it stumbled forward and fell, the acrid aroma of its burnt flesh rising in smoky wisps.

As the twin moons cleared the clouds, their silvery surfaces illuminating the field, the wraithwolf struggled up onto its legs. Smoking stumps were all that remained of the arms. No blood flowed from the wounds. Ryne's lips twisted into a hideous smile with the knowledge that the cauterized wounds wouldn't allow any living appendage to grow back.

The wraithwolf teetered for a moment before steadying itself. Frothing slobber flew from its maw, and with a piteous cry, it pushed off those powerful legs and flew headfirst. Ryne leapt up on currents of air essences, one with the Flows. His sword swooped down like the leathery wings of the legendary Hengen etched into his Scripts. No sound passed from the monster as the head went spinning. The black–furred body shriveled and dissipated.

Shuddering, Ryne turned to face the other wraithwolves. The fight had taken longer than he wanted. The beasts, however, stayed on the other side of the trail, pacing back and forth, green–eyed gazes never leaving him. Within moments, several darkwraiths joined them. These too did not cross the threshold. Instead, they waited.

Ryne's insides burned with the craze. He hadn't killed enough to abate its pull. His body trembled as he fought to resist the urge and rush into a headlong attack. Cackling maniacally, he focused on the gathering shadelings. They would be his release. Here, he would begin to avenge Carnas. Here, he would make right what happened to Kahkon. Here, he would appease his power.

If he died in the process, then he would finally be released from a world that never was his. A world where he'd wreaked havoc, where he'd sown suffering, fear, and grief. Such a fate would be just repayment. Faces of the dead flitted through his mind. The time was now. He commanded his Scripts.

The second voice came roaring into his mind, this time it didn't gibber or plead. It questioned and ridiculed his foolishness. What of the good he'd done? What of the many lives he'd saved over the long years? Did those not counterbalance the suffering he caused? What of his purpose? What of the one who would show him the way that Halvor mentioned? Was he willing to die without knowing? What of the shadeling army and the suffering and chaos it would bring?

Caught between the warring voices, Ryne threw back his head. He didn't abandon his hold on his Scripts. Instead, he pictured those depicting the Forms—the earth, the mountains, the metals, the trees and brush around him. Through the Scripts, he drew on the essences of the earth that pressed dirt into stone, stone into metal, and metal into precious jewels. The power of the Forms built within him like the vast Nevermore Heights to the north. With it came strength, an unwavering determination, steadfastness to match the very bedrock forming those mountains.

The fire of his kill craze and his rage slammed into the wall he erected. The Streams tried to envelop the Forms, tried to melt the stone, but was instead absorbed and spread across the wall's surface. The heat within him subsided, held at bay for the moment. Ryne inhaled deeply, his body trembling and weak with exertion.

Mind clouded with doubt, Ryne studied the gathered shadelings. In his weakened state, he couldn't trust himself not to succumb to the will of his power, to revel in his bloodlust. He took hold of the light once again and Shimmered away until he crossed the field into a stand of trees, occasionally glancing behind him to make sure the shadelings still waited for the ones lagging. Satisfied, he headed to the biggest tree he could find.

Ryne's head throbbed and his arms and legs felt like large logs he could barely lift. He made sure he was deep enough within the tangled growth around him to remain hidden from the shadelings. Once more, he touched the Forms and Forged, pulling stone and earth, roughly his size, from the ground. His mind touched the drawings of men on his body, Forging the rocky mass into a construct in a man–like shape. With the last

bit of strength borrowed from the Forms, he slammed both the
light and earth essences into the construct. In the same act, he
Shimmered high up into the tree branches.

Once secure, he sent the construct sprinting away from
him and out the stand's other side. As he did so, he collapsed
against a thick branch, the last of his strength spent. His gaze
followed the aura from his construct as it sped across the land.

Behind him, the shadelings wailed.

Not long after, the trees shook and brush thrashed as
the creatures chased after his creation. Ryne counted them to
make sure they all passed by. Still, he refused to move from his
precarious perch slumped against the branch. Whether it was
from sheer exhaustion, caution or both, he couldn't tell. He
simply waited. Laying there with his face against the rough bark,
he lost track of time.

When the howls and wails sounded miles away, he heaved
a sigh. He mustered what strength he could and clambered down
from the tree, breaking branches along the way. Close enough to
the ground that he could do no great harm to himself, he pushed
off and let himself fall. He hit the ground with a thud and a
grunt.

Climbing to his feet was an exercise in pain. Ryne gritted
his teeth against what felt like broken ribs, his breath wheezing
through his lips as he used stunted trees for support. When he
found some semblance of balance, he stumbled more than he
walked or ran through the woods. He couldn't grasp the elements
for help, not even if he wanted to. He fought tooth and nail not
to fall on his face no matter how much the ground called to him.

The lump that spoke of Sakari's location grew larger as
he traveled. Hours later, after crossing too many pastures and
copses to count, he arrived at a steep cliff face. He followed an
old goat path along the cliff's base until he came to a small slit.
There, he waited until the moonlight beamed on the crack in just
the right way.

A hand appeared from the crevice and snatched him
inside. Brief disorientation followed.

"I watched you through the link." Sakari's voice sounded
distant. "You almost gave in to the craze."

Ryne shook his head against the cloudy focus in front
his eyes as if he peered into a foggy mirror while a muted buzz

played in his head. He took in his surroundings.

They were in an Entosis similar to the one Halvor had hidden inside. Moonlight sparkled from above, lighting crystals along the walls that glowed in sparkling pinpoints. He lay at the edge of a pond. Somewhere close by, night insects chirped.

"What were you thinking, drawing so much Mater with your Scripts?"

Ryne's lips were chalk, parched and dry. A million cobwebs enveloped his mind. He tried to shake his head again, but the motion became a feeble tilt. "I wanted to st...to stretch muscles..."

"Stretch them? You almost ripped them asunder. Some poor village or city would have felt your wrath then, to the tune of thousands dead."

Ryne sensed concern in Sakari's voice. He almost smiled. It was the first time he'd ever heard any change from the man.

Sakari continued, "Do you feel this?"

A hand passed across Ryne's chest. He frowned at the sudden feel of cool air. Confused, he looked down to see his chest piece had been removed. "Yes. I'm cold."

"No," Sakari corrected, "Not just cold. You are sweating. You broke the seal on your body when you did the last Forging. Mater is leaking from you. If you had held onto the essences much longer while creating the construct you would have perished or gone insane."

As if I'm not insane already. Ryne eased up to a seated position. "Praise Ilumni I didn't succumb then. May he keep it so."

Ryne fell forward and Sakari caught him. This time he didn't push his companion's hand away. Not that he could even if he wanted.

"Relax, we need to stay here a few days for you to mend," Sakari said.

Without trying, Ryne could feel the Mater around him. Similar to the other two Entoses he knew of, the elements gathered here in their most primal forms, stronger than any normal places in Denestia. They seeped into him as they worked to mend the damage to his body and mind. He wanted to tell Sakari they couldn't spare even a day. Instead, he lay back, looked up at the sky, and allowed the elements to do their work.

CHAPTER 27

Shin Galiana Calestis made no attempt to lessen her harsh tone. She spoke slowly, stressing each word as if trying to drill them into Headspeaker Valdeen's head that shone with the sheen of sweat. "You were given specific instructions to make sure the boys came back with you. How could you let this happen?" She rapped her staff on the Council chamber's floor as she counted off each issue. "Deliver the kinai. Allow the boys some pleasure. Bring them home. Simple tasks."

Edwin Valdeen dabbed at his bald head. His other hand fidgeted on the tabletop. The man had arrived late that night without the boys. Galiana had called the meeting immediately, but it took several hours before all the Council made it to the Whitewater Inn. Outside, a rooster's crows announced the lateness or rather earliness of the hour.

Valdeen's eyes and mouth twitched as he surveyed the other Council members. Without his preening arrogance, the man was a sagging shell. His gaze settled on Galiana for a brief moment before he looked away. "I–In case you didn't notice, they're not boys anymore, they're men. And they follow whatever Ancel does. He and his friends decided they wanted to stay for a few extra days. What was I to say? No? You yourself know the mood he's been in. Who knows what he would've done if I tried to stop him."

"Bullshit," Devan Faber blurted. Mirza's father stared down the Headspeaker, his eyes cold pits.

"A moment, Devan," Galiana said, and Devan nodded. Galiana knew Edwin's real reason was more the fact he wanted Ancel to have nothing to do with his daughter. She took in the Headspeaker with an unwavering stare. "I would advise you not to forget yourself when you address me, Edwin. As for him being a man, you are correct. I had hopes his involvement with your daughter would help, but that does not appear to be the case. We shall give them another week before we send to Randane and have the regiment escort them home."

"And you better pray to Ilumni nothing happens to our sons," Devan Faber warned.

"What about these other reports," Guthrie asked. The portly innkeeper, and Danvir's father, whose inn they used as a meeting place cast his gaze around the large lamplit room to all the other Council Heads at their respective seats. All but one were dressed in their red Dagodin uniforms. "Should we send out our own patrol to meet them along the road?"

"I don't know about you, Guthrie, but I'm all for it. I'm not willing to risk my son's life if some renegade Dosteri have decided merchants are fair game," Devan said. Where Guthrie's unrestrained eating habits shaped him, years toiling in the cliff quarries and mines marked Devan. Since taking over as mine foreman, he worked even harder, and his boulder shoulders and arms banded with thick muscular slabs had grown. "He may not act his age, but he's still my son," he added.

Guthrie nodded.

A smile, quickly masked, played across Shin Galiana's face. In the bright light provided by the lamps in their sconces around the walls and on the table, she studied the two men. They had always been close, and they would have already discussed this action between them.

"I think you two are exaggerating as usual," Rohan said. Galiana found herself leaning forward to hear the man's thin, reedy voice. "I don't believe the Dosteri would be so bold as to strike this far north. And it's not like our boys cannot protect themselves. They have all almost completed their Dagodin training. As for the rumors from Ostania, the last real threat to us was what…over seventy–five years ago. The Bastions and the Vallum protected us then, and they will now. If the Tribunal felt an army in Ostania was a threat, they would've sent for us."

Rohan took a sip of water when he finished.

Stefan laughed, but neither the sound nor his piercing emerald eyes held any mirth. "The last thing the Tribunal wants is to include us in any plan of the sort. Not only are we old and retired, but have you forgotten who we are? We may have come a long way in our relationship with Granadia, but the Tribunal keeps its plans to itself and protects their interests first. The rest of Denestia is secondary. As for the Dosteri—"

"Which is why I agree with Rohan," Jillian interrupted. The woman had ever been staunch opposition to the Dorns. "If there was a serious threat to Granadia or our children, we would have more than just Shin Galiana here. They also would have sent more than the one High Ashishin for the negotiations." She glanced in Galiana's direction. "No insult intended."

"None taken," Galiana replied. "Continue."

"My eagles have given me no reports of any Dagodin movements other than the recent legions the Tribunal sent across the Vallum. Even then, there's nothing unusual about such a stationing." Today, Jillian was dressed in an extravagant dress with purple, silky folds, split and rejoined between the legs for a billowy, trouser–like effect.

Galiana said nothing, but she knew differently. The Tribunal feared what the Chronicles prophesied: the advent of the shade, an army of Amuni's Children, the return of the Erastonian tribes and the end of the Tribunal's reign. Chaos would follow. So far the first two events may well be occurring if the reports were indeed true. Those Dagodin legions had been deployed well before the first news from Ostania arrived and in far greater numbers than was required for training. And High Shin Jerem had sent Irmina across the Vallum a year prior. Ashishin or not, the girl still had not returned. That in itself troubled her. For all his many secrets, if Jerem said Ancel's survival relied on Irmina's success, then it was so. Sacrifices were sometimes necessary.

"Be that as it may, I feel the same way as Guthrie and Devan." Stefan stood. His soft yet commanding tone and the golden knots on his scarlet uniform commanded attention. "I want to know my son is safe. It's not as if the Dosteri representatives will tell us the truth. But where rumors spread like flies, there must be an inkling of shit. If I have to send my own guards, so be it. I prefer caution when in doubt. I won't feel comfortable until our sons are home."

"Well, we should bring the matter up for vote," Jillian said.

Stefan waved her off. "There's no need for a vote. Either we send a patrol or I'll lead my men from the winery myself."

"B–But what about the kinai crop…the wine…the juice for the Soltide Festival?" Edwin stuttered.

"Soltide can go to Hydae and rot for all I care." The vehemence in Stefan's curse brought gasps from around the room. "This is my son we're talking about here. All of our sons."

"Too bad it has taken our suffering as well as possibly losing a child of your own to feel this way," Jillian said, scowling.

Stefan whirled around, his face mottled with rage. He took several steps toward Jillian until he towered over her. Thania rose to her feet and hustled to her husband's side.

Eyes icy, emerald barbs, Stefan glared down at the scout leader. "Repeat that if you dare."

Jillian opened her mouth, but Shin Galiana had seen enough. "Stop it, both of you," Galiana commanded. "Jillian, we may no longer be in the old lands, but Stefan is still your Lord. Show appropriate respect." Jillian sniffed, but Galiana ignored her and continued, "There's no time for petty arguments. Despite what you feel Jillian, I must agree with the men on this. We have not taken risks in the past three hundred years, and we will not start now. I suggest you send a patrol and your eagles."

Stefan's arms trembled, and his fists clenched. His wife rested her hand on his shoulder as she reached up to whisper into his ear. He caressed her hand in response and gave her fingers a light squeeze. His eyes closed, and a deep, drawn out breath left his lips. When he opened them again, his eyes were serene. Turning away from Jillian, he strode to a window overlooking the Eldan Road.

Thania Dorn looked down on the scout leader, her gray–blue eyes as cool as early morning mist. The lines about her cheeks and lips creased with the hint of a smirk. Her well–tailored silk dress with its linen ruffles swirled about her when, with a parting shake of her head, she joined her husband.

Rising to her feet, and making a point of not looking in Stefan's direction, Jillian said, "I will do as you request, Shin Galiana." After a bow, she strode toward the door. As she twisted the knob, she glanced over her shoulder. "I almost forgot to mention, some fool named Captain Wendel Giomar has been attempting to recruit our youth for Sendeth's squabbles with Doster. I tried to talk to the man, but he is beyond arrogant. I'm sure you've seen him strutting around town."

"Yes, I've heard the complaints from a few," Shin Galiana said. "I shall deal with him." She inclined her head to the others and gestured toward the door. "Now, if the rest of you will excuse me, I need to speak to the Dorns."

Jillian bowed again and left. Chairs scraped and murmurs followed as the other Council Heads said their goodbyes and filed out soon after.

Shin Galiana shuffled to the top of the stairs and made sure they had all descended and left through the Whitewater Inn's front door before she spoke. "So many years and still Jillian has not forgiven you."

"It's only become worse since the Shadowbearer War," Stefan said. He and Thania had taken their seats once more.

"It didn't help when we took her last surviving family member and raised her," Thania added. She tapped a finger to her lips as she spoke. "When Irmina's parents died, Jillian expected she would take the girl in. It would have been folly, but she has never seen it any other way. Sometimes I wonder what will become of her hate for the Dorn clan. When will she realize we may be the last free Setian, that she is a part of the clan, and has been ever since she decided to flee with us to seek safety?" Thania shook her head.

"I still remember trying to soothe Irmina when her parents died," Shin Galiana said as she returned to her seat. "She blames Amuni's Children and the shade as much as she blames the old leaders of the Setian themselves. She has used her hate as fuel for her training."

"It still surprises me that with all her misgivings about the Dorns, Jillian has not yet revealed who I am to Irmina," Stefan said.

"Which is why I keep asking how you and Jerem could send her to Ostania," Thania said. "Who knows where her mind is now, and our Ancel is worse off for it."

"Bah. You know better. You of all people. I can no more change Jerem's mind than I could force water come from a rock.

I did what I could when I learned where he intended to send her."

"I know," Thania said. "I've written to Jerem myself and asked. The response has always been the same. Anything he did should not be questioned, and it was crucial for Ancel and the clan's future."

"Speaking of which, with these reports concerning the sudden rise in aggressive Dosteri tactics, I will assume the negotiations did not go well?" Galiana asked.

Stefan shook his head. "No, they didn't. I don't think the Dosteri ever had any intentions to bargain in good faith. They were more interested in how the Tribunal felt. The High Shin didn't appear to support one faction or the other, insisting they find a way to settle their differences."

"Did you suggest you would give Doster part of our kinai harvests or wine at a highly discounted rate?"

"Yes."

"And what were their replies?"

"They want land allocated to them with several hundred thousand acres worth of kinai crop and our people to tend it."

Galiana raised an eyebrow. "I am sure the Sendethi nobles were not pleased."

"Not in the least," Ryne said. "Their denial was, shall we say, pronounced? After that, the Dosteri walked away from the table. They said they would resolve their issues their own way."

"Well," Galiana said, "I guess that explains this recruiter and the Dosteri actions in Sendeth."

"You promised Ancel would be safe," Stefan said, his voice grim. "We sent him to Randane for that reason. Now that we haven't found any credible threat, I wonder if sending him was the correct decision. We've placed him in the middle of a brewing war."

"He is quite safe, I assure you."

"If my wife didn't insist on my trust in you, or hadn't given him a *divya* token so we know Ancel's alive, I would be dispatching a patrol instead of blowing hot air at the Council so Guthrie and Devan don't send their own men," Stefan admitted.

"Although I do not approve of what you did, Thania," Galiana admonished, "I understand. However, the one we have sent to guard him has yet to fail. Not only will Ancel be safe, but he will return a new man, having put Irmina behind him."

"I still say we should send out a few soldiers from the town watch along with my own men to secure him and his friends in case the Dosteri do the unexpected," Stefan said. "You haven't drilled me in the Disciplines to have me forget them now, Galiana. Your sayings about coincidence and well laid plans are forever etched into my mind."

Galiana smiled. "I am sure they are, but no, do nothing of the sort. Not with Ancel coming into his power. There are more subtle ways to act that would not draw the attention of the Tribunal's Pathfinders here. I have a solution in mind." Tension eased out of Galiana's back as she thought about what she intended.

"Always the secrets." Stefan shook his head. "So what of the other report Edwin brought back?"

"I've sent an eagle with a message to the Tribunal at Coren. I also dispatched a messenger by dartan. As soon as word comes back, we shall know if there is any truth to an attack in Ostania and if shadelings were involved. Until then, all we can do is wait."

"And be cautious," Stefan added. "I have an ill feeling about all this."

"My dear husband, you always have an ill feeling."

Stefan shrugged. "If you say so, my dear heart. What about this Giomar? We ought not to sully our good relations with the King, but this recruitment cannot be allowed."

"My solution will see Giomar handled while taking every precaution with the boys." Galiana couldn't help the smile on her face at the frowns on the Dorns'. "As you said, Stefan, deception has always been my strongpoint. Now, unless there is something else you wish to discuss, I must see to this Captain Giomar."

The Dorns shook their heads and stood. Galiana followed suit.

"With Ilumni's Blessings, until the next time," they intoned almost as one with bows to each other. They left the Whitewater Inn.

CHAPTER 28

Galiana shivered despite the warm breath of wind that stirred the dust along the Eldan Road's cobbles. Although dawn tinted the sky to the east, blue lights still illuminated the streets and buildings. To the north, above the Kelvore Mountains, dark clouds boiled and lightning flashed as a storm brewed unlike any in recent memory. And it was not yet winter. There was still a whole season to go before northern Granadia should be seeing its usual fierce winter weather.

The reported events in Ostania were forcing her to move sooner than she wanted. Something she didn't much like. Added to those events were the recent reports of merchants murdered by Dosteri from Sendeth to as far south as Ishtar and its port cities. After each killing, they left a quote from the Chronicle of Undeath. Could this be Jerem's doing? If so, it was certainly a risky maneuver considering the Pathfinders were already inquiring about students from the Mysteras across Granadia. Why draw more attention? Would that not lead to greater scrutiny?

In some ways, she could understand why Jerem would see it as a sound strategy. Not only would these killings, which were spread over a great area, delay the Tribunal's Pathfinders, but the Chronicle of Undeath and any knowledge of Mater fascinated Ancel. This could function as a way to draw him back into his studies. But at what cost? Sacrificing someone to guide Ancel was one thing, but risking his discovery was folly. One issue was clear. If this was not Jerem's actions, then she needed to take any possible measure she could in case the Dosteri had indeed infiltrated this far north into Sendeth.

Galiana was so deep in thought, she hardly noticed the early risers around her going about their daily activities. Or those hurrying along to early morning prayers at the Streamean temple. She raised her hand or nodded her head out of habit as she traveled down the street. Not even the clangor from a blacksmith's hammer interrupted her musing. Preoccupied by her thoughts, Galiana arrived at Eldanhill's south end.

She gazed across a field at the regiment's encampment. Torches stood out on tall posts, and patrols strolled around the perimeter. Standards displaying a black boar charging across a green pasture under blue skies flew from many tents. Others had the banners and flags from minor nobles flapping in the light breeze. Next to those, and flying higher still, was the Silver Spear—a fist enclosed around a shining lance set against a black backdrop—King Emory of Sendeth's banner.

Galiana shambled toward the tents, relying heavily on her staff. Her fingers tightened on the weathered wood at the thought of this Captain Giomar adding to the present troubles. She did not appreciate having her hand forced like this.

Today, she'd made sure to wear her long, flowing crimson dress with the one silver sleeve and its short, white stripes. Five stripes marked her as one rank below a member of the Tribunal. Embroidered onto the breast in gold and white was the Lightstorm insignia. She hoped they would be enough to serve her purpose.

She headed across grass flattened by constant travel toward the largest tan structure, more a pavilion than a tent, positioned at the encampment's center. It was one of the few with light inside. The Charging Boar and the Silver Spear flew at the same height in front the tent. A sign of this man, Giomar's arrogance, to fly his standard the same height as the King's.

To one side of the field, dartans picketed in neat lines stamped and mewled impatiently. One of Eldanhill's small dogs barked at the creatures, until they showed their fangs, trilled a warning reply and tore at reeking pieces of meat piled on the ground. The dog ducked its head, whimpered, and slunk away, its tail between its legs.

Soldiers, in blue and green or gold surcoats emblazoned with the Charging Boar and worn over chainmail, moved about the camp with a purposeful bustle. Lancers, in burnished armor, practiced formations under the supervision of a stern–faced man–at–arms. Another group copied sword forms taught by a swordmaster. A few dozen murmurs followed her as she passed, but no one questioned her. Several soldiers knuckled their forehead, or nodded slightly, and she acknowledged them in kind. Hopefully, she could affect the Captain in the same manner and with as much ease. From what she'd heard, the man brandished his insolence as much as his sword. Like so many others accustomed to command, he wouldn't be easily intimidated, and he was loyal to a fault.

Therein lay her biggest obstacle—his blind loyalty to the King. The same King who had made his displeasure with the Tribunal's lack of direct interference to resolve the issues between Sendeth and Doster abundantly clear. In fact, he went so far as to declare his dislike for the Tribunal and Matii as a whole. In his words, if they wouldn't help him, then why should he tolerate them? He was not the first ruler to make such a declaration, but once the Tribunal turned their attention on those monarchs, they had a habit of changing their minds. All this meant she would need to give Giomar a stiff reminder of her status. There was something to be said for small dogs with big barks.

She stopped at the tent's entrance where a grizzle–faced, bone of a man stood at the slit for a doorway. His eyes shifted as his gaze followed her, but nothing else moved. She announced herself as Ashishin Galiana, Eldanhill's mender and a Teacher. The man blinked. He nodded and ducked inside to relay her arrival. Returning shortly after, he beckoned her in. She shuffled inside past the guard, and he let the flap fall behind him.

Captain Giomar stood next to a table poring over Granadian maps by lamplight. Among the maps and papers, she noticed a half–rolled glossy sheet of paper with the King's Seal.

The spacious pavilion contained two other tables, a bedroll, and a stand with a black and green suit of armor embossed with the Charging Boar on the chest. One table held food—two roasted quails, bread, gooseberries, kinai fruit and two pitchers filled with wine, one yellow, and one red. A longsword rested on the other table along with gauntlets, greaves, and a gorget, all matching the armor on the stand.

"Good day, Mender Galiana, or would you prefer Teacher Galiana. Better yet, Shin Galiana?" he asked, in a smooth tone without taking his eyes from the maps. A smirk played across his lips. "I tend to forget myself sometimes when it comes to addressing your kind. I seem to have a difficult time deciding which title is appropriate. You tend to have so many it can be quite confusing to one as simple as myself."

She dismissed the man's blatant attempt at disrespect, refusing to let any emotion show as she stepped up to the table. "You shall address me as Shin Galiana."

Giomar straightened to his full height. Any other time, she would have chuckled at the man now towering over her. Men often felt their great size and height over women affected a meetings' outcome. She smiled inwardly with the thought and leaned even more heavily on her staff. Most men could be such fools. He strode from behind the table with a smooth, arrogant grace, his beady eyes studying her. She met his gaze with a blank expression.

"My humble apologies, Shin Galiana. Although, I thought the title of Shin was reserved for those still in active service. Anyway, where are my manners? May I offer you a drink?" She shook her head, and he continued, "I always wondered what became of you Matii once you were of no more use. Imagine my surprise when I discovered you're relegated to teaching young pups in the most obscure parts of Granadia."

"Let me guess, you could not muster a good enough score to be admitted to one of our Mysteras." Galiana said, unblinking. "So you resort to snide remarks in hopes you can bruise a Matus' pride while your envy is plain to see." She shook her head in disdain.

Giomar smiled mirthlessly. "I have no envy toward the Matii. You're as good as any other watch dog. You keep the nobility safe from the other dregs of society. You enforce the iron rule of the Tribunal and maintain the blessings of the Streamean temples. I simply feel you should be treated no different than a wolf hound. Once its day is done, the animal needs to be put to pasture. Why King Emory allows your school in Sendeth is beyond me. And if you are still a Shin, rather than one of these so called Teachers," he almost spat the last words, "tell me, why are you in Eldanhill? There are no nobles to be protected in this useless town."

"Despite what you may think, it is an Ashishin's duty to

represent all. Whether they are lowly peasants, soldiers led by an overzealous Captain, or the King himself. Everyone is afforded the same protection and counsel," Galiana said.

The lines about his eyes tightened, and a fire flickered in them for a brief second. *Good, now he knows where I stand as far as he and King Emory are concerned.*

The dark haired man schooled his face to calm as he replied, "It seems the King's name does not ring out as it should within the Whitewater Falls despite it being part of Sendeth."

"The people here do not take kindly to badgering, not even from the King's men."

"Are you saying their refusal was warranted?"

"I'm saying Whitewater Falls folk and those in Eldanhill in particular have provided more than their fair share to the King's coffers. That has never changed. Not when they suffered the worst winter storms in years or when pestilence struck their crops. As such, they should be treated with respect. Yet, you approached them with hostility and demands as if they were beggars and thieves. What did you expect? Wine, women, and song?"

Giomar shrugged, but the lines about his eyes tightened. "I expected them to obey. Everyone faces trials and tribulations, but there's one defining constant. This entire area is within Sendeth's borders, and thus under the King's rule. I am but an extension of the King's arm, and he decreed I should recruit, so I obey."

"Is that the excuse you used for trying to secretly recruit Eldanhill's youth without their parents' permission?"

"You're all part of Sendeth, aren't you?"

"I see you miss my point or you are simply a blind fool. I'm positive King Emory advised you of my presence here. But, you decided to do as you wished in his name. Only idiocy could promote such an action."

Giomar scowled, his face becoming a dark shade of red. "I would watch my mouth if I were you. The Tribunal has decreed they will not interfere with the local government within the kingdoms, and this is a local matter, Ashishin." He hawked and spat to the side. "My orders were to seek new recruits, and I will leave with as many as I deem necessary."

"About new recruits," Shin Galiana held the man's gaze

and hardened her voice, "You will not recruit Eldanhill folk." She drew herself up until she no longer leaned on her staff. Giomar's eyes widened. "I shall send word to the capital to address the people's concerns about recruitment. You and your men can make yourselves useful by keeping Eldanhill safe in the meantime. I'm sure you have heard the rumors."

Giomar's body stiffened at her command, and he strode to the pavilion's other side. "Galiana, is this the Council's decision?" The air in the tent stilled as he turned to face her, his eyes blue ice, his hands balled into fists. "If so, it is treason against the realm to deny a royal decree."

"Treason?" Curling her lips in as contemptuous a smile as she could manage, she allowed Giomar's anger to wash over her. "Captain, is it? You seem to have lofty goals for a man of your rank. Well, I suggest you allow me to assist you with them."

"Gal—"

She waved her hand and cut him off. "The decision was made by me, Ashishin Galiana Calestis as the Tribunal's representative here in Eldanhill." She refused to allow the man any attempt to recover. He needed to be humiliated. "Should you," she paused, pointing a finger at the man, "choose to meddle in the Tribunal's affairs, rather than provide Eldanhill with protection, you will feel mine and their wrath."

"How dare—"

"Before you utter another word, Giomar." She realized now her words nor her uniform would be enough. She gave the essences around them a subtle touch. "You say you possess a royal decree, yes?"

Giomar's face bloomed almost purple with the struggle to restrain himself. He gave her a single nod.

"Good. You should know every decree bears the Seal of Light, approved and signed by the Tribunal. Yes?" She dipped her head slightly. The man nodded, his skin flushed as if was choking. "Every Royal decree contains instructions on who could override its order and who should be treated with as much respect as the King himself. I suggest you look at your Seal."

As she spoke, she made a delicate Forging. A slight amount of water from one of the pitchers on his table, a tiny amount of dust to give it substance, and the singular shade she could touch to give her creation its color.

Giomar reached among the maps on the table and picked up the half–rolled sheet of glossy paper she'd noticed earlier. Unrolling the lower part, he uncovered the Seal and the names listed there. His eyes narrowed, and then he gaped.

"Overstep your bounds Giomar, and you shall answer to me," Shin Galiana said in a soft tone.

"Yes, Blessed High Shin. My humble apologies, Blessed High Shin." Giomar's words almost tripped over each other with not a single hint of divisiveness attached. His shoulders slumped, and he looked as if he lost a foot or more in height.

Galiana smiled. With Giomar's spirit broken, her task became simple. "Now, here is what you shall do. This year we sent an unusually large amount of kinai wine and juice to King Emory. As the Dosteri have decided to slay Sendethi merchants, we would not want one of our own to be mistaken as such. You would not want them to lay their hands on Lord Loriz after the failure of the negotiations. Yes?"

Giomar's face blanched. He nodded weakly.

Galiana continued, her voice soft but nonetheless filled with the authority the Captain expected. "You will leave Eldanhill at once and proceed toward Randane to escort the Lord as normal. Your purpose will be twofold. See to his safety and make sure the Eldan Road is safe from here to the capital, sending men to escort any of our people you may meet on the road. You will maintain the King's peace for at least two weeks."

"Yes, Blessed High Shin," Giomar answered as if in a trance, his gaze locked on the Seal.

Now, for the most important and delicate part. "You will forget we had this conversation or that my name is on the Seal. When asked you will state your actions are a part of your orders to strengthen the King's regiment." She couldn't help but smile. The man's own blind loyalty would be his undoing.

"I hear and obey, High One," Giomar intoned. He bowed from his waist.

Galiana gave him a mere dip of her head and strode from the tent.

She left the stunned man still staring at where he thought he saw her name signed after the King's on the royal decree.

CHAPTER 29

Ancel and Ryne retreated from the army of shadelings surrounding them. Ten thousand throats wailed. The army washed over them in a black wave.

Irmina started awake. Yet, she couldn't see. No, that wasn't entirely true. She could see, but her eyes wouldn't open. Raising her brow to force her lids apart made no difference. They refused to budge. Brightness shone through the skin of her lids as if someone held a torch inches above her eyes. She would've pried them open with her fingers if her hands didn't also refuse to do as she bid. With each failure, her heart raced, and her breaths came in short, panicked gasps.

Perspiration poured down her face, and chills wracked her body. Despite the sweat, she felt as if she stood outside during one of Eldanhill's fierce winters.

Take a hold of yourself, woman. She reached for that cold place deep within her mind and found calm.

Her concern drifted to the rest of her body. She was in her small clothes. From the smell, someone had changed her bandages. The wounds no longer lanced with pain as they did earlier, and their ache was now a dull throb. Something soft, maybe layered furs or rugs, lay beneath her, a blanket hugged her body, and a pillow cushioned her head. She again attempted to open her eyes, but managed no more than a flutter. When she tried to push up onto her elbows, she failed.

She would have frowned if she could. The last she remembered, she, Ormand, and two surviving Dagodin Knights were fleeing toward the Vallum of Light. *Why am I now in a bed?*

Attempting to conjure a memory of how she arrived here proved futile. Something rustled above her. She held her breath. Fingers like old leather stroked her face.

"Shin Irmina, you must rest. Go back to sleep," commanded a motherly voice tinged with steel.

Irmina didn't recognize the woman. In her mind, she frowned. *No one commands me.* She made another attempt to rise to her elbows and tell this person as much. She barely managed to twitch a few fingers and her leg. Nothing more. Helplessness overwhelmed her. Unbidden tears welled up in her eyes, and her mind drifted to Ancel. She wished he was there to help.

"You will be fine, young Shin. I will take good care of you. Rest," the woman coaxed.

The voice sounded so sincere, so tender, Irmina couldn't help the contented smile that played across her lips. She obeyed. The brightness outside her eyelids faded.

Irmina woke from another fitful dream. This time, her eyes eased open. Morning sunlight drifted through a window across from where she lay upon a few soft furs. Her wounds no longer ached, and she felt no stiffness. The room smelled of old blood, herbs and mending. The odor reminded her of Galiana's hospice back in Eldanhill.

Glancing down, she saw she was now dressed in the crimson and gold uniform of a Raijin. Her legs were covered in tight leathers that reached high up her thighs, and a leather skirt split on both sides to give an apron like effect covered her waist and loins. A belt with several *divya* discs to collect and store Mater kept the skirt in place. Light, elaborately crafted gold and red chainmail hid her breasts, but left her stomach exposed for ease of movement. The same pliant armor—rerebrace on the upper arm and vambrace on the lower, crafted as one with plate mail at the elbow for added protection—covered her arms up to her finger–less leather gloves.

"Ah," the motherly voice called, "Finally, you wake from your long rest."

Instinct taking over, Irmina reached for her sword but found nothing.

The voice chuckled. "Your weapon and your Ashishin and Raijin pins are over here. You may take them at your leisure."

Irmina sat up with a grimace.

Sitting in a chair on the other side of the room was a woman dressed in homespun linen. She was so old she appeared more like one of the ancients or crones from a story. What hair she did have was as white as sun bleached bones and hung in sparse wisps about her wrinkled face. Her bald patches bore speckled brown splotches, some the size of a coin. Her arms were frail things that looked as if they belonged on some featherless bird. Her skin had the appearance of old, cracked leather.

"Who are you?" Irmina asked, eyes narrowing into slits.

"Only the person who saved you, dearest Shin." The old crone's words broke into a toothless cackle, her watery white eyes shifting unnaturally.

Irmina fought the apprehension knotting her stomach. "No. Your name," she said, trying to sound braver than she felt as she studied the woman. Whenever their gazes met, Irmina glanced away. *Stop it. Look her in the eye.*

"Names are of no importance, but if you must, you can call me Tae." She flung Irmina's sword and pins to her with a strength beyond her apparent fragility.

They landed next to Irmina. She eased her hand over until it rested on the comfort of sword's pommel. Her gaze still locked on the woman, she picked up the weapon and the insignias. Savoring the feel of the hilt against her palm, she stood, belted on the scabbard and stuck the pins to the leather patch woven into the pliant chainmail pauldrons at her shoulder. As she did so, visions from her dreams assaulted her. Each appeared more real than the next. From her office, to the shadelings' attack, the fight with Jaecar, her Forgings and her flight from Ranoda. Recognition of each grew. They were no mere visions, she realized, they were real. Her head throbbed.

"Where am I?" Irmina massaged her temple through the mass of her dark hair.

"You're somewhere safe."

"How long have I been here? And where are my men?"

"Long enough," Tae said. "As for your men…" Her smile was a dark slit. "They're dead. They gave their lives for you."

Irmina stiffened, ice freezing her veins with Tae's words.

"What do you mean?"

"Think about it," Tae said. "I know you remember. You were dying. So were they. You needed to live. They didn't. So I did as needed. I fed them to you."

Irmina's stomach lurched, and bile rushed up into her mouth in a bitter torrent. Retching, she bent over. No. This woman had to mean something different. Right hand tight around her sword's hilt, Irmina wiped the acrid taste from her mouth with her left.

When she managed to speak, Irmina's voice was hoarse and cracked. "Speak so I can understand, woman. How do you mean, you fed them to me?" She opened her Matersense. A tingle of anticipation tugged at her as she prepared to Forge.

Around the room, the essences beckoned. She couldn't help the gasp that escaped her mouth as her sight passed over Tae. A staggering mass of essences gathered about the woman. More than she'd ever seen even around Jerem when he touched the elements.

Tae gave a knowing smirk. "You nor your men didn't escape. You were allowed to go. A test of sorts to see how well the shade's weapons worked. You were all poisoned by the shade's taint. You were either going to die and be used as fodder, or you yourself were going to be transformed into shadelings."

"Impossible," Irmina managed to whisper, her voice a disembodied shell of itself. The news of shadeling creation caused the essences she saw around the old woman to shatter into a million pieces as she lost her grip on her Matersense.

"Who's to say what's possible? Be that as it may. That's where you were headed, or into the belly of the beast."

Somehow, Irmina found a breath despite the lump caught in her throat. "I–If this is true, then h–how did you save me? Why couldn't you save them?"

"Aha. There lies the question. You needed an infusion of sela essence to drive the taint from your body. It didn't matter where it came from, as long as you received it. I couldn't save you all, so I did the most prudent thing. I fed their sela to you."

"You're—" Irmina wheezed, before she sitting down flat on the furs, any semblance of reason or coherence fleeing her mind. She clawed for a sense of calm to grasp the elements again, but her dread had a steel grip on her senses.

"A daemon? A Skadwaz? Fear not my dear, I'm neither."

Irmina could only sit and stare. Finally, she found words. "Then how...?"

"It's an ancient art." Tae chuckled. "I would say lost, but that wouldn't be true would it? Well, as you see, I'm very old." Tae's eyes changed colors rapidly from gold to green to white to blue.

Irmina fought against the urge to crawl away, but she couldn't help cringing as the memory of Sakari's eyes came to life. Something inside her made her believe Tae. Why would the woman save her only to kill her now? At last, when she found a sense of calm, she asked, "Why has no one used such a skill before?"

Tae arched an eyebrow at her. "You're presumptuous, aren't you? Who says no one has? If you could do it, you could live for a thousand years."

Irmina covered her open mouth with her hand. "You're speaking about the Tribunal aren't you? An–And the Eldanhill Council leaders."

Both of Tae's eyebrows rose. "Am I?"

"Are you?"

"Infusions of Mater could accomplish the same thing. If you knew how to make people ingest enough. Even those who couldn't possibly touch the elements." Tae smiled wickedly, her brown gums failing to come together, leaving a dark hole in her mouth.

Irmina frowned. What could she be hinting at? She'd discovered just how old the members of Eldanhill's Council and members of the Tribunal were. Some could be traced back at least a millennia according to the records she'd smuggled from among the Pathfinders. How they'd accomplished such a feat was unclear. "Why are you telling me all this?"

"Because one day soon, my dear Shin, you will need to use this knowledge to save many lives."

"When? What can I do against Matii who are practically immortal."

Tae chortled, a carefree rasp of a sound of someone trying to hide amusement but failing. "Dear, dear one." She shook her head, her mouth split again in a morbid grin. "No one is immortal. Hard to kill? Yes. Immortal? No." She chortled again. "Relieve a person of their head or their heart. No one can survive that. Destroying their brain works just as well too." She subsided to a low chuckle before she cut off.

Irmina's expression soured. "If it's so simple why don't you do it? Why tell me?"

"Because my part in this is done for now. As for you, you're special as you well know. As your parents and much of your lineage were before you. It's why the shade sought them out."

Irmina trembled with the mention of her parents in the same breath as the shade. Her anger lent her strength. "What do you know of them?" she spat. "They walked in the Ilumni's light and were murdered to hide the Tribunal's secrets."

Tae shrugged. "I know much. However, I'm not allowed to involve myself further than the message I need you to deliver."

"What message?"

Tae's eyes and voice became grim. "You must repeat my message exactly as I will tell you."

Taken aback by the intense expression on the old woman's face, Irmina offered a nod.

"Tell Jerem one among Amuni's Children not only can use, but has perfected the Bloodline Affinity. Tell him they've taken Kahkon."

"Gods be good," Irmina whispered. For the second time, she found her mouth agape. Not just because this woman knew her master, but because the Bloodline Affinity was a powerful Forging used by Pathfinders to track those they sought. Once triggered, they could retrace not only a person's entire lineage but also any living kin.

But no one had ever mastered it.

Just to use such a skill, the person would need to be at least as strong as a High Ashishin. To master the ability would require someone stronger. The thought of one so powerful among Amuni's Children chilled her to her core.

"I see you understand what this means."

Dumbfounded, Irmina nodded.

"Good. I would expect nothing less from one of Jerem's students." Tae tilted her head to one side. Her eyes slipped through their many changes before focusing on something Irmina couldn't see. Tae cleared her throat in annoyance. "They've brought one who can sense me. It's time you leave."

In desperation, Irmina pleaded, "Please, no. Not yet. Tell me what you know of my family."

"That is not for me to tell."

"Then why mention them?" Irmina's voice was shrill. "Why tell me this now? Why not inform the Tribunal or some High Ashishin? If they're those among Amuni's Children as strong as you say, who know the secrets of the Bloodline, who can transform people into shadelings, why did they wait until now?"

"Harmony, my dear. There hasn't been enough power, enough Mater, in Denestia, or in any of the realms to begin such an undertaking. Not since the gods were sealed in the Nether thousands of years ago."

"And now there is?"

"See? You're catching on."

"How come?"

"Ah, my dear. That's where I have to draw the line without breaking the rules. It's time to go. Don't worry, the shade won't find you. I'll scatter your scent to the thirty–two winds. Ride for the Vallum of Light. And avoid the Bastions. You wouldn't want to draw the attention of the Pathfinders while you're on this side of the wall. Oh, one more thing. Tell Jerem we're even."

With those words, Irmina's world swirled and went black. Before she could react, a sensation came as if a great wind snatched her and threw her from a mountaintop. Heart racing, an unreleased scream stuck in her throat, her stomach attempting to spew its contents, she fell.

And lurched to a head–snapping stop. Black became light. Light slowly evolved into the world once more. When she came to her senses, she was unsure of her location.

Far off, a speck in the distance, a bright line sparkled and followed the land along the horizon. She knew that line. The Vallum. Attached to the wall and rising into the air another hundred feet was one of the Bastions of Light.

CHAPTER 30

A ncel kicked at a rat crawling across his filthy boots. Boots he'd taken from a dead soldier. The rodent's squeal joined the multitude of squeaks around him. He didn't need to look hard to see the numerous rats, some almost as big as man's thigh, that scurried along the sewer tunnel. Covering his nose and mouth against the overwhelming stench of shit, sludge, mud, and only the Pits of Hydae knew what else, that clung to his boots and pants almost to his waist was futile. The air stank worse than a week old corpse. Breathing served to have the odor become a foul taste.

They had made good their escape through the canals and into the extensive drainage system under Randane. Dodged patrols, loud footsteps, shushed breaths, shadowy hiding places, and incessant bell tolls filled their flight. When they couldn't escape a patrol's path, Kachien commanded them to stand still wherever they hid, often around the corner in some alley and against a building. Tense moments edged on achingly as the soldiers would run by, passing them as if they were not standing in plain sight.

Mirza and Danvir huddled nearby, their forms silhouetted against the light provided by the tunnel's opening. Outside, the rain fell in glinting sheets, and lightning crackled across the dark quilt of clouds covering the heavens and blotting out any signs of the morning sun. Separating the three of them from Kachien was a knee–deep flow of filth. At all times, Charra kept himself between Ancel and her.

There had been no chance to speak during their escape,

and in fact, this was their first respite. Still, Ancel refused to talk to the woman. Not that he didn't want to, but whereas his Kachien had been a tender, breathtaking, seductive flower with more than a touch of flame, this woman, this killer, was as hard as silversteel and colder than the Kelvore Mountains' highest peak.

Six times on their way here, she'd slunk off to kill a patrolling regimental guard. Each time, she returned impassive and wordless. Not once did she shy away from Ancel's accusatory gaze. He found it was he who broke contact whenever their eyes made four. *How can you possibly be the same woman who shared your fears and tears with me?*

"What've we done? What've we done? Gods be good, what've we done?" Danvir muttered.

"Survived," Mirza answered, his voice thick.

"No." Danvir trembled. "We killed men. Merchant's guards. Do you know what that means? We murdered them."

"It means you saved my life and probably Ancel's too. The guard was going to run me through if you and Charra hadn't interfered." Mirza's gaze shifted to Kachien for a brief moment. He sounded steadier by a hair than Ancel felt until his voice cracked. "A—And without her, the rest of them would've finished us. I—I thought I was dead for sure." His eyes shone with wetness in the dim light. He scrubbed at his face.

"What happened up there?" Ancel gestured outside with a nod, rubbing at his folded arms as he thought about what he heard and saw. "All I remember is them hitting me, then Charra's growls and the sound of fighting."

"You resisted and they beat you." Mirza's voice regained some of its normal smoothness. "Then one sliced at me just as Danvir and Charra leaped on him. Your woman showed up then. And well, you saw the results."

"Why'd it have to come to that?" Danvir's words were a hoarse whine. "What did you two do?"

"Us?" Ancel gave him an incredulous stare. "We did nothing. We heard the screaming and ran outside. When we got there we saw someone huddled over the merchant." He glanced at Kachien. "The guards found us in the alley and thought we did it. Although Master Callan told them different, they wouldn't listen. They tried to arrest us."

"Why'd you have to fight?" Danvir moaned. "Look what

you made me do." He looked down at his hands, horror written across his face. "The King's regiment could've easily settled the matter when they arrived. They would've known you had nothing to do with the killings."

Ancel shook his head. Their encounter and flight replayed through his head. "You don't get it, do you? At first, I thought they were just merchant's guards. But in all the running here, I realized they wore the same armor and emblems as the King's men. The Silver Spear, the Charging Boar, the Mailed Fist, the Leaping Hound, the Hunter's Bow, the Executioner's Axe. All the King's men."

"That doesn't make sense," Mirza said. "Why'd they think we had something to do with the killings?"

"They did not," Kachien said. Her voice had its usual lilt, but she sounded much more in command, harder. Her gaze locked onto Ancel. "Those who seek you grew tired of me killing everyone they sent. So they chose to have the King's guards do their work."

"What?" Ancel couldn't help his shocked expression.

"Who's after him? Better yet, why?" Mirza asked.

"Neither is for me to say. I simply follow orders."

"Listen, you whore!" Mirza snarled, utter disdain twisting his features. "When Teacher Calestis asked me—"

A slap rang out. Ancel hadn't seen Kachien move. One moment she stood on the opposite side of the stream of waste, and the next, she was in front of Mirza, backhanding him.

"You will learn to respect me." Kachien kept her hand raised for a moment before lowering it.

Charra released a low growl and shifted position slightly. Without thinking, Ancel reached out and grabbed a handful of fur.

Sullen–faced, Mirza rubbed at his cheek. "I–I'm sorry," he muttered.

Charra strained against Ancel's grip, but he held firm. "What were your orders?"

"To protect you even if it should cost me my life." Kachien remained neutral, almost bored, as if reciting an instruction to continue travelling in one direction over another.

Danvir was still blubbering in the background about killing a man. His eyes shifted constantly, and they were blank, lost.

"Slap your friend," Kachien said with an annoyed glance in the broad-shouldered young man's direction.

"Why would—" Ancel began.

Another slap rang out. Mirza shrugged in response to Ancel's glare. The muttering stopped, and Danvir peered down at them as if he woke from a dream.

Kachien stared at him, her yellow-brown eyes glowing in the dim light. "Do you wish to see your home again?" Danvir nodded. "Good. Then act like a man. You saved your friends' lives. If not for you and the pet, they would be dead. Killing is never easy, especially not your first. Weather the storm. Think of the good you have done to save them."

"Why did we need to kill them?" Danvir whispered.

"Because they were bad men. Evil. Their kind needs killing. You will soon see."

Ancel couldn't believe this was the sweet girl he had taken to. "Who gave you orders to protect me?"

"Shin Galiana Calestis."

Danvir and Ancel gaped. Mirza had no reaction.

"She's a Teacher," Ancel blurted. "She hasn't been a Shin in over twenty years."

"If you say so," Kachien answered, but her face left no doubt as to what she thought. "I shall tell you as much as I am allowed. Some time ago, Amuni's Children crossed from the Rotted Forest. They—"

"So now you're trying to convince us with some peddler's tall story?" Ancel made the contempt in his voice plain.

"No," Kachien said, "With the truth. They destroyed several towns and clans. Mine included. Unfortunately for me, I was sent to protect a boy and watch a man at a village named Carnas in Ostania." Kachien's voice wavered. "Because of that, when my people were massacred I was not there to die with them in honor. They were the second family I have lost."

"What happened to this boy and man?" Ancel asked, oblivious to the change in her state.

"I failed to protect the boy. They took him. So I was summoned here and instructed to protect you. I was told if I failed again to take my own life."

Ancel snorted his disbelief. "As simple as that?"

"Yes. Still, if you do not believe me about your teacher," her eyes shifted to Mirza, "You can ask him."

Ancel's eyes almost popped out of his head. Then he remembered Mirza's earlier outburst. The meek expression on his friend's face said the rest.

Danvir stared as much as Ancel did. "Is it true, Mirz?"

Mirza fidgeted for a bit, then he squeezed his eyes shut, inhaled deeply, and opened them again. "Yes. I mean, I'm not sure of the bits about Amuni's Children, but what she said about Shin Galiana is true." Mirza's body deflated with the confession.

Seeing his friend's face was one thing, but hearing Mirza actually confess brought a sudden anger coursing through Ancel. "Why didn't you tell me?" He balled his hands into tight fists, fingernails digging painfully into his palms as he tried to focus on anything other than hitting his friend.

"I–I wanted to. But I couldn't. She ordered me not to." Mirza scrubbed at his face again. "What was I to do? You tell me. Someone who you knew as a Teacher reveals they're still a full Ashishin following the Tribunal's orders. What choice would you have?"

"What'd she tell you to do?" Ancel's lip curled.

"She said she knew how concerned we all were for how you've been lately, since, you know…" Ancel nodded. Mirza continued, "Well, she told me to make sure you met her." Mirza gestured with his head to Kachien.

Mirza's story made sense. *He knows I love learning about Ostania. And that I can't resist a challenge. No wonder he took the bet.* His anger still smoldering, Ancel turned to Kachien. "So it was all a lie then? Everything between us?"

Kachien looked away. When she spoke, her voice was quiet. "Yes. At first."

Ancel's world crumbled. The colors he experienced the last few days swirled across his vision. They roiled all around Kachien and the others. Even the filth within the drain glowed. He closed his eyes and shuddered. Remembering what Kachien told him, he sought the calm he used when he trained by forcing all his emotions into the deep pools within his mind until they became a light buzz. A sense of emptiness filled him, and he opened his eyes.

Kachien tilted her head. "Do you remember what happened when we…" Her voice trailed off, and she looked at the ground.

Ancel's answer slipped out before he could think. "Y–Yes, I do."

"Well, the power you have, Amuni's Children want it. They desire you enough to have brought whatever shadelings escaped with them into the Broken Lands back across the Rotted Forest. And whatever they want, the shade wants."

"How could you know this?"

"I did not. Not until you told me, and I felt what happened at the river. Whatever power came alive in you then, someone else here must have sensed it before. Remember what I told you about controlling your power. About what my people practiced. I am not supposed to be telling you this much, but…" Her gaze rose to meet his once more. "At first, you were a task, and like most men, a slave to your lust, to your weakness for female flesh. The best way for me to get close to you was in the bed. The other part of what I did was to help you grow. By bringing out your emotions I could help your power along."

The words stung and added to the empty space in Ancel's head and chest.

"But you became more than that." Kachien's face wrinkled in confusion. She heaved a sigh. "I have never had a man touch me the way you have. Make me feel the way you do. This is something new for me. All the others are just sex and me keeping up my disguise." She closed her eyes as if it had taken everything for her to make such an admittance.

"Fuck. You," Ancel growled. "No one is that hardened. Now, I'm supposed to believe someone may be after me from this side of the Vallum also? Why should I believe anything you've said. You've already proven how well you can lie. You all have." He scowled at them.

"Not me," Danvir protested.

Ancel spared him a glare that could have shattered glass.

"If I wanted you dead, you would be." Tears flowed down Kachien's cheeks as her impassive tone wilted. "If I wanted to take you, I could have done so outside the city, and no one would have known. Where I am from, you must be hard to survive or the land breaks you. If I did not feel as I feel, I could act if you were nothing. But I cannot." She wiped at her face.

A part of Ancel wanted to doubt Kachien, but the look on her face touched him. He remembered all the time they spent together, the dinners, the music, their laughter, and lovemaking. That couldn't all be a lie? Could it?

Outside, the storm raged, and the winds howled. Rain drummed harder and lightning rippled angrily.

"I believe her," Mirza said, the sudden flashes illuminating his grim face. "I've kept it to myself all this time. But when Mother died my father would have nightmares for weeks after. He often talked in his sleep. He'd always say he was sorry to my mother over and over again. He blamed himself. One night, he mentioned how if he knew Pathfinders would've come for mother he would've ran away. When—"

"Pathfinders?" Danvir blurted. "Why would Pathfinders take your mother? She never used Mater to break the law." He paused, a questioning expression on his face. "Or did she?"

"No," Mirza said firmly, but his voice echoed his pain. "Mother never did any such thing. When I asked my father about it, he made me swear not to say a word. He said if I ever did, to anyone, they'd take me next. I still remember that night. How he cried."

"What'd he say?" Ancel asked.

"That Mother lost control. He said at her age, it sometimes happens, so the Pathfinders came to take her where she wouldn't be a danger to anyone. It's the reason I've always pleaded with you to continue your training. I'd hate for the Pathfinders to come for you too."

"Mirz, I...I...This can't be real. Only criminals need fear the Pathfinders. Why would they—" Ancel remembered the conversation with Kachien then. How she asked about those who lacked emotional control, or those who failed the trials, or touched Mater on their own without training. His doubts withered and died.

"Besides she saved my life," Ancel heard Mirza say as he regained his focus. "Ancel, I believe what we saw in the Greenleaf Forest *were* wraithwolves?"

Kachien's attention snapped to Mirza. "Where? Here in Granadia?"

"Yes. Near our home."

She shook her head. "No. I doubt they were. Shadelings cannot cross the Vallum of Light."

Mirza gave a snort. "If you asked me several years ago, I would've said Pathfinders are good people, not some all powerful Ashishins who come and snatch your loved ones in the night. Until today, I believed Amuni's Children wanting Ancel and the shade appearing again was impossible too. Not anymore."

"Let's not jump to conclusions," Ancel implored. "If my father said they weren't wraithwolves then we should believe him."

"Like he told you the truth about yourself? About why they sent you here?"

Glowering, Ancel balled his hands into fists. The mere suggestion his father was somehow involved in this mess made his blood boil. Again, he subdued his emotions.

"You know, you're my friend, Ancel. My best friend. But you can be naïve at times," Mirza added.

"He's right," Danvir said.

"Listen, if *Shin* Galiana knew about her and asked her to come protect you, then it's obvious your father knew." Mirza turned his hands palm upward. "It makes me wonder what else they're hiding."

"Regardless," Ancel said, his voice tight as he resisted the temptation to touch his mother's pendant, "We need to head home. That's the only place we'll find answers. And the only place I'll be safe. What do you suggest, Kachien?"

"There is a way out." She pointed outside into the pouring rain. "We need to cross this canal to the tunnels on the other side. They lead to the river. I shall warn you now. You will need to swim and dive near the end."

Ancel almost gagged at the prospect of swimming and being submerged in the canal's filthy water.

"So what're we waiting for?" Danvir took a step toward the tunnel's entrance.

"If you leave, the soldiers waiting above on those banks will cut you down."

"They know we're here?" Danvir eased back from the opening.

"Maybe not, but they are covering this way," Kachien said. "I have seen their helmets bob up and down too many times now."

"So what do we do? You brought us here. I assume you have a plan?" Ancel raised a questioning eyebrow.

"Yes. I do." Kachien closed her eyes. "Any moment now."

Yells sounded toward the opposite end of the tunnel where the drains twisted and turned. Bells began ringing once more. Outside, orders rattled out above them. Sure enough, what seemed like several hundred helmets bobbed from along the canal's walls and ran in the direction of the shouts and away from where they hid.

"Give them a few minutes," Kachien said. "Then we run."

"What did you do?"

Kachien smiled. "They think they see what they do not see. Once they realize they are chasing stone, it will be too late."

Ancel's face twisted in confusion, but he got no chance to ask.

"Go. Now," Kachien ordered.

They ran for the entrance, Charra bounding ahead of them, cold rain and winds buffeting them as they left the tunnel's shelter.

Ancel's heart raced, each splashing footstep sounding as if the entire world could hear them. *Dear gods, please don't let them hear us.* Rain soaked him within moments, but he didn't care. He pushed his tired legs harder and harder through the filth around them. The muck sucked at his feet, conspiring to slow his progress, but he fought against it. Several times, he stumbled, but somehow managed to regain his balance. His breaths came in burning, ragged gasps. He thought he heard a shout, and he drove his legs even harder.

The safety of the drainage tunnel on the other side seemed miles away. In his mind, they were not getting any closer. He closed his eyes and prayed some more while pumping his legs. Then, in one sudden step, the rain no longer wet him.

Ancel opened his eyes. They had all crossed. He grinned, and so did the others. But Kachien was frowning with her head tilted to one side.

"What's wrong?" As he asked the question, the noises reached Ancel. The squeals of thousands of rats and a distant roar.

"What's that?" Concern filled Kachien's voice.

"Th–They opened the dam," Ancel sputtered. "These tunnels will flood in minutes. We'll die here if we don't make the river in time. Run. Run for your lives."

They ran.

CHAPTER 31

Darkness engulfed them as they plunged deeper into the sewers. Cold seeped through Ancel's soaked boots, and already, the water in the central channel had risen to overflowing, causing filthy liquid to lap at the sides of the tunnel. Although only ankle deep at the moment, the sewage was still rising. With only the entrance behind providing dim light Ancel followed his friends' silhouettes and footsteps splashing ahead, the stench of weeks old waste near impossible to breathe in. Making the mistake of sucking in too much air brought on coughing fits. Behind them, the crush of rodents fleeing for safety wailed a squealing chorus like an out of tune takuatin. The oncoming flood played the accompaniment in a muffled roar.

"This tunnel will lead us to the river," Kachien yelled a few feet from Ancel.

"What do we do when we get there?" Ancel shouted. Rodents swam or scurried by him, oblivious to his presence, intent on their escape.

"I have a small boat hidden near the river bank. We use it to cross the Kelvore River. On the other side, I have dartans ready for us."

The level of Kachien's preparation left him taken aback. "Why not stay on this side of the river? There's a few farmers I know who don't live far from Randane. I could get us mounts there."

"No. The King has men already searching the Randane Road."

"How do you know this?"

"A guard told me."

Ancel could only imagine what she did to obtain the information. "Well, we could skip across the Randane Road when it's clear of soldiers and head into the Patchwork Forest. From there we can make the Greenleaf and the Eldan Road in a few days. It's a quick run home after that. Still a lot faster than crossing the Kelvore."

"No."

Ancel opened his mouth to protest.

"Think about what you said and what has happened so far," Kachien said.

In the deepening dark Ancel gave his plan some thought. If they somehow managed to sneak across the Randane Road, past the King's regiments, they would still need mounts. Chances are soldiers were watching the farms in the area. Worse yet was whether the creatures he and Mirza saw were wraithwolves. Even with Charra and Kachien's protection, taking to the Patchwork and the Greenleaf Forests no longer seemed a good idea. Unfamiliar mounts in unfamiliar territory chased by shadelings. Ancel cringed.

"You're right," Ancel admitted. "Crossing the Kelvore is the best way." In the dark, he could see the white glint of Kachien's teeth.

"I know," she said.

The water had now swirled up to their shins. Ahead, Mirza and Danvir labored. Wet, cold, clothes clinging to his body, Ancel found himself breathing harder and struggling to find purchase for his feet. Next to him, both Charra and Kachien sounded as if they had little trouble. The tunnel's entrance behind was a mere pinprick. Darkness swathed everything else.

Not inclined to more conversation, Ancel focused on moving forward. He tried to ignore the overpowering squeaks and the sound from the oncoming flood behind. But he couldn't. A lump formed in the pit of his stomach and continued to tighten and grow as the waters rose and the noises increased. When he dared a glance over his shoulder, blackness greeted him. Shivers wracked his body in a blend of chill and dread that he couldn't separate. Either didn't matter. He wanted out.

Is this all that's left for me? Am I to die swarmed over by ten thousand rats and drowned in shit and filth? Never to see Irmina again? Never getting to learn more of Kachien? Will I ever get to see my parents again? My home? The Soltide Festival? Taste kinai, practice the sword, finish my Mater training? Am I doomed to die without becoming a Dagodin or an Ashishin? He squeezed the likeness of his mother that hung from the chain around his neck.

His thoughts did nothing for his clenched gut. In the stories, the Dagodin Knights were always gallant, saving some village from raiders or slavers. Never did the stories tell of them or Ashishin in situations such as this. Ancel's lips twitched. That he would find himself in such a crisis felt too comical to be true. Cold water rising to his groin quickly diffused the humor.

Squeals from the rats and the water's roaring counter dominated the air. No longer able to hear the splashes of his friends or their breathing, Ancel forced himself forward, now having to wade as the water reached his stomach. His sword constantly snagged on debris, threatening to drag him under or forward with the current. Left with no other option, he unbuckled the swordbelt and let the water sweep it away.

Freed up of the burden, travel became a little easier. Batting at several huge rodents as they swarmed by served to infuriate them. Charra's growls did little to help. More than once, Ancel felt sharp teeth and nails. His breathing grew labored, his heartbeat sped and thumped, and blood rushed to his ears.

"Ancel," Kachien shouted. "We will not make it if I do not do something. Go. Swim now, it is faster. Do not wait for me. You must reach the point where the tunnels slope down. I will catch up."

Ancel squeezed his eyes tight against the words. Mustering all the will he could, he prevented himself from going to Kachien. She knew what she needed to do. In this situation and in his current state, he was of little help. He locked his jaws against the need to gag up the foul water and swam away.

When he'd gone some two hundred feet or more, there came a rumble like a great waterfall. The tunnel trembled. The noise reverberated through Ancel. He looked back and gasped.

Daylight bathed Kachien as she stood with her hands outstretched to the sides, a gaping hole above her. The mossy walls and the black–covered water crawled with rodents. Sandstone bricks crumbled all around as the tunnel collapsed on itself and around her.

A moment later, she was gone from view as the tunnel

inclined, and Ancel dropped below eye level. He was thrown into complete dark again. Even if he wanted to go back to her, he couldn't now. Not against the current's pull. Allowing the water to take him as it pleased, Ancel squeezed his eyes tight. The tell tale warmth of tears washed across his face. He prayed to the gods he hadn't lost another woman he cared for.

Ryne woke to the pull of the essences around him and the baking sun.

Close–by, Sakari sat on a large stone; a cookpot, branches empty of kinai and fleshberries, and the remnants of a fire at his feet. Not far from him, stood Thumper, chewing on whatever tidbit Sakari had given him. "How do you feel?"

Ryne sat up among short, lush grass, drawing a breath at the sweet scents of fruit and roasted meat. "Like a new man."

This Entosis was much bigger than the one where he met Halvor, but it was smaller than the one he'd woken inside seventy years ago in Granadia. The lily pond he remembered from the previous night, its clear water now reflecting the sunlight, was several hundred feet below him in a small glen. Deer, slainen, and grazing animals he didn't recognize, drank from the pool or frolicked among fields, fruit plants and trees that thrived in the area. The plant life grew until they touched the granite and feldspar cliffs rife with mineral deposits. At a glance, he identified gold, silver, and the sparkle from precious gems.

Ryne stood and did a few stretches. All the while, the essences thrummed, tugging this way and that, or caressing his Scripts. Not once did his bloodlust surge to their pull. Although his power offered subtle whispers within him, he didn't feel the compulsion to answer its call. Not even when he pictured the faces of Carnas' slain. He soon found himself deep within his sword arts, flowing through various Stances and Styles. When he finished, he was more refreshed than when he began.

"Sakari. It's time we left," Ryne said as he headed toward Thumper. "We have work to do. A city to warn. A war to prepare for. And someone to find who can show me who I am and help guide me to my power's full potential." When he reached the dartan, Ryne rubbed its nose and flanks before reaching up to his bags and removing two water skins. "Gather some kinai from below." He pointed among the fruit trees. "Make sure Thumper eats his fill. When we leave, link with him. Have him use his power so we can reach Castere by noon tomorrow. We can't afford four more days travel."

"As you wish."

On his way to the pond, Ryne reveled in the feel of the primal essences around him. He didn't need his Matersense for them. They swirled, and spun, tickled and tugged, dipped and rose in an exotic dance around his body. He wondered if the time would ever come when he could sense and see them all joined together in their full elemental states. He relished the thought.

The animals drinking from the pond acted as if he was one of them, hardly batting an eye at his presence. Ryne filled the water skins with the cool water and took a long drink. When he finished, he poured what was left over his head before refilling the container. With a cursory bow to the gathered wild life, he strode back up the hill.

Ryne took a seat near the dead cooking fire and picked up the pot. Inside was a stew made with wild potatoes, seeds, and brown meat. The spicy food set Ryne's taste buds tingling, and he recognized the stringy composition and succulent taste of slainen flesh. By the time he finished the meal and washed it down with water, Sakari returned with Thumper.

As they mounted to leave, curiosity nagged at Ryne. He opened his Matersense. Essences flooded him immediately. His Scripts responded with more than their usual eager ferocity and life–like writhing. Somewhere deep inside him, his bloodlust resonated. The craving to kill rose, but with ease, he gathered the essences he could and thrust them into his center. Despite the violence of all the individual essences and the elements they formed, Ryne's core became as calm as the pond down in the glen. He smiled. "I'm ready."

Sakari was silent for a moment. Then, as if whipped by a fierce storm gale or shot from a massive bow, Thumper bounded through the Entosis' entrance. Outside, the hills, the fields, trees, grass, the ground, and the sky stretched into one multicolored mass with the speed Thumper ran.

CHAPTER 32

Coughing and sputtering, Ancel crawled away from the riverbank. The wind gusted, flapping his shirttail and trouser legs and pressing the wet material against him. He shivered as rain peppered him with cold, pebble–sized drops. Beside him, Charra followed with slow steps to match his own. The daggerpaw's head shifted from Ancel and out toward the marshy land along the city's bulwarks.

Lightning lashed the shrouded sky, its afterimage burning into his eyes before fading in a blink. Just ahead of him, Danvir helped Mirza to his feet. To their left, and several dozen feet behind, water rushed from the large sewer drain set into Randane's towering wall, spilling filth and rats into the dirty, foamy swirls of the Kelvore River. Ancel thanked the gods for the winds and the rushing water that swept away the stench.

He still remembered the drop into the murky depths. For too long to measure in the dark, he'd allowed the current to take him when a pinprick of light grew into the sewer's exit. The speed of his descent increased until he was tossed every which way the sewage wished. He spun, darkness became light, the cramped tunnel became open air, and he flailed as he fell. A splash, a roaring in his ears, and he found himself battling for breath, his lungs burning as he swam for the surface.

Ancel retched, breaking off from the memory. Struggling to his feet was an agony–filled exercise, his body feeling as battered as if he trained nonstop for an entire day. Step by painful step, he teetered to where his friends huddled with their backs against Randane's granite wall where it curved away into a long expanse with towers dotting its length. If their appearance was any judge, they all resembled disheveled beggars. At least the river had taken care of most of their smell. And, blessedly, they were alive.

Ancel looked toward the water pouring from the tunnel into the river below. Each splash of anything large enough to be a small person brought hope. Not one turned out to be Kachien. With every disappointment he sunk further into himself.

Mirza was the first to speak up, his voice cracked and hoarse. "So what do we do now?"

"Find this boat of hers and cross the river," Danvir said, his white–blond hair plastered to his cheeks much like Ancel's dark layers felt.

Seeing his bear–sized friend hug himself and rub his arms made Ancel even more aware of the chill. Another too cold summer day. Ancel surveyed the land around them. "I doubt it'll be that easy," he said.

The bloated waters of the Kelvore River carried on for miles before dwindling around a curve. Stunted trees, marsh reeds, humps, and hills provided more than adequate hiding places. Besides the threat from flooding, there was also the threat of discovery.

"I'd say go to the ferry, but that area's sure to be watched," Mirza added. Red bled into his shirt from his hair—an oozing head wound that caused Ancel's heart to skip before he realized it was the dye.

"Of course, it is watched."

Ancel's heart leaped at Kachien's quiet voice. Danvir and Mirza started while Charra whined.

Soaked to the bone, she threaded along what was left of a thin embankment of rock and sediment as if the slippery formation was the most stable surface in the world. Her long, golden hair hung in wet strands about her face, and her dark breeches and shirt clung to her body. Rents in the fabric revealed her tan skin. Not even her tattered cloak could dispel her serenity or her beauty.

"You three are lucky there are no guards in the tower above you. If there were, the entire regiment would be here with the noise you have made."

Ancel snapped his mouth shut. He made an effort not to glance up at the tower. Hopefully, if his features were as dirty as his two friends, the muck hid his blush.

With a dainty leap, Kachien flew over a break in the rock, landed on the riverbank, and joined them. "The boat is hidden along the wall there under those reeds."

Resisting the urge to touch Kachien, Ancel followed her gaze to the plants and trees in question. They looked as normal as any other, if a bit more disheveled from the weather. "What happened in the tunnel?"

Kachien shrugged. "I used the Forms to destroy the walls and build another path for the water and the rats to follow."

"You're an Ashishin?" Mirza and Danvir blurted all at once before covering their mouths.

"Keep your voice down!" Kachien warned. "No, I'm no Ashishin." She looked away from the recognition on Ancel's face.

Ancel remained quiet. Now he knew why she'd avoided his question about if she could touch Mater. He also understood her fear for him. Her emotions were written plainly in her eyes. She lacked the control. That's why she had to kill when she helped them escape. She was a Deathbringer. What she must have suffered tore at him while at the same time the horrific things he imagined she did gave him pause.

"You sure that didn't let them know where we were?" A slight doubt creeping through his insides, Ancel placed himself between Charra and Kachien.

Kachien didn't hide her pained expression. "Maybe. But it was the only way for us to escape. We will not be here when and if they do come." She walked a wide arc around Charra and headed to the hiding place she mentioned.

"What's with you three?" Mirza glanced from Kachien to Charra to Ancel.

"Nothing." The secret was hers to reveal. Her hurt look at his wariness bothered him. If she lacked the control to decide who to kill she would have murdered them long ago. Besides, why would Teacher Galiana trust someone who was this unstable? Exhaling deeply, Ancel tried to shake his uneasiness. "Let's go."

They followed Kachien, staying close to the wall. Rain beat down on them, and the constant grumbling of thunder and the dark clouds skittering across the sky showed no signs of letting up. Although Ancel was sure it must be afternoon by the now, the dim light made the time of day seem more like evening.

Kachien wasted no time in sloshing through mud and water pooled near the reeds and small trees. Without waiting for help, she began to drag the well–crafted covering of branches and leaves away. Soon, a small rowboat not big enough to carry all five of them became exposed.

"The guards should still be occupied trying to capture what I left them. But to be safe, when we lift the boat to the river, stay close to the wall. We will follow the tide. When we are hidden from view of the city's towers, then we will cross."

"What about Charra?" Ancel asked.

"He will swim."

Charra was a strong swimmer, but he hated water. Convincing the daggerpaw could become an issue, but Ancel could see no other solution.

"There's one small problem," Mirza said as they bent to pick up the boat. "How do we get across against the current?"

The Kelvore River, usually three quarters of a mile across, had swollen to almost twice that size. Muddy brown water swirled around hidden rocks before rushing off farther south. The roar of the rushing river was only drowned out when thunder pealed. With the current's ferocity, crossing would be near impossible.

"Let me worry about that," Kachien said reassuringly. "There are three paddles in the reeds. You will help keep us straight, but I will do most of the work."

None of them bothered to ask how. They already knew. Instead, they concentrated on their footing across the muddied ground.

"What about the cost?" Ancel said from his position at the hull.

Danvir had the middle, supporting the majority of the weight on his beefy shoulders.

"You have nothing to worry about there. I can maintain until an opportunity comes." The brief closing of her eyes and her reluctant tone said Kachien didn't relish the thought.

"What cost? What're you two talking about?" Mirza said, his voice strained and taut.

"You can tell them." Resignation inched into Kachien's

tone. "They deserve to know."

As they set down the boat where they'd sat moments before, Ancel told them about what Kachien's people, the Alzari, believed, and how they handled those who could touch Mater but lacked control. His two friends gave her wary looks and tried not to be obvious about the space they kept between her and them.

"Are you safe to be around?" Mirza finally managed.

"Safe enough. I decide who needs to die to appease the essences. Here in Granadia, there are more than enough enemies. I will not be driven to madness and harm you."

Mirza and Danvir's worried expressions smoothed. Danvir went off to get the three wooden paddles as Ancel, Mirza and Kachien eased the rowboat into the river. Kachien held a tether in one hand.

"Ancel," Danvir began when he returned, and they climbed in one by one. "I know he's strong, but can Charra swim against this current?"

"Make sure he stays close," Kachien said before Ancel offered a reply. "If he does, he should be fine."

They all looked at each other but said nothing. Kachien leaped into the boat last. From the riverbank, Charra growled.

"Follow," Ancel commanded.

Charra whined and leaped after them as they pushed off from the shore. He landed with a splash and paddled beside the craft.

They kept as close to the bulwark as they dared. Danvir sat in the middle as the counterweight to Ancel and Mirza at the ends. Kachien took up a position near Mirza, her eyes focused ahead. The first few hundred feet went smoothly. When they reached the sewer exit, they worked hard to stay as close to the city's walls as they dared. The sewage roared out as they passed, and the swirling currents from its collision with the river careened the boat, sending the bow high in the air before the vessel crashed back down, and the stern lifted from the water.

Ancel frantically switched his paddle from side to side in order to help prevent the craft from capsizing. He considered shouting to help them work in concert, but not only would that prove fruitless with the water roaring around them, there was the risk of alerting a guard. He struggled on, the pain in his arms and legs a dull throb. When at last they passed the danger, he blew out a deep breath. Allowing his shoulders to sag never felt so good.

His relaxation was short lived as the speed at which they traveled increased. They were pitched to and from the stone edifice without mercy. Keeping the boat on course became more difficult than he could have imagined, and he resorted to shorter strokes as the waters conspired to slam them into the stone. Luckily, the city's bulwarks shielded them from the wind that howled as if possessed by some wraithlike creature, venting its rage at the fact they didn't have to deal with its swirling eddies and the treacherous waters at the same time.

Occasional spray and the rain tempted Ancel to wipe his eyes. He resisted. Instead, he focused on the task at hand and his friends in front. The muscles on Danvir's back and arms threatened to burst through his dirty silk shirt. Ancel's shoulders, back, and legs burned even more than before. Mirza's red head bobbed this way and that as he worked. Kachien simply watched.

Foot by foot, their speed grew until they hurtled by stone and debris alike. Charra somehow managed to keep up with them. At any moment, Ancel expected the river's fury to smash and break them against the wall. But as if by Ilumni's good grace, they avoided their demise, often only by inches. Ancel managed a glimpse of Kachien. Her forehead was furrowed in concentration and her eyes narrowed. He was certain whatever she did had to do with Materforging.

His arms feeling as if they would fall off at any moment, Ancel battled on. Legs wooden, breathing ragged, back aching, and hands raw from the constant fight with the paddle, he lost track of time. The only things that existed was their craft tipping toward the wall, his strokes to push it away, then his work on the opposite side so they wouldn't be swept out into the middle of the river.

Without warning, they passed the bulwark. Moments later, the river flung them around a sharp bend. Icy wind whipped into them like frozen daggers. The front of the boat turned and it keeled to one side. At the dizzying speed they traveled, the craft twisted the opposite direction, toward the foaming violence at the river's center, yawing listlessly. There was no way to stop the movement. They were going to flip over.

We're going to die here.

Just as abruptly as the wind began, it stopped. The boat

lurched upright.

"You no longer...need to...paddle," Kachien said, an edge to her voice as if she'd fought a great battle.

Ancel hissed at the sight of her haggard, pale face. He wanted to reach out to her and stroke away the wild strands of hair from her cheeks, but his arms were too heavy to lift and his legs too numb to move.

Then, the impossible happened.

The craft veered out into the river. And was not swept away. It sped along as if the day was a calm, sunny one, and they were out on a leisurely boat ride. The oncoming water never struck them with more than a gentle lap. They cut across the river's heart like a sharp blade through silk.

Ancel stared, his mouth open. Danvir plopped down into a sitting position. Mirza cackled, his head thrown to the sky.

And somehow, next to them swam Charra, his golden eyes focused on Kachien.

Ancel looked back behind them. A fog had risen along the riverbank they just left. The gray, cloying mist spread down the entire length of the city and up, obscuring the wall and its many towers. Faded orange light marked where torches dotted Randane's fortifications. Ancel almost whooped.

A ragged gasp came from Kachien. Her face had grown even paler. Her chest heaved the same as when a farmer stuck a pig and allowed its blood to drain until the animal died. Spittle bubbling at her lips, sweat pouring down her face at such a rate not even the constant deluge of rain could hide it, she stared straight ahead, her body rigid. Her breaths came harder and faster.

Ancel pined to go to her, but if he moved, he would upset the boat's current balance. He forced himself to hold his position and watched, his hands clenched, his eyes moist, and his heart feeling as if someone stabbed him.

The boat struck the far bank. Kachien flopped to one knee in a boneless heap.

Ancel tried to yell, but the words he uttered were a dull croak. "Help her."

CHAPTER 33

Early the next morning, Ryne and Sakari emerged from the Sang Reaches and entered Astoca. They crossed the wide Tantua River, which meandered through the Mondros Forest miles to the east, before it split into several smaller tributaries forming the Sinking Swamps and the Great Rainbow Lakes to their immediate south. Skiffs, fishing boats, sleek river dancers, bulky ferries, and the occasional warsailer traversed the Tantua's murky waters. Most headed in the direction of Castere. Ryne skirted the swamps, and they soon arrived at the citadel built between the Rainbow Lakes.

The rising sun sparkled in dizzying colors off the glassy stones littering the lakes' floor. The sight took Ryne's breath away. Boats by the hundreds dotted the expanses of water. Twin gigantic statues, one of Hyzenki and the other of Aeoli, both holding massive swords raised to the heavens, adorned each lake.

Perched on the islands between Lake Benica and Venica sat Castere. The city's Outer Ring to its Inner Ring rose in a mountain of structures which began with wooden shacks followed by stone edifices in blue and violet shades and culminated with the spires and towers of the King's castle at the city's peak. Tiles or shingles covered roofs that sloped down or peaked up. Even this early, people streamed like foraging ants across the white bridges spanning the many tributaries, streams, and canals that carved paths through the city's Outer and Mid Ring.

The Mid Ring began where the Outer Ring ended a mile into Castere at the first of the city's two encircling ramparts.

The hundred–foot edifice marked the Mid Ring's border, and although considered one wall, it was two, separated by huge gates in each cardinal direction. Once, what was now the Mid Ring had been the poor slums of the Outer Ring until Castere rose to prominence and the hovels spilled outside the first wall. Stone structures had replaced the shanties, and the slums had shifted until the Outer Ring lay outside the fortification. Ryne could see the process may well repeat itself again.

Two miles inside the Mid Ring stood Castere's second rampart, two hundred feet high, which encircled the Inner Ring. This structure only had two gates located at the north and south ends. Guard towers and crenellations spread across both walls. From atop the hill they traveled, the ramparts resembled a giant eye with the lakes at its corners and the city as the iris. *The Crying City, indeed.*

Ryne pictured himself marshalling legions to defend the city. The mountainous design and its position with the lakes defending its flanks made the citadel difficult to take. As Ryne descended down to Lake Venica's shores, he couldn't help but wonder if an army the size of the one Jaecar reported could sack Castere.

"Anything that rises may fall. Whatever man has built, the gods will tear down," Sakari said.

Ryne frowned. Had he spoken aloud? Or was it just Sakari appearing to read his thoughts again? He gave his friend a sidelong glance. "Either way, it would take a long siege even with the numbers Jaecar described."

"Maybe." Sakari pointed across the multicolored stones littering Lake Venica's shores out to the glittering crystal waters. "Will they help them?"

Ryne eyed the towering statue of Hyzenki, his beard to his waist, rising in the middle of Lake Venica. "Have the gods ever helped anyone?"

"Yet, you pray to them."

Ryne could just see the tip of the sword the statue's twin—the goddess Aeoli—held high in Lake Benica. Against the backdrop of the wall across the lake stood the ordered temples dedicated to the two gods of Flows. "Maybe, I'm just hopeful."

"Or maybe you believe," Sakari replied.

Ryne opened his mouth, but before he answered, he

realized Sakari was right. He'd seen too much not to believe in divine power or the gods' hands meddling in men's affairs. Why he himself prayed only to Ilumni, he didn't know. It just felt right. He shrugged the thought off and peered out across the lake to the massive docks that stretched over five hundred feet out into the lake.

Longboats, ferries, and flat cargo carriers sailed between Castere and the outlying settlements along the shores or sat at docks. Rows of oars rose and fell in a rhythm more like flapping wings than wooden planks. Vessels approaching Castere had to travel between the passage the Mid Ring's ramparts formed a quarter mile into each lake. The passages led to the Eastern and Western gates and the docks beyond. Each gigantic metal portcullis and the chains and gears that hoisted it, said to be imbued with Mater so the gate would never rust, was the only way to reach Castere proper from the water.

"Do you think the walls, the gates, and those would be enough protection?" Ryne pointed to the Astocan warsailers—sleek ships with easily dismantled square sails—practicing formations. The Waterwall—a depiction of a huge ocean wave with a storm brewing above—emblazoned the sails.

"I would not attack Castere from the water. The lakes themselves would prove weapons for Astoca's Namazzi Matii."

"Indeed," Ryne agreed. "But the question remains still. Would it be enough?" A wide Cardian vessel bearing sails with the Maelstrom emblem of Cardia steered a wide berth around the warsailers.

"I doubt it. Eventually it will depend on sustenance."

Ryne grunted in agreement. Castere would be able to hold as long as they had supplies. Once they used up their stores, the real fight would begin.

They continued past Lake Venica onto the wide, main causeway. People in the thousands from across the kingdoms traversed the road. Were those Alzari in their tight–fitted garb among the crowds, with their heads down, feet dragging from their defeat? They looked like them, but Ryne couldn't be sure since they wore no war paint. His attention shifted across the masses to swarthy Harnans, some near as tall as he, ebony–skinned Cardians, aloof Astocans, hairless and yellow complexioned Banai, tall, slim Felani with their short, cropped hair, and even pale–skinned and fair featured Granadians.

Various languages and too many accents to count filtered from the crush of people calling to each other or involved in murmured or heated conversations. Wheels trundled on earth and flagstones, hooves clopped, feet shuffled and stomped, beasts of burden called, all coalescing into an unintelligible tumult. Sweaty odors, the aromas from scented oils and perfumes, and the smell of animals and their droppings combined for a hodgepodge of scents.

One constant held true along the road. People made way for Thumper and Ryne. They both dwarfed any other creature on the causeway, be it dartan, slainen, or horses drawing wagons. After another hour of travel, they reached a queue of wagons and drays at the Outer Ring.

Guards in azure armor, the Waterwall insignia on their surcoats, inspected each wagon. This lent to the crowds bunching closer to a makeshift wooden gate built on the main causeway. The other smaller roads were also guarded. Normally, there were few guards and few inspections until the main gates at the Mid Ring. To one side, soldiers questioned several travelers who Ryne could now confirm were Alzari from the smudged remnants of war paint on their faces. Other soldiers spoke to any man or woman wearing armor or bearing arms. These, they led away down a clear side of the causeway separated from the main by wooden barriers. A few soldiers pointed in Ryne's direction, hands reaching for sword hilts while others unlimbered their bows.

"Looks like they've received word," Ryne said.

"So it seems," Sakari replied.

An Astocan officer with multiple knots on the shoulder of his sky blue uniform approached Ryne on a speckled dartan. The man's dark brown skin had a polished sheen to match the pebbles he had for eyes. "Ryne Waldron?" The sweaty, round–faced man's nostrils flared, and the slits on the side of his neck opened and closed in slow flutters as he took a deep breath.

"Yes?" Ryne answered. From his books, he'd learned that unlike most others, Astocans and Cardians smelled more than they saw features.

"I'm Lieutenanat Rosival, I have orders to escort you to the King's Audience Chambers."

Ryne nodded. "Lead on."

"This way." Rosival's hand beckoned toward a side path with a smaller gate.

Rosival led at a gallop, and Ryne and Sakari followed. The many streets within the area the Lieutenant took them appeared deserted. The noise from the crowds became nothing more than a muffled buzz as they crossed small bridges over the drains and canals lining the rank streets. Along with Forgings by the Namazzi, levies controlled the streams and small rivers during the worst weather. Ryne envisioned the liquid within the drainage system used as weapons during any attack.

Cracked and pitted cobblestones marred the Outer Ring's narrow roads as they continued to follow Rosival. One in every three buildings were in a state of disrepair, paint peeled and reduced to faded blues and whites. Refuse lined more roads than not. Flies buzzed about, and small dogs and large swamp rats dug or scurried among the garbage.

Disgusting. Ryne shook his head. He abhorred the thought that the less fortunate should be forced to live in squalor. What upset him even more was how the rich contributed to the situation. He'd seen Castere during the storms or hard rains. Filth would run into the slums carried down by the drains from the Inner City. He gazed across several canals and culverts where workers dug trenches while other laborers loaded refuse onto a flat cargo vessel. *Well, at least it seems they're addressing the situation.*

They soon reached the bulwark at the Mid Ring. Lances dotted the battlements, and guards patrolled atop the walls or kept a vigilant eye from the many towers. Here, they encountered workers collecting garbage in two–wheeled drays pulled by dartans along roads in much better condition. Once loaded, the dartans headed toward the Outer Ring. The streets here had also been cleared of regular folk, restricting passage to soldiers.

When they came upon the Inner Ring and its crenellated rampart, the streets became spotless, paved with large flagstones in mosaic designs. Villas dotted the hundred–foot wide avenue, their deep blue and violet walls gleaming. Spires stretched twice the height of the two hundred–foot walls, and sunlight reflected from the buildings' glass–covered facades. Fountains lined the main road, and small ponds filled with fish decorated some areas. Pillars adorned the entrance to each villa with manicured gardens hedging most properties.

Another thing stood out to Ryne within the Inner Ring—the number of soldiers. They marched through the streets or stood in lined formations numbering in the tens of thousands. Infantry, dartan divisions, archers, and several cohorts who displayed the Waterwall insignia of Astoca's Matii, the Namazzi, crowded the squares. Ryne smiled at the occasional shift or fidget among the troops when Thumper rode by.

They turned onto a marbled colonnade, wide enough for twenty wagons to travel abreast, which led to the castle's main gates. Immaculate flagstones, and even more fountains sprouting water at timed intervals, decorated the area. Manicured gardens, much more beautiful than any before, spread to the sides. Guards stood at attention along this path, tasseled lances held high.

Looming ahead was Castere Keep, its towers and spires extending a thousand feet into the air as Astoca's dedication to Aeoli, its walls glittering in silvery blue. Disguised within the beauty were arrow slits, murder holes, and sally gates. Twin barbicans guarded the raised, heavy gate and portcullis. The Waterwall fluttered from multiple flag posts. Ryne saw the castle for what it was—a fortress.

They rode through the gates into a courtyard and past two matching guard formations standing at strict attention to either side of the walkway that ended at the stairs to the castle itself. Ten servants in white livery ran down the wide stairs. Rosival dismounted and passed his reins to two such. Without being told, Sakari hopped down and Ryne followed suit, handing Thumper's reins to a wide-eyed young Astocan who stared, openmouthed. The young man's partner nudged him in the side. Still staring, the youth muttered an apology. After quick bows, the servants led the mounts toward a path on one side.

Rosival turned to Ryne and said, "Master Waldron, as a safety measure it is requested you leave your weapons here with the guards. Due to the nature of recent events, only the Royal Guards are allowed to be armed in the King's presence."

Ryne did not bother to look at the Lieutenant. "In that case, I'll be leaving." He raised a hand toward the servant leading Thumper away. "Hul—"

"Wait." Rosival wiped sweat from his forehead. "Allow me to pass word of your arrival."

"We'll be sitting on your pretty stairs waiting. If you take too long, I'm leaving." With that, Ryne strode to the steps and sat.

Rosival spoke to a guard, and then hurried inside.

From where Ryne sat, he could see through the gates and down into the city and land for miles to the northeast. From this vantage point, someone in Castere must have seen the smoking clanholds. That would explain why the soldiers were questioning the Alzari at the gates. The King was already aware of the threat.

"You may enter," Rosival said when he returned soon after.

They followed the Lieutenant up the stairs and through a wide gateway manned by several guards in bronze armor. Hands on swords, they stared straight ahead as if they saw nothing. Not a single guard reached higher than Ryne's chest.

The entrance opened into a long hall of marble and paneled wood, polished until it could hold a blurred reflection. Tapestries and murals illustrating great battles hung above the paneling. The most prominent depicted the gods Hyzenki and Aeoli at war, commanding storms and seas in battle against the Eztezians—a race of giants the size of the Svenzar. A few displayed the King on his hunts.

Along the length of the hall, stone columns supported inlaid vaulted ceilings with lamps in sconces adorning each pillar. Ryne's feet made little to no noise on the lush carpets. Every fifteen feet, guards stood at attention on alternating sides.

Doorways, with the Waterwall standard draped above, intersected the hall at regular intervals. Liveried servants ran back and forth from rooms or bustled up and down the hall. Some carried food, others drink, and yet others held trays of fruit. The sweet aromas wafting from the dishes made Ryne's stomach grumble. Rosival led them straight ahead into the Audience Chamber.

Dignitaries and nobles in extravagant clothing crowded the hall. Long coats reaching down to their knees, skin like polished copper, heads shaved on one side, marked Felani from the west. Harnan Lords, their skin tanned to ebony, puffed about in embroidered jackets and dresses buttoned to the neck, dabbing at their heads with scented scarves. With one side of their chests exposed, often with nothing more than painted stripes across the skin, Cardian Lords and Ladies prowled in bright colored, sheer satins and linens that did little to hide their bodies. Colorful tattoos on baldheads indicated the Banai nobility among the crowds. Most listened to an Astocan in gold and white silks who stood on a dais at the room's center.

The Audience Chamber contained more vaulted ceilings, paneled wood, silk and satin drapes, and tiered chandeliers. Huge marbled pillars marked the first two hundred paces into the room like monolithic sentinels. Representations of Hyzenki and Aeoli peeked from the tall, stained–glass windows partially hidden by satin curtains. Smaller windows with barely discernible images of Humelen, Liganen, Ilumni and Rituni were located just below the others. A flowered rug ran all the way to the dais.

"Sacrilege," said Sakari, his voice still passive, his gaze fixed on the smaller windows. "They are a token gesture to the other nobles here, nothing more."

Rosival missed a step and glanced back at Sakari.

"I wondered when you would say something. Maybe, you're getting old after all," Ryne replied, but Sakari offered no response as they stopped among the pillars.

King Voliny sat sprawled on his throne, a hundred feet from the room's center. The large marble chair, with a likeness of a Waterwall carved into it, stood on a raised platform several feet higher than the dais where the Astocan spoke. Dressed in pristine cerulean blue, with gold scrollwork running up his coat sleeves, the King made for an imposing figure despite one sleeve ending at the elbow. A beak for a nose and hard angles highlighted his clean–shaven face, and his russet skin shone like oiled leather. Silver highlights set off his black hair, which was pulled back into a tight braid. A foolish person could mistake his lazed sprawl for inattention until they met those piercing blue eyes. His body shifted ever so slightly when his gaze crossed Ryne.

For an instant, the King's aura appeared to change shades. None of what Ryne saw was malevolent, but something about the aura felt out of place. It tickled some familiarity in the back of Ryne's mind. *Where have I seen such an aura before?* Try as he might, he couldn't dredge up the memory. For the moment, he dismissed the thought.

There were no guards visible, but he could sense and see their auras all the same. They were positioned next to the pillars he and Sakari stood among and at various locations throughout the room. He found King Voliny's choice for Royal Guards to be ironic. The man held Hyzenki and Aeoli in such high esteem, yet found it prudent to send Namazzi Matii whose strengths all lay in Forging the Flows, to be trained by the Svenzar in the elements of Forms. The same Svenzar who stood behind their Formist beliefs in their worship to Humelen and Liganen, and who the Astocans and their Flowic beliefs disdained.

Nevertheless, what these Matii did despite their weakness in the Forms impressed Ryne. Maintaining a constant Forge drained a person until they collapsed. Push beyond those limits and they would die, their aura torn in such a fashion their Mater spilled from them until they expired. Instead, these Namazzi had each placed a single Forge on themselves and the surface they used to Mask their presence. Then, they stood absolutely still in order not to disturb the Forge. The smallest motion other than breathing would reveal them. At least ten guards were Masked at the pillars behind Voliny. Ryne counted another fifty throughout the room. *Impressive, indeed.*

Ryne's attention shifted to the Astocan on the dais.

"It is for this reason I believe we cannot wait," said the powder–faced Astocan Lord. "If this threat is real, we should marshal our forces and strike first." He waited for the King's nod and stepped down.

A Cardian Lord came forward but dipped his head and averted his eyes as the Astocan passed him. He made a great show of bowing to the King and the other Astocans in the chamber. Ryne shook his head at the gesture. Cardians believed their distant cousins to be of lesser stock, but ever since the Astocans defeated them in their last war, Cardians showed deference to them. Except in their clothing. Cardians wore bright clothes to show off what they called their 'purity of color'. Ryne couldn't see himself bowing and scraping to any man, for any reason.

This Cardian was dressed in vibrant yellows and reds that highlighted his ebony skin. "King Voliny and my esteemed colleagues, the question is whether the threat is real to anyone but the Alzari. Did they finally run afoul of those who inhabit the Nevermore Heights?" His already harsh voice was made more so by the growling way Cardians spoke. "Could it not be the savage Harnan tribes from within the Mondros or the Nevermore? Why should we defend the Alzari after all they have done in the past?"

Those comments brought shouts from the Harnans, proclaiming their innocence and decrying the Cardian noble's insinuations.

King Voliny's sharp voice echoed through the chamber. "Whatever they may be, I saw the smoke with mine own eyes and several of my spies reported the clanholds did fall. Whomever the invaders, they are a threat to us all, Lord Traushen."

Traushen dabbed a cloth over the wet slits on his neck, which opened and closed in a slow rhythm. "The Cardian Council hears this, but in light of the past differences between the five territories, we ask for time to consider and gather evidence on our own."

"You ask for a commodity we may not have," Voliny stated with a wave of his hand and Traushen stepped down from the dais.

A wide, bald–headed Banai ambassador stepped up after Traushen. He made a sweeping bow to the King before he began. "Your Majesty, our concerns differ somewhat." The Banai's voice, like so many of his people, was soft yet impressionable. "Memories of Amuni's Children and before them, the Setian, still ring fresh among us Banai. We believe this threat is real. It has been foretold in the great carvings of Humelen and Liganen. The day when the dreaded Eztezian giants return draws nigh. On that day, gods and daemons alike shall cross the darkness of the Nether and chaos will rule our lands. Should we not band together, Ostania will fall and the rest of Denestia with it."

An uproar followed the ambassador's words with many a voice decrying the Banai as a race, and shouting for him to have his people go back to hiding in their mountain cliffs and forests near the Broken Lands. Astocans yelled profanities about him mentioning the gods of Forms within their sacred halls.

"You dare to speak of the Eztezians to us?" berated Lord Traushen. "The ones who betrayed all? Who deserted their duties, allowed the shade to breach the Nether and enter Denestia in the first place? Those who fell from grace, whom the gods cursed with disease until their kind was culled from the land? You dare!"

"Enough!" King Voliny's voice cut through the din. "There is a reason I commanded this audience every day. Debate and division has ever been our failing. I waited for someone that none of us can deny, in hopes my messengers would reach him, but it seems he is here even before they reached his home. Step forward, Master Ryne Waldron."

"Wait here, Sakari," Ryne said.

If there were any complaints during the King's last speech, they died at the mention of Ryne's name. Breaths sucked in and quiet chatter followed. As Ryne strode forward, silence grew heavy in front of him. Faces hardened then melted like wet snow when he strode by them. Some noses turned up, followed by a few sniffs. Ryne felt his lips curl. He must smell like an old dartan over a hunk of rancid meat. Postures of many around the room made an audible shift, some into defensive positions, and others as if they were ready to flee. When he passed, the murmurs spread behind him. Many mentioned his sword. Expectant eyes watched from all angles as he stepped onto the dais.

"Your Majesty," Ryne said and inclined his head to the King.

"Master Waldron," Voliny replied, "You have served the kingdoms well in many…endeavors. As can be expected, where there is strife, you appear. I assumed one as traveled as you would have heard about the clanholds, and I hoped you would come here. Thank the Flows my prayers were answered."

Ryne nodded. "Yes, I heard what happened to clanholds. I got a firsthand account from an Alzari fleeing with his family to the Vallum." A few whispers followed. "Then I saw what these invaders can do. My home, Carnas, is no more." The murmurs increased to a loud buzz.

"Silence," the King commanded. When the noise died down, he continued. "I'm sorry for your loss. May the Flows bless those who perished and keep their souls safe. Did you see this army when it attacked the clanholds?"

"No, but they wield the shade and use it to slaughter. The Alzari I met described Amuni's Children. Everyone in Carnas is dead."

Loud gasps and prayers trickled around the room. A voice he recognized yelled, "What about the women and children?"

Ryne turned toward Traushen. "They spared no one."

More shouts and cries followed that statement. This

reminded him so much of the Council's squabbles in Carnas that Ryne's stomach roiled. He held up a hand and all quieted.

"The choice is yours to work together. Eventually, they'll strike again. The invaders already took the clanholds, and I'm sure the dullest among you understand the gravity of such a situation. You've been weakened even before the first sally."

"The Alzari clans got nothing more than they deserved," yelled Lord Traushen.

Ryne shrugged. "Maybe they did, but if this force can take the clanholds, what chance does the pitiful Cardian dregs have?"

The Cardian's face reddened. On one side of his neck, the three slits flared open and closed.

Ryne gazed around the room. "I never understood why so many of you hate the Alzari so when you made them the mercenaries they are." There were a few murmurs and nods of agreement. "It's quite simple. I studied the possible defenses here in Castere. While you could hold out for years, you would eventually fall once your resources ran out. By destroying the clanholds, the Ostanian kingdoms have been weakened enough that an army as large as the reports given will sweep across the land. Even if you band together, you'll only be able to hold them but for so long. With the Svenzar staying hidden in their mountain homes, I suggest you send to Granadia for help."

Shouts and curses spilled from most around the room in a thunderous roar. Arguments for never allowing Granadia to command any more of Ostania than it already did ensued. Yet, the King appeared calm.

Voliny's voice rose above the din. "My generals agree with your position." The noise died down. "A few days after the attacks, we sent a message to the Vallum by Envoy, asking for assistance. We await the Tribunal's answer."

Silence swept across the room. Doubtful expressions crossed the faces of many. Only a few seemed to back the King's decision.

Good, at least word has reached the Vallum already. I'll leave today to see what legions the Granadians have. Now for the worse news. Now to tell them what they didn't wish to hear. "A wise decision, Your Majesty. This army does indeed possess shadelings. Wraithwolves, darkwraiths and at least one daemon."

"Blasphemy," someone shouted.

"No one would dare, not after the War of the Remnants or the Shadowbearer War," yelled another.

"They cannot be enough of them left after the wars to even matter!" shouted another voice.

"But you said, you never saw them," countered Traushen.

"I said I didn't see the army when they attacked the clanholds," Ryne corrected. "But I fought a few of them on my way here."

"You fought a daemon?" Traushen's forehead creased with doubt.

"No, but I faced several wraithwolves. And there were more than a dozen darkwraiths. They've been ravaging farms in the countryside to supply their army. Every farm I passed has been stripped bare. In Carnas, I saw men, women, and children with their sela gone. You decide—"

"Oh gods, there's an army approaching from the south," a frantic voice yelled.

The chamber erupted into chaos.

CHAPTER 34

From her position at one of the tall windows on the topmost floor of the Streamean temple's clock tower, Shin Galiana rolled the words in the letter through her mind again. Rain pattered a staccato rhythm on the roof as the wind howled outside, whipping the deluge sideways.

Shin Galiana, I am sorry to disappoint you and how you thought this would end. But I am under orders from the King.

Thank you for helping to show how your Tribunal would usurp every authority. At this point, Sendeth and its allies stand against you. You and your people are required to surrender Eldanhill to the rule of Sendeth and King Emory.

Shall you choose to not hand over the town within the next few days, we will take it by force.

Captain Giomar.

Foolish man. Through the looking glass, the army massed to the south of Eldanhill, its bannermen carrying tall lances bearing the standards of Sendeth, jumped into sight as if she stood a few feet from them. The rain lashing down did nothing to stop the blustery wind from sweeping the banners to flap into the air. The Charging Boar outnumbered the others. Flying the highest was the Sliver Spear. Then, there was the Bloody Lance of Descane, the Crossed Swords of Parisan, the Night Sky of Bardes, the Red Bull of Loreth, the Gray Wolf of New Paltz, the Mailed Fist, the Leaping Hound, the Hunter's Bow, the

Executioner's Axe, and many more minor standards on display. Indeed, King Emory had summoned the strongest of his regiments from every major Sendethi town and city.

Three thousand feet outside Eldanhill's southern exit wagons and drays by the score blocked the road. Gathered behind the makeshift blockade thousands of men and young boys toiled in the storm as thunder and lightning warred in the sky. They built spiked, wooden barricades to stretch through the fields on that side of town. Women and those too young or old for the strenuous labor of fortifying the town's defenses ferried water and food to those who worked.

Rank upon rank of once retired soldiers and trainees, many in mismatched pieces of armor, stood at attention. Separated from them in several cohorts, their crimson armor spotless, were all the retired Dagodin Eldanhill could muster. Lined behind the Dagodin were over two dozen retired Ashishin who worked to lessen the effect of the raging storm. Galiana knew it was more the threat from the Matii that kept Sendeth's forces at bay than anything else.

"I thought you said this Giomar would do as you wished?" Stefan stood next to Galiana with his half of the tall windowpane closed.

The mosaic imprint stained into the glass depicted one of Ilumni's triumphs over Amuni. *Maybe that is a sign for us,* Galiana thought as she passed the looking glass to Stefan. "I used Manipulation on him. By all means, it should have worked." Her frown betrayed her confident voice. How could her Forging not work? There were no signs to say differently. The patterns of essences in his mind had been clear and concise, and she pulled the correct strings to touch off his fears, his need, and his own beliefs. Failure should have been impossible.

Stefan's thick eyebrows drew together. "You used Manipulation, and he was still able to defy you? A Buffer, maybe?" He put his eye to the looking glass and grunted.

"I was just thinking the same thought. But that would mean a High Ashishin within the Tribunal is making a play for power now rather than later. Who would betray them?"

Stefan slid the looking glass closed and gave her a sidelong glance. "You mean besides us and Jerem?" He shrugged. "Take your pick."

"Our reasons differ though," Galiana protested. "How long did they expect people to stand idly by while they leeched life from the lands around them for their attempts at immortality? And then destroy those who brought their concerns before them?"

Stefan stroked his gray–streaked beard. "Yet, what we do to fight them hasn't proved to be much different, Galiana. What makes what we do right?"

Galiana leaned on her staff, the scented incenses and the lightstones inserted at regular intervals along the walls reminding her of where she was and her purpose. "We have never killed a single person in Ilumni's name. We were forced into this position. Seems the burden of what we do has made you forget. How could we fight near immortality without doing what we have done?"

"Saying we've never killed anyone is Ilumni's name is stretching the truth just a little don't you think? Even so, it doesn't make what we do right."

"Sometimes, it is not doing what is right that saves man, but what is necessary."

Stefan gave a snorting chuckle. "I'm sure they would say the same."

"What they've done to remain in power all these years is evil, dating back to what Nerian began with the Erastonians. What he forced upon you, the lives he snuffed out with his wars. Sometimes you have to fight shade with shade. Isn't that what you once said to me?"

"I'm just weary of it all." Stefan sighed. "All these centuries planning and waiting and to see light at the end of the tunnel, only to have things start to spiral out of control. If we allow what the Tribunal has done to continue, Denestia will be forever mired in darkness. They must go. The fact they've abused the Chronicles to choose the path they did only proves the point more. I want this to end already."

"Patience. The Setian will be the spearhead of the war to come. The Chronicles do not lie," Galiana said in an effort to soothe Stefan's frustration. "We need to be strong for when the shade does come. If that means dealing with the Tribunal a little longer, then so be it."

"Maybe. But you and Jerem keep so much hidden it's

hard to keep the faith." Stefan pointed out toward the massing army. "I doubt it's a coincidence they're here at a time we may actually gain the upper hand. And who is to say what other allies they have? Barson, for sure. They've always made their hate for the Tribunal clear. Maybe Danindad or Calvar? Who knows? Then there's the Dosteri. All signs from our agents point to them knowing the importance of our kinai."

"When surrounded by enemies, choose a path no one expects," Galiana quoted from the Disciplines.

Stefan shook his head and gave a wry smile. "Is there such a path? Crossing too far down the Kelvore leads to territory caught up in the battles between Doster and Sendeth. The mountains, as you well know, leads to the feuding clans. We could ask them for help, but why should they help us? Giomar's failed attempt to demand their obedience to a King they don't recognize may have ruined that chance. Going west would be to enter Barson, which is forbidden territory for us. Has Jillian sent eagles to the Iluminus?"

"Yes. As soon as word arrived about the army. It will be at least a week and a half before the eagles arrive and we get help."

Stefan opened the looking glass and studied the opposing forces once more. "A week and a half we don't have. This has been almost perfectly orchestrated. The Tribunal is so blinded by their schemes in Ostania they've missed the real threat."

"But we cannot afford for them to lose beforehand," Galiana added. "So for now, we need to do what we can. We need them as much or more than they need us." Although she wouldn't admit all to Stefan, Galiana agreed with everything he said. Events were falling out of their control. Without word from Jerem, her hands were tied. They would need to sit and wait and hope reinforcements from the Tribunal arrived in time. Their outlook was bleak.

"Have you heard from your agent about my son?" Stefan closed the glass once more and turned to face her. He looked as if he aged ten years as he mentioned Ancel. Even within his crimson uniform, she could tell his shoulders slumped. Bags marred his face under his eyes.

Galiana sighed. She'd hoped Stefan wouldn't bring this up now. "No. Not yet."

Stefan's eyes hardened. "So not only are we faced with this, but Ancel may be hurt or imprisoned for all we know. How can we save the people if we can't even save my son?"

"Well, we know he is not dead."

"I thank my wife for that every day," Stefan muttered,.

Galiana's heart ached to see Stefan this way, but he wasn't thinking clearly. "Has the Access Key changed?"

Stefan touched his sword with its hilt of chased gold. "No."

"And Thania has not felt him pass?"

"No."

"Then he is not dead. Held captive would make more sense. It would give another reason why Sendeth's army has given us a few days to make our decision. They could be bringing him here to bargain."

That set Stefan's eyes smoldering. "Or they could be waiting for the arrival of their own Matii. The Pathfinders may have done a good job culling those without control, but we all know they didn't capture every single one. Regardless, if Sendeth has my son, I will give up Eldanhill for him."

"As would I," Galiana said. "He is too important not to. But I fear if they do have him they will not surrender him."

"I'd announce my rule and flay them all if they tried to keep my son from me. Or if they hurt him." Stefan's hands balled into fists.

Galiana didn't doubt the man. He'd lost one family before to the Tribunal's schemes with Nerian. She'd spent too many centuries plotting with him not to know the look his face bore. People were going to die. A great many, if they harmed Ancel. "I beg you to be patient. Wait and see what other terms they send while we build our defenses here. In the meantime, you plan a way for us to escape."

"I've been thinking on that." Stefan's forehead furrowed. "There's no way for everyone to escape. The best we could hope for is to defend Eldanhill until we find out where Ancel is, collect him, then you Materialize him, Thania and the Access Key somewhere safe." Stefan's gaze met hers in an intense stare.

"You know what you're asking?"

"Yes."

Galiana's shoulders slumped bonelessly. To use

Materialization, she would break the last bonds of her control. The Pathfinders would come and put an end to her. "If that is my fate then the sacrifice would be worth it for him, for the world."

Stefan nodded, reached out, and gave her a firm squeeze. The sadness of her possible death radiated from his eyes. *What's done is done.* She prayed that somehow Kachien had taken Ancel to safety.

CHAPTER 35

R yne took note of the Astocans, with regalia on
display, who had continued to talk and partake
from the supply of food available as if no one had announced
the presence of an encroaching force. He allowed his lips a slight
twitch. *So, Voliny still keeps his Advisors and Generals mingled within the
crowd, and he obviously knew of this army's approach beforehand.*

Speculation still ran rampant despite the announcement
the reported army was Granadian. Many fidgeted or dabbed at
sweaty foreheads, and hushed murmurs swept through the room.
The anticipation within the air grew palpable, and all heads faced
the wide door to the chamber.

Marching footsteps sounded from the hall, the door
swung open, and a gold liveried servant with the Waterwall
insignia stitched to his breast entered. "Knight Commander
Varick of Granadia, Your Majesty," announced the servant. He
shied away from the entrance.

A sweaty Lieutenant Rosival entered and stepped aside.

Following Rosival was a wide–shouldered man in silver
armor filigreed with an embossing of the sun and lightning
bolts striking in front of it on his chest plate. Short, gray hair,
interspersed with white streaks, perched on his head and matched
the scraggly growth on his chin. His hair bounced with each
robust stride. Eyes like flint stared straight ahead at the King as
the man strode down the hall. Varick had aged since Ryne last
saw him, but those hard eyes remained the same. The Knight
Commander carried a silver helmet under one arm. Although

unarmed, he moved with a predator–like grace in his calf high sabatons, his gait and his expression daring anyone in the room to challenge him. The man's eyes gave a slight twitch when his gaze crossed Ryne.

Knight Commander Varick stepped onto the dais and bowed from his waist to the King. "Your Majesty." He gave a mere nod to the rest of the room; his gaze strayed to Ryne for a moment. "People of Astoca and those of the other Ostanian Kingdoms, I thank you for accommodating me." His attention returned to the King.

Without standing, the King gave a slight bow. "You're always welcome Knight Commander. I hoped for a quick response, but this is faster than I expected."

"We could have come directly, but we did not wish to create alarm or provoke any attacks. A High Ashishin brought us as close as he dared, Your Majesty. The Tribunal recognizes the threat we all face. I've been ordered to help in whatever way I deem necessary."

The King stood. "In that case, would you all please excuse us?" He gestured to everyone within the chamber. "The ambassadors who represent the interests of the other four kingdoms can stay."

All the other nobles, dignitaries, and their translators bowed to the King and filed out of the audience chamber. Those still left were the representatives from Cardia, Harna, Bana, and a black–coated Felani Lord. The King's Advisors and Generals stayed. Ryne turned on his heels to walk from the room.

"A moment if you will, Master Waldron," Voliny said.

Ryne stopped and turned to face the King. "Yes, Your Majesty?"

"Would you stay and lend an ear to the proceedings?"

"No," Ryne said. Face a blank mask he met the King's stony gaze. "You know my opinion, and even without me you already sent word to the west. His presence," he gestured to Varick, "means the Tribunal's offer of support is genuine. Now the strategy is up to you. I was never good with that sort of thing."

The King eyes tightened, but Ryne didn't flinch. "That is not what I have heard when my soldiers faced you. However, I will not try to force you into something you do not wish. Yet, can

I ask…will you fight for us?"

Ryne sensed a subtle shift in the Royal Guards hidden around the room. A touch on his arm announced Sakari stepping up next to him. Ryne's hand rose to the scarred left side of his face, and he stroked the old wounds. "Yes."

Sighs rolled around the room like whispered hisses as the Royal Guards relaxed.

"Master Waldron," said Knight Commander Varick in his familiar gruff voice, "I'd like to speak to you after this meeting."

Ryne still stared at the King who finally looked away. "Sure, I'll be outside when you're finished." Ryne's gaze brushed Varick long enough to see the twinkle in the Knight Commander's eyes. "It'll be a pleasure." Ryne strolled from the room.

Almost three hours later, with the sun waning in its dying throes, Ryne and Sakari rode with Varick toward the Knight Commander's encampment accompanied by Rosival. They left the lights and sights of Astoca behind them to the north. Rosival took his leave when they reached the encampment comprised of several hundred white tents with the Tribunal's Lightstorm standard flying high above.

They dismounted, and several Dagodin took their dartans. Knight Commander Varick led the way through the neat tent lines. The camp reeked of the droppings from gathered mounts mingled with the sweet aromas of food for a stifling contrast. Soldiers acknowledged Varick with a bow or knuckled their foreheads. Many relaxed at fire pits, either cooking or sharpening weapons, while others practiced the sword using wooden lathes. The clack, clack of the weapons played a soothing beat. Almost every soldier they passed studied Ryne, often fingering their weapons. They ignored Sakari.

"I had no desire to speak around Rosival," Varick said.

"I figured as much."

"I was surprised to find you here. And discussing war no less. I thought you retired?" Varick led them to a tent about twice the size as the others.

"I did."

Two lance–wielding guards stood at the pavilion's

entrance, snapping to attention at the sight of Varick. The Knight Commander nodded to each man in turn.

"Knight Cosar," Varick said to the one on the left. "I'm as hungry as a starved bear. Send for food."

The soldier bowed, leaned his lance on the canvas with care, and strode away toward the cook fires. Varick entered the tent.

"I'll wait out here," Sakari said.

Grumbling to himself, Ryne raised the flaps and ducked low as he stepped inside. Too often, he had to keep his body hunched and head down when standing inside one of these contraptions.

"Sorry about that." Varick pulled off his gauntlets and threw them on the plain, wooden table. They thudded next to a bright lamp and Ostanian maps. "If I knew we would've found you, I would have had the tent raised."

Ryne grunted dismissively. "You would think I'd be used to it, but it's been too many years."

"Now, that's the truth." Varick turned to face Ryne. Smiling, he held out a callused hand. "It's been too long, old friend."

"Indeed." Ryne clasped the shorter man's arm. "Way too long."

"Well, at least the years have been good to you. You haven't aged a day since we first met."

Ryne grinned. "I wish I could say the same for you. Your hair is almost as white as this tent."

"Don't let the white hairs and wrinkles fool you." He looked Ryne up and down. "I could still manage a blow or two on you." Varick released the handshake and faked a strike at Ryne.

Leaning away from Varick, Ryne held up his hand. "I'd never make such a mistake, old timer."

Varick wrinkled his nose. "Although, I would have to beg you to take a bath first."

They both laughed. Ryne sniffed himself. The smell of death and days without a bath clung to him still.

Varick took a step back and studied Ryne. "So, are you joining with the Astocans?"

"No."

"But, you said—"

"I said, yes, I'll fight. Meaning I'll fight for the Alliance. If he took my words to mean I'd fight for Astoca…" Ryne shrugged. "I didn't want to cause trouble, so I said it in a way he'd want to hear. After I came here, the plan was to go find you."

"Oh?" Varick removed his sword and strode over to a bedroll, the only other contents in the tent. "The gods work in strange ways. Before I received the message from the Tribunal, I planned to come to Carn—."

Ryne took a deep breath at the mention of his home, his hand tightening on his sword.

"I'm sorry," Varick said. "I forgot. You feel like talking about it?" He carefully lay his sword down on the bedroll.

"Not much to talk about. They didn't leave anyone alive. Not much different than what I've done in the past."

"You shouldn't compare yourself to them. You've always fought for the light, for Ilumni." Varick headed to the table and its maps. "There's nothing but darkness in what they do. We've both seen it, Ryne. They have to be stopped, or else we all fall."

Stooping slightly, Ryne moved close to the tent's center to better accommodate his size. "I just don't understand the point to all of this. The killings, the wars. Is it just for territory? For power? If this is all part of a divine battle in preparation for the day the seals break, wouldn't Amuni secure his powerbase in Hydae first, before he tried to claim Denestia? What of the other gods? Where do they fit in? If Denestia is Ilumni's, why does it seem we're always defending? When do we attack? Is this really about divinity or just some story drawn up for us to spill blood so one kingdom can claim another in the name of religion?"

Varick remained silent for a moment. "You're asking questions I can't answer. I'm just a soldier who's been fighting for too long. The Tribunal points, I attack. This is the way things have always been."

"You ever questioned it?"

"Question who?" Varick grunted. "The Tribunal? That's not my place. I'm not you. I can't defy them. If I could kill a Pathfinder, maybe. But look where doing so got you. My tasks are simple. I see a threat, and I respond. We've both seen enough to know they're greater powers at work here. You've always sought answers since I met you, Ryne. More answers than most. You say because you can't remember who or what you are. Yet, even after your pardon, you refused to go whenever the Tribunal asked for an audience. I've backed you in the past against them, but you've never said wh—"

"Because it's not up for discussion." Ryne's hands clenched around his sword once more. After all these years, Varick was still insistent. "The High Ashishin Tribunal is not all pure like they make people believe."

Varick shrugged. "None of us are. But we do what we must, as they do what they must. I don't think you'll ever get the answers you seek without going to them. Demand bravery by conquering your fear. Remember? It doesn't only apply to grooming troops. Hiding across the Vallum will only work for so long. Sooner or later, you'll have to go to them."

"Well, let's just hope it's later. I'll continue searching for my answers elsewhere. Speaking of which, why were you looking for me?"

"Well, there's two parts to that. First, The Tribunal has sent several legions across the Vallum in the past few months alone. Many of them raw recruits. Trained Dagodin, yes, but hearing what I did today, training will only take them so far. So—"

"So you were going to ask me to train them, or at least to help." Ryne smiled. This fit what he needed perfectly. A glimmer of vengeance to come warmed his insides. "How's the Tribunal feel about that?"

Varick gave Ryne a sidelong glance and a smirk.

"I see. What's the second reason?"

"Not only did they dispatch these new legions but they also ordered all Dagodin Imbuers to begin crafting *divya*." Varick paced back and forth from the table to a cot in the corner. "It really became strange when they managed to drag Dagodin Lucina Adler from wherever she retired to train these new Imbuers."

Ryne frowned. "*The* Lucina Adler?"

"Yes."

"Too much of a coincidence. It reeks of the Tribunal knowing what was about to happen here. Always plotting," Ryne mused, stroking his scars.

Varick nodded in agreement. "Even so, once I heard they'd dragged her from wherever she was hiding, I thought of you. She's one of the few people who may be able to tell you the origins of your weapon. And not go running back to the Tribunal, that is."

Ryne perked up, possibilities flitting through his head. "So where can I find her?"

"She's in Felan Mark. I figured it being in Ostania would give you a better chance to talk to her before anyone could do something about it."

"Why would they send her all the way there?"

Varick's face brightened. "Oh, I don't know. Some commander reported he needed the weapons as soon as possible. The Tribunal agreed."

Ryne couldn't help his grin. Varick had a way of seeing he got things done just the way he wanted them. Ryne's face grew serious. "You'll need those *divya* more than you know."

"Really?"

Drawing a deep breath, Ryne told him what had happened. He started with Mariel then continued on with the missing villagers, the murdered men, the golden-haired stranger, the infected lapra, the Alzari, the wraithwolves found in the woods, the darkwraiths and his battle. He left out Halvor and the Entosis.

Varick's expression went from wide-eyed shock to disgust until his brow furrowed tightly. "Mariel, you say? I almost forgot. There was a third reason I needed to see you. A couple months before I left the Vallum, there was a slim, dark haired woman with gold eyes like an eagle's looking for you. Claimed she was a Devout named Mariel. I had one of my men look into it. She was really an Ashishin named Irmina, well on her way to becoming a Raijin. One of the Tribunal's favorites or so I've been told."

Ryne ground his teeth. Not only was the woman an Ashishin, but she was training to be a member of one of the deadliest assassin corps in Granadia. *I knew I should've killed her.*

CHAPTER 36

From Irmina's vantage point atop a hill, travelers and soldiers alike approaching the main fort appeared as small colored figures dwarfed by the Vallum of Light's size. In groups, they disappeared into the two–hundred foot wide mouth of the passage that served as the only exit or entrance through the wall. The Vallum itself stretched three hundred feet into the air, its white alabaster, feldspar, and steel, shining with an ethereal glow. Irmina knew the radiance for what it was—light and fire essences imbued into the structure.

In truth, the fort was two Bastions—Hope and Forlorn—like every other Bastion named for whatever the High Ashishin who undertook their construction felt they represented. The oval edifices, with their lines of crenels separated twenty–five feet between each, extended another hundred feet above the Vallum, and were positioned to the left and right of the entrance to and from Ostania proper. Not that the land spanning from the Vallum west to the Sea of Swirls was not part of Ostania, but as that swath was currently under Tribunal rule, it was often considered Granadian territory. The fact the local Ostanian kingdoms disagreed with such considerations was of no consequence.

As the setting sun painted wispy clouds purple and orange, Irmina rode down from the hills toward the throng of travelers heading to and from locations beyond the Vallum. Those without an armed escort were already preparing camps not far from the wall's protection. Wagons rolled along, and those on horses, dartan or slainen galloped by those on foot in an attempt to reach the gates before the call to close the entrance sounded.

The activity around her droned on in an incomprehensible racket. Peoples in fashions she didn't recognize, various skin colors from pale Granadians to ebony Cardians, and languages and dialects she couldn't begin to understand, journeyed the wide road. Quick bows came from those who glanced up and saw Irmina's crimson Ashishin uniform as Misty sped by.

Irmina followed the path set aside for nobility and military, red armored Dagodin greeting her with salutes. As she passed the first massive gate set into the wall, Irmina cringed. Unlike other gates, this one was all stone—a part of the wall—and required an Ashishin to trigger the wards that closed and opened it. She had once seen what would happen to those caught between when the massive slabs slid together. Dark red splotches marked the most recent occurrence.

Neither lamp nor lightstone lit the passage, but the glow from the essences within the structure made the inside as bright as early afternoon. Murder–holes and arrow slits dotted the walls and the bridge above that spanned between the two Bastions. With a soft trill, Irmina urged Misty to go faster. Minutes later, they crossed the five hundred foot tunnel and out into the open air. Tension eased from Irmina's shoulders, and she allowed herself a deep breath.

Ignoring the people either heading to the closest encampments of travelers or continuing toward the town in the distance, Irmina veered right. Spread below in a vast field were thousands of tents, many with the Lightstorm insignia flying above. Barked orders, the clash of steel, and the synchronized stomp from Dagodin practicing formations rolled through the air. She rode abreast the Vallum, bathed in its white glow, until she reached the rounded granite structure where the Bastion Forlorn began. The Dagodin outside snapped to attention as she dismounted and dropped Misty's reins over one of many hooked spikes set into the wall.

The gravity of the news she brought crawled within her as she entered the building. Before long, her hurried footsteps became a run. Several winding stairs later, she reached the well–guarded communication center.

The room's rough–hewn, feldspar and steel blocks rose

into a dome far above her head. As with the passage, no lamps hung along the walls, but the room was bright all the same. A lone man, with a round, too–smooth face, wearing a long robe with colorful sashes embroidered in diagonal patterns that identified him as an Ashishin Herald studied the message map on the floor.

This was not her first time inside a Bastion, but she still found herself muttering prayers to Ilumni and casting glances at the glowing walls around her. Sometimes, the light felt like a great weight upon her, and she would rub her shoulders. The feeling diminished the longer she remained inside the Bastion. She waited to the side as the Herald studied the message map. Every so often, he stopped to stroke his thin, forked beard, which was in odd counterpoint to his cheeks and even rounder bald head.

Created from metal, wood, and stone, the map spanned almost the entire floor. Life–like replicas of the cities and other important locations jutted into the air inches off the stone. They appeared real and solid as if she could reach out and touch them. If she did, her hands would just pass through them. Irmina didn't need to open her Matersense to see that an intricate Forge created the effect. Like almost everything else within the Bastion, the message map was a *divya*.

Lightstones in various colors gave off a sharp gleam, highlighting the major cities in Granadia. Others matched the location of every Bastion along the Vallum as well as those built within Granadia. Lesser lights between the cities moved on their own accord, following Envoys' movements. Across the entire message system, every map and their stones were designed from the same *divya*. This intricate network never ceased to amaze her.

Irmina made sure to remain a few feet from the map. Heralds took their jobs to heart and considered it blasphemous for anyone not of their own calling to tread upon their work. She'd thought about becoming a Herald once, until her calling showed her another path.

The man continued to study the map, ignoring her presence. Every time he moved, his robes flowed around him and made the sashes appear to swirl all the way to just below his waist. Irmina tapped her foot and coughed.

Herald Bodo looked up from the map. "Ah. Shin Irmina." He signaled to the two Dagodin standing just inside the door. "Leave us and close the door behind you." The men bowed and did as asked. Bodo waited a moment with his eyes closed. When he opened them again, he took her in with a wry smile and a twinkle in his silver–blue eyes. "I see you've done away with that farce of a Devout uniform. Does Jerem approve or will I be visiting you chained to a wall? I'm sure the old coot must have had a heart attack."

Irmina smiled. Bodo was one of few she ever heard speak of her master in anything close to affection. Most others simply cowered. "He doesn't know yet. That's to be part of my message. I fear the rest isn't so pleasing."

"Well, considering if your wearing a Raijin uniform when you haven't graduated yet is to be considered 'pleasing', I cannot imagine what other ill tidings you bear."

She told Bodo about the little she discovered about Ryne, before she gave him the news of the attack on Ranoda by the shadeling army and Amuni's Children. Herald Bodo handled it well, nodding and grunting while stroking his forked beard. When she relayed her rescue by Tae and the message the old woman wanted her to deliver to their master, Herald Bodo's face paled. He paced back and forth across his message map, his robes swishing through the replicas in colorful swirls as if they didn't exist.

"May Ilumni help us all," he uttered when she finished.

"I understand shadeling creation shouldn't be possible in Denestia, and the chance of one among them being as strong as a High Ashishin is daunting for sure. But we should be able to handle this if we act now," Irmina insisted.

Herald Bodo paused for a moment, listened, shook his head then continued pacing and muttering to himself.

"Bodo?"

"You don't understand just how dire our situation is, do you?" He stopped pacing for a moment before he began again.

"Actually, I think I do, after all she told me. Why else would she have risked Materialization to get me here so fast?"

The Herald paused again at the mention of Tae's Materialization Forge. His mutterings grew more pronounced. "You're the closest we have to this situation. I would risk telling you, but not without our master's permission. A moment, if you will." He stepped onto the path built around the map.

Irmina embraced her Matersense. As if a fog lifted before

her eyes, all around her came alive with new clarity. The walls of the Bastion thrummed with essences so bright she squinted. On the message map itself, essences matching those that made up the actual cities filled their ethereal counterparts. Mater flowed from point to point like blood running through veins. And Herald Bodo manipulated them all.

The Forging he made was so complex she lost track of the strings of essences in their intricacy. As usual, her own power surged within her, begging for release. Already within the Eye, she ignored it. Control was hers, and she wouldn't relinquish her hold. The scale of Bodo's Forging built to incomprehensible proportions. Irmina felt her bonds begin to weaken, and her resolve grew tenuous. Before she could lose control, she cut off her Matersense. Everything faded to a pale, washed out version of what she'd witnessed, and the essences vanished.

Bodo's ragged gasps made Irmina look toward the man. "What was that all about? Do you need to use that much power for a message?"

"No," Bodo said, still breathing heavily. "But in order to hide this particular message, it had to be done. No one can see what I sent except Jerem."

"What now?"

"We wait. His answer—" Bodo paused, his eyes trained on the map. "Ah, permission has been granted."

Irmina frowned. What could be so important all of this needed to be done?

Bodo paced back and forth again. "Where to start? Where to start?" he said to himself.

Irmina swallowed. "He wants me to get rid of the Raijin uniform doesn't he?"

"Actually, no. He didn't bother with that."

"He didn't?" Irmina gave a slight shake of her head. Her work entailed the use of many a disguise, but anything above a Devout's garb, from Raijin to Exalted, was expressly forbidden and punishable by a pain penance at the very least.

Bodo stopped pacing. "Ah. What do you know of the Eztezians?"

"History was never my area of expertise, Bodo."

"Still what do you remember from your schooling."

Irmina shrugged. "They were the appointed Guardians

of Denestia responsible for sealing the gods in the Nether. The very same gods that appointed them. Later, driven insane by their own power, they fought against each other and brought about the Great Divide in which they almost destroyed the world. What do they have to do with anything? They're long dead."

Bodo's eyes twinkled, and he gave her a knowing smile. "Therein is your first mistake. Not all the Eztezians are dead. And they weren't just the Guardians of Denestia. They were the direct descendants of our so called gods and also their Battleguards."

Irmina tried to grasp the concept of humans being the gods' Battleguards. "So you're telling me every scholar, every book, every school, every story about the Eztezians' existence are all wrong?"

"Not wrong, but purposefully misguiding. Do you know how the Eztezians sealed the gods?"

"They used some kind of powerful *divyas*. There are no real records of the *divyas'* creation or their names. At least not that I've seen."

"Well yes, but the *divya* were people. The Eztezians themselves were the *divya.*"

Irmina stared in disbelief. "How's that possible?"

"By use of Etchings. Our gods were created in the Nether, out of the bodies of netherlings by the One God. The netherlings—"

"The same netherlings which were later used to help create the first shadelings?"

"Precisely so. And they never forgave the gods for such misuse, for the destruction of millions of their kind to create the armies of the shade. The gods warred among each other using these forces. Until the netherlings decided to rebel. They used their control over Mater in its most primal state to bestow power comparable to the gods unto the Eztezians. Many of the Eztezians themselves had grown weary of the constant war and the destruction of all they'd grown to love about the worlds. So, they allowed the netherlings to Etch this power into their core. On the very strongest of the Eztezians, the Etchings also included the seals. With surprise on their side, they betrayed their forefathers and trapped the gods in the Nether."

"How do the Etchings work?"

"No one really knows. There's no record to be found

of exactly what they looked like or what they did. All we know are some of the results. Of course, they were those among the netherlings who didn't agree because they too reaped benefits from the constant death and destruction of the wars."

"What could one gain from all that death?"

Bodo raised his brows. "Why sela of course. Forged the right way, sela can be a source of near immortality. I know you're thinking no one can Forge sela. The truth is, it can be done. But in order to reap the rewards, a living being has to die. The more death, the more sela gained. So for the sake of eternal youth, we became fodder. Bred and raised to die."

Irmina cringed at the idea of being bred like cattle. "Is that what the Tribunal does and others like yourself to live as long as you do?" Maybe Bodo would give her the answer Taeria wouldn't.

"The Tribunal, yes. Me, no. There are other, safer ways now."

"Yes. I stumbled upon one," Irmina admitted, now convinced of what the Eldanhill Council and Setian's old leaders did. "Using kinai products to feed the masses then leeching Mater from them to halt aging." She ached to tell someone, anyone, how she knew. The revelation and the side effects of the process had been her parents' work. They'd died because they believed it was unjust and wished to expose the Tribunal. The Dorns had issued the execution order. Irmina took a deep breath, forcing the sudden wave of heat deep inside the Eye.

"…simple way to put a complex process, but yes, in short that is how it works," Bodo finished.

Irmina needed to change the subject. "If the Eztezians aren't dead, what happened to them?"

"They sealed themselves and hid the memory of their locations. But there was one thing they forgot to account for."

"What?"

"The Chroniclers."

"The Great Tomes?"

"No. The Chroniclers. The men and women who wrote the Chronicles within the Great Tomes. The lost descendants of Eztezian and netherling couplings. They decided it was their duty to walk the land and record all past, present and futures. They passed their knowledge down inherently. After thousands of years, their offspring became the Matii we are today. The Ashishin, the Namazzi, the Svenzar, the Alzari, the Skadwaz and others who shall remain nameless."

Irmina frowned. "So what makes the Chroniclers so important?"

"Well, if you could find the descendants of the Chroniclers, then you could find who now holds the histories. In turn, you could find out where the Eztezians are hidden."

Everything fell into place for Irmina now. "And by perfecting the Bloodline Affinity, whoever it is among Amuni's Children now has the upper hand in locating the last Eztezians. Kill them, and they break the seals."

"Precisely so."

Something still didn't make sense to her. "But who has enough power to kill an Eztezian. Not even a High Ashishin could. One of the Exalted, maybe?"

Bodo paced once more. "Several Exalted may stand a chance. It's more likely all this has been put into play by a netherling."

"Merciful Ilumni," Irmina whispered. "A netherling, here in Denestia? But that would mean the seals have weakened enough for them to breach the Kassite and pass into any of the Planes of Existence."

"That, is just the beginning of the horrors that could be unleashed on our world," Bodo said, his round faced now haggard and grim. "We don't think the seals have weakened to that point yet, but we believe some netherlings have always been here since the sealing. We don't know how to find them, but as of now, we suspect only the weakest creatures can cross the Kassite as it is attuned to stop the strongest threats.

"However, as the seals continue to weaken, not only will stronger shadelings pass through, but we will face daemons and the Skadwaz themselves. Denestia will fall to a horde of shadelings under their power. Eventually, the seals will be broken, and the gods will come to seek vengeance. So, you see our dilemma. We ourselves need the help of the Eztezians. It's why Jerem has ordered you to approach this man, Ryne. You need to find a way to have him trust you. Jerem believes this Ryne to be a direct descendant of an Eztezian."

Chapter 37

Ancel shifted his butt around in an attempt to find a more comfortable position in the corner of the old barn, brushing away the offending sprigs of hay that poked at him through his clothes. Kachien, her face a pale imitation of its normal coppery color, lay asleep next to him. Her chest rose and fell in a steady rhythm, much better than the shallow breathing she'd suffered from as the night had turned to day and she pointed the way to this abandoned farm and its ramshackle buildings. Now, dusk had come again, but at least this time they'd found shelter. Charra stood guard near the door, his eyes focused out into the night's encroaching darkness.

Earlier, they'd managed to find an old oil lamp and enough fuel in a metal drum to keep it alight. Mirza, his hair now a faded scarlet, stirred the coals in a fire pit they'd dug after clearing out the hay from the stall he and Danvir occupied. The small fire flared and smoke wafted through the air, finding its way out a nearby window. On a spit, Danvir turned several mutton haunches, their juices sizzling when they touched the glowing coals. The meat's mouthwatering aroma set Ancel's stomach grumbling.

Ancel made certain Kachien still rested comfortably before he stood and walked over to his friends. He took a seat next to them on the barn's earthen floor, the fire's warmth a welcome comfort.

Danvir nodded toward Kachien. "How's she doing?"

"Much better. I still don't think we'll be able to leave tonight like she wanted."

Mirza stirred the coals again, kicking up sparks. "As long as we get to eat first, I don't care. I've never much liked this side of the Kelvore River."

Danvir grunted in agreement. The two of them had kept up a constant vigil since they crossed the river. Although still in Sendeth, Ancel couldn't blame his friends for their apprehension. They weren't far from Randane, but this region may as well be unclaimed lands—the result of frequent skirmishes between Dosteri and Sendethi troops.

"I still can't believe what she did," Ancel said, his low voice filled with awe. "To be able to hold the currents of a river at bay. To calm storm winds. To go against the natural flow of Mater. Can you imagine if any of us could do something like that? I wonder how strong she is?"

"Stronger than an Ashishin, I think," Mirza said.

Danvir took down the hunks of sizzling meat. "Maybe. And right now, I don't care. I just want to eat and get home." He dropped the haunches into two large pots they'd found inside the farmhouse.

Echoing his sentiments, Ancel nodded and eyed the food. They'd discussed staying in the farmhouse until they ventured inside past the broken down front door. A weeks old corpse sat rotting in a chair, a huge gash across the chest, head lolled to one side. The place reeked of death. They took only what they needed to prepare their food and left. Ancel cringed with the memory and almost lost his appetite, but his need for sustenance overrode his revulsion.

"Do you think they're looking for us back home?" Mirza stared out through the lone window.

Ancel followed his gaze. The twin moons hung low in the sky. On clear nights after a storm, if one saw the moons before they reached their zenith, their huge silvery–blue forms gave the impression they were close enough to reach out and touch.

"They must be by now. I'm sure my father's people in Randane dispatched eagles," Ancel said.

At least that's what he hoped. But suppose they didn't know it was him and his friends that the King's men sought? Then word wouldn't reach Eldanhill until too late. How long before the soldiers discovered what they did? He thought about his father, his mother, his classes, Teacher's Calestis' tutelage, and the long ride in the morning that comforted him so much. Would they ever see their homes again?

"I'm sure by now my Da has either sent men or is on his way to Randane himself," Danvir said as he fanned the hot food with the flat back of an old chair.

"I'm worried about that too," Mirza said. "None of our people are safe in Randane or anywhere in Sendeth for that matter."

"You know what this all means, right?" Ancel said glumly. He stared off into the distance. "It means more war. To think King Emory's involved with the shade. Wouldn't it have been easier to seize us when we delivered the kinai? It's not like Headspeaker Valdeen could've stopped them. Either way, they'll all answer to the Tribunal."

Danvir growled. "They can keep their bloody war. All I want right now is to eat." His broad shoulders flexed as he ripped chunks of meat from the bone.

Following their friend's lead, Ancel and Mirza went to the pots and prepared themselves their own meals. Before long, they sat drinking water and eating in silence.

Ancel found himself thinking about Kachien's power again, and his own recent manifestations came to mind. From the way Kachien had grown weak from her Forging, he knew she would soon need to kill to appease whatever her power required as a price or she would either go insane or die. He shuddered to think what she went through. If he was to ever control what grew inside himself, he needed to practice in earnest. Tonight, he would begin the task until the ability to step into the Eye's calmness became as easy as breathing.

After he finished eating, Ancel cleared old furniture and wood from the far side of the barn. He found a thin branch among some firewood. Using a rusted knife he'd found in the barn, he whittled the stick until its weight matched his sword. Satisfied, he stood and shifted into a ready position, his right foot forward, facing straight ahead. Most of his weight rested on his back leg, firm to the ground like tree roots. He kept his front foot balanced on the ball with the heel slightly raised.

In quick motions, he began to move, shifting his front

foot to copy likely scenarios, to compensate for balance or to pull back as if he slipped. Adding his rooted back leg to the movements, he pushed off into lunges, side steps, and blocks, his charm bouncing on his chest. At times, he dropped his weight onto his front foot to press forward. The entire time, his legs remained slightly bent, his joints loose, his back straight, body facing forward and his arms relaxed. He imagined his father or Teacher Calestis calling out the positions from left, right, back and front as he ran through the exercises called the Bonadotors, his feet making precise steps in every direction, his arms whipping out, loose and fast.

"Dexterity and sword handling are as important as strength. Speed kills," his father would say. *"The Bonadotors are the keys. Practice them daily."*

He repeated the Bonadotors several times before he moved into basic swordplay. First came the eight basic parry positions, from head, to shoulder, to flank and to his legs on each side. He imagined his assailant attacking him from each position, and he defended. When he found his opening he struck with the cuts, slices, and thrusts he'd been taught. Elancose for all attacks on the right. Carnean for those on the left. His repertoire sped faster and faster, and he hardly noticed the sweat on his brow.

The burning in his arms and shoulders became a sweet sensation, the weight of his legs, a feather. The stick became a sword in truth.

He shifted into the Stances his father had taught him. Flowing like water, absorbing every attack was the art of the Namazzi. Rumbling and strong, strength like the mountains themselves was the Svenzar. Swift, faster than an eye could follow, like light itself, were the Ashishin arts. If only he knew the Styles to go with each. Regret touched him as he realized how far along in his training he could be at this moment.

Teacher Calestis' voice echoed in his ear. *"Your sela isn't just a combination of life and death essences. It's the combination of your heart and mind, as your gaze is your perception and sight, as your hearing is a connection to locate anything close, as your touch can be as useful as what you perceive. Thrust all you sense into yourself, so deep until you reach a calm pool. There resides your sela. All that makes you who you are. Embrace it. When you have, then you will have attained the Eye. Within the Eye, all and nothing exists. There is no speed, no strength, no dark, no light. There is just you and what your heart desires. Commit to that and what seems impossible will become possible. Ultimate control will be yours to reap."*

Ancel embraced the Eye, and floated upon the calm pool at his center. Outside, all his emotions and feelings raged. They tugged at him from every direction. He could pluck any he wished to use or none. In the Eye, control belonged to him.

As before, at the river with Kachien or when he was overcome with emotions, a sight rose within him. Every living thing glowed with their own luminescence, with their own shades, like an aura of light around a candle, lightstone or lamp.

The glow drifted over Mirza and Danvir in vibrant hues. Ancel could tell them apart like the calluses on his palms. Whites, reds, and blues swirled around Mirza as if he was swathed in fire then surrounded by sky and clouds. Danvir's was heavy with browns and greens, which somehow reminded Ancel of the mountains and forests. When he turned to Kachien, he stared with his mouth open.

Colors roiled around the woman as if they fought for supremacy—a white glare, many shades of brown, yellowish light, faint blue. And dominating them all, squeezing them in was darkness. Ancel knew the darkness for what it was. Shade. Somehow, he knew. This hue was what encroached on her sanity, made her kill, caused her lack of control. And as he watched, the shade was devouring the other colors in tiny increments. Ancel wanted to run to her, to hold her, to tell her she would be fine. He could tell the pain being inflicted on her by the battle around her body. Each time the shade gained ground, a near imperceptible shiver passed over her body, too tiny for a normal eye to notice but not for his new sight. Not able to bear anymore, he tore his eyes away from her.

His gaze passed over Charra, and he lost a hold on the Eye. The glow around everything melted like snow into a geyser. But he knew what he witnessed, what caused him to lose his grip on the Eye in the first place.

Charra had no hues. Looking at the daggerpaw had been like looking at a blank slate. How could there be nothing?

A groan from Kachien broke Ancel from his thoughts. Her eyes opened.

Danvir and Mirza rushed to her side. Ancel looked on, not quite sure what to do now he'd seen the suffering existing around her. After a moment, and one more glance at where Charra lay, he joined his friends.

They prepared a meal for Kachien and helped her get comfortable. She ate, and before long, she was shooing them away.

"You three remind me of Tae, one of the old menders in my village. Fussing over me as if I am about to die. I am fine and strong." Kachien stood.

As Ancel and his friends watched, she closed her eyes and danced. First left, then right, back, front, a side step, her shoulders dipping or rising with each rhythmic movement. Her movements were achingly slow at first, mesmerizing. She swayed delicately, but not as sensual as the Temtesa. Her movements were sharper, more pronounced. Ancel found himself smiling as he recognized what she did. The Bonadotors, but in a more flowing way than he'd ever seen, like the lapping movement of tiny waves on a calm sea. In tiny increments, she sped up, until she flitted so quickly he could no longer follow her movements. When she finished, he and his friends stood jaws unhinged in awe. Kachien bowed.

How she could perform as she did with what Ancel witnessed around her, he didn't know, but for now he possessed no desire to question it. She appeared fine for the moment.

"Now that you three are done staring, it is time to go. The dartans I have hidden are not far from here. They should still be safe." Kachien headed to the door. "Come, we must hurry. The other part of me is in need."

Ancel squeezed his eyes shut. Although she hadn't said it, he knew. Kachien's power needed to be fed.

CHAPTER 38

Just before dawn, Ryne received Varick's summons. Twilight tinged the cloudy horizon to the east in deep orange, while above the encampment, the skies remained dark, the moons having already fled from view to the west. The camp bustled with preparations of a mass exodus. Firepits smoked and smoldered, and the sweet aroma from early breakfast lingered on the air. Already soldiers on horseback, followed by those on dartans, formed a long line, all facing west. Behind them, Dagodin infantry stood in neat rows, most appearing bored and impatient. Varick's tent was the only one still standing.

With a nod to the two guards, and a signal for Sakari to wait, Ryne ducked inside. Varick, in his resplendent silver armor, the Lightstorm insignia engraved into the chest plate in gold, stood at his table tracing a finger along a map next to his helmet. He glanced up when Ryne cleared his throat.

"Ah, you're here. Good," Varick said. He went back to his map for a moment. "What do you know of a town named Ranoda?" His attention remained on the map as he spoke.

"Small town as Ostanian towns go." Ryne joined Varick at the table near the tent's center where he could finally straighten to his full height. "Up northwest, not far from the Nevermore Heights. There's a Granadian barracks there. Well fortified from what I could tell the last time I passed anywhere close. Why?"

"The Tribunal has ordered us back to the Vallum. There's been trouble at Ranoda."

"What kind of trouble?"

Varick looked up then, his face grim. "Shadeling and Amuni's Children kind. According to the report, the entire town has been wiped out."

Ryne sensed there was more, so he waited. Ranoda was less than a day's travel from where he'd left Jaecar, his family, and this Ashishin, Irmina. Being able to strike there as well as destroy Carnas and raid the farms along the Astocan border meant this army now moved on several fronts, and still their forces had been sizable enough to take a town with an entire Dagodin legion as well as one Ashishin.

"This Irmina I told you about delivered the report at the Vallum. She was the only survivor." Varick's blue eyes hardened, his gaze grew distant. "Lost a lot of good men. Men I knew. Some I trained myself. Her report claims your Alzari and his family were involved in the attack. According to her, she barely escaped the man."

Ryne frowned. "I saw the man. He's an assassin, sure, like all Alzari, but an ally of the shadelings? No, nothing I saw about him indicated such." As he said the words, doubts skittered across Ryne's mind. What about the golden–haired woman and how her aura simply disappeared? What of the recent odd sightings of auras that came and went like flitting shadows? Auras he somehow didn't remember when he'd not forgotten a single one since he woke. Until now.

"Be that as it may," Varick said. "I have little reason to doubt the woman if the Tribunal believes her. I've been given orders and I obey. We leave this morning. I called you here because they sent a High Ashishin to take me and my Knight Generals to the Vallum. They want us there yesterday. I want you to make the trip with us."

The muscles along Ryne's jaw tightened with his grimace. Varick was asking not only to expose him to a High Ashishin, but to allow the Matus to Materialize him. The last High Ashishin Ryne encountered, he'd killed the man. That act and the scores of Ashishin he'd killed in his refusal to be captured were part of the reasons the Tribunal sought him. Varick's intervention had bought him a pardon until he decided he no longer wished to work as the Tribunal's hand of vengeance. Until he made the choice to atone for the many atrocities he committed under their orders, for the deaths he reveled in when his power took him.

Varick paced to the tent's entrance and peered outside. "I knew how you'd feel. But this man you can trust. He has no interest in what the Tribunal seeks you for."

"I don't think this is a good idea."

"Look," Varick turned to face Ryne, his eyes pleading. "I need you. I'm getting old. I fear I won't survive another war. I have a wife and a son back in Eldanhill. I'd like to see them again. Near eighteen years since I last saw them." Varick paused, regret written clearly on his face. "There's not been a greater warrior than you since the days of the Shadowbearer War when Nerian struck down all before him. Watching you fight always reminded me of him. The difference is you're on our side. Not only will I need you to train the men, but should this army attack as soon as expected, we can use you at the front lines. *I* can use you and that brain of yours."

Ryne closed his eyes, mulling over the choices. The very reason he intended to head to the Vallum lay before him. Vengeance for Carnas' people. Now, he was also being offered a chance to repay an old friend who stood for him when no one else dared. But could he take such a risk? If he suffered one of his recent cracks in control when in the presence of this High Ashishin, there was no telling what he would do. Would the control he'd found first in Halvor's Entosis then in the one Sakari nursed him back to health within, hold?

"Besides," Varick added. "This way you'll get to Imbuer Adler faster than you thought."

Too many chances were converging at the same time. Ryne shrugged off his lingering doubts. A step lay before him to be sure he could master himself in the way he'd found in the Entosis. And another led to a possibility of discovering the past that haunted him. "Fine. I'll go with you."

Varick let out a deep breath. "Good." His teeth showed in a relieved grin. "Well, now's as good a time as any to meet High Ashishin Jerem."

As if on cue, a gauntleted fist held the tent flap to one side. A frail looking man stepped inside. He appeared ancient, wrinkles and lines by the dozens marring his features. The skin of his face hung loose about his cheeks and neck, in stark contrast to the skin pulled tight and shiny on his hands. His hair, so white it shone like new snow, reached down to his waist. A long wispy beard adorned his chin and stretched down to his stomach. When the man's gaze passed over Ryne, his thin eyebrows rose. A glint of recognition flashed across his eyes. Eyes as hard as ebonsteel that sparkled with a youth the man's apparent frailty belied. Where silver flecked Sakari's eyes, this man's were pools of liquid silver that radiated intelligence.

"High Ashishin Jerem, meet Ryne," Varick intoned with his head bowed.

Despite his appearance, and long, flowing crimson and white robe, the High Ashishin's robust stride resembled a young man in the prime of his youth. "I have heard much about you." He crossed from the doorway to stand in front of Ryne. His head barely reached Ryne's chest, but if he was intimidated by Ryne's great size, Jerem didn't show it. He looked Ryne up and down as if inspecting a strange creature he'd read about. His eyes drank in everything.

"I've heard nothing about you," Ryne answered. Jerem's aura shone so bright he almost averted his eyes. Instead, he forced himself to ignore the glare and meet Jerem's uncomfortable, assessing gaze. Even without his Matersense, Ryne felt the power rolling off the High Shin in waves. He tensed as doubt crept into his mind once again.

Jerem smiled, exposing perfect teeth. "My anonymity is as it should be. I tend to keep myself from the forefront." Stroking his chin, he inspected Ryne once more with the temerity of youth rather than the caution of a seasoned old hunter, making several grunts of approval before he nodded to himself.

"If that's the case, why're you here?" Ryne snapped. He frowned. He'd spoken without thought.

Jerem's expression soured. "To the point. I admire that in a man."

At first, Ryne thought his response was his lust rising. But as in the Entosis, the feeling was buried deep down inside. Sure the craving resonated, but it did nothing more. His answer to Jerem had simply been his own annoyance. "My apologies. Events have been hectic. And if you know me as well as you say, you know I have no great love for Ashishin or the Tribunal."

Jerem's face brightened. "Hmm. I see you have some restraint after all. Good. You will need it."

Ryne found himself intrigued. "Why? What do you know that I don't?"

"Well," Jerem shrugged. "If you are to fight again, if you are to seek the vengeance which drives you, you need to be able to control your power. Destroying entire towns would only serve the shade's purpose. Not to mention, such events would turn the entire world against you. Being able to restrain yourself while the power of Materialization pulls at you will indeed be an important step in your growth." Ryne opened his mouth, but before he could utter a word, Jerem continued, "As for what I know? I know events are at play here you cannot see or begin to fathom. A day will come when you will seek me. But until you learn to trust one such as me, that day is still a long way off."

Manipulation, and feeling like his thoughts were plain, needled Ryne. He regarded Jerem with a flat, dead expression. "A day like the one you speak of will never come. Not after what your people did to me."

"I assure you," Jerem said, his face softening, his eyes piteous. "Those were no people of mine. For now, let's begin anew with today, Ryne Thanairen Waldron."

"That isn't…" Ryne almost said it wasn't his name. But Thanairen sparked a memory within him. A memory of a different time and place. Of a castle, courtyards, peoples who bowed to him. As quick as the memory came, it fled.

"Who are you?" Ryne whispered.

"Me? I am a humble High Shin who wishes to see Denestia prosper as she did in the days of old. Before Materforging corrupted the gods and the great Eztezians. When men lived in peace and our world was joined as one." Jerem gave Ryne a knowing smile. "Denestia needs you for what is to come as she needs every man, woman, or child of any power. Allow me an inkling of trust to take you with us. If you trust me this once, you may find you may need such services again. Services I would willingly give in your quest to discover your past."

Instantly wary, Ryne frowned. "In exchange for?"

"Like I said, for our world's prosperity."

Ryne was tempted to ask Jerem for his assistance, beg him for his knowledge, but the pain from his torture hung like a cloud about him. He would trust Jerem to bring him to the Vallum, but nothing more.

Jerem cocked his head to one side. "Enough talk about days long lost for now. We leave for the Vallum immediately. The Knight Generals are here."

As Jerem's words ended, the tent flap opened. One by one, Knight Generals filed in. First entered a meaty–nosed waif of a man whose white armor inlaid with gold appeared too big for his frame, but somehow he still managed to puff up his chest. Behind him strode a broad–shouldered, red headed man with bushy eyebrows. His armor was scaled leather with several metal clasps at the joints of his elbows and knees, each carved in the shape of dartans. The last Knight General was a man with multiple scars across his face and missing an ear. His left eye was so bloodshot, red liquid floated on his eyeball, and the heavy crimson armor he wore seemed not to hinder him one bit. Each man carried a sword at their hips and held their helmets under one arm. The Lightstorm insignia stood out upon each breast.

The men bowed first to High Shin Jerem, then knuckled their foreheads to Knight Commander Varick. Their gazes took in Ryne, and their expressions varied from lips curled in scorn from the Knight General in white armor, to wariness for the one in leather, and indifference from the scar–faced man.

"Are we ready?" Jerem looked from one to the other.

"Not quite," Ryne answered. He linked with Sakari and told him to enter.

The tent flap fluttered ever so lightly as Sakari glided into the tent. Feet shuffled for a moment, and the Knight Generals gave Sakari uneasy glances, hands hovering over sword hilts. Then they suddenly relaxed and breathed easier as if Sakari was some peer they recognized.

"Now, we're ready," Ryne said.

Jerem nodded, and his wispy brows drew together.

Ryne chose the same moment to open his Matersense. If he was to test his limits, then touching his power while the High Ashishin Forged was the best way.

Mater swirled about Jerem, gathering in thick bands of varied colors. The essences flowed in such a condensed form Ryne found it difficult to tell one from the other.

Ryne's Scripts writhed, and his bloodlust seethed, so he sought the calm pond as he did when he lay in the Entosis. The voices called to him, one yearning for violence, the other for peace. He allowed the differing pulls to mingle with one another. As they drew together, they stilled each other, and the craving within him dwindled to a dull warmth lost deep in his mind. At peace, he focused on Jerem.

The High Ashishin smiled and thrust his hand out, palm open.

Reality tore. It was as if the air in front of them split down the middle. The world screamed. Vertigo took over and with it came a falling sensation.

A moment later, in bright morning sunlight, the entire party stood at the Vallum.

CHAPTER 39

Ancel inched forward on his stomach among the tall brush until he lay where he could see down into the camp. To his left and right, Mirza and Danvir took up similar positions while Charra guarded their rear. Below them, wispy smoke curled up from the remnants of the campfire's smoldering coals before dissipating into the still air. Overhead, gray clouds hung near unmoving, heralds of more stormy weather. The four Sendethi soldiers camped below hadn't stirred in hours, and even their watch appeared to have nodded off. Dampness on Ancel's back came from a combination of the wet blades of grass and his perspiration. Despite the cool predawn air, sweat rolled down his face. He licked his salty lips both from a need to moisten the dry clay his mouth had become as well as from the anticipation sidling through his body.

Swathed in darkness so she appeared no more than a silhouette, Kachien crept from brush to small tree a few feet from the camp. The lookout's head dipped a few times, each time stopping before his chin hit his chest. Snorting, he shook his head. Kachien froze. The man mumbled to himself, shifted for a more comfortable position, and settled down once more. Moments later, a snore rose from his position.

Kachien darted out from her hiding place, her body leaning forward, an arrow destined for its target. She moved as swift as a striking viper. The soldier didn't even manage a grunt before Kachien's hands swept across the area of his throat. Ancel could picture those black blades she used, hidden right now by the darkness, slicing through flesh and artery. The man slumped forward. Kachien caught him and eased him to the ground.

Slowly, she stretched upright, her head arching back to the sky, and rolled her neck from side to side. Ancel shivered to think about the enjoyment that seemed to ripple through her body. When her stretch ended, her head pointed toward the camp and the unsuspecting soldiers.

Watching in silent horror, Ancel tightened his grip on the small sword she'd given him. His stomach clenched. Gasps to either side of him matched his own emotions as Kachien snuck in utter silence to the first sleeping soldier.

Again, there was a small movement, followed by a jerk from the dead man.

Without pausing, she eased forward, a silent silhouette of death in the darkness. A slight motion and a mumbled curse that died in his throat, the next soldier's flesh met her blades. The noise woke the third Sendethi.

Judging from her earlier speed, Kachien could have reached the man before he rose, but she didn't try. The soldier leaped to his feet, fumbling about in his boiled leather armor, the still smoldering coals painting his bearded visage with its ruddy glow. He snarled and snatched his sword from his scabbard.

This time, Ancel couldn't suppress his own gasp with the swiftness in which Kachien moved. Her form was a blur flashing by the firepit. The Sendethi's hand rose to swing. He never finished the attack. Black blades flashed across his armor parting it like paper. With a gurgle, he collapsed.

Bile rose in Ancel's throat, not just from seeing the murder, but sick from what Kachien represented. He bit back the sensation, the sour taste filling his mouth. Struggling to remain calm, he eased down the hill the way they'd come, his legs and thoughts wooden. The feel of the grass and uneven ground were distant brushes against his boots.

How could he have fallen for this woman, this heartless killer? The quick deaths he witnessed moments ago, and the times she'd run off back in Randane replayed over and over. Was this to be his destiny? To be caught within the throes of his power with death being the only way to appease it. He squeezed his eyes tight against the thought.

Despite the revulsion he harbored toward Kachien's acts, he also pitied her. To be unable to function properly until she answered her power's craving was a burden he couldn't begin to comprehend. How did she manage to live in such a way? Even as he thought it, he knew he'd do the same if given no other choice. The idea of killing himself to be free of such a curse was beyond him.

I must've been a fool to think I could control such power. Look what a monster it has made of her. What chance do I stand if and when the power takes me in the midst of my emotions?

When they'd fled back in Randane, the fear of capture had been overwhelming. Watching her moments ago, tension worming its way through his stomach, had brought on the same effect. Both times, all he could do was watch. Could he really find the Eye in the heat of battle, in the flames of rage, in the icy clamminess of fear? Uncertainty filled him as he trudged through grass laden with dewdrops toward the small hollow where their dartans were tethered.

Ancel glanced over to Danvir. He now understood how his friend must have felt in the tunnels when he'd openly wept about having killed someone. Not far away, Mirza strode, his face blank, gray eyes empty. Whining, Charra padded next to Ancel. He reached a hand out and trailed his fingers through the daggerpaw's fur. No matter what, Charra was always there for him with no concern for what he faced.

They soon reached the dip in the land where they'd left the dartans. As they often did when Charra approached too close, the creatures mewled. Ancel and his friends hurried over and shushed them. Charra stayed just below the top of the slope watching the way they'd come as nearby trees cast long shadows with the orange hues of dawn now tinting the sky. Far east, red mountains loomed in innumerable plateaus and ridges, their ranges spreading north until they met and became one with the Kelvore Mountains.

Danvir gripped the reins of his mount and drew the beast close. "Did you see how she moved? How can any human be so fast and kill without flinching?"

"Of course we did," Ancel said. "But at this point, it doesn't much matter. She did what she needed to bring herself under control."

"And you're fine with it?" Danvir protested, his lips curling around the words, disgust twisting his features. "We just watched her murder four men."

"I thought you'd gotten over this already?" Mirza said, eyebrows raised quizzically. "At least she didn't turn on us. Not that I think she would, but if this is anything like Ancel said, then it's the risk we have to live with in order to get home safely." His voice was hard but calm. "You know, when she used her power to save us at the river, it was fine. Now it's not. You need to wise up. You seem to forget the Sendethi soldiers have tried to kill or capture us. I, for one, intend to survive this. I want to see Eldanhill again. With you two by my side. I'll pay any cost."

Ancel blinked at Mirza's words and his temperament. Mirza, who was so excitable, taking much for fun, who'd been fearful when they were in the glen, had become a different person. The events in Randane had changed him. Ancel hoped he could carry himself in the same way when the time came for him to take a life.

A low growl from Charra announced Kachien's return. She appeared at the top of the slope and jogged down to meet them. The occasional twitter from an early morning bird interspersed the still air as they waited. Somewhere, an owl that should have been asleep already, hooted.

Ancel forced himself to meet Kachien's eyes. The tight lines from earlier no longer marred her features. As much as she'd appeared haggard, now she was the opposite—calm, serene and full of energy. Her face betrayed no emotions as she stopped next to her own mount.

In one hand, Kachien held several sheets of paper. She waved them before her. "These soldiers were looking for you." Her unyielding gaze took them all in.

Ancel took the papers, reading them wordlessly before passing them around. Drawn on the first sheet was a likeness of him and Charra. On the others were Mirza and Danvir. Mirza hissed and Danvir swallowed.

"And they carried a map of this side of the river. The path they have marked leads to your home," Kachien added.

All Ancel's earlier worry about Kachien's darker side fled him, replaced by concern for Eldanhill. She'd saved their lives yet again. Ilumni smiles on those who follow him in many ways.

Maybe Kachien was his way of smiling on them. Either way it was an issue for him to worry about later. He turned to Mirza. "How far are we from the bridge?"

"At least three days."

"I still think using the bridge is a mistake," Danvir said. "I have a feeling either Dosteri or Sendethi troops will be there."

Mirza shook his head. "Unlikely. You've taken that route yourself many times. Only the quarry workers and miners use the path through the Red Ridge Mountains down to that bridge. All others take the ferries. If we stay as we are, we'll skip the ferry landings." He looked from Kachien to the map she held. "May I?" She passed the map to him. Mirza opened it up. "Look." He pointed as they drew closer around him. "Here and here are the landings." The areas he indicated were farther north and toward the Kelvore River. "We're about here. From the route these soldiers marked, they assumed we would go for the ferries. We stay wide, push hard and we make the bridge. No one will be the wiser."

Kachien nodded, a respectful gleam in her eye as she regarded Mirza. He'd discussed this idea before, but she'd insisted on them heading to the ferries instead of the old bridge.

"I agree with you, Mirza," Kachien conceded. "This way will be safest."

Danvir groaned. "That's all we need now. Someone telling him he's right. We won't be able to live this down for a week."

Ancel couldn't help his smile. Mirza gave Danvir a smug look and shrugged. In return, Danvir snickered.

Kachien climbed onto her dartan, the beast's massive carapace dwarfing her slight form. "We have no time to waste. I intend to not only reach the bridge, but be in your home in three days."

Ancel's brows climbed his forehead. "You plan to push us until they drop?"

"If I have to. These soldiers weren't alone. There must—"

Charra's low growl cut her off.

Ancel's head snapped up as his daggerpaw bounded down the slope to them. Kachien had already whipped her reins and sent her dartan galloping up the hill. Everyone else followed suit. Before she reached the hilltop, she dismounted and snuck up the remainder of the way. Without thinking, Ancel did the same.

When he peeked over the other side, he was at a loss for words. At least forty armored soldiers, with the Charging Boar flying high, trotted toward their position on horses. One of them, in leather rather than the chainmail the others wore, dismounted and inspected the ground. He stopped, stared toward the hill where Ancel and Kachien hid, and pointed. A tracker. The soldiers kicked their horses into a gallop.

Kachien's hand pulled at Ancel. "Go! Now! We have to flee." She ran for her mount.

Wide–eyed, Ancel scrambled onto his dartan. "It's a regimental squad," he said to the bewildered expressions from Mirza and Danvir.

Recognition and fear swam across their faces.

"Mirza," Kachien called from her mount, her voice a little more than a whisper. "Lead the way. Push as hard and as fast as you can. Our only hope is to tire their horses."

Behind them hooves drummed and armor jangled. Shouts rose from over forty throats as the soldiers urged their mounts on.

Sweat beading his forehead, Mirza maneuvered his dartan to face the north and slapped his reins. The beast took off. Hands tight on his reins, Ancel followed.

CHAPTER 40

"You should at least hear the message she carries," Knight Commander Varick said from the tent's rear as he scratched his scraggly beard.

Ryne's eyebrow arched. "That a command, Varick?"

The Knight Commander smirked and removed his gauntlets. "As if you would follow it anyway. All I'm saying is if the Tribunal sent her, at least hear what they propose."

"Because I allowed High Shin Jerem to bring me here doesn't mean I trust the Tribunal. Even assuming they're who sent her, I've heard enough from them," Ryne snapped. "If she makes a single threatening move, I'll kill her. I'm giving you and them, fair warning. There's been enough grief wherever she's shown her face. You yourself said she's almost a Raijin."

Varick drew a deep breath. "I've tried sending men to talk to her, but so far they've been unsuccessful. At this point, if the Tribunal's High Ashishin did send her, and you kill her, they'll just send someone else, someone worse. Maybe Pathfinders or even a full Raijin. It won't be like last time."

Ryne shrugged. "Then I'll pray for Ilumni to show mercy on their souls like the others."

"Listen to yourself, Ryne. Killing won't stop them hunting you like it did in the past. It's not that simple anymore. They won't grant you a third pardon. No matter how many battles against the shade we win." Varick scowled and paced to the table with its maps of Ostania showing military positions.

Ryne strode to the front of the tent. Unlike before, he

didn't need to stoop. Outside, a few feet from the entrance, Sakari sat on a crate, staring at the thousands of white canvas spread below the Vallum of Light. Sunlight glared from the towering, ever–shining wall in a near blinding effect.

"Death's always simple, Varick. We spend our entire lives dying."

Varick snorted. "Easy for you to say. Try telling that to the mothers who watch their children get slaughtered in these forsaken wars."

Ryne turned back to Varick, crossed the distance to the table, and pointed to the locations listing the shadeling army's last known positions. "Exactly why I refuse to go to the High Ashishin. I'm more important here than I ever will be answering questions about a power I don't even understand. I'm needed here, at the front lines. We both watched too many die, friend. My soul craves for revenge. It sings for battle against the shade. I can no more shun its calling than you can relieve yourself of command and leave your soldiers here. Or leave these people to the shade's mercy."

Varick sighed. Even in his intricate silver armor, Ryne could tell his broad shoulders slumped. "Ryne, there's going to come a time when the High Ashishin will no longer accept no for an answer." The aged Commander craned his neck and gazed into Ryne's eyes. "It's not like you can hide."

Ryne met the smaller man's hard eyes with a cold stare of his own. "I'm done hiding. And I'll kill anyone who gets in my way."

"Even me?" Varick asked, his voice dangerously quiet.

Ryne refused to answer. The tight lines around the Knight Commander's eyes softened. Ryne looked away from Varick and pushed the thought of ever having to fight the man from his mind. "I'll think about it on my way to Felan Mark."

Knight Commander Varick let out a whoosh. He sifted through the papers on his table and handed Ryne his personal pass—a gold insignia engraved with a sword surrounded by lightning. "Show this to the guards, and only state once that you're there to see Miss Adler."

Ryne nodded and strode toward the tent's entrance. "Varick."

"Hmm?"

"Warn her. Let her know I decide when I feel like meeting." Ryne didn't wait for an answer. He raised the tent's flap and ducked outside.

Several hours later, Ryne shook his head at Irmina's annoying persistence. She'd followed him from the Knight Commander's encampment all the way to Felan Mark. She tried to hide among the mix of Ostanian locals behind him, but her aura stuck out like a bright light.

Ryne linked with Sakari, who milled in the crowd nearby. "Keep an eye on her until I return." He stepped to the head of the line preparing to enter Felan Mark's main fort.

"As you wish."

Ryne broke the link.

"Sir, do you have business here?" asked one of the four scarlet armored Dagodin guards with his neck craned to peer into Ryne's face.

"Yes." Ryne produced the pass for the guard's inspection. "I'm here to see Miss Adler."

The guard eyed Ryne's leather armor and his sword suspiciously. After a moment, he said, "Follow the long hall. Don't touch your weapons as you walk and you'll be fine. Someone will meet you once you've passed inspection inside."

Ryne nodded, and the guardsman signaled behind him with his silver spear. The soft clink of well-oiled metal gears churned within the armory's thick, steel walls. The massive gate slid open with a brisk motion, and the spiked portcullis rose. Ryne entered, and the gate and portcullis slid shut.

Metal walls surrounded him, drab, gray, and featureless. A long, well lit hallway stretched ahead, lamps in metal sconces hanging at measured intervals. The hallway continued as far as he could see. Ryne made sure to keep his hands away from his sword as he strode forward.

Half an hour and a few twisting halls later, Ryne stood
at a bladesmith's shop within the armory. In front of him stood
a short, gray–haired woman, lines creasing her forehead, nose,
and beneath her eyes. The woman's young student, a girl with
smooth, pale skin and long blonde hair, cast nervous glances in
Ryne's direction. A few feet from them, a bulky smith wearing a
thick apron poured molten silversteel into a cast. Ryne opened
his mouth.

"Shh," the wrinkle faced woman said. She gestured to
the girl. "Close your eyes, Millie. Feel the Mater flowing within
the metal—the elements that make everything what it is." Her
voice had become a hypnotic drone. "Seek each individual
essence of Mater as they form the solid blade. You need to find
the light among those essences. When you do, guide it, help it to
flow apart."

Ryne searched both the teacher's and the student's face
for any kind of strain he would have felt. The goading power, the
struggle for control, the emotional battle he experienced when he
touched Mater. In their faces, he saw none. The same as he noted
with most Granadian Matii he met.

The bladesmith held the cast steady, and the diminutive,
old woman's voice murmured like a gurgling brook in the
background. His focus fixed on the mold, Ryne lost himself in
the teacher's voice. The liquid metal's acrid smell hung so strong
he could taste it.

The teacher's soft monotone continued. "Just as the
Mater is about to complete the weapon's creation, gently guide the
light you separated back into it. That will complete the imbuing."

Ryne found the calm pool in the center of his being.
He opened his Matersense, his bloodlust a distant buzz he
easily ignored. Essences around him and within the molten steel
bloomed. They swept about the room in sharp–edged transparent
swirls, enhancing his vision.

Each essence became vivid despite their transparency.
Streams of fire flared, melting the metal and rising in waves, the
heat, light, and energy essences all working together. Water and
air essences flowed to make up the liquid byproduct and steam.
Both the Streams and Flows worked to create the superheated
air in the smith's shop. The liquid began to solidify giving it the

element of Forms.

Light in a white luminescence intertwined with everything in intricate patterns. Shade essences filled the void in the shadows cast by flames within the forge and lamps on the walls. They too, a part of the Streams. A flow of light slid away from the whole and formed a thick ball.

"Guide the light into the metal now," the gray–haired teacher whispered.

The elements of Mater snapped together. As they did, the light rotated and slammed into them. A tiny concussion of air brushed Ryne's hair from his face. A small section from the ball of light dissipated and joined its origins.

In the mold now sat a shining, silversteel core. Light glowed from it in flickering waves.

Ryne's eyes widened at the newly imbued metal. It was the first time he'd seen an imbuing. He released his Matersense, and the glow disappeared, the metal appearing as ordinary, highly polished steel.

"Next time, be more gentle, my dear. The light essences will pass into the steel without force. The gentler you are, the stronger the imbuing will be, and the fewer essences you will lose. In turn, the stronger the *divya* you will have created."

"Thank you, Miss Adler," the girl said, her broad smile lighting up her face.

Miss Adler gave the girl's shoulder an encouraging pat. "Now, watch as the smith crafts the weapon." She turned to Ryne. "Follow me."

She led them from the room and down a long, lamp lit hallway with vaulted, steel ceilings. Miss Adler walked with a swift, purposeful gait unhindered by her long dress, but Ryne still needed to shorten his steps by a great degree to make sure he did not pass her. As they walked, he couldn't help but open his Matersense again with the reaction of his Scripts to all the Forgings around him.

Beneath his feet and through the steel floors, he sensed the magmatic essences of fire powering the armory's vast forges. Water essences ran through pipes around him to every room. Forms abounded and metallic scents permeated the air as hammers rung on metal, and steam swished from bellows.

Craft rooms lined the hallway, each occupied with a

Matus and a smith. Some contained three people—a teacher, a student, and an artisan. In other, much larger rooms, there were double bellows, and those rooms held up to four Matii and several weaponsmiths. All around, Matii drew on the essences as they imbued weapons into *divya*.

Signs above the doors announced shield, axe, hammer, sword, and scythesmiths. Figures painted on the thick steel walls in reds, blues, and yellows next to each door depicted the artisans. The clangs and rings from the metalwork flooded the hall in a ceaseless din.

Ryne followed Miss Adler to the end of the hall. Two Dagodin, in white uniforms with red stripes on the arms—a stark contrast with the dark gray metal around them—stood in front of a blank wall. One soldier moved his silver–hafted lance to one side, turned to the wall, and a heavy metal door slid open. Ryne and Miss Adler passed through. The door slid shut behind them, and the sounds from the smiths cut off abruptly.

"So, Knight Commander Varick sent you?" Miss Adler said as they continued down another hall.

"Yes, he said you were the one I needed to speak to."

"Oh? How's the old bat doing anyways? The last I saw him, his face looked like old leather, worn and dry. Tried to convince him to eat more and maybe take a break, but he refused."

Ryne smiled. "Much the same. Grumpy, rude and still in command at the Vallum."

"Good to know much hasn't changed with him." Miss Adler stopped at a door and pushed it open.

Ryne ducked inside. Miss Adler entered, locked the door behind them, and dropped a steel bar in place.

"One can never be too cautious," she said in response to Ryne's questioning look. She took a seat at a large oak table. Filled bookshelves lined the walls behind her, and in one corner sat a small cot. "I would offer you a seat, but judging by your size, you wouldn't fit in any chair I own."

Ryne shrugged and stood across the table from her. "It's fine. I'm used to it."

"So, why'd Varick send you?"

Ryne unsheathed his greatsword. With a quick move, the old woman brought a longsword up from beneath her table.

"Like I said, one can never be too cautious," she said at Ryne's raised brow and kept her longsword between them.

With great care, Ryne laid his sword lengthways on the table. The grip stretched a foot past one end, and the blade stopped at the other. Ryne fixed his gaze on Miss Adler's piercing blue eyes. "Varick said you're the only Dagodin he could think of who may be able to tell me about my sword."

The wrinkles on Miss Adler's face doubled as she frowned and pointed at the runes running along the blade and hilt. "What are those?" She rested her sword next to Ryne's weapon and traced her fingers along the markings.

"Scripts," Ryne said and paused. Miss Adler raised her face to him and squinted. Ryne continued in answer to her apparent confusion, "I can use them to manipulate almost any element of Mater to empower my sword. It's like imbuing except my weapons are already crafted."

Miss Adler's head jerked back ever so slightly. "I've never heard the like. I don't think it's even possible. Imbuing can only happen when the components are at their base levels. Before Mater has already formed the item." She shook her head. "As I look at your sword, I see nothing but a plain, oversized greatsword. It's not a *divya*."

Ryne reached down and held the sword's hilt. Through the Scripts on the sword, he touched the light essences around him. The Scripts shifted and swirled as he drew light into the weapon until first its Scripts, and then the sword itself glowed white. Miss Adler gasped. Ryne released the weapon, and the white light faded as the Mater receded back into the air around them.

Miss Adler stared from Ryne to the sword. "I've spent over seventy years creating *divya*, and I've never seen anything like those Scripts. There isn't an Imbuer or a Dagodin I know who can manipulate Mater within a *divya* that way. We can only imbue and wield them. Once a *divya* is created, only the essences imbued within it can be used. We cannot increase or change their properties. I would've said no one can but..." She gestured to Ryne. "A long time ago, I read about something like this, but I always thought it a myth."

Ryne's heart leaped. After so many years searching, he would take even a myth if it meant progress. After all, he was living proof myths held some semblance of truth. "Where? Can you show me the book?"

"It's in the possession of the Tribunal at the Iluminus' great library. I could request—" She stopped talking, her eyes narrowing as his body stiffened at the mention of the Tribunal.

Taking a deep breath of resignation, Ryne forced his body to relax. "Miss Adler?" He picked up his sword and sheathed it.

"Yes?" Miss Adler's gaze met his.

"Please don't mention—"

"You don't need to say it. With Varick sending you like this, and your reaction, I know not to say anything to any Ashishin or to anyone else." A pained expression crossed her face. "I still remember what I went through in my younger days when they found out I could imbue. Yet, only with their training did I finally understand my power. You'll need to face that decision some day. I wish you the best when that day comes. To think I almost asked your name. Now, I'm glad I didn't."

He nodded, unlocked the door, and ducked outside.

Trudging through Felan Mark's crowded streets did little for Ryne's troubled thoughts. Here, he'd finally found some information which he hoped would lead to more about himself, and it was in the Tribunal's hands. Years of fruitless searching boiled down to him having to deal with those he despised the most.

He let out a weary breath as he took in Felan Mark. The fortress city's steel walls shone with the setting sun's purplish hues. The same colors lit up the Barrier Mountains and their long dead volcanoes sprouting to the north. Ryne often wondered why the Felani built everything with metal in a land plagued by flash thunderstorms. Massive steel frames highlighted towers under construction around the city, and immense statues portraying Ilumni decorated the metal city's central spire. Here and there, a person stopped among the bustling crowd to voice a brief prayer to the god of Streams.

The crowd gave Ryne ample space along the street's

flagstones. Being shunned felt strangely familiar even after so many years in Carnas. Many in the crowd murmured or gaped at his great size. Among the throng, Ryne could pick out the dark linen coats without buttons donned by Felani men, and the earth tones favored by their women in their airy cotton dresses. Their height and their favored braided hairstyles had drawn him to them in his search, but that led nowhere. Sprinkled among them were a few bald-headed Banai, slit-necked Cardians and Astocans, and he even spotted a huge Harnan, his skin the color of bronze.

The Granadians among them stood out, preferring brighter, often multicolored, brocaded silks, extravagant and frilly. The men's patterned shirts and trousers and the form fitting breeches the women flaunted made the colorful garb of the Cardians seem dull by comparison. They kept their hair cropped neat and short, and a few heads were shaved on one side—a sign of nobility.

Peddlers shopped their wares, and criers yelled for attention as they announced one shop or another among the spice, fruit, and fabric storefronts lining this district. Patrons visited the various steel and iron buildings in steady streams. Despite the variety of peoples around him, more than Ryne's great size stood out. In one town, long ago, the children called him tapestry man. Ryne smiled.

Foghorns from Felan Mark's vast docks broke Ryne from his thoughts, the stench from offloaded composts rising strong on the warm air. Neither the salty sea spray nor the many smells from the spice vendors could hide it. Unnoticed, gray twilight had crept in as he walked. He narrowed his eyes and turned his attention ahead.

Sakari's link bloomed in Ryne's mind. The man, who now looked like a typical Felani, tall and thin, eased his way through the shoppers and vendors alike. "You have company, and it is not her. From the markings they have disguised, they may be Alzari."

"I see. Wait for me at the gates."

Sakari melted into the crowds. Moments later, the link broke.

Ryne made purposeful stops at several vendors, haggling with them then storming off in a huff. Soon, he was able to tell who followed him. Their auras roiled with the same tainted shade he'd seen from the Alzari in the Fretian Woods. He counted ten in all. His brow furrowed. Could it really be them? Here in the city? How? He continued to walk as if he didn't notice them.

From the corner of his eye, an aura fraught with light bloomed. It flared brighter than any other within his range. The aura followed those tracking him.

Irmina had returned.

Ryne hurried toward the stables. The last thing he needed was to draw more attention than he already commanded. If there was to be a fight, he couldn't risk such a battle within the city. Especially if he lost control. There was no Entosis close by if he were to expend as much Mater as he did against the shadelings. He would need to give his power its due if he failed to restrain himself. He glanced behind him to see the Alzari split up. Two trailed him. Behind them, Irmina followed.

When he reached the large stables, one of the few stone buildings in Felan Mark, he paid the stable master and checked on Thumper while tracking his pursuers. Easing farther into the stall, Ryne waited for the two men who followed him to enter the stables. As he continued his inspection of Thumper's chain bit and reins, he watched without drawing attention to himself as the Alzari hurried to their own dartans. Satisfied, Ryne mounted just as the Irmina entered.

Their gazes met for a brief moment. The woman's brown eyes narrowed, but she made no move toward him. Instead, she rushed in the opposite direction toward another line of dartans.

Ryne shook Thumper's reins, and the dartan mewled before plodding to the stable's wide entrance and out. Without a backward glance, he headed toward Felan Mark's gargantuan main gates along a road reserved for riding. This close to moonrise, few riders traveled the flagstoned streets in the direction of Felan Mark's gates, so he made good time.

"Are you certain you want to leave at this time o' night?" drawled a Dagodin guard at the gates. The man gave Ryne's armor and sword a long look over.

"Yes. I'm sure I can get hired on with them." Ryne motioned to a heavily guarded supply caravan the Dagodin were allowing to pass through a wider than normal sally gate.

"I guess. It's your life." The man shook his head, signaled, and let Ryne by.

A few hundred feet from the walls, Sakari waited. When

Ryne reached him, his companion leaped onto Thumper's back behind Ryne and shifted around for a moment before he settled down.

The caravan peeled off toward the east, following the Felan Road, while Ryne headed north toward the Barrier Mountains silhouetted in the distance. Thumper picked up speed until he flew by the sandy plain's sparse grasses and shrubs. The first deep hollow that hid them from Felan Mark's towers soon came upon them, and Ryne stopped. He stared back toward the city.

Behind him, the ten Alzari left the gates, riding hard. Soon after came Irmina's aura.

A tingling sensation ran through Ryne's body as battle energy filled him. He tilted his head back, a grin spreading across his face at the sensation. With a last look at the oncoming mercenaries, he wheeled Thumper and rode toward the mountainous foothills.

CHAPTER 41

Irmina followed the dust clouds from the men hunting Ryne toward the Barrier Mountains, flying by short, hardy grasses decorating the red and beige sands in faded browns and greens. Days had passed since the last of the areas common thunderstorms, and despite her light linen and cotton fabrics, sweat trickled down her temple. She pulled her scarf up to protect her from the flying dust. Misty sped across the undulating plains with such ease Irmina had to hold back so she wouldn't catch up to the bandits.

Wreathed in shadow, rocky foothills appeared ahead of Irmina. *Fool. Why would he come to such a remote location rather than stay in the city? Worse yet, why go into the bandit's own territory?* Even in her brief time in Ostania, she knew about the bandits who hid among the Barrier Mountains, raiding any caravans or traders who dared travel without a heavy guard contingent. She'd seen Ryne fight, but to take on ten men? The man must be insane. Jerem said he believed the man a descendant of the Eztezians, but they were supposed to be twenty feet tall. Even if it were true, surely he couldn't hope to survive against ten men? Not even with his strange bodyguard. Battling animals was one thing, men, another. She shrugged the idea off as preposterous.

By the time she maneuvered Misty past old volcanic outcrops, the moons hung above the mountains, one chasing the other. Eerie shadows abounded, mixed with the many fissures within the rocks, and a brisk wind carried sulfur smells from the ancient volcanoes. Somewhere farther north, a grunting bark echoed. Misty issued several piercing whistles at the disconcerting bark.

Up ahead, dark silhouettes resolved into the bandit's mounts. Irmina trilled twice to Misty—the sound coming as four, fluttering, shrill tones—swung her legs over to one side, and dismounted. The only movement ahead came from the bandit's dartans twisting long necks to look at Irmina. The men had left them unguarded. Crossing the path she slipped by the creatures while Misty hung back close to the rocks, obeying Irmina's command to stay.

Irmina crept among the shadowy rocks but saw no sign of the ten men. A slope jutted up ahead of her, and she darted across glassy volcanic stone until she crouched below the hill. After a few furtive glances, she crawled up the slope, careful not to slip on loose shale.

Below her, Ryne stood in a clearing at the center of a hollow, a mountain of flesh, sword, and tattoos. On the ground, a lightstone illuminated his features and the surrounding area, throwing long shadows from the skeletal trees scattered in patches around the clearing.

The dark–garbed bandits approached him from four different directions with swords out. Three stood behind one of the dead trees a few feet from the clearing's edge. Another two squatted within the shadows provided by some tall bushes close to those three. Across the hollow's far slope, the other five bandits slunk among the sparse vegetation. Despite the gravelly, uneven ground, the men moved in silence, their steps ghostly silent despite the slate and shale.

Irmina narrowed her eyes at the men's unusual, noiseless movements. Brow furrowed, she engaged her Matersense.

Around her, the night bloomed with individual colors that represented Mater for her. Brown shades signified Forms. Streams hung colorless but sharp. Moonlight gave off a soft, perpetual white glow. Many other colors she couldn't apply to an essence swirled around her. She focused on the bandits and gasped. Shade clung about them and their swords. These men possessed shaded *divya*.

Shade stymied the lightstone's illumination in thick, impenetrable black blankets, except several feet from Ryne. There, the shade dissipated as if the light gobbled it up. Outside that area, shade essence sat unmoving among all others like dead weight, and these men used it to creep closer to their quarry without a sound. It appeared as if they walked on shadows.

Irmina shifted her gaze to Ryne. The giant man appeared unperturbed, the odd tattoos on his arms and the artwork drawn all over his leather armor glinting with the moonlight. He held no power from what she could tell, and yet he stood with quiet confidence as the men approached. He neither moved nor looked in any particular direction, and his oversized sword still rested in its scabbard.

Strangely, Silvereyes was nowhere to be seen.

The bandits on the hollow's far side sneaked close enough that with a few strides they could attack. Ryne still didn't move. Within the open space, they would surround him with ease.

Heart racing, Irmina took a deep breath. She'd never failed to carry out her orders before, and she intended on maintaining her reputation for success. Without her help, Ryne wouldn't survive. She edged backward from the hilltop.

As she retreated, still facing the slope's crest, the sound of clashing steel and muted, choked off cries rose from the hollow. Light bloomed from below, illuminating the night air. The essence washed out the shade. White images burnt across her vision before they faded. The sheer force of the power sent a tingle through her body as she remembered what she'd seen and felt Ryne do in the Fretian Woods.

Turning, she scrambled the rest of the way down and signaled to Misty with a single low trill, this time two wavering tones. The dartan ambled to her without a sound. She swung up onto Misty's back and took her bow from next to the big saddle. Her hand touched the reassuring hilt of her longsword.

Battle sounds continued to surge. Then, as abruptly as they began, they stopped.

No, he mustn't die. No. She urged Misty toward the hilltop. As they topped the rise, three trills undulating from low to high to low in a bird like song, left her lips.

Misty charged.

Irmina's gaze flitted to the clearing, and she pulled back hard on her reins. The dartan reared to a halt with its two front feet in the air, shale and slate kicking up. Irmina gaped at the scene below her.

Ryne sauntered to the center of the clearing with his sword still sheathed. The ten men lay dead in the clearing. Each corpse lacked a head.

Ten men.

He'd defeated ten men in minutes and walked as if he was out on a leisurely stroll. Irmina snapped her mouth closed.

In each hand, Ryne carried a shaded *divya*. One by one, he dropped them to the ground at the middle of the clearing. He turned, his gaze rose to her, and his sword left its scabbard with a move her eyes couldn't follow. Near blinding light flashed around the weapon. She gasped and covered her eyes.

The clang of steel on steel rang in the air. She dropped her hand from her eyes. His sword, covered in smooth light essences, rose and fell, shattering each *divya*. The light winked out when he finished. Another indiscernible motion followed, and his sword appeared in its scabbard once more.

"My master wishes for you to go to him," said a soft voice behind her like ice trailing along her skin.

Irmina turned slowly, keeping her reins steady so Misty wouldn't panic. Dressed in a long, dark Felani jacket and matching trousers, Silvereyes stood next to her. His face was all hard planes and angles, and his sandy hair was longer than she remembered. He appeared taller also. Locking gazes with her, he smiled, the expression one that could curdle milk. Her hand tightened on her bow.

"My name is Sakari. I mean you no harm." He ignored her and glided noiselessly down the hill, his feet appearing not to touch the shale.

Irmina squinted at the places he stepped, but saw no sign of him using shade to move. She hesitated for a moment, her gaze drifting from Sakari to Ryne.

"It's not safe out there," Ryne called, in a voice that rumbled like a slow peal of thunder, yet clear and distinct.

The grunting bark she heard earlier echoed again, but this time from more than one direction. She peered around but saw nothing. The barks came again, this time tickling some familiarity at the back of her mind.

Lines creasing her forehead in a tight frown, she trilled once to Misty and sent her down the slope. They weaved their way past the dead trees and dry brush to the two men. As they passed the corpses, the cloying smell of blood hung thick in the air. Misty tried to reach her neck out to the fresh meat, but Irmina pulled her away. She stopped a few feet from the men, replaced her bow next to the saddle, but didn't dismount. Broken *divya* glinted near where Ryne stood.

Close up, Ryne was even more formidable than he appeared from a distance. She barely reached past his midsection, and he was as wide in the chest as Misty with slabs of banded muscle covering his arms like metal plastered over flesh. The tanned skin of his face and arms—the only places not covered by armor almost matching his skin color—shone. His head actually reached past Misty's withers by a good two feet. He kicked away the splintered *divya*, his leather armor shifting as if molded to him when he moved. This close, she couldn't see a place on the armor that wasn't covered by intricate artwork matching the tattoos on his skin. Black hair in a single thick braid, and tied with a string, hung to the middle of his back. Scars streaking from his left ear to his chin marred the sculptured planes of his face.

He whistled and his dartan trotted out from amongst the trees to him. The blue and green creature stood several hands taller than Misty. The lightstone dimmed, its Mater waning.

"How did you manage that?" She pointed at the ten corpses.

He shrugged. "I was faster than them."

She eyed his massive frame, but a picture of him moving with the speed needed to kill ten men in a straight fight wouldn't form. Sure, she'd seen him run across the Orchid Plains, but such speed was nothing compared to what would be needed to kill these men. Sakari must have helped. Or maybe Ryne was an Ashishin. But that didn't make sense either. She wouldn't be here if he was one of the Tribunal's Matii.

"Didn't Varick tell you I might kill you if you came close to me without my permission?" Ryne's cold, emerald eyes shone with the moonlight.

"Your bodyguard just told me to come to you." She eased her hand to her sword.

"I would not do that. My master does not like threats." Sakari's voice and eyes were lifeless pools.

"Yes. He did ask you to come to me, didn't he?" Ryne's white teeth showed in a humorless smile. "You've followed me all the way from Carnas to here. Tell me, Mariel, are you an Ashishin?"

For a moment, she considered lying to him. But his mention of Varick bothered her. Had he told Ryne her identity? Ryne's head cocked to one side as he waited, but neither his eyes or his relaxed posture gave away anything.

"Yes," Irmina replied. "I am Ashishin Irmina Nagel."

Ryne's eyes became cold pits of ice. "Good. If you'd lied to me, I would've killed you for sure. Now it seems as if you do have some sense in you. I wondered if you did when you decided to chase after ten Alzari in the employ of Amuni's Children." His eyes drifted to the corpses.

Irmina beat back the urge to suck in a breath, giving the bodies a level look instead. "I thought they were simple bandits. Besides I couldn't sit by and let them kill you."

Ryne shook with his sudden chuckle. "Even if it cost you your life?"

"Yes."

His eyebrows rose steeply at her reply. He turned to his mount and reached into his bags. For the first time, she noticed the firewood near Ryne's feet as his hand came away from his bags holding flint and tinder. He tossed them to Sakari.

Within moments, a fire roared a few feet from them. Deep eyes glittering with the flickering flames, Ryne regarded her with a bemused expression. The grunting barks sounded again, this time form several directions. He gazed up the slope. Why did those barks sound so familiar to her?

"You should dismount," Ryne said, his tone neither a command or a request, but a voice that expected to be obeyed nonetheless.

She frowned at him. "Why? Around you I feel a lot safer mounted."

"Sometimes you should just do as you're told. It can save your life." Ryne swept away the remainder of the broken weapons with his foot before he made his way to the fire with effortless grace, his muscles rippling under his armor with his motions. The movement enhanced his tattoos and the artwork on his armor, and she found it difficult to tell where the pictures on the armor ended and the tattoos on his arms began. The two were seamless. Even the orange reflection cast by the flames failed to diminish the rich colors.

She dismounted and trilled twice to Misty. Her dartan drifted next to his, and they mewled at each other and touched necks. She noticed Ryne's smile at the two mounts.

That one tender look somehow gave her a degree of trust, however small. Irmina took a couple steps closer to where he sat next to the fire's warmth. A sweet, musky smell drifted from the man. Even sitting he was almost as tall as her. Never before had she stood next to someone this large. He was neither handsome nor ugly. Except for his scars, his face appeared rather normal, nothing that would stand out in a crowd other than the size.

Ryne reached a hand out close to her and Misty warbled. Irmina took a step back. Ryne picked up a few fragments from the broken *divya* and tossed them aside.

"It's fine, girl," Irmina said, and made four short trills. Misty settled down.

"You can speak to her?" Ryne frowned and glanced at Sakari.

"After a fashion. I've trained with them all my life. I guess it just comes naturally." She had no intention of telling him about her ability to commune with beasts.

Across from her, Sakari stared her down, eyes flat. She sat where she could keep an eye on them both.

"So," Ryne began, his tone casual. "I'll be honest with you. If you lie about anything I ask, I *will* kill you."

Irmina stiffened, but nodded.

"Do you know who I am?"

"Besides that you're called Ryne? No."

"Well that makes two of us." Ryne gave a wry smile. "Why have you been following me?"

"I was given orders to find you and return with you to my master."

Ryne snorted. "You said master. You mean the Tribunal?"

"No. I don't work for them."

Ryne's brows drew together. "But you're an Ashishin. All of you belong to the Tribunal."

"In a sense, that's true but not all of us work toward the Tribunal's cause. Some Ashishin take individual masters within the Tribunal. A well–known practice. This way, we retain some semblance of freedom."

"Ah," Ryne said. "So your master works for the Tribunal then."

Irmina shrugged. "When their needs suit his, I suppose. I've seen many times where he does things contrary to what they wish."

"So what's your master's interest in me?"

Irmina held Ryne's gaze as she spoke, trying her hardest not to flinch or look away while at the same time maintaining a neutral tone to match his. "He believes you're a key to our future. To surviving what is to come. He says he knows who you are. More to the point, what you are. He says he has the answers you seek."

Ryne's eyes twitched with her last words, a spark shining deep in his emerald eyes, but then in the next instant, it was gone. "That's the second time in a few days I've heard that. Strange considering it's been seventy years with no one having a clue. Regardless, you'll have to give me more than that if I'm to follow you. Tell me, Irmina. Did you have anything to do with what happened at Carnas? With the Alzari?"

Irmina's brow furrowed. *What was the man talking about?* "No. I sent a warning to Bertram about the infected lapra. And I knew nothing of these Alzari until the one I met in the Mondros who spoke to you. This Jaecar—" Memories of what occurred rose from where she'd blocked them off, freezing her where she stood. Ryne had befriended the man in the Mondros. Could he be a part of this advance of Amuni's Children? Everything had happened so fast, she'd forgotten about Ryne's connection to Jaecar. Her hand edged to her sword.

Sakari's iron grip on her hand stopped her. She flexed against his hold, but his fingers never budged. She met his gaze, and he shook his head. He didn't release his hold even after she relaxed.

Ryne regarded her with narrowed eyes, his back stiff. His deep voice was steel. "What do you mean you sent a message to Bertram about the lapra?"

Irmina chose her words with care. "I sent Kahkon to tell him I'd seen the infected lapra. To keep his people away from the forest. I also sent a warning about a golden–haired woman I saw.

She was always near where they would find those bodies." The confusion on Ryne's face registered with her. "Bertram didn't tell anyone?"

Staring off at something distant, Ryne shook his head.

The night air hung heavy and again the grunting bark sounded. This time closer. Irmina wiped the sweat from her forehead with her other hand.

Finally, Ryne spoke. "You mentioned Jaecar. What did you do with him?"

At the mention of the man's name, the attack in the office came roaring back. Irmina squeezed her eyes shut for brief moment and took a long breath. "N–Nothing." She opened her eyes and steadied her shaking voice. "Although I wish I had. He tried to kill me in Ranoda. He brought an army of shadelings and Amuni's Children down onto the town."

Ryne was shaking his head, brows drawn together in a lumpy frown. "I saw no ill aura around him except—. His aura was as normal as—."

She gasped as his hard fingers engulfed her arm, replacing Sakari's, and snatched her to her feet. She hadn't seen him or Sakari move.

Misty warbled a warning.

The grunting barks came again from multiple locations almost on top of them—too many to count. Irmina's eyes narrowed. She recognized those noises.

Ancel's daggerpaw made the same sound when he hunted.

"Pay attention, woman." Ryne's eyes bored into hers as he held her by one arm. "They're here. Don't do anything. Don't even speak."

CHAPTER 42

R yne's fingers were coiled into a steel bracelet of tight control that dwarfed Irmina's arm. The woman's golden–brown eyes flashed, but she said nothing. After a moment, he released his grip. Wincing, she rubbed at her arm.

The realization Bertram was somehow involved in the attack on Carnas had rocked him to his core. The mayor's aura had appeared so perfect to him—same as it had been around Jaecar—except for those few times that he'd attributed the slight shift as a trick of the light or an emotional reaction. How could the man have hidden his intentions for so long? All the smiles, the banter, the annoying yet welcome arguments. Had Bertram really taken his hate for the Tribunal to such a level he doomed Carnas in the process? Ryne balled his hand into a fist and focused on the present danger.

Atop the hills, scores of daggerpaws appeared. Soon after, men in dark armor rose beside the beasts as if they grew from the earth.

Battle energy thrummed through Ryne's body. "Remember, do not move or speak."

More men riding horses or dartans crested the hill in front of him. Two dartan riders guided their mounts down into the hollow while the others stayed at the top. There had to be over a hundred of them by now. Upon reaching the clearing's edge, the two dismounted.

Full helmets made from hard leather, dyed green, hid their faces. Silver rivets covered the interlocking leather plates giving the helms a layered effect. Only their eyes showed between six thin straps connecting one side of the helm to the other and serving as a faceguard. They were equipped as well as any soldier in Varick's army, with deep green chestpieces and spaulders. Spiked bracers adorned their arms and fists. Cuisses at their thighs covered kilts that looked more like an apron, and under the kilts, leggings showed, all made from the same hardened leather in layered plates. Their soft leather boots made little noise against the clearing's black stone and sandy shale. Short, double–bladed axes hung from hasps at each hip.

Both men pulled off their helmets. The taller of the two reached Ryne's shoulder. He was a young man with an angular jaw, squared chin and a black braid wrapped in a small bun. He shook his head and the braid fell down his back. Hard, golden eyes studied Ryne. His aura writhed about him with a strength few possessed. Something about the man's face seemed familiar.

The other man had long, white hair done in numerous, small, intricate braids. Unlike the young man's smooth features, scars marred this man's face on both sides before they disappeared under the leather at his neck. His left side lacked an ear. On the same side, his eye proved nothing more than a closed lid. The old man gazed at Ryne without blinking. The man's single golden eye with its few silver flecks reflected the flames.

Ryne knew that eye, and the smooth aura, even if it was sixty years later. Tension eased from his shoulders.

The old man smiled. "Ryne Waldron, the Lightbringer. If I hadn't seen you with mine own eyes, or is that eye?" He chuckled. "I wouldn't have believed." His voice came in slow, raspy gasps, stretching into a hiss at every pause. Not like Ryne remembered. "So I left relative safety to see for myself. And here you are, looking as if you haven't aged a day since you saved my people."

"Edsel Stonewilled," Ryne said with a shake of his head and a smile, his battle energy seeping from him.

"Yes, my old friend." Edsel pointed at the young man. "This is my son, Garon. I've told him more times than I can count he wouldn't exist without you." He gestured around the hilltops. "None of us would."

Garon bowed. "May Ilumni's and Humelen's blessings always shine on you, Lightbringer, for what you've done for the Setian." His deep, strong voice emphasized the reverence etched in his words.

Irmina gasped, and they all looked to her. The Ashishin's hand edged toward her sword. Garon's eyes narrowed. Ryne shook his head, and her hand stilled, but her face still creased with worry.

Breathing easier, Ryne shifted his attention back to Garon. "Please, just call me Ryne. I told your father the same thing sixty years ago."

Edsel nodded toward Sakari. "I see you still travel with the silent one." He turned his head and his good eye to Irmina. "Who is the young Beastsinger?"

"Irmina, Irmina Nagel," she answered before Ryne could reply.

Ryne grimaced.

Edsel circled her. Every step included a small limp. "What's your business here Nagel Beastsinger? My son has watched you following the Lightbringer. He also saw you Forge. By your skin and eyes, you're a Granadian Ashishin. Did you know this, Ryne?"

"Yes. We were just discussing it when you came." Ryne paused and shot her a meaningful glance. "Edsel, she's a friend for now. Extend the same protection to her as you would for me and Sakari."

Both the Setian's heads snapped around to Ryne. Edsel's one eye stared for a moment, and then he bowed. "As the Lightbringer wishes." Edsel's gaze brushed over the corpses. "I see you took care of what drew us here in the first place." He pointed at the daggerpaws. "They're drawn to the shade like rot flies to decayed flesh." His eye shifted to Ryne. "It must be the Chronicle's work to find you here. Come, there's something you must see. On the way, you can tell me how you survived when you were taken by the Ashishin." His eye shifted to Irmina, and he smirked.

"Give me a moment," Ryne said.

Edsel nodded, signaled to his men and they mounted and rode up the hill.

"You're not considering going with them, are you?"

Irmina cast a venomous glare at the back of the Setian.

"If Edsel says there's something I must see, then it must be important. It would help if you either shut up or chose your words more carefully."

Irmina gave him a sullen look and opened her mouth before snapping it closed again. Face red, she stood quietly.

With a nod at her acquiescence, Ryne said, "You two help me get these bodies into the fire. I'll leave nothing the shade could possibly use."

As quickly as they could, they dragged the bodies, piling them around the fire. When they were finished, Ryne embraced Mater and stoked the fire's essences. Clothes, armor, and flesh burst into flames, spewing out a heated backwash and smoke that reeked of the substances the fire consumed. Within moments, the corpses of the Alzari were nothing more than charred, oily ash, and the flames had diminished. Ryne kicked shale over the fire until it sputtered and died.

"Mount up, let's go," Ryne ordered. "And remember to watch what you say, Irmina."

Torches lit the Setian convoy when they joined them on the other side of the hill. The winding line of dartans and lights stretched ahead. Ryne and the others rode up to the front next to Edsel and Garon. At a slow walk, they headed deeper into the mountains with the daggerpaws and their handlers bringing up the rear.

"Edsel, I still can't believe you're the Barrier bandits. Why the raids?" Ryne asked.

"Did the Setian ever need a reason for slaughtering innocent people?" Irmina scoffed.

Ryne shook his head.

A scowl twisting his face, Edsel made a point of ignoring Irmina. "At first, we needed to keep our people supplied until we could survive on our own. But that was long ago. Since then, we've carved our own lives out of this harsh land. We've had scouts return from Ranoda, Astoca, and the Alzari clanholds. We know of Amuni's Children and the shadeling armies. Every raid we've done has been on supplies meant for them. None else. Some who died may have appeared innocent, yes, but they were helping Amuni's Children. Whether they knew it or not makes no difference."

"How noble of you," Irmina said mockingly. "If not for your people, the shade wouldn't have a toehold on these lands."

Ryne sighed. The woman didn't know when to shut up.

"It's obvious you cannot see past what lies you were taught. You only see the picture's frame instead of the delicate artwork." Edsel shook his head. "Although your argument does have some validity, there's much you don't know. The Setian were in some ways responsible for the shade's coming. In turn, without the Shadowbearer's advance, Granadia too, would have fallen to the shade."

"So now you would have me believe your kind saved us? Ha."

Edsel tilted his head, his gold and silver eye unblinking as he studied her. He offered no reply as they weaved their way up into a narrow, rock–strewn pass scattered with occasional giant boulders. The Setian traveled between the mountainous silhouettes looming around them with the surefootedness of a well–known path.

After a few moments' silence, Edsel pointed to his face and throat, then to his people riding ahead. "Here is my reminder of my people's failure, but also of the torture yours inflicted on mine. This is all that's left of a once thriving people. So save your talk about slaughter and reasons for someone else. You Granadians are no more innocent than we, even if you fail to see it."

A sneer twisted Irmina's features. "Your people destroyed your own, and killed thousands of mine. You wiped out most of Ostania with your conquest—"

"Did we? Or did the shade?" Edsel sounded as if he were chastising a naughty child. "Were your people any less the executioners? Let me guess, your vaunted history books tell you different. I see the Tribunal has perfected the business of poisoning young minds."

Irimina's voice rose. "My people?" Eyes ablaze, her voice sizzled with hatred. "My parents were Felani. Your people killed most of my family with your invasion. How can you defend what you did? Countless innocents, countless Ashishin and Dagodin slaughtered. Your people, under the Shadowbearer's banner did that. You abandoned Ilumni and served Amuni. What did you expect? Mercy? Your people deserve to be wiped from Denestia."

Garon hissed and reached for his axe.

"Don't Garon," Edsel said, his voice quiet. "Beastsinger, there's much for you to learn. You rage against us with righteousness, but do your people really follow the Streamean Tenets?"

Ryne thought about Halvor. *Why did he make me repeat light's Tenets? Could anyone follow all the Tenets without breaking one?*

Edsel continued before Irmina answered, his tone almost conversational. "Many Setian killed were fleeing the shade and Nerian. Those of us who didn't turn were forced into the Shadowbearer's war. But then you know this, or you should. His armies held our children and the elderly hostage. We either had to fight or watch them die. I witnessed my children suffer, flayed limb by limb. What would've been your choice?"

Irmina's body shook, and she opened her mouth.

"What he says is true," Ryne said. "I wasn't a part of the war, but I saw what came after. Many Setian died by my own hand after I joined one of the Dagodin cohorts hunting them down. We slaughtered them by the thousands." *Never again.* "But just as many Setian were innocent, not turned by the shade. I fought against killing the innocent, but the Granadians wanted retribution. So did the other Ostanian tribes. They intended to kill every Setian and wipe the land of Seti from the map.

"One day, we came upon Edsel's clan hiding within some marshes and swamps. We hunted them down, dragged them out, and lined them up. Edsel begged for mercy. He spoke of all his clan had suffered in their efforts to refuse serving the Shadowbearer's purpose. I could see they were good people. I begged the soldiers to stop, but they began to kill the men first. Then they raped the women and children. The muddy marsh waters ran red with blood." The visions of that day spilled through Ryne's head. *Never again.*

Ryne's voice was as hollow as an empty grave. "What they did was no better than what the Setian and the shade's minions had done. Finally, I could take no more. I intervened, and in doing so, was forced to kill several Ashishin and Dagodin to help Edsel escape."

"Why would you help murderers?" Irmina's high–pitched voice broke in. "They wiped out whole cities! They deserved no better than they received."

Several Setian paused or stopped. Edsel flicked his hand out, and they continued riding.

"Because," Ryne answered, "The killing needed to stop, Irmina. Who did the children—the babies—kill? It needed to stop. For the sake of all the people, not just yours or theirs."

"I still remember those days." Edsel's soft hissing voice echoed in the pass. "We ran for weeks, fighting, dying, eluding regular soldiers, Dagodin and Ashishin alike. A month later, we reached Coronad Port and took a ship. But the Tribunal's armies caught us. I took as many as I thought we needed to start anew. Lightbringer stayed with my people who volunteered to defend the docks in order for our ship to escape. Four High Ashishin arrived and the massacre of the remnants of my people began, until Ryne alone battled them. Then he was gone from sight. I still don't know what happened after that, Lightbringer. I've heard stories, but they always seem more legend than life."

Irmina's wide eyes regarded Ryne. "You alone stopped four High Ashishin?" she whispered.

Ryne held her gaze for a moment before she looked away. "Me and Sakari. We fought until the barriers Edsel's people had Forged gave out and exhaustion took us. I was ready to accept death then. I deserved it for the lives I took. They sent me before the Tribunal, and although they condemned me to death, the High Ashishin didn't kill me. Instead, they imprisoned me in the Iluminus for years. I didn't see Sakari again until later, but I could feel him being tortured. The things they did to him…"

He remained silent for a moment before he continued. "As for me, they tried torturing me into telling them how my power worked. Day after day, they beat me with *divya* whips. They tried to strip the skin from my flesh to inspect my Scripts. When that wouldn't work, they beat me some more. Then they mended me and started all over again." Ryne shuddered as the lashes from the whips seared fresh across his flesh.

Irmina's face held a pitiless expression. "You killed Ashishin and fought alongside the Setian—"

Ryne cut her off. "No matter how I tried, I couldn't grasp Mater to defend myself. It seemed always out of my reach."

"No…" Irmina's face that seconds ago was red with anger and contempt paled to a pasty white. "They wouldn't."

"I found out later they had Warped the Mater around

me, twisting the elements so I couldn't touch them."

"But, Warping requires sela," Irmina said slowly. "They would need to have killed someone to gather the power to work such a Forging. One person's sela could maybe Warp enough Mater for a week. If they kept you imprisoned for years, then hundreds of people...Oh, Ilumni." Tears came to her eyes.

The pain etched on Irmina's face reminded Ryne of his own shame for the atrocities he'd committed. He wished he knew a way to console her because his next words would make her feel no better. "When they saw the torture wouldn't work, they brought in scholars to study me. They too were left stumped. A few months later, a High Ashishin visited me escorted by several of his Pathfinders. My Scripts raged out of control at their presence, threatening to destroy the Warping because I saw these men for what they were. Those men, supposed servants of Ilumni, were all under the shade's influence."

"Another High Ashishin and Pathfinders serving Amuni? Like Nerian? No, no that cannot be." Irmina's voice was a mere shell.

Ryne shook his head. "It's true. I tried to tell the guards but they didn't listen. They said I was mad. Then he had my guards replaced with his own."

Edsel studied Irmina for a moment, a smug expression on his face. "So you see, everything is not always what it seems to be. Even among your own people."

Irmina returned a stunned look. Her mouth opened and closed, but she uttered no words.

They reached end of the pass and entered a valley. Below them, thick grass and large trees hugged the slopes. A river's rushing waters sounded in the dark.

Appearing to have recovered her senses somewhat, Irmina asked, "How...How did you escape?"

"There came another meeting with the Tribunal. They decided that instead of killing me, they would put me to use. My new punishment was to help purge Ostania of both the Setian and the shade beyond the Vallum. The next day, the tainted High Ashishin returned with his Pathfinders. They chained me in *divya* chains and put me on a ship with Sakari. For weeks, we sailed with them only bringing me up once a week for fresh air. I fought madness daily, with my Scripts feeling as if they wanted to tear off my skin. Every time they took me upstairs, I opened myself to my Scripts. I learned that although I couldn't grasp Mater; my Scripts could, but I would need to give in to them. I allowed them to store as much essences as they craved.

"During the trip the High Ashishin studied me for hours on end. Three months into our journey, I overheard the guards mention we were soon at our destination. But I knew they would never take me to the Dagodin and Ashishin armies. So, the next time they brought me up for air. I let my Scripts loose.

"To this day, I've never felt such power. It almost tore my soul and my body apart. I still cannot remember what happened. Somehow, I woke floating in the sea on a piece of driftwood left from the ship. Through my Scripts, I drew my armor and my sword to myself and swam to shore. Sakari found me there soon after. He nursed me back to health."

"That part of the sea still glows today," Edsel said. "You can see it from Felan Mark's towers. From what I felt that day, Lightbringer, I suspected you were alive."

Ryne gave Edsel a small smile. "In my attempt to escape across the Vallum I ended up at Knight Commander Varick's encampment during a shadeling attack. Sakari and I helped him fight, saving thousands. He vouched for us and we earned a partial pardon. Afterward, we were offered a full pardon if we served the Tribunal in its endeavors here in Ostania. As my power craved to fight the shade, I accepted."

Ryne became deathly silent. Farther north, grasslands and forest sloped gradually until he could no longer see them. The Vallum of Light rose at that end of the valley, its glow dominating the land in the distance.

Edsel called for a stop near the forest. The daggerpaw handlers fanned out into the dense trees. Several other Setian dismounted and followed the handlers, torches bobbing about within the woods.

"This is why I said the Chronicles must have a hand in your being here, Lightbringer," Edsel said. "I always knew you lived. I felt it in my heart. When my son described you, I had to come to see for myself. Come, we're here."

Ryne smiled. He still remembered Edsel's constant mention of the Chroniclers. *I searched for over twenty years, my old friend, and not once did I find proof of the great record keepers of history.*

Just rumor upon rumor of their existence.

Garon dismounted and helped his father down. Ryne, Sakari and Irmina also dismounted. They followed Garon through the long grasses and into the dark forest, sweet scents of blooming flowers and the chirping of insects greeting them. Two daggerpaw handlers flanked the group on each side. The men's heads moved from side to side as if they expected an attack at any moment. Irmina's hand strayed close to her sword.

Edsel gestured around the valley as he hobbled. "This valley is one of the few fertile ones in this part of the Barrier Mountains. No one would've ever suspected the Setian of being here. After all, we're all under the shade's influence." He cast a quick glance and a wry smile at Irmina.

She met his gaze for a moment, and then she looked at the ground, her pale cheeks flushed.

As they progressed through the woods along a path lit by torches and lamps, Ryne opened his Matersense. The forest came alive around him, the essences swirling in multiple eddies. A breeze picked up, but this time the flower scents were gone. Instead, a fetid, moldy stench assaulted Ryne's nostrils. His eyes narrowed.

Irmina sniffed. "What's that smell?"

"That's the reason for all the torches and lamps. The reason we now stay together at all times. The reason we brought you here," Edsel's voice hissed.

Battle energy flooded Ryne.

CHAPTER 43

Irmina's hand darted to her sword's hilt. Garon snatched one of his axes, clearing the clasp on his hip before his foot landed with his next step. Ryne stepped in between them.

"Stop it," Ryne ordered, his outstretched arms keeping them apart. "If they meant us harm, there'd be no need to drag us all the way out here." Ryne held Irmina's small hand against her hilt so she couldn't draw the sword.

After a moment, tension eased from her flushed face, she relaxed her grip, and he released her hand. Still glaring at her, Garon put away his axe. Ryne took his hands from the man's chest.

They continued forward, the decaying, moldy stench growing stronger as they advanced. Ahead, lamps hung from branches, lighting up the forest. Pines and oaks appeared, leaves frail and gray, trunks sporting rotted, discolored masses. The flowers and plants close by were wilted and brown. Edsel led them past the line of unhealthy trees into wide, open land.

A kinai orchard spread as far as Ryne could see. What looked like red spider webs covered the ground. Fungus engulfed the trees so dense in some parts it hung like thick, mottled beards.

A choked sound uttered from Irmina, and her hand covered her mouth. "Oh, Ilumni."

Every kinai plant was dead. Some fruit appeared half–eaten or simply squashed. Shade clogged the other elements within the plants. The air itself appeared dim. At their core, most trees lacked their sela.

Ryne's thoughts raced. Heat crawled along his skin and not only did his Scripts roil, but his bloodlust tried to rise. After a moment, the feeling passed. Something squeezed Ryne's hand, and he looked down. Irmina's clammy fingers clung to his. She caught herself and released her grip.

"Did you see what did this?" Ryne asked.

Garon nodded. "Follow me."

The tall Setian edged around the dead orchard with Edsel hobbling after him.

As Ryne turned to follow, clumps of shade among the dead kinai drew his attention. He squinted. Wraithwolf droppings. Ryne signaled to Sakari who nodded, then the two of them hurried to join the others with a pale–faced Irmina in tow.

"I wasn't here when this first happened," Garon said when they caught up. "The daggerpaws picked up on them. My father sent a team out, and they found this." He stopped at an unusually dense thicket with ashy, motionless leaves and black trunks.

Ryne recognized the way the trees appeared as the same as those he'd found in the Fretian Woods when he discovered the missing villagers. The essences within the trees were smudged the same as he remembered from Carnas and the kinai orchards at the Astocan farms.

Irmina gasped. "Wraithwoods. How's this possible?" Her trembling voice was a barely audible whisper.

The name itched with familiarity to Ryne. But he couldn't conjure the memory of where he heard it before.

"That's not all." Garon brought his hand up, and his brow furrowed.

Light essences swept up into the man. His hands moved with a circular motion, and he pushed the Forging out. A swath of light cut into the wraithwoods, and the trees released a soft, whispering wail as if spirits sighed through the forest.

Ryne frowned at what Garon had done, then it clicked. The man's golden eyes, his unusually strong aura, and now this. Garon was a Setian Ashishin.

Garon stepped forward into the path he cut into the wraithwoods with Ryne and the others following. The ground and trees around them smoked, filling the air with the smell of burning wood. Heat rose in waves from the earth, warm even through Ryne's boots. Charred stumps were all that remained of some trees; the rest were ash rising on the wind. Ryne anticipated a reaction from Irmina, but she seemed too stunned to think.

Within the thicket another scent consumed the air. A choking stink like old corpses left out on a battlefield. The others coughed at the stench and held their hands over their mouths and noses. Ryne breathed through his mouth to lessen the putrid smell as he eyed the jumbled fleshy mess in the thicket. His bloodlust rose screaming, and his Scripts squirmed about his skin.

Bodies of Setian men and women lay on the dark, soggy ground. Maggots crawled from their flesh, and black fluid seeped from their wounds. But their chests rose and fell in a slow rhythm. Black tendrils connected them together. Close to them lay half–formed wraithwolves.

Retching, Irmina turned away, spewing the contents of her stomach.

Ryne folded his mouth in against the urge to inhale. "Not only have the shadelings left the Broken Lands, bypassed the wards in the Rotted Forest, but they've also breached the Vallum of Light."

"T–That's…not…possible." Irmina said. If she was pale before, her face was now a sickly white.

Ryne gestured to encompass the area around them. "It shouldn't be, but the proof lies before us. Worse yet is what could have extracted sela from the kinai."

"Now you know why I said there's something you must see," Edsel explained. "They're few things I know of that can harvest sela."

"You're speaking of daemons aren't you?" Irmina blurted out. "How?" she added at Ryne's nod.

Spreading his hands helplessly, Ryne said, "I don't know." His Scripts roiled again. As at the other wraithwoods, he knew there was only one thing to do. "I need you all to leave here."

"But—" Garon began.

"Leave now," Ryne ordered without raising his voice.

Sakari stepped in between everyone and Ryne.

Edsel took Garon by the arm. "Do as the Lightbringer says."

"You too," Ryne said, without looking at Irmina. His Scripts continued to flit and shift around him, responding to the shade.

Irmina said nothing. Her face finally regaining some semblance of color, she left with the others. Sakari followed her.

Ryne studied the wraithwoods. He didn't understand how the shadelings could've reached this side of the Vallum. Not to mention that they were advancing at a far faster rate than he could have imagined. However they were managing the feat, it didn't matter. They had to be stopped. And soon.

Where Garon's power had struck, the wraithwoods were already growing again, blocking outside influences of light. Ryne touched his Scripts, drawing on the ones depicting the sun and the twin moons. Light and fire essences rushed into him. The voices skittered through his mind, but he brushed them aside, and unsheathed his sword. The essences spread within him like flames through dry brush. He pushed them into the weapon, and it burst alight with a soft, white glow.

Around him, the shade–filled leaves wilted. The grass beneath his feet disintegrated into smoking ash. Skin peeled from the bodies of the Setian and wraithwolves alike, and the stench of burnt flesh and hair replaced the reek of decay. The trees themselves seemed to shrink back from the light. He bent and slammed the sword into the earth. Still holding the hilt, he linked with the earth and sent the light and fire through it. A breath left his lips, and at the same time, he triggered the power his sword held.

A noiseless concussion shook the trees. Light swept around him in an incandescent pillar that spread rapidly with him at its center. The Forms and Streams mingled in the earth and carried the Forging to its purpose.

Shade shattered.

The wraithwoods, the bodies, and the shadelings crumpled and turned to ash. Air rose as wind and took the ashes with it. The pillar of Light shot up into the air.

A clear, circular area, devoid of vegetation with Ryne at its center and steam rising in a dreary mist, replaced the wraithwoods. Ryne's sword winked out. In one motion, he pulled it from the earth and sheathed the weapon. As he released his Matersense, he took several deep breaths to steady himself, and strode from the trees toward the others.

Irmina gawked. Edsel and Garon's eyes shone with

reverence as they regarded Ryne. They both bowed. Sakari regarded him with a blank expression.

"Are there anymore wraithwood manifestations?" Ryne asked.

"Yes, three more, across the valley to the east," Garon said as he led them from the forest toward their mounts. "I can have the scouts lead us there—"

"No. I can find them on my own. You need to get to your people now. Head to the Vallum. It'll be the safest place for you."

"Our homes are in the mountains, right next to the Vallum," Edsel said, a hint of pride in his voice as they reached the dartans.

Irmina's head snapped around to the man.

Edsel shrugged and a smile played across his lips. "There's no safer place than under the noses of your worst enemy. It's the last place they would expect. What's your plan, Lightbringer?"

"I'm going to destroy the other woods before they're put to anymore use. Then I'm going to hunt the daemon responsible," Ryne declared.

Silence hung heavy in the air with his words. No one spoke until they reached the mounts.

Garon felt around inside the bags on his dartan and pulled out a map. He studied it for a moment then pointed at three locations. "Here, here and here. That's where you'll find the other manifestations. Please, Lightbringer, let some of our men go with you. The daggerpaws can track the shadelings better than any man. Besides, I've been trying to tell you—it's no daemon that did this. It was a man."

"Are you sure?"

"Yes, we watched him for days. Every time he came and left, the wraithwoods grew."

"Did your men try to stop him?"

"Several did. He killed them with a mere wave of his hand. My father decided then we needed to find you."

One man who could create wraithwoods or somehow help them grow? This had to be the Skadwaz he and Sakari suspected or worse some High Ashishin who'd turned traitor. Ryne studied the Vallum. *What in Ilumni's name was going on?* "Did he Forge shade?"

Garon nodded. "Some yes, but he mostly killed with a Forge of light, fire and earth essences."

Ryne's eyes widened, and he glanced to Sakari who gave him a simple shrug. Edsel's face mirrored Garon's words. Irmina's hiss said she too knew what it meant. Only the most powerful could Forge two or more different elements of Mater at the same time.

"Ryne," Irmina said, her eyes wide with sudden fear. "I need to speak to you now." She looked at the others. "Alone."

Edsel led Garon away and Ryne nodded to Sakari.

Irmina made sure they were out of earshot before she began. "With all that's been happening, it slipped my mind. But I started to think. I–I met a woman who told me about this. About the creation of new shadelings using people."

"What woman?"

"Her name was Tae." She paused for a moment at his narrowed eyes before she continued. "She saved my life. She's the reason I survived Ranoda. She said there's now enough power in the world for such an undertaking. She mentioned a skill being used among Amuni's Children that only one as powerful as a High Ashishin could use. I–I think there's a Skadwaz here in Denestia. That must be who did this."

"Or a Shin who's been turned." He kept his face impassive despite the sharp look she gave him. "What did this woman look like?"

Irmina described Taeria down to her leathery skin. First, Bertram, and now, Taeria. *Hagan, you and your pipe, always generous and willing to help those in need, among the first to accept me. Vana and Vera…* The faces and names flooded Ryne again. He rubbed at his temples as if it would push the memories away. "First I'll take care of the wraithwoods, then we'll warn Varick," he said, his voice strained.

Irmina nodded, and they walked off to meet up with the others. Over in the trees, a bright light sparked from the direction of the kinai orchard. A crackling sound reached them from the same area.

"We're burning the kinai," Garon said, in response to Irmina's frown. "This way whoever he is cannot use these plants again."

"Listen," Ryne said. "What I'm about to do will draw this man's attention. Pathfinders will come here soon enough anyway with what's happened. You need to move your people now." Ryne took in the stubborn set of Edsel's jaw. "There's no other way to ensure your safety and force his hand at the same time."

Edsel's jaw relaxed and his eyes softened. "If times were different, I would've insisted on coming with you. However, I have a people to preserve. We planned for a new place to settle when this first began. We'll travel farther north along the Vallum. We should be safe enough that way."

Ryne grabbed Thumper's reins and turned to Irmina. "Take Thumper—"

"I'm coming with you."

Ryne opened his mouth to disagree. Her willingness to help him even if it meant her death came back to him. "How about this? I promise to return with you to your master if you go with the Setian."

Her forehead wrinkled. She studied his face for a moment, then nodded. "If you're not back by dawn, I'll find you."

"You won't need to. Sakari is going with you. He always knows where I am." Ryne noted Sakari's quick glance in his direction. He linked with him. "Stay with them. They may need more protection than I do."

"As you wish." Sakari bowed and strode over to Thumper.

After brief goodbyes, Ryne waited in the open plain while they rode away. The line of Setian dipped from sight below a distant hill, and he took out the map. He memorized the wraithwood locations and crossed the field into the forest.

Almost an hour later, Ryne destroyed the last wraithwood manifestation and inspected the area around it. Unlike the other two, fresh paw prints angled deeper into the forest. From the tracks, at least two wraithwolves stalked somewhere within the valley. A screeching wail echoed from farther south. Another answered closer to him within the woods. As expected, the shadelings had sensed his use of Mater.

Battle energy coursing through him, Ryne craned his head to the twin moons' circular contours between the branches. Stars twinkled like diamond pinpoints. He called on his Scripts, linking with the moonbeams that filtered through the dark canopy and interrupted the dominance of shadow in the forest.

Glancing back down, he picked out the shade residing within all shadow. The malevolent essences beckoned to him, but he knew better than to touch them. Not with the wraithwolves using shade for their eyes and ears. Ryne drew light through his Scripts and pictured himself soaked in its glow. The Scripts responded and did as he requested, swathing him in luminescent essences, giving him the appearance of a ghostly presence. Now that he'd made himself invisible to the wraithwolves' senses, he mapped the moon rays illuminating the ground and branches around him.

He Shimmered.

With each Shimmer, his Scripts called on light and pulled him to a designated moonbeam. He flew up into the trees, from one patch of light to the other, making certain to avoid the shade. Each Shimmer brought him closer to the wraithwolves. Already linked with the elements around him, he soon found the first one.

The black–furred beast, almost Ryne's size, stood on muscular hind legs like a man, staring at the trees below. The shadeling whined and snarled, flexing long, oversized arms tipped with sharp claws that dangled past its knees. Glowing green eyes changed from orbs to slits, back to orbs. The wraithwolf's pungent, moldy stench wafted up to Ryne as he listened to the whines and snarls below for the change in pitch that would tell him the creature sensed his presence. No changes occurred.

Obviously bewildered by Ryne's disappearance, the wraithwolf stared around for a few more minutes. Another wail sounded from the south. The shadeling Blurred away toward the sound. A smile touched the corner of Ryne's lips. Unseen among the tree branches, he followed in silence.

The wraithwolf Blurred from the forest into the wide, open plain, and bounded across the long grasses to where its counterpart stalked. The second shadeling was a foot shorter than the first, and loped a few feet to one side then back, first on two legs then on all fours. When the beast dropped onto its arms like forelegs, and then rose again, it sniffed the air and whined.

Ryne frowned. Why would the creatures go into an open field where moonlight reached with ease? The lack of shade within the field played to his advantage. Ryne's lips curled into a lazy smile. This Skadwaz had to be close by, waiting for Ryne to engage. Ryne reached his senses out, but found nothing unusual other than the wraithwolves. Still, an uneasy prickle raised the hair on his arms.

A stiff wind rose at Ryne's back, and a distant rumble echoed in the air. Ryne Shimmered to a new position, eyeing the northern sky. Onyx thunderheads with blue lightning radiating within them rolled across the heavens. Ryne grunted his concern. When the blanket of clouds crossed the moons, they would cast the land into darkness. Shade would envelop everything. Whoever his hidden adversary, the man was no fool.

Ryne knew he couldn't afford to wait any longer.

He Shimmered twice out onto the plains toward the wraithwolves. The smaller one rose up onto its legs as he landed. In one fluid motion, Ryne unsheathed his sword and triggered its Scripts. He took the shadeling's head before it stood fully erect. There was no sense of impact as the body crumpled to ash.

The bigger wraithwolf Blurred away to the forest's edge. Sheathing his weapon, Ryne faced the beast. The shadeling Blurred, this time toward Ryne, its form appearing to stretch into a long silhouette. Ryne's gaze followed. Only one patch of shade was big enough to hold the creature. It emerged from Ryne's shadow.

As the shadeling appeared, Ryne drew his sword and sliced through the shadow. The wraithwolf issued a plaintive cry. Still wreathed in shadow, its body shriveled, the ash of its remains dissipating on the storm winds.

Ryne spun in anticipation of his hidden foe. But no attack came. Eyes shifting from side to side, he rotated slowly.

The thunderheads began to cross the moons, lightning radiating from within them in ever increasing beats in time with the growl of thunder. Rain pattered to the ground and darkness swept in. Ryne's Scripts writhed about him, pulling at his skin as if they could peel from him. The two warring voices came screaming into his head, and his bloodlust rose in a vicious torrent that almost made him stumble, but he made no attempt to calm them, instead reveling in the power they bestowed.

Disturbed Flows of air and the interruption of the raindrops' steady rhythm was his only warning. He swung his sword up.

Light met shade in an embrace of white and black sparks. Steel rang with a reverberating echo, the impact vibrating through Ryne's arms.

Illuminated by the glow from Ryne's sword, a black-armored assailant darted away, hooded cloak billowing, then circled. The man's height brought him past Ryne's shoulders, and he appeared powerfully built matching in Ryne in size. Not even his eyes showed. In one hand, the stranger held a wide, five foot-long blade with distinctive glyphs.

How is it that I can't sense this man's Mater or see his aura?

Lightning flashed and the man struck again. Low then high. Ryne parried the blows with ease. His attacker leaped back before Ryne could counter.

Ryne's eyes narrowed. He ignored the raindrops drumming his head and water dripping down his face. The stranger moved faster than anyone he'd ever faced. But why was he using the most basic strikes?

Again, the dark man swept in, this time with four strokes alternating from torso to head to legs. Still, just the basics.

Ryne parried each strike and swept in for an attack. The man Blurred away. Ryne hadn't felt him draw any shade when he used his ability. Worry chilled Ryne's bones and crawled down his back. His heart raced. Whoever this attacker was, he possessed skills beyond any Ryne remembered encountering.

The black armored man circled once more and shifted, this time into a more advanced Stance—Earthtouch. Ryne countered the man's Stance with Voidwalk, ready to use air's weightless Styles to counter earth's solid strength. Ryne smiled inwardly. Now he knew who'd taught the Alzari he fought.

Before Ryne could move, the man disappeared again in the darkness. Ryne sensed essences being drawn in a Forging he recognized. Unable to Shimmer, he sprinted in the direction he felt the Forging.

As quickly as it began, the thunderstorm ended. The clouds bypassed the moons, and moonlight illuminated the field once more. Able to use his power now, Ryne Shimmered to the location of the Forge.

The man was gone, and from the residue left from the Forging, Ryne knew he wouldn't be back. For a moment, Ryne stood surveying the valley and its forests. Life, he knew, had just become more difficult than he could've imagined. With a sigh, he Shimmered to the north and the relative safety of the Vallum of Light.

Ryne stood in a field below the Vallum with his sword in hand, the white stone and steel wall stretching several hundred feet above him. It had taken him another hour to reach Irmina and the others. The Setian camp spread behind him, close to the towering *divya* wall, but out of sight of any Bastions. There were no tents, just bedrolls containing sleeping people and guards patrolling with daggerpaws.

Dawn hovered on the air, but the sun still lay beyond the mountains and horizon to the east. The silver–blue moons had already deserted the sky, leaving a slate–like blanket of gloom. Loose strands of hair fluttering with the wind, Ryne adhered to his own regimen and practiced the sword under a gray cloudless sky, feet swishing through wet grass. Sakari watched his every move.

Ryne flowed through every Stance and Style memorized from years of unending practice—most of those years hidden in a fog of lost memories. Thoughts of his murderous past, of Carnas, of Bertram's betrayal, of Taeria's secret, of his failure to save Kahkon, haunted him. No matter how he tried, he couldn't banish those memories this dreary morning. He brought his sword work to a halt as Edsel, Garon and Irmina strode to meet him.

"Glad to see you're alive and well, old friend." Edsel's golden eye shone as he spoke. He clasped his hand over Ryne's when he reached him.

Ryne returned the gesture. "Yet, I failed," Ryne said solemnly. "I managed to destroy the wraithwoods, but the man escaped."

"How?" Garon asked with an incredulous stare.

"He was stronger than a High Ashishin. I too couldn't sense when he drew Mater. I could only sense what he Forged after the fact."

Garon's eyes widened even more. Irmina's expression radiated fear.

"You'll have to take your people away from here. He *will* come back," Ryne stated.

Edsel nodded. "I figured as much. I had already planned on it. What do you intend to do?"

"I'm going to warn Knight Commander Varick. He needs to inform the Tribunal about the Vallum's breach."

Irmina scowled. "So much for your promise."

"I promised I would come, I never said when. Besides, warning Varick is more important than going with you."

She opened her mouth to speak, but Ryne stared her down. "That man could be anywhere by now. He Materialized," Ryne said in a soft voice.

Irmina's mouth went slack. "But, but only High Ashishin or Exalted can use that ability."

"Exactly, my point."

CHAPTER 44

A blast of icy wind swept down from the snow–capped shoulders of the Kelvore Mountains. Shin Galiana shivered. The air was too cold by far for summer, unnaturally so. The gale cut through cloak, cloth, leather, and mail alike as it chased bloated, gray clouds before it, harrying them across the dark sky. Steamy breaths rose in the air as men shifted uneasily or stomped their feet, shoulders hunched, intent gazes focused across the battlefield. Bonfires along the lines of archers did little to stave off the chill, their heat swelling for a moment before the wind swept the warmth away into the night. Knight Captains barked commands at the soldiers to remain vigilant, to ignore the cold. Often, the response was chattering teeth and stomping feet. Although used to the harsh winters northern Granadia brought, their bodies were not prepared for the sudden change of weather.

Shin Galiana's dartan mewled behind the lines of its fellow cavalry. Ahead of them, row upon row of armor clad novices and trainees interspersed by spear and sword wielding Dagodin formed. She wished she had all Matii for the task at hand, but such wishes were miracles the gods granted. In her time, she'd seen too little of miracles. Barely enough for her to keep her faith.

At least the supplies they'd collected for years would finally be put to good use. Not at the original time as they'd planned, but that made no difference right now. Plans of men were inconsequential things and made to be changed. Resplendent in new green cloth, painted leather, shiny chainmail or glittering steel, a full legion of Dagodin stood ready. In contrast, the retired soldiers, novices, and trainees had to resort to whatever armor they could muster or what could be hastily crafted. One cohort still wore the crimson of Granadia's Tribunal.

A white battle standard depicting a forest split down the middle by a great quake flew high in the air—the colors and insignia of the Setian. A long time since she'd seen such. A somber smile touched her lips. Despite her regret at days long gone, she still found herself riding with her back a little straighter, and her chest out. The standard was a pronouncement of independence, of a return of an old kingdom, of a reclamation.

Stefan had insisted on the display. Why, she wasn't certain. He'd assured her it was worth the risk if Eldanhill and their people was to survive the siege and the uprising of the other Granadian kingdoms. Eagles had been dispatched to the other Mysteras to make them aware and begin their exodus before any repercussions or suspicions took place. She'd also sent word to Jerem so he could activate and dispatch the Sleepers within their network to begin their whispers while relaying tidbits of proof that would point to the Tribunal's many atrocities over these long years. Whether the Setian were ready or not, war had once again come and no way existed to avoid it. *When warranted, strike hard with subversion, fire, and steel and let those in your way tremble at your bold stroke.*

Again, she wished the time could've been more ideal for this revelation. Indeed, many in Eldanhill had been in shock. But after seeing the few who'd surrendered to the encroaching Sendethi forces have their heads removed and hung on tall pikes, they'd understood their plight. Fight or die.

The Tribunal would be none too pleased by Eldanhill's proclamation or King Emory's actions, but faced with rebellion from so many other fronts in Granadia they'd have to consider who to take on first. Their reaction may well be one of immediate retribution. Of course, there was the chance the Granadian kingdoms banded together to crush their old enemy the Setian. Another risk the Tribunal couldn't afford, and yet they couldn't be seen to openly support the revival of the Setian. Ah, well, one worry at a time.

The problem at hand lay several thousand feet on the

other side of the makeshift palisade where thousands upon thousands of Sendethi soldiers gathered. Twice the battle standards as before flew high, buffeted by the strong wind. Flying not far from those were a few Barsonian banners. More than she'd expected. This was to be the first statement in overthrowing the Tribunal's iron grip, it seemed. Eldanhill was to be the example. Her lips curled in a cruel smile at that last.

She eyed the sky above once more. Of all times, this Sendethi army had chosen the Spellforge hour to attack. They were playing into the strength of the Matii. Whoever led this army hadn't done their research. The strategy may be sound against a normal army, but not Eldanhill's. Could Giomar really be this stupid? Her forehead creased with lines. No. The man didn't appear the type. After all, he'd already outmaneuvered her once.

Emerald eyes shining from within his silver helmet, icy flecks dotting his beard, Stefan brought his dartan closer. "Something isn't quite right, Galiana."

"Yes. That's what I was beginning to think."

Stefan signaled for Guthrie, Devan, Jillian, Rohan and Edwin to join them. All now appointed as Generals, they rode over and formed a small circle, misty breaths of men and mounts rising in the air, leather and armor creaking. The musky smell of dartans filled the area.

"Why would you choose to fight Matii at the Spellforge hour?" Stefan scanned the Sendethi forces.

Jillian cocked her head in that odd way of hers, the beak upon her leather helmet making her appear as aquiline as one of her pet eagles. "Maybe they have Matii of their own?"

Edwin snorted. "Where would the Sendethi acquire Matii? The Pathfinders have weeded out every single one who's come into their power."

"That may be true," Guthrie stated, his paunch making him appear to lean unsteadily in the saddle. "But the question still begs to be asked. And the answer Jillian gave seems the most plausible one."

"I say we take no chances," Devan said, his hulking form matching his gruff voice. He rode the biggest dartan of the bunch, an animal that dwarfed the others. "Act as if they do have Matii. Prepare our Ashishin to counter rather than attack."

Galiana nodded. "I agree. If they'd smuggled in Namazzi or Alzari we would have known. And well, the Svenzar fight for no one but themselves." Her cloak flapped in the breeze, and she pulled it tighter around her. "But I see the Golden Tide banners of Barson among the Sendethi forces. The Pathfinders have never penetrated their borders. I do not think now is the time to act without caution."

"Well," Guthrie said, "They have our ten thousand outnumbered by three to one. If our original plan can't work, what now?"

"We split forces," Stefan said. "Make them move their army."

Edwin's brow rose. "How do we do that? And why we would we split when our strength lies in our numbers."

Stefan smiled, all teeth. "*Their* strength is in their numbers. Ours isn't. Our strength is maneuverability, our Ashishin, Dagodin and what *divya* we've mustered. Our mounted divisions are groomed for speed. Their heavily armored horses are no match. Today will prove their downfall. Horse against dartan. There's no contest."

Everyone nodded their agreement. Galiana could see part of the plan clearly now. But where would they leave Eldanhill vulnerable?

As if seeing the question written on her face, Stefan answered. "We keep several Ashishin here. Fire the tar and oil pits. Let the battlefield burn even before they charge. Why wait? Have the Ashishin maintain the blaze. There's no way those horses will charge through fire like dartans would. Their infantry certainly won't. We have the river's protection on one side of Eldanhill. Put a small force there led by Jillian in case they decide to use the river. Her eagles can keep her abreast of anything they see across the Kelvore.

"The remainder of our forces we take west to face the Greenleaf Forest. They'll have to change positions. As they do, we spring the traps we set in the fields to that side. If they have Matii, they'll be forced to respond then. When they do, we strike. Our Ashishin will counter their Matii as our archers pick their infantry and cavalry apart from atop the dartans. Then it will come down to infantry versus infantry. Our Dagodin versus their regiments." Stefan drew a line across his throat with his thumb.

Galiana almost grinned. As she'd thought, even after fifty years without his active involvement in a war, Stefan hadn't lost a step. The best General to serve under Nerian the Shadowbearer was proving his worth. The best Knight Commander ever to don the Tribunal crimson was now in his own element.

With the decision made, they ended their meeting and joined their individual cohorts. Nervous mutters abounded as new instructions were given. Galiana passed the word to the green and white clad Ashishin spread to her left and right. Once, they'd all been warriors, trained for worse battles than this, until they took on the task to be Teachers. Now, they were being drawn into what they loved the most, what their power often cried for. She nodded at the stern faces all around.

"Archers! Light!" Guthrie's voice boomed, silencing the shift of cold feet, the clink of armor, and the restless murmurs of men and women.

All across the lines, archers dipped arrowheads into fires. The ones who needed to move did so quickly and efficiently, rejoining their rank with practiced smoothness.

Galiana opened her Matersense. All around her, she felt Ashishin do the same. They seized essences of fire from the Streams and essences of air from the Flows. The orange flames at the tip of the arrows bloomed into phosphorescent spheres, sealed off and fed by air. Shadows fled before the luminescence.

"Archers! Ready!"

Longbows arched into the air as bowstrings drew taut. The creak of wood stretching whispered along the archer lines. Flames illuminated faces strained in concentration.

"Loose!"

The twang of several thousand bows reverberated through the air. Burning arrows streaked high, illuminating the heavens with its multitude of thunderclouds boiling in a dark stew. The shafts sailed over oil–filled moats, the chasm of palisades and spiked barriers between Eldanhill and the Sendethi army, and down.

Galiana focused on the army, picking out movement among the cavalry. She squinted and brought her looking glass to her eye.

Hooded men stepped forward from around the Golden Tide banners. Hands raised in the air, they moved up in front the

Sendethi horse.

"Ashishin!" Galiana yelled. "Shield those arrows. Now!"

A nimbus glowed around the men and women as they quickly linked for the undertaking. A dome rose up in the air above the arrows.

Thunderless lightning cracked across the sky. The bloated clouds tore open, and icy rain fell in a silvery sheet. At the same time, the wind picked up into swirling eddies, buffeting cloaks and spilling hair about the faces of those who went helmetless.

Just as sudden as it began, the storm cut off as the barrier closed above Eldanhill's forces. The tempest, Forged by the Barsonian Matii, battered against the shield created by the Ashishin. Lightning lanced across its surface, and water flowed off, revealing the shape of the immense oval dome in streaming rivulets.

The shield held. Galiana smirked.

The fire arrows landed with a whoosh.

Flames roared up where the arrows struck oil and tar, racing across the ground in every direction until a curtain of fire, a few thousand feet thick, separated southern Eldanhill from the Sendethi forces. Heat shimmered and swelled to devour the cold that dominated only moments ago. The essences worked into the blaze gobbled up the Mater in the air, and an inferno bloomed, white–hot and eerily quiet. Eldanhill's army cheered.

Guthrie and the others wasted no time. Orders barked out in quick succession, and their cohorts split.

"Ashishin Berg, Maurer, Jung, and Finkel," Galiana yelled, voice carrying over the march of the departing soldiers. "Choose five more to feed the fire and maintain the barrier." She waited as they complied. When they were ready, she nodded her approval of their choices. "The rest of you with me." She shook her reins and headed toward Eldanhill's west side.

As she moved, she heard someone yelling and pointing. *Why was the town lit up to the west?* A sinking feeling grew in the pit of her stomach.

Screams echoed from the same direction. Above those cries came frantic orders. Those on mounts gathered in formation and charged. The infantry quickened their march toward what Galiana knew now to be flames. Eldanhill's western flank was under attack.

Slapping her reins harder, she broke into a gallop. Rain and biting wind lashed her as she left the protection of the shield. Coupled with the icy water and howling gale, the fear crawling through her stomach chilled her to the bone. She huddled in her saddle, cloak streaming behind her as her dartan dashed headlong along the slick road. Behind her, the remaining Ashishin followed toward the new threat.

Lightning continued to flicker angrily across the sky, but this time thunder bellowed its response. Galiana ignored the tempest, knowing the Barsonian Matii couldn't be controlling this portion of the storm. Unless they were stronger than she thought. But the elements within the weather brewing above them now was natural and not a Forging. The change was subtle, like the difference between the smoothness of wet clay and grainy texture of mud, but it was there.

She turned off the Eldan Road onto Market Row and kept pushing west. Small houses along tight alleys huddled against the streets in this section of Eldanhill. Sewage and debris spilled onto the lanes from swollen drains, clouding the air with their stench. Along with the icy sheets the freezing rain had created, this made the going much more treacherous. The occasional gust that found its way down the alleys whipped anything not heavy enough into the air.

The trip all seemed to be taking too long. Ahead, the glow from the fires increased. The cacophony of battle rose on the wind—steel clashing against steel, screams of terror, groans of the wounded, and the ripped cries and gurgles of the dying.

Above those sounds rose something terrible.

Inhuman wails, howls and shrieks that scraped along Galiana's skin. Despite the cold and the rain, sweat beaded her forehead. She knew those sounds. Hundreds of years spent from one battle to another had etched them into her mind, into her core. They were a part of her as surely as her thoughts.

Shadelings.

She burst from an alley out onto the main avenue of the sparsely housed western outskirts of Eldanhill. And into a scene from a nightmare.

Dead bodies littered the cobbles. Blood colored the water runoff, painted the street red, and pooled in any dip or crack, its cloying scent hanging in the air, adding to the stench of shadelings.

Highlighted against the backdrop of burning homes, wraithwolves and darkwraiths fought soldiers and civilians alike. Black blades or claws and fangs ripped into the unprepared and untrained civilians with ease. Desperate townsfolk preferred to run into the blazes of their homes, creating their own funeral pyres, rather than die to the shadelings.

Dagodin fought in small groups to stave off the attackers, boots splashing through bloody pools. Advancing among the shadelings were Sendethi soldiers, mounted and on foot, laying about them with shields and swords. With every kill, the wraithwolves put their cavernous maws to the storming sky and howled.

At first, Eldanhill's soldiers faltered. On many a face, Galiana saw fear, the kind of raw fear that paralyzes a man.

But Stefan, Guthrie, Devan and many others had seen this sort of battle before. Undaunted, Stefan barked orders and his Generals obeyed.

Dagodin formed ranks among the chaos. Sword and spear gathered in ordered lines. Galiana recognized several of Eldanhill's Weaponmasters at the forefront of each group and behind them, several rows of archers. Guthrie shouted an order and arrows loosed, struck true and made pincushions of shadeling and Sendethi alike. Pained howls and shrieks ensued.

The response of Eldanhill's defenders stemmed the tide of the battle for the moment. The advancing army paused.

Wraithwolves and darkwraiths by the hundreds turned to the new threat. Green eyes glowed above elongated snouts and red eyes shone from within the black depths of smoky darkwraith hoods. How could there be so many? She and Stefan had made preparations, assuming but hoping against hope the shadelings hadn't crossed the Vallum. But now, the proof lay before her, the stench from the wraithwolves holding dominion over the smell of burnt wood, cooked flesh, offal and blood. The shrieks, howls and wails from the shadelings drowned out the crackle of the blazes, the clash of weapons, the marching feet, and the cries and moans of the wounded and dying.

How did the shade breach the Vallum of Light? And without anyone's knowledge?

Galiana didn't spare another moment. She leaped from

the back of her dartan. When she landed, she shouted, "Ashishin, dismount! Form ranks!"

She didn't need to look behind her to know the other Ashishin had dismounted and formed an ordered line behind her according to their strength. As in the days of old, when the shade ran rampant, they did as she commanded.

The shadeling and Sendethi forces recovered from their momentary lapse. A command bellowed out. Swords and shields rose, pointed toward the Eldanhill lines. With howling screeches, the enemy charged.

"Hold!" Stefan yelled as his dartan swept up and down the Eldanhill ranks.

In front the other cohorts, Devan, Guthrie and the Weaponmasters stood, repeating the same command.

The rumble of a thousand feet and hundreds of shadeling cries drowned out the thunder that pealed in the heavens. Boots shifted uneasily. Eyes showed uncertainty. However, not one Eldanhill defender broke formation. Not one raised a hand to wipe away the rain running down their helmets onto their faces.

Galiana's smile tipped imperceptibly at the edge of her mouth, and she waited. Stefan and the army became as still as a venomous snake just before it struck.

Goaded by their bloodlust, the wraithwolves bounded ahead of men and darkwraith, maws spread wide, white fangs gleaming. Driven by the need to sink their black blades into living flesh, the darkwraiths sped even faster like oily, black smoke blown by a fierce wind.

The first wraithwolves Blurred, and the darkwraiths followed their lead.

"Now!" Galiana yelled. She opened her Matersense and the other Ashishin did the same.

Shade lay in thick blankets around the Sendethi, wraithwolves, and darkwraiths. Galiana ignored the Sendethi for now. The shadelings posed the real threat. Picking out the telltale trails of the Blurs, she split her Forge into several hundred different strands, loosing light and fire essences. The strands flew like incandescent arrows. When they connected, the trails blazed.

At the same time, the Ashishin behind her took a hold of the storms above. They linked the lightning with Galiana's

Forging. Several others pulled fire essences from the flames around them and added those.

When the shadelings emerged from their Blurs, sheets of lightning and balls of fire greeted them. The blazing trails coalesced amongst the creatures with loud booms. The concussions from the blasts rocked the beasts and any nearby structures, blowing holes in limbs, wood and stone alike.

The carnage didn't deter the remainder of the shadelings or the Sendethi. If anything, it incensed them. They surged forward, screaming curses, eyes aglow with hate. Unflinching, Galiana's Ashishin continued to tear into the shadelings. Masses of acrid smoke billowed up into the air.

The black beasts that managed to reach the first wave of Dagodin were met by silversteel *divya* weapons. In unison, as if a part of a synchronized dance, spears stabbed. Any shadeling that cleared the spears were met by swords.

But the creatures moved with an uncanny speed many were unprepared for. Soldiers fought to find purchase on the slippery ground as they tried to fend off the attacks. Exploiting the weakness they didn't share with Eldanhill's defenders, the shadelings remained in perpetual motion. As many shadelings killed, twice the number in Dagodin and soldiers died, gutted by claws, throats ripped by fangs or sliced to shred by black blades. The darkwraiths moved like greasy death among the Eldanhill forces, side stepping attacks to slice into a soldier or Dagodin who was too slow to defend.

The Sendethi soldiers reached the Eldanhill lines, engaging with wild abandon.

"Single target attacks only," Galiana yelled. She dared not use the same Forges this close to their own forces now. The results would be catastrophic for all.

Single firebolts or balls and streams of light shot forth from the Ashishin into individual targets. Each strike sent a shadeling or an enemy soldier crumpling to the ground. Galiana concentrated on helping the trainees and lightly garbed defenders.

Stefan, his Generals, and the Weaponmasters were at the forefront of the battle. They protected any small pockets the shadelings and Sendethi came close to overwhelming. Stefan's sword darted and sliced faster than her eyes could follow as he danced between the enemy, taking arms or spilling guts with deadly efficiency.

A darkwraith flowed toward Stefan, and the graying man turned to meet the creature. His silver armor glinted with the flames, the green insignia on his breast standing out.

Black, Hydae–forged ebonsteel lashed out as the shadeling struck. Stefan parried the attack, his *divya* sword flashing up. Sparks cascaded into the air.

The darkwraith circled Stefan, its movements as quick and elusive as its sword rose and fell, stabbed and sliced. Stefan was a picture of concentration and calm. He slid between the attacks, parrying each with not much more than a step or a shift of his body. The darkwraith howled in frustration.

Attacking faster and faster, its black arms a blur, its iridescent black blade near invisible at times, the darkwraith drove forward. Stefan's defensive speed increased to match.

Then, as if the creature wasn't pushing him back, Stefan shifted his stance, positioning his front foot forward. At the same time, he stepped to the left. The darkwraith, still in all–out attack, couldn't compensate. Its sword flashed by where Stefan's body once was. Stefan's sword swung above the blow and took the creature's head. Stefan whirled around looking for his next target.

A roar and thundering boots on cobbles sounded behind Galiana. She turned to see the heart of the Eldanhill infantry led by old man Rohan, in golden armor chased with silver, charging between the homes and alleys. They joined the fray, beating back the attackers.

But the damage had been done. More than a third of the Dagodin lay dead or wounded.

A trumpet sounded from the dark out toward the open fields. The Sendethi stopped and turned to flee. A few of Eldanhill's defenders gave chase before the Generals yelled for them to stay their ground. What remained of the shadelings were nothing more than piles of wet ash. By now, the rain had abated and the remaining fires petered out. Blackened frames and timber filled the spaces where homes once stood. The retreating soldiers ran or limped to meet the main Sendethi army gathering in the fields.

Groans and calls for help rose from the wounded. Dagodin strode out among the carnage while unseasoned defenders still stood in place, dazed. When the Dagodin found a wounded Sendethi, they put them down with a swift stroke to the neck. This brought on fits of retching by the novices and trainees. Others who held their composure helped wounded Eldanhill defenders to their feet. Calls came for carts to move those who couldn't walk on their own.

"Ashishin, assist with mending," Galiana ordered. She strode to meet with Stefan and his Generals.

The former Knight Commander drew them aside, the concern in his eyes plain for all to see. "How in Ilumni's name have shadelings managed to breach the Vallum?" Blood splatter dotted his filigreed silver armor.

Shrugs and dumbfounded looks on faces dripping water and sweat were the answers he received. Brows wrinkled with worry and anxious gazes turned to Galiana.

Just as baffled as they were, Galiana shook her head. "I have no idea myself. There is no mention in history of them being able to cross the kind of wards built into the Vallum. My other worry is if they can cross the Vallum, why not come in greater numbers?" Galiana's brow wrinkled as another thought struck her. "Where is the daemon that must have created the darkwraiths? Can they too cross the Vallum? If they can, why allow the shadelings to attack without guidance? The fight was too easy. Not once did they try to come after us."

Guthrie whispered a prayer to Ilumni. A few others touched fingers to their lips, then their foreheads and their hearts in their own reverence to the god of Streams.

As if in answer, trumpets blared from the Sendethi army in a long bray. Wails, howls and screeches answered from somewhere within the Greenleaf Forest's darkened interior.

A flood of black–furred bodies, forms that moved with the fluidity of smoke, and those covered in dark armor, spilled from the Greenleaf. At their head, on a large dartan, rode a figure silhouetted in shadow and swathed in the blackest armor Galiana had ever seen. It was as if all light shrunk away from the man. A huge sword stood out at his hip.

"I guess we have our answer," Stefan said, his hand on his sword hilt. "Dagodin, Ashishin! Form ranks! We won't be easy meat." His voice boomed with unnatural power. "Shin Galiana, you remember during the Shadowbearer War when you sent signals by shooting those great balls of fire into the air?"

Galiana raised an eyebrow. Why would he require such a thing now? She nodded.

Stefan's emerald eyes were cold steel. "On my order, spring the traps. At the same time have several of yours shoot three fireballs as big as they can make as far into the sky as they can. Whatever happens after that, do not attack the Dosteri."

Dosteri? Galiana opened her mouth, but another blare from the trumpet stopped her question.

Across the field, the black armored man whipped his dartan into a gallop. The shadelings charged with him. Behind them, the Sendethi followed suit, the earth shaking as thirty thousand Sendethi feet and hooves thundered.

"Go, now," Stefan commanded.

"May Ilumni help us," Galiana prayed. She ran back to meet her Ashishin who were scrambling to form up once more and pointed to the five closest. "When we spring the trap, launch three of the largest fireballs you can Forge into the sky."

"Yes, High Shin," they replied as one.

Over the din of the oncoming forces and the storming weather, Stefan's voice rose, clear and deep. "Ashishin, ready."

Galiana linked with the other Ashishin. For this, they would need her complete guidance. She reached through the ground, gathering essences of the Forms. Earth and metal stood most prominent, mixed in with the Flows of rainwater. She felt for the weaknesses out in the fields that she'd painstakingly Forged over the last few days. The Forgings of the other Ashishin followed hers. They'd taught these exact skills to manipulate Mater for years now. It came as second nature.

When her power touched the thirty pillars she'd Forged to give the ground the impression of solidity, Galiana paused. She waited for the others to grasp the supports as she did. Then with a squeeze of her mind, she used the Forms to crush the pillars of earth.

A chasm several hundred feet wide and a hundred feet deep opened up beneath the onrushing army. The hole swallowed those too slow to react. Cries and wails of triumph and bloodlust abruptly changed into panicked screams.

Orange light bloomed, illuminating the carnage within Eldanhill and the roiling mass of shadelings and men trapped on the chasm's far side. Three fireballs the size of wagons sailed into the sky, before arching down toward the rent in the earth. They passed below the lip and a loud thump followed. More screams rose. Flame tongues licked hungrily from the lips of the chasm.

The majority of the shadelings either Blurred to the top or across the trench. The earth opening up had missed their leader altogether. The man came on undaunted, cloak flying behind him, the fiery backdrop highlighting his charge like a god out of a storybook.

From the north rose a roar as if from several thousand throats—loud, barking grunts, growls and men's battle cries. Galiana's head whipped around.

Across the field, on the Eldanhill side of the crevasse, rumbled several thousand white–furred beasts. Some were smaller than the wraithwolves. Others were larger still. Along most backs rose dagger–like ridges made of bone. Galiana's eyes widened. She'd never before seen so many daggerpaws and mountain wolves. Big men, wearing mostly fur and leathers rode several of the beasts. Charging behind them came at least a legion's worth of soldiers in blue and gold armor. A battle standard of a wall with a shield and a sword in front of it flew high in the air—the Guardian Wall—the Dosteri insignia.

Galiana inhaled sharply. How had Stefan managed to bring together both the mountain tribes and the Dosteri? How had he managed to convince the Dosteri to fight for Eldanhill in the first place?

"In the name of Ilumni, the shade shall fall," yelled Stefan. He charged toward the oncoming shadelings and their black armored leader.

CHAPTER 45

Overhead, an eagle screeched a warning. Chest burning, Ancel gasped for air, but he couldn't allow his aching, mud spattered legs to stop moving. *Up, down, up, down…Don't you dare fail me*, he begged, his footsteps and ragged breaths thundering in his ears with the rush of his pulse. Sweat mixed with rain poured down his forehead, the liquid trickling down his nose onto his lips. Hair and clothes already sodden, he lumbered forward one agonizing step after another.

The bridge was only a few hundred feet away from them. Close, but the distance felt more like a mile. Ancel thanked the gods the earlier storm had ended, and the rain was now no more than a drizzle. Still, slogging through mud proved more difficult than he could have imagined; each step he took came with a soppy slurp that made him yank his booted feet free of ankle–deep muck. At least he didn't have to fight against the cold and fog with the sun having risen some time ago and burning off both. Of course, that didn't account for the wind, which whipped at him mercilessly as if conspiring to push him away from his intended target.

To his left, the Kelvore River roared, its banks swollen from the earlier deluge, the fresh smells of wet earth filling the air, pieces of trees and driftwood swirling about in the rushing brown and gray waters. Way beyond the Kelvore, plumes of smoke still billowed into the air from Eldanhill's direction. The same direction from which they'd heard war trumpets earlier that morning. Then, they'd seen the horizon light up and soon after, the smoke. His stomach churned with the memory even as he clung to hope. He dared several glances over his shoulder. Mirza and Danvir labored not far from him, their clothes and countenances covered in thick mud. Farther behind ran Kachien and Charra.

The Sendethi cavalry topped a hill several thousand feet behind them. How had the men caught up? Kachien had made them push their dartans until the animals collapsed, but somehow some of the soldiers had been able to maintain their pursuit on horseback. Ancel's throat constricted and his already straining heart thudded harder still—a rapid booming drum within his chest. Colors bloomed as far as his eyes could see.

Squinting, Ancel picked out a darkness roiling around the men similar to what he'd seen around Kachien. But this was darker, blacker, yet shiny like polished obsidian. The same aura encroached around the soldiers' mounts. A lump formed in his throat at the sight. Ancel stumbled and almost fell, breaking his vision. Swallowing, he turned his attention to the bridge and the muddy ground once more. They weren't going to make it. At the speed those horses traveled, he and his friends would be caught at the bridge or on its wooden planks. The eagle screeched again.

Run, damn it. Run. He willed his legs to keep going. Maybe, if they reached the bridge they could fight off their attackers. The span was wide enough for only one man on horseback or two on foot. With Kachien's help, they might hold their own in such a tight space.

"Ilumni shine on us. Let there be some help," Ancel prayed.

The strange dizziness he'd experienced when last he'd been home swept through him. Ancel stumbled again, but this time he went down to one knee, mud squishing beneath him. Strong meaty hands that could only be Danvir's grabbed him and helped him up. On unsteady legs, he nodded to his friend, and they broke into a run again.

He could hear the horses now. The sloshing hooves and the soldiers spurring them on beat a death knell behind them.

Stumbling more than running, he and his friends reached the bridge. Below them, the Kelvore River roared and raged—a great caged beast thrashing against the barriers of the banks that imprisoned it. Occasionally, spray flew into the air as some debris crashed into one of the bridge's thick, timber supports. As they began to cross, the closing rumble of hooves drew Ancel's eyes. The soldiers were only a few dozen feet behind and closing fast. The rope and wooden structure swayed as Ancel shambled across in a futile attempt to increase the distance between their pursuers.

"Keep going," Kachien yelled from behind. "Do not stop. Do not look back."

Ancel opened his mouth to say they could stop and fight, maybe hold the soldiers back, but all that came out was another gasp for breath from his burning chest. He cursed his cowardice and lurched on, grabbing the ropes to steady himself.

Charra burst into barks and growls.

Hooves sounded on wood. The bridge gave a sudden heave. It swayed as violently as when they rode the boat across the Kelvore, the motion forcing Ancel to grab onto the ropes tighter. The clop of hooves became rapid peals of thunder.

Charra's barks changed into snaps, grunts, and snarls heard over the din of rushing water.

Once again, an eagle screeched its warning, louder and closer this time, as if it flew directly above them.

A horse whinnied. A man screamed. Steel clashed in metallic chimes, and Charra was all snarls now.

Refusing the urge to look back, his heart pounding and pounding, blood a rush in his ears, Ancel focused on the far side of the bridge and possible safety. At the end of the bridge, a figure rose before him dressed in boiled leather and chainmail with a surcoat he didn't recognize—a forest split by a great rent in the earth. Rain dripping from his outstretched arm, the figure held a long bow, fletching drawn to ear.

Another man stood beside the first, and another, and another. It was as if they appeared from the ground itself. Every one held a long bow, drawn and ready to loose.

Ancel's heart felt as if it thumped to a stop in his chest. He staggered to a halt, causing Danvir and Mirza to crash into his back.

"Why'd you stop? Go, go," Danvir pleaded. "Oh merciful Ilumni." His voice dropped to a slight whimper.

They all stood stock still, not daring to twitch. Out of the corner of his eye, Ancel took in the raging torrent of the

Kelvore River below him. If he jumped, there was no way he could survive.

Dozens of hard eyes watched them under hardened leather helmets. The moment seemed to last an eternity. Ancel and his friends still, their breathing labored. The soldiers ready, their faces grim.

The first archer's arm flexed. The world slowed. Water sprinkled to the ground from his leather gauntlets as he let out a long breath, and his body sagged into relaxation. His fingers loosened near the arrowhead, and his bowstring twanged. The other bowstrings joined his to ring out the same deadly chorus.

Ancel closed his eyes, threw his arms out to protect his friends, and waited for the pain.

Screams and gurgles pierced the air.

But not from Danvir or Mirza, behind them. Ancel spun to see several dozen arrows punch into the Sendethi soldiers, through armor, throats, and eyes. Blood spurting, the men fell like target dolls. Ancel gaped.

"It's good to see you're safe."

Ancel's eyes went wide as he turned to Jillian's voice. An eagle screeched once more, so close it made him jump. A moment later, the great bird flew down and landed on Jillian's outstretched, gloved, arm. She stood before the men, garbed in form–fitting leather armor that hugged every curve. On her head perched a helmet in the shape of an eagle's visage.

"Praise Ilumni," Danvir cried and rushed headlong toward Jillian and the waiting Eldanhill men.

Ancel and Mirza followed, both dumbfounded. He recognized some of the men now. Many were the soldiers he'd often seen being trained by Jillian and other Weaponmasters. Without awaiting any command, the men drew and released another volley of arrows.

"Save the pleasantries for later," Jillian said, her tone stern. "My men have work to do. Sendethi dogs to kill. Cade, get them some mounts. You young men need to get to Eldanhill as soon as possible. This is no place for you."

"But our friend—" Ancel protested, looking back.

"We won't harm her. We saw her save you three," Jillian answered.

Halfway down the bridge, Charra and Kachien were

running toward the Eldanhill archers. More arrows tore into the Sendethi soldiers who had crowded around the bridges entrance. As more fell, they retreated out of bow range.

"How'd you know we would be here, Mistress Jillian? We saw smoke and heard trumpets this morning. In Randane, the King's regiments attacked us and—" He cut off at Jillian's tight eyes and pained expression.

"We didn't know," Jillian said. "We were sent to protect the river and this old bridge because the Sendethi attacked Eldanhill this morning."

"What?" Ancel blurted.

Gasps rose from Mirza and Danvir. They all clamored to ask if anyone had been wounded. Anyone they knew.

Jillian held up a hand and they quieted. "This isn't the place or the time. You three head home now." Her gaze strayed to Ancel. "You need to visit Shin Galiana's. Your father will be there."

Shin Galiana, not Teacher Galiana, Ancel noted just as Kachien and Charra reached them. Jillian studied the smaller woman, and Kachien did the same, the two like female mountain cats when they crossed paths. The moment hung in the air tensely, then it was gone. A look of mutual respect passed between them. Jillian nodded, and Kachien returned the gesture. Ancel was still frowning at the brief exchange when Cade returned with four dartans.

"Peace be with you, Alzari," Jillian said as they mounted. "Many thanks for bringing them home safe."

"You and yours are most welcome, Setian." Kachien replied. May the Streams and the Forms defend you always."

"Now, go," Jillian commanded. "Galiana and the others will be waiting."

Speechless at the reactions and words between the two women, Ancel whipped his reins and sent his dartan running through the slight drizzle, the muddy ground squelching beneath its feet. Behind him, the others followed. One thought swelled in his mind. *Why had Kachien addressed Jillian as Setian?*

They travelled in tense silences, punctuated by failed attempts to start conversations until they reached Eldanhill. All other thoughts fled Ancel's mind, and he could only stare.

Charred woodpiles, chimneys covered in soot, and gutted foundations marked where houses once stood. Smoke rose from the ruins, and in some places people still put out flames. Hairless bodies lay in a line, once pale skin now black, brown, or red and cracked to reveal tissue underneath. The nauseating stench of cooked flesh still hung in the air, comingling with the smell of burnt wood.

Ancel's legs felt like blocks of stone. If not for the dartan under him, he would've stood frozen. He mouthed a prayer as they trotted to the second square and its myriad wagons prepared for Soltide. He hardly recognized this part of Eldanhill. Or, what remained of it. Even the cobblestones here seemed different, as if seen through a foggy dream he couldn't quite remember. What, in damnation, had happened?

Dagodin soldiers piled the blackened corpses onto a dray. Menders picked their way among the wounded still lined on the street. Lives and homes lay shattered around them, reduced to charred ash piles and sooty sandstone. Lives of people he knew. The Bergs, the Durrs, the Finkels, the Jungs, the Maurers—on and on the names flashed through his head. His mind spun with the scope of the burnt out, empty shells and blackened foundations.

Some family members dug among the ruins, salvaging what they could. No children played along the main road. No dogs ran back and forth making a friendly nuisance—or even barking and sniffing at Charra as they often did. No music drifted through the air to announce Soltide. No blacksmith or stonemason hammers clanged. Only the mourns of the mournful, the mutterings of the hopeless, and the prayers of the faithful sighed through the air, punctuated by the cries and blubbering sobs of grief.

A dark pall lay across the town along with the acrid, smoky smell clinging to the air. A soot–covered child stumbled from among burnt rubble and collapsed. Several menders rushed to help.

Horse–drawn drays, stained black and red with blood

and filled with corpses, groaned down the Eldan Road, following woodcarts lugging burnt timber and debris from the ruined structures. Townsfolk trudged behind the two–wheeled carts, tear–streaked faces sooty, somber, and sullen. Novices and trainees dumped the woodpiles from the carts at the town's outskirts to the south, adding to a bonfire already raging there. At the sight of the pyre, a woman wailed and fell to her knees.

Ancel clutched at his charm. *Dear Ilumni, let my parents be well.* He glanced toward the Streamean temple. White banners flew the same insignia he'd seen on Jillian and many of the Dagodin in Eldanhill. Next to them flapped the Dosteri Guardian Wall. *Dosteri in Sendethi territory helping Eldanhill?*

Weak sunlight glinted from the armor and helmets of the Dagodin cohort standing at attention to Eldanhill's westernmost outskirts where most of the damage and corpses lay. What was more surprising were the large, rawboned men in furs and cloaks made from pelts who were standing behind the Dagodin or rode upon large daggerpaws. Mountain wolves were sitting on their haunches next to some, tongues lolling. The animals pawed the ground or frolicked with each other, their dog–like reek unmistakable. A few gave coughing barks or whined in Charra's direction. Charra growled his reply. Apparently, someone had managed to bring the Seifer and the Nema together.

Ancel's regret at not being there when the Sendethi attacked rose again. He could have helped somehow if he'd been here. Maybe he could've saved some lives. The thought twisted in his gut. He shook his head and glanced around, just now realizing they had crossed the town. Behind them, three plumes of smoke marked where the majority of the attacks occurred. The rest of the town was untouched.

Scratching at his beard, he followed Danvir and Mirza down the road toward Shin Galiana's. He spared Kachien a few glances, thoughts about what she said also churning through his mind. They continued down the twisting path between older houses, many just one or two stories tall. This part of town lay so close to one of the Kelvore River's tributaries he could hear the rushing waters. Townsfolk shambled by, some weeping, others with grim expressions on their faces. Some gasped or skirted around Ancel and their friends when they saw Charra. A few reached for or hefted weapons. The daggerpaw ignored them.

They rounded the last corner, and ahead stood the squat sandstone and granite structure of Galiana's hospice. For the first time, Ancel thought about why he needed to come here to meet his father. Why not at the Whitewater Inn? Or their own home? Was his father hurt in the fighting?

Trying in earnest to dismiss the thought, Ancel dismounted, and tethered his dartan. People trudged by them, some struggling to carry several buckets to where dartans waited. Others wore bloodied bandages, their clothes torn and disheveled as they shambled up the cobbled streets from the direction of Shin Galiana's. Drays carrying wounded men, women and children rumbled down the road toward the hospice. Where some faces showed despair, others bore a fierce determination. On one side of the street, a man comforted a woman with a tear–streaked face and clothes covered in blood. Everywhere Ancel looked made worry for his father come crawling back to the surface.

"Things are worse than I could have imagined," Kachien said, her voice grave.

Ancel gave her a questioning frown.

"The wounds on many of those bodies and on some of the people." She squinted at a cart carrying injured folk. "Those are not just from normal steel. I know wounds caused by wraithwolves and darkwraiths when I see them."

Ancel sucked in a breath. "Are you sure?" A quick look at Mirza's wide–eyed expression and Danvir's pale face told him they'd heard.

"Yes. I have no doubts."

"That's impossible," Danvir whispered. "The Vallum protects us against shadelings. There's no way…" His voice trailed off at Kachien's wilting stare.

"I told you," Mirza said in earnest. "Still, why aren't there any Tribunal Ashishin here already? You would think this place would be crawling with them."

"Maybe—"

"Ancel, there you are, young man," Guthrie Bemelle's voice called.

Ancel turned to see Danvir's father striding toward them. The owner of the Whitewater Inn no longer wore his usual extravagant loose silks. Instead, a full suit of shining, blood red, Dagodin plate armor covered him, the noonday sun glinting off the polished steel, patterned swirls and lines on the breastplate. Already a wide man, the armor enhanced his size. In one pudgy hand, he carried a wide–bladed, two–handed greatsword. Gold embossing covered the scarlet scabbard.

"Da!" Danvir exclaimed, his eyes watery. He ran to his father and the two of them hugged. Somehow, Guthrie appeared the smaller of the two even in his armor.

The innkeeper looked his son over, his hanging jowls flapping against the collar of the gorget at his neck. "Glad to see you're well." He beamed. After a few more hugs and wiping of tears, he released Danvir and turned to Ancel. "I've been searching for you since Jillian sent word. Shin Galiana needs you." He eyed Kachien. "You must be the Alzari. Shin Galiana said to expect you. If you don't mind, my son and Mirza will see you to the Whitewater Inn. Galiana will meet you there." After Kachien's nod of approval, Guthrie locked gazes with Ancel, but his eyes betrayed nothing. "Ancel, if you will?" He turned and strode toward the hospice.

"Wait here, Charra," Ancel said. After a moment to make sure the daggerpaw complied, he hurried to catch up to Guthrie. "Master Bemelle, are my parents well?"

"Your mother is fine." The man tilted his head toward Ancel. Dark lines tugged at his slanted eyes instead of their usual smile. "Your father—"

"Is my father hurt?" Ancel's heart skipped a beat.

Guthrie stared ahead. "I'd rather Shin Galiana speak to you about that. Things are already hectic enough as it is."

Taking in deep breaths, Ancel attempted to calm himself, but he couldn't help the sinking feeling or the great weight on his shoulders. Guthrie's lack of an answer didn't help nor did the weariness tugging at his body. The feeling grew as they walked.

Outside the hospice, a line of townsfolk stretched from the wide front door, past the porch, down the stairs and out into the street. Dagodin and Shin Galiana's apprentices were turning back many of the injured after a brief inspection. Alys stood among those apprentices.

"Why are they turning people away?"

"We've resorted to only mending those who bare the shade's taint in their wounds. Even then, the mending has stretched Shin Galiana and the other Ashishin to the maximum.

We've sent to Calisto for more menders, but they're still several days or more away. In the meantime, those with normal wounds are being treated by the apothecaries and their apprentices." Guthrie nodded to the guards, bypassed everyone on the line, and strode to the stairs.

"Guthrie is my fath—"

"Alys," Guthrie said, signaling to the flame–haired young woman. "Take Ancel down to see Shin Galiana." He turned to Ancel. "Everything will be fine, my boy." Guthrie wiped sweat from his forehead and left.

Wordlessly, Ancel stared at Alys. They had not spoken since the night at the inn. Dark rings spread under her eyes, ash smeared her cheeks and hands, and soot coated her sunset hair in gray streaks. Her mouth was downturned, and after a moment, she averted her eyes.

"This way," Alys said, hurrying inside.

Ancel wanted to ask after his father, and find out how Alys was doing, but he had no idea where to start. Instead, he kept his mouth shut and occupied his mind with his surroundings as he staved off the need to rush inside to find his father.

Shin Galiana kept a tidy home. Each item had its place. Every piece stood in coordination with one another in blue and brown tones. Neatly aligned bookshelves bordered the living room, and rugs highlighted its wood floors. Center tables sat at the middle of the rugs, and evenly spaced chairs surrounded the main dinner table. They passed through the main room into a small hallway with a door on each side. The one open door revealed a comfortable kitchen and a hearth. They continued straight ahead to the end of the hall and a staircase leading down to the cellar.

To Ancel's surprise, the cellar contained the hospice. The last time he was there, Shin Galiana tended the sick in a backroom upstairs. The area below spanned about twice the house's size, he realized, as they traveled along a wall to an open door with a wide hall. Against a wall, appearing haggard and frail, leaned his old Teacher.

"Wait here." Alys continued down the hall to Galiana.

Downstairs, white dominated the décor. It appeared as if nothing became soiled or remained dirty for long. Even Shin Galiana's white dress didn't have a speck of dirt, medicine, or stains. Ancel made sure to keep his hands to himself and resisted the urge to touch anything.

A brief conversation ensued between Galiana and Alys. The Ashishin's tired golden eyes in a face fraught with more wrinkles than he remembered, regarded Ancel for a moment. She nodded. Alys gestured for Ancel to follow.

They entered a wide room that had a small fireplace at the far end. Next to a table, upon which sat a tray and cups, was a large, comfortable–looking, cushioned armchair. Three smaller chairs were spaced around the table, and a teakettle sat above the fireplace.

"I'll make some tea." Alys moved toward the fireplace and the table, leaving him to follow Teacher—no, Shin Galiana.

Without a word to Ancel, Galiana crossed the room and entered a door to their right. Ancel followed. The urge to rush past his Teacher and find his father gnawed at him, but he resisted it. She would probably just snatch him by his ears. If his father was wounded and his situation dire, she wouldn't be taking her time.

Through the door, several cots set up in the same orderly fashion as the rest of the house occupied the room. Eldanhill women and Teachers inspected one cot after another and tended the wounded. The sickly stench Ancel expected from those on the cots didn't reach him. Instead, a sweet smell like flowers on a spring day filtered through the air. Around the room, at specific intervals, candles and herbs burned, thin smoke trails carrying the flowery scent. Ancel recognized some of the women fussing over the wounded—Emlyn, the miller's wife, Mosel's wife Brandi, Clarissa, and Robyn, cousins to the Bemelles. Sad, lost eyes looked back at him for a moment before the women returned to their work.

Ancel could just make out the butcher, Cell, on a cot with his wife Renee above him. Heide, the old peddler's wife strode from one cot or another as well as Idna, Tarka Sonet's wife. She stopped at one cot and brushed her hands over the soiled bandages hiding the person underneath, then promptly burst into tears.

A lump formed in Ancel's throat with the sight of the men. Except for Cell, the other forms on the cots were unrecognizable, layered bandages hiding even their faces. The visible parts revealed swollen, purple and black bruises. Blood and fluids seeped into the bandages. Bile rose in Ancel's throat, and he cupped his hand over his mouth.

Guthrie's words about those wounded by the shadelings echoed in Ancel's head. He sought the Eye and opened his Matersense. Around him, every wounded person showed the taint of shade crawling within his or her wounds. It tried to spill out, but the light from wards within the room forced it back.

To the rear of the room, a familiar form drew him. Dressed in the tattered remnants of a crimson uniform and swathed in bandages around the chest, neck, and arm, the man groaned and muttered. Like the others, shade clung to his wounds. Dark hair with touches of silver hung in unkempt wisps. The usually neat mustache and beard was scraggly and flecked with blood, and the man's eyes were closed in a face haggard and gray.

His father's face.

CHAPTER 46

"No! Dear Ilumni, no," Ancel cried in a hoarse croak, bursting into tears. He rushed past Shin Galiana to his father's side.

Stefan's chest rose and fell in ragged, shallow breaths. Beneath his closed lids, his eyes shifted quickly. Squeezing his father's cold fingers tight, Ancel got down on one knee beside the cot.

Ancel glanced up when soft hands squeezed his shoulder. "Teacher Galiana. Is he dy—" He choked up, unable to bring himself to finish the words.

"I do not know." Her dark–rimmed eyes regarded Ancel. "I have done what I could. The rest is up to him."

"But, his breathing and the shade and—" His father's gray face brought a desperate dread rushing up into him. *If she can't, then I have to help him. I can't let him die. O Ilumni, help me.*

A spinning sensation filled Ancel. His grip tightened on the bed and his father's hand. Somehow, Ancel found the Eye, and he opened his Matersense. Power tugged at him.

"Our power is yours to use," clamored a sultry voice in a seductive drawl. *"I can grant you unending strength and the means to mend your father."*

"And in return you'll be forever sealed to us," another voice, this one lighter, said with a hint of a chuckle. *"Is that what you want?"*

"Your father is dying. Save him."

"And doom yourself."

"Look at his face. Yes, our power, you need it."

"Our power is not always what you wish, but it is there for you, if you know the risks. Kachien has told you of the risks. Choose."

Ancel chose.

Light streamed into his body. He opened himself to bathe within its incandescence. The one Forging he'd read about in the Tome of Undeath brushed his thoughts. Snarling, he thrust the light toward the shade dominating his father's wounds.

A blow to his back knocked Ancel to one side, slamming him into the wall. His Forging shattered, and his hand fell away from his father. Air essences held him against the wall behind the cot.

Dazed, he stared at the Forge holding him. He reached for light again. Another blow rocked him. Stars danced before his eyes. Blood filled his mouth. He lost both his grip on his Matersense and the Eye.

A blurry form blocked his father from his sight. Ancel shook his head and focused. The form resolved into Shin Galiana standing over him with her fists at her hips, her golden eyes ablaze.

"Have you learned nothing this past year?" Shin Galiana scolded. "Master yourself, child. Ignore the temptations. Take a closer look. Do not just think of light's first Tenet. Remember Mater's first Principle."

Light to balance the shade. But wasn't that what I did? No, the first Principle. The elements must exist in harmony.

Remembering not only Teacher Galiana's but Kachien's warning about control and the way Kachien looked when she gave in to her power, Ancel took a deep shuddering breath. His heart was still pounding as he sought the serenity he used when he practiced. Wiping away the blood from his mouth, he pictured a tranquil lily pond. His heart calmed. Once again, he found the Eye.

He opened his Matersense and traced the essences in his father again. The shade dominated all else, seeping in and out of his father's wounds. Light waxed and waned like dusk's weak fingers trying to penetrate thick, dark clouds. "I can't tell…the shade…Why not just strip the shade from him. It's killing him."

"Concentrate; remember all living beings need the harmony of all the elements, all the essences to live, even the shade." Her voice sounded tired and distant. "Banishing the shade as you suggest and tried would only ensure his death."

Ancel focused, and then he saw it. The shade in his father resided in clumps within the wounds and prevented them from mending. At the same time, the essence helped to keep the rest of his body sealed against disease while restricting veins for proper blood flow. Light essences worked to ease certain blockages to increase the flow, or open shade's seals and force out possible infection.

He could also see how water, air, and flesh came together, but most of it was so complicated, the workings were a blur. One thing became obvious. If shade was completely removed, the body's balance would fail, as the harmony of Stefan's Mater would be irreparably damaged. Instead, the Forging Shin Galiana used allowed the light to work with the taint, pushing it back to where it belonged—balancing it. In turn, the Forging mended the wound while maintaining his father's life. Ancel couldn't see all the intricate strands Forged together to accomplish this, but he was no less awed. He released his Matersense.

He realized something else. By focusing on what ailed his father, he had fully calmed and his emotions no longer controlled him. He faced Galiana and smiled. "Thank you, Shin Galiana."

She gave him a weak nod. "I wish I could do the same for all the others." Her gaze swung around the room, and her shoulders sagged.

Silence hung around the room like the somber weight of gloom at a funeral. Every eye watched them. The faces were expectant, forlorn, many without hope. From his brief memory of what he'd seen, Ancel knew the majority of the wounded in the room would die. He squeezed his eyes shut. *Da, please survive this. I pray the gods make it so.*

The lost eyes and pained expressions still lingered as people returned to tending the wounded and dying. Prayers and whispers resumed, building into quiet sobs and soft wails.

"Shin Galiana, how did the shadelings manage to cross the Vallum?" Ancel asked, still holding his father's hand.

She regarded him, strained lines etching her eyes. "I do not know, but I intend to find out. Alys should have his medicine shortly and something for you also. I need to go meet with the Council. I shall return." She gathered her white dress and strode from the room.

A mender's apprentice, in their customary blue garb, brought Ancel a chair. Ancel thanked the woman and sat next to his father. It took a great deal of effort for him not to open up to his Matersense again. He reminded himself trying to help might hurt his father more.

Still, nothing about his father's appearance eased Ancel's concern. Only a head shorter than Ancel himself, his father's frame appeared not only shorter but smaller. Sunken cheeks and bones protruding at his jaw line didn't help. Neither did his unintelligible mutterings.

"The Tenets, no, the Disciplines…Ancel…We're free. The kinai…how? Jeremiah, are you there? They seek us. They created a breach…" *Who were they? Who was Jeremiah?* The unfinished sentences continued. "The Eztezian…Ilumni, O Ilumni save…Thania, are you there?"

"No Da, mother isn't here." Ancel grabbed his father's hand and squeezed. The flesh was now hot to the touch like heated waves above a roaring hearth.

His father's garbled words continued. Tears came to Ancel's eyes at his delirium.

Sweat beaded Stefan's brow, and his eyes shot open. "The keys…Ancel," he whispered and his eyes closed again.

"I'm here, Da! It's me," Ancel exclaimed but his pleading went unacknowledged. *What's he talking about? What's he trying to tell me?*

Just as sudden as the mutterings began, they stopped. His father's breathing evened out. Ancel touched the back of his hand to his father's head. It was cool to the touch, almost normal. A relieved sigh escaped Ancel's lips.

"I've brought his medicine." Alys' soft voice sounded behind him.

Ancel turned to face her. Her eyes shone wetly. In her hand, she carried a tray with two teacups.

"And a cup for you. Shin Galiana said it will help with what you feel now." Alys' gaze met his for a moment before her attention shifted to his father.

Ancel nodded, released his father's hand, and pushed his chair out of her way.

"Could you please help me with him?" Alys stepped

up to Stefan and placed the tray on a tiny table next to the bed. "Sometimes when he mutters like this, he fights when we try to give him his medicine."

"What do you need me to do?"

"Just hold him up while I feed this to him." She leaned down as she spoke, and her hair brushed past Ancel.

Her hair carried the perfumed scent of bellflowers. Ancel fought hard against the urge to touch her hair, instead reaching down to his father. Stefan's weight mattered little as Ancel drew him up into a sitting position. Ancel frowned at not only his father's weight, but also at Stefan's body, which was now not just cool, but cold like the icy chill of death.

Hands trembling, Ancel tried to keep his father steady as Alys held his mouth open. With a teacup in her other hand, she poured red tea down his throat in short doses. From the tea's scent, Ancel knew it was kinai tea. One of Shin Galiana's favorite mending tonics. When Alys finished, Ancel laid his father back down. Color returned to Stefan's face, and his body warmed in that small period. Alys studied his father, and after a moment, she nodded in satisfaction and picked up the tray.

"This is for you," she said, holding the other cup out to Ancel

He almost protested, but he remembered Shin Galiana's words. Moreover, Alys had made the tea. Things were already bad enough between them without him making them worse. He took the cup and sipped. The warm, sweet tasting tea slid down his gullet, and its warmth invigorated and calmed him at the same time.

Her green eyes met his. "Ancel, I'm sorry. I shouldn't have—"

"It's fine, Alys…" No, he couldn't lie. "I mean, it's not fine, but I understand."

A deep breath released from her at his words. "You've never been the same since—"

"I don't think I'll ever truly get over her, Alys. I'm sorry if I led you on, but that's the way of things. Whether I like them or not."

Her lips trembled and her eyes became downcast. "I know. I just hoped…I won't ever forgive her for leaving, for what she did to you."

Ancel smiled and touched Alys' hand tenderly. "Thank you for that. Maybe you're stronger than I'll ever be."

A faint smile crossing her lips, she gave his hand a brief squeeze.

"I'm glad we had this talk," Ancel said.

"Me too."

"How're you handling all this." Ancel pointed to the other cots.

"I'm managing. Barely. How could this happen, Ancel? Without anyone knowing?" Alys' eyes glistened.

"I–I don't know. Have you heard anything from your father about Council's plans?"

"No, they've been in meetings all day. Mother has been quite flustered though. And Shin Galiana has acted strange. She's been staying close to your father ever since they brought him in. A few times she wrote something down during his rambling but later burnt it."

Ancel studied his father's face. Since drinking the kinai tea, Stefan had regained some of his color and his chest rose and fell in even breaths. Why did Shin Galiana write down what he said?

A commotion to the other side of the room drew Ancel's attention. About twenty Dagodin followed a senior officer with the crossed swords signet on his arm that named him a Knight. The black–haired, hook–nosed man strode next to a mender who pointed out men on cots. Two Dagodin marched to each cot chosen, positioned themselves to either end, lifted and headed to the hall leading upstairs.

"What are they doing?" Ancel asked, amid women's panicked wails from across the room.

Each time the menders pointed out a man, cries burst out from a woman. A few tried to reach the cots picked out, but the soldiers restrained them.

"When someone dies from the taint they're cremated. Shin Galiana hasn't given a reason for this, but her orders were explicit." Tears streamed down Alys' face.

Ancel watched in stunned silence as the Dagodin took ten dead men. He took a step forward, before he fought back to urge to help the townsfolk, his arms tight from the effort. An Ashishin's orders were not to be disobeyed, no matter how gruesome.

"I have to go console them," Alys said, her tone painfully soft. She crossed the room and spoke to the women, touching a shoulder here, squeezing a hand there, or whispering in an ear. Sometimes, the sobs increased, and she would hug that woman until her display of grief lessened.

Another Dagodin squad entered, and the process repeated. Ancel swallowed the sudden lump in his throat and scrubbed at the wet warmth that ran down his face. He reached for his father's hand. *Dear Ilumni, spare my father such a fate.*

Ancel's head spun for a moment. This time he quickly sought the Eye and brought himself under control. He frowned. Was it the third time that had happened? All after a prayer to Ilumni? He said another prayer in his mind for the well–being of Eldanhill, but nothing happened. Shaking the idea off as ridiculous, Ancel returned his attention to his father. Anything so he wouldn't count how many people he knew were being cremated.

His father's confusing words continued from time to time. Often his face would revert to its pale appearance. Every hour Alys dosed him with kinai and the color returned. Eventually, Ancel took over the doses.

Ancel was sipping his second cup of kinai tea when Mirza and Danvir visited.

"Sorry, Ancel. We didn't know." Danvir patted Ancel's shoulder.

"Not many did," Ancel said.

"How's he doing?" Mirza asked, his gray eyes steady.

Ancel shrugged, trying not to show how torn up he felt inside. "Not as bad as some. He keeps coming in and out of consciousness."

Dagodin carried away another group of men.

"What's that about?" Danvir nodded at the commotion and crying women.

Ancel explained Shin Galiana's orders. Both his friends stared.

"Any idea why?"

Ancel shook his head.

"Hmm, I'll ask my father when I go home, see what he says," Danvir mused.

"How's everything outside?"

Mirza raised his eyebrows and shook his head slowly. "Bad. They deployed Dagodin to the south of town. The Sendethi have gained reinforcements. But there's no sign of the shadelings. You should see all the lightstones and lamps they have out there. You can hardly tell moonrise is com—"

"M–m–moonrise?" Stefan sputtered painfully.

"Da!" Ancel exclaimed.

His father's face had retained its color since the last kinai dose. The man's cheeks appeared fuller even as his emerald eyes watered. He gripped the sheets as a spasm wracked his body.

Ancel squeezed his father's arm. "Take it easy, Da."

"An—" His father coughed. "Ance, Ancel what are you doing here. W–w–where is your…mother?"

"She's fine. At least that's what Guthrie said. Why—"

His father struggled to sit up. "You need to go to your—" He coughed. "Your mother. S–s–she will need your help. Get… get to her before moonrise."

"Da—"

"No, boy." His father's voice became steel. He hacked another cough. "Take my sword. It's a *divya*. You'll need it." He pulled the sword, in its white and gold scabbard, from under the sheet. With his other hand, he made the sign of an X over his heart. "Release—" He collapsed.

White heat flashed through Ancel. "Alys! Alys!" he yelled. The heat sucked at him as if it wanted to swallow him. Chest heaving, shoulders knotting with strain, he fought against the feeling, and it subsided to a comfortable warmth. Warmth he could sense outside himself, on his chest, and in his father's hand.

The sword and the pendant. He could sense them. Ancel's eyes bulged.

Alys appeared by his side. Danvir and Mirza tried to help, but she shooed them away. She motioned for Ancel to help her with the medicine, and he did, all the while hoping to ignore what he felt. His father sputtered as he drank.

Stefan's hand rose feebly with the sword in it. "Go," he whispered, then his body sagged and his eyes fluttered shut.

"No. No. Alys is he…"

She touched his neck. "He's asleep. What happened?"

"He woke and asked after my mother. Then he said she'll need my help and to take his sword." Ancel refused to touch the weapon, but he could feel it all the same. "He said I needed to reach her before moonrise." He wiped tears he didn't realize he'd shed from his face.

"He always feared this." Guthrie's grim voice sounded from behind them. He still wore his armor. His massive greatsword rested on his shoulder. "Take the sword. If we're to save your mother, we must go now."

CHAPTER 47

Irmina stood in the Bastion's s main envoy room. Like the others, the room's white alabaster, feldspar and steel blocks formed a dome. No lamps hung along the walls, and neither the Dagodin guarding the room nor Herald Bodo bore lightstones, yet the room was bright all the same. She waited to the side for the Herald who still read the message map.

Somewhere above her, Ryne was meeting with Knight Commander Varick and his Knight Generals. The man had pushed the dartans hard, not stopping to rest or talk.

"You seem impatient," Herald Bodo intoned. Whenever the man spoke, he sounded as if on the verge of some important proclamation.

"I don't know if it's impatience as much as it is worry." Her thoughts still hovered around the discovery of the shadelings, the wraithwoods, the breach of the Vallum and the powerful man Ryne had fought.

"Rest assured the High Shin isn't ignoring you. Your message has more severe implications than the last." Lights flashed across the map in an ordered sequence, and he frowned.

"Then why so long for Jerem's reply?"

Herald Bodo stroked his forked beard. "According to the message I just received, there have been similar occurrences in Granadia."

Irmina gave him an incredulous stare. "What? When?"

"In close proximity to several northern towns in Sendeth and Barson. Right now, the Tribunal is still discussing the best course of action." His attention remained on his maps.

Irmina's eyes grew wide. "In Sendeth? Which town?" A chill crept along her spine.

The Herald strode across the map from the Ostanian side into Granadia. After a moment studying it, he pointed at a location to the extreme north of Sendeth's capital, Randane. "Eldanhill, in the Whitewater Falls region, if I am not mistaken." He paused for a moment and raised his gaze to her. "And I am never mistaken."

The chill became ice, freezing her in place with her mouth slack.

"Are you familiar with this town?"

"Yes," she whispered. "It's my home."

Through window slits atop the Bastion, a cool wind brushed Ryne's face. Dappled shadows covered the land below, yet he could shoot an arrow straight to where Sakari waited if he chose. Clear skies stretched for miles, the stars a twinkling carpet. A good night for a battle. Ryne wished Knight Commander Varick could have addressed his findings right away, but what lay before them on the war map was of immediate concern.

Six shadebanes marched on four major Ostanian towns held by the Granadian armies. At possibly five thousand shadelings and Amuni's Children for each bane, it made for an imposing force. Still, the numbers fell short of what he knew would've been needed to take the Alzari clanholds. Where was the rest of the army?

"Here and here," Knight Commander Varick said, pointing to two spots to the east as he walked across the map, his feet passing through its life–like replicas.

The Herald's eyes tightened, but he said nothing. Varick had already dismissed the man's colleague who'd voiced his displeasure at the Knight Commander setting foot on the maps. The two locations Varick pointed out, close to two towns, Bastair and Cendos, were the only ones without a scout's markings.

"We need to know what's happening there before the High Ashishin arrive," Varick said.

The three Knight Generals, Strom, Clovis, and Refald nodded, their armor reflecting colors from the lightstones decorating the war map.

"I can take my force here," said Clovis in his white armor, inlaid with gold. The hill he pointed out was west of Cendos and closest to the Vallum, near a town named Sandar.

"And I'll go here," Strom said. He pointed a few miles south of Clovis's position. "I can help Clovis, then we can head north to defend Dastan together."

Clovis nodded, brow puckered in thought. "Yes, yes. With your faster dartans, you will easily catch my heavy armored cohorts. It looks like your light cavalry may prove useful after all."

Strom grunted and cast a sidelong glance at Clovis. "A dartan's shell is more than enough protection."

Clovis opened his mouth just as lights from the scout locations marked on the field blinked. Herald Jensen stepped forward, his robes with its sashes that reached his waist swirling about him. After a moment studying the lights, the bald man nodded to Varick. Each man knew what that meant and stepped off the war map.

Herald Jensen waved his hand over the three scout locations near Sandar and Dastan. Light and shade spilled up into the man. A small slit Materialized in the air and widened to about the size of a palm. Individual blades of grass and bleached white sand showed beyond the tear. A small, folded paper slipped through the hole, and then the breach twisted back into a slit and snapped shut. Ryne arched an eyebrow. A basic Materialization like the one Herald Jensen just Forged was almost as impressive as the one Jerem used to bring him to the Vallum. The Herald passed the paper to Varick.

The Knight Commander unfolded the paper and studied it. "Hmm, the scouts confirm the bane locations at those two towns" As he spoke, Jensen waved a hand and new enemy markers appeared around Sandar and Dastan. Your plan is even more feasible now, Clovis and Strom."

The two Knight Generals nodded and smiled, clapping each other's shoulder.

"Refald." Varick eyed the scar–faced man in heavy crimson armor. "You keep the Dagodin infantry ready and waiting. When we give you the locations, the High Ashishin will

Materialize your legion in to close the traps. My legion will take Bastair and Cendos, and then we finish whatever dregs are left. What do you think, Master Waldron?"

"Seems as fine a plan as any," Ryne said. "There's no reason it shouldn't work." He ignored the grimaces and narrowed eyes from Clovis and Strom.

Varick nodded. "Well then, that's it until the High Ashishin arrive. You three go prepare. Master Waldron, with me."

The Knight Generals struck fist to hearts and stalked off.

After they left, Varick strode to the window slits overlooking the landscape below. Miles in the distance, twinkling lights marked a few towns or cities.

"Those two dislike you. I almost expected you to react."

Ryne shrugged. "Demand discipline, but first show mastery of self. Men tend to dislike what they can't understand. They're new enough to this to feel the way they do. Like the others, they'll come to understand me. If they live long enough."

Varick smiled. "Sometimes I wonder if you weren't born to lead, old friend."

"I wish I knew what I was born for," Ryne said staring out into the darkness.

Varick stepped up next to him, the cool wind ruffling the white–streaked hair he had left. "This feels like a bad one, Ryne. The word you brought made it no better. And the Tribunal hasn't responded to my report yet. You would've thought they'd have the High Ashishin here already." Varick's eyes hardened. "I've received word there were other shadeling attacks in Granadia itself. I have an ill feeling about all this. That's why I'm sending you to Bastair where the banes are closest together."

An hour later, near a rocky crag of the Dead Hills, Ryne hugged the slanted ground in the shadows of an incline. Sakari crawled next to him. Ryne had avoided Irmina following him by Shimmering down from the Bastion. *Thank the gods.*

The stench of burnt flesh drifted on the cool night air. Screams rose from the town below as swirling winds whipped at Ryne's cloak. *O, Ilumni, please bring them a quick death.* Even as he prayed, Ryne knew no one listened. The god of light offered no mercy this night.

Children's cries and babies' frantic bawling reached Ryne where he crept along the slope. Undetected, he eased up onto the peak of the crag and looked down.

Bastair was in shambles. Greasy smoke and ash billowed into the sky from fires illuminating broken buildings with their ruddy glow. Huge sandstone blocks littered the ground where homes once stood. Piled rubble marked other foundations as if those structures had been ground to sand in a gigantic hand and poured from it. Many houses left standing lacked roofs or walls. Wide, gaping holes big enough to swallow a building marred the ground in several places. In the town square, a gigantic oak tree burned.

Corpses littered the cobbled streets, some dressed in shredded, scarlet uniforms and others in the tattered trousers and tunics of townsfolk. Bodies clothed in black armor lay close to those in red.

Rank upon rank of black armored Amuni's Children wielding long, sooty-looking spears herded disheveled survivors into the town square. Once there, the soldiers ripped babies from the arms of wailing mothers. They separated crying children from adults.

Ryne clenched his fists against the urge to charge down into the square.

Men and women surged toward the soldiers who carried the young off to one side. Spearmen intercepted them, dark lances stabbing legs and arms of those who protested as Amuni's followers restored order within a few minutes.

A few hundred Amuni cultists formed ranks between the adults and children. In unison, they ground their spear butts at their feet. The flames roaring from the oak tree illuminated the spears, which stretched several feet above the soldiers' heads. Ryne narrowed his eyes at the smoke rising from the wavering black blades.

Several soldiers stepped forward, placed long horns to their mouths, and blew. One, long, shrill note keened.

Among the shadows in the square, darkwraiths appeared by the hundreds as if from nowhere, long cloaks flying in wispy swirls with the strong wind, black blades hanging from scabbards at their hips. Smoky darkness wrapped their entire countenance like waves of black heat.

Screeching howls echoed from within the dark forest surrounding Bastair. From the tree line loped several wolf–like forms, green eyes glowing. Ryne counted forty wraithwolves in all, running like men on two muscular legs. Black hair covered their bodies, and they sprang with long, leaping bounds that could outpace a horse's gallop. With each leap, they dropped to all fours, and their arms helped propel them into the air. After they landed, they sprinted on two legs again. In minutes, they reached the town square and the captives.

The beasts stalked among the adults, sniffing at each. People cowered away or tried to run but Amuni's Children quelled such attempts. When the wraithwolves found what they sought, they dragged that person kicking and screaming to the center of the square, a few feet from the massive, burning oak tree. After they completed the separations, the wraithwolves raised their noses to the air and began a rhythmic, keening wail.

A distortion appeared in the air in front the burning oak as if Ryne saw it through a cloudy glass. The blurred area swirled and turned black before eventually splitting into a thin, horizontal slit.

As the slit widened, one long, obsidian leg stepped out, and then several arms and legs followed in quick succession.

Ryne sucked in a breath, his bloodlust immediately roaring to the forefront of his mind as his power surged within him. The voices began their bickering, but this time they were of one thought. Destroy. Ryne sought the calm center of himself, picturing the pond within the Entosis, and forced the lust and the voices down.

A slender body, rippling with sinew, slithered out from the portal. The daemon stood over eight feet tall on four misshapen legs. Four disproportionate, claw–tipped appendages stuck out chest high. Its slender body glowed with its blackness, and two small wings hummed on its back. A flowing mass of fleshy locks adorned its head, hanging down past those wings. Many–faceted, lidless eyes glowed, and dripping mandibles squirmed in its grotesque face. The shadestalker's locks flicked up and across the eyes as if shading them.

The cultists and the shadelings bowed low before the

daemon. Screams and cries rose from the captives, and several of them fainted.

The shadestalker's locks dropped away from its face, and its head swiveled around to the townsfolk near the tree. They cowered away from the daemon. A few attempted to flee, but the wraithwolves quickly caught them.

"I can distract while you take care of the stalker," Sakari whispered.

Succumbing to the voices screaming once more in his head and the pull of his lust, Ryne agreed. "Yes." He pointed toward the forest. "You take them there. I'll be able to strike and get out before they react."

Opening his Matersense, Ryne prepared to Shimmer into the square. Sakari's cold hand on his arm made him stop. In that instant, his Scripts rippled.

Ryne frowned at his companion. Sakari pointed to the square.

A man garbed in black appeared next to the shadestalker. He carried a wide blade with distinct glyphs. Ryne knew that blade. With the recognition, Ryne's Scripts writhed violently.

The daemon prostrated itself before the man, its body spread like a giant insect on the flagstones. Everyone else but the captives followed suit. The newcomer strode down the line of prisoners then stopped, his head suddenly rising toward the woods at the town's opposite end. His cloak swirled for a moment, then he Blurred away to an unknown location.

The daemon eased up from the ground, and its locks stretched out. At the tips of each, tendrils of shade rose like wispy smoke. The locks grew longer, and snaked toward a few of the captives until they hovered before their chests.

Those townsfolk shied away. The appendages touched each captive chosen. All wriggling stooped; each became deathly still. A wail rose once more from the daemon's minions.

The shadestalker snapped its head back, and the locks ripped through the townsfolk, turning their torsos into pulpy masses. Blood flew and bodies crumpled. The other survivors bawled.

Sela glowed at each tendril's tip.

Ryne choked at the sight, his gut clenching. Was this what had happened at Carnas? His body and head felt as if soaring flames roared through his body.

He took a deep, shuddering breath, struggling mightily to calm himself. Within the square, a black slit appeared in the air, and opened like an eye turned sideways. An impenetrable darkness showed within.

The glowing sela flew into it. The slit snapped shut.

Shade billowed from the shadestalker in waves, blotting out the orange and yellow flames from the tree. Ryne frowned at the shadelings as they grew larger.

The shadestalker's size increased to over ten feet. It flung its locks out, and shade flew into the air in multiple directions. Shrieks echoed from those same locations, a lot closer than they should have been.

Ryne recounted the shadeling armies' positions from the war map and cringed. *They're all heading to Bastair.* He eased away from the ledge, worked his way across the Dead Hills and down onto the plains where Thumper waited. He mounted and galloped toward the Vallum of Light.

Goaded by the urgency of his discovery, Ryne pushed hard for the wall's soaring spans glowing several miles away. Even at this distance, Ryne could feel the Streams radiating from it. The twin moons' light enhanced the Vallum's Mater and bathed the hills, lone trees, and brush in slivery–blue. Questions tumbled through his head. Who was this man who made his Scripts react in that way? Was he Skadwaz, High Shin, Exalted or something more? And what was the black hole that devoured the sela? Was it the god of shade himself? No, it couldn't be. If it had been Amuni, darkness would have devoured the world by now. Ryne shook his head. Whatever the phenomenon was, the daemon and the shadelings had gained more power from the feeding.

Up and down the grassy knolls, Ryne ran, the wind whipping at him as Thumper's massive legs churned through the grass and sand. The only hope left for Bastair lay in reaching the army in time. The fate of the innocents flooded through Ryne and left him shivering.

Not long after, Ryne reached the first sentries a few hundred feet from Varick's encampment. He rode straight for the

Knight Commander's tent.

Along the way, soldiers in the same scarlet uniforms he saw at Bastair saluted him. Others ate at the many fire pits. In their heavy crimson armor, infantrymen practiced formations in a clear training area. The first row consisted of shieldbearers carrying large rectangular tower shields and wielding short swords. Pikemen with lances twice their heights made up the next rank. The final rank bore lesser armored Dagodin carrying long, shining scythes with wicked blades.

Ryne pulled up in front Varick's tent. One of the two guards turned inside to announce Ryne's arrival. The other stood with his hand on his sword hilt—a customary gesture. Ryne dismounted just as the first guard returned.

"You may enter, Master Waldron. The Knight Commander is expecting you." The young soldier nodded to the tent's entrance.

"Thank you." Ryne pushed the flaps aside and entered.

Knight Commander Varick stood at a broad table in his suit of embossed silver plate with his maps spread before him. His beard was now trimmed into a neat V. Ryne smiled. The man disliked going to war with an uncouth appearance. Three helmets rested on the table beside the maps, and next to Varick, stood Clovis and Strom.

"Greetings, Master Waldron," Varick said without looking up from the maps.

"Greetings, Knight Commander. Clovis, Strom." Ryne stepped closer to the tent's center.

The Knight Captains nodded.

Varick turned his gaze up to Ryne's face. "So, what news of Bastair."

"Not good. They've captured the town. I saw shadelings, one daemon and—"

Varick frowned. "What kind exactly, and in what numbers?"

"About forty wraithwolves, several hundred darkwraiths, and a shadestalker," Ryne answered. Clovis snorted and opened his mouth to speak. "They also had about four thousand Amuni's Children. Not your typical ones either. These were soldiers, all equipped with *divya* spears," Ryne finished before Clovis could utter a word.

Strom's mouth dropped open. "That's more *divya* than we currently have."

Varick stroked his beard calmly, his eyes not betraying the same concern as Strom's. "A few cohorts of Amuni's Children and nowhere close to the full bane of shadelings rumored to be advancing." He grunted. "The daemon is worrying but I've dealt with its kind before during the War of the Shadowbearer. That wouldn't make you rush back this quickly, Ryne. If you're the same man I remember, with those numbers, I would've expected you to attempt to kill the daemon even against the darkwraiths. There's more isn't there?"

Ryne stared into Varick's sharp eyes. "Yes, the shadestalker began a sela harvest. It took fifty the first time. There's still about a thousand townsfolk left, but the daemon has already called to the other banes. They'll make it to Bastair within the hour. Also, there was a man who could well be a Skadwaz."

The men gasped.

Outside, shrill horns keened. Within the camp, warring trumpets blared.

CHAPTER 48

Ryne's head snapped around at the sound of the horns.

"They're here?" Strom's eyebrows rose.

"Maybe they have some secret," Clovis sputtered, his earlier bravado gone. "How else could they…? Dear Ilumni."

Varick tilted his head and regarded Clovis with cold eyes. "Calm down, Clovis. These aren't those Svenzar raids you're used to where you sit and chat after a show of force, man. This is real war. Get a fucking grip on yourself or return to Kalir where you can be coddled."

Sweat trickling down his brow, Clovis knuckled his forehead. "Yes, Knight Commander. I–I'm sorry, sir."

"Leave it to the Tribunal to send an inexperienced officer," Ryne said under his breath with a shake of his head.

Varick gave a slight nod and sighed before returning his attention to the map. "Ryne, this doesn't make sense. Even if all their banes came here with every *divya* they have, they couldn't hope to win, not this close to the Vallum."

The tent flap ruffled and a guard stepped inside. "Sir, an Envoy is here."

"Send him in," Varick said without taking his eyes from the map.

The guard stepped outside, and a sharp–eyed young man in the green shirt and dark blue trousers of an Envoy entered. He made several nervous bows to the men inside.

Varick waved the man to the table. "Report."

"Herald Jensen says the scouts have reported multiple enemy movements. The shadebanes are no longer at the other towns. They're concentrated near Bastair and Cendos, sir." He indicated an area between Bastair and Varick's encampment. "The army of Amuni's Children has formed here."

Varick nodded. "In what numbers?"

"Three legions, sir. Scouts estimate four thousand per legion. And at least one full shadebane."

"Cavalry?"

"Yes sir, three dartan cohorts. Four hundred mounts per cohort."

"Thank you, Envoy. Dismissed."

The Envoy bowed, turned away from the table, and strode from the tent.

Clovis drummed his fingers on the table. "Sir, we should use the advantage of the Vallum and crush the cultist force. If we're able to also defeat that shadebane, it would be a huge blow."

"Huge blow for whom?" Ryne asked. "Are you even paying attention?"

Clovis hissed. "Do not speak—"

"Oh hush, Clovis. Ryne knows more about war than you've seen or read in your lifetime twice over," Varick said. "Now, do as he says and pay attention. To have moved so many men so fast means only one thing. It's as you said, Ryne. There are those among the shade who can Materialize."

Clovis offered no response, but his pasty face was almost pink. He gave a hesitant nod.

"Interesting," Strom said. He traced his gloved fingers along the map from Sandar and Dastan to where the enemy force was now positioned. "As unlikely as it would seem for someone that powerful to be helping them, it must be a consideration. Could it be this daemon or maybe some old remnant from Seti?"

Varick shook his head. "I've approached the Tribunal about this in the past. They seem to think no Ashishin or daemon powerful enough to have such a skill still lives in Ostania, and that they eliminated the few Skadwaz from Denestia a century before the Shadowbearer. This may be just what I need to prove them wrong. Any suggestions, Ryne?"

"It's simple," Ryne stated. "Whoever is leading the shade knows we would love a chance to take out a bane. He also knows he would lose in a fight here due to the Vallum. Using a full bane to lure our forces is a smart maneuver. Almost irresistible. However, it's all a distraction."

"I disagree—"Clovis began.

"As you would. This trap would work perfectly on someone as foolhardy and unblooded as you." Ryne stared at the man until Clovis averted his eyes. "This is a distraction. A simple sacrifice." Ryne stepped up to the table and pointed out the locations on the map. "With the numbers they needed to defeat the Alzari, they could field a larger force, but instead they send this group. Why? They intend to finish the harvest at Bastair, and then move on to Cendos. By the time we defeat their forces blocking us, the deed would be finished. And the other five banes would be that much stronger for it. They will then escape with ease, Materializing to safety."

Varick grimaced. "Hmm. In one move, they would have reinforced five banes. We can't afford that."

Strom regarded Ryne, one thick brow raised. "What do you suggest, Master Waldron?"

"Leave Clovis with his heavy armored dartans here." Ryne indicated the Knight General with a tilt of his head while pointing at the location of the shadebane and the enemy army. "Have Refald assist him." Seeing Refald's infantry at work should lend some backbone to Clovis. "Let Refald engage first, and Clovis can flank them in a simple pincer."

Clovis opened his mouth but Ryne continued, speaking to Strom. "We take your light cavalry and Varick's legions and engage the banes at Bastair. That'll force the other two banes moving to Cendos to help. Then we can crush all five. If the High Ashishin shows up by then…" Ryne shrugged. "All the better. They can bring reinforcements."

The tent flap whipped aside. In strode High Shin Jerem, his silver robes flowing about him, followed by Irmina. "A good plan, but there's one issue." He made his way to the table.

Ryne's eyes grew wide at the sight of Irmina. Her armor left her entire stomach exposed and accentuated her breasts. Her leggings appeared as if they were molded to her skin, and around her waist hung a belt with several disks. A kilt barely managed to cover her privates. The most heavily armored part of her body was her shoulders and arms, which were covered by pauldrons and vambraces made from some pliant material that glinted like polished steel. The crimson of the armor set off her pale skin. A sword hung at her waist.

"Blessed High Shin and Raijin," the other men intoned almost at once while bowing.

High Shin Jerem coughed.

Blushing, Ryne tore his eyes away from Irmina and the slight twitch of her lips.

"As I was saying. Your fight is elsewhere, Master Waldron."

Ryne frowned. "There's at least one daemon at Bastair and maybe a Skadwaz. Why would I go some place else to fight?"

High Shin Jerem's bony hand snaked out of the flared ends of his robes' sleeves. "Study the map once more." The markers for the enemy forces repositioned again. "Think about how many they needed to destroy the Alzari. Then consider how many Alzari now possibly belong to the shade. What do you see?"

Pursing his lips, Ryne counted a third of the Alzari as having succumbed to the shade's influences. With the mercenaries among them, this army was unlike anything he remembered encountering. So if they wanted Cendos and Bastair so badly why not bring all their forces? Why send what may well be only a third? Was it a trap? Where was the remainder of this army? And why avoid all the towns and cities they had, leaving the chance to be struck from behind by the massed Ostanian armies?

Ryne's eyes narrowed. "It's a double feint. Cendos and Bastair aren't their true targets either. They want us to fight there." He traced a straight line across the map from the two towns to a city thousands of miles beyond them to the northeast. "Their target is Castere."

Breaths drew in from everyone but Jerem. The old High Ashishin smiled. "I knew you would see it if nudged a bit. However, it's worse than you think. It appears Castere was already being ruled by one of Amuni's servants."

"Voliny?" Ryne scrunched up his face.

"Or Mayor Bertram if you would rather," Jerem said.

Breath quickening, muscles tightening, Ryne's bloodlust rose in a red torrent, filling his body, his eyes, stiffening him. *Hagan, you and your pipe. Vana and Vera…*

Ancel reached a tentative hand to his sword. It had become a habit although he didn't need to touch it to tell the weapon was there. The soothing warmth of his bond to the sword told him it sat in the scabbard at his hip. The same for his mother's charm around his neck. He could feel the warm link of his mother through it, calling to him in earnest.

"We go on foot from here," A grimace played across Galiana's pale face as she dismounted on the path several hundred feet before the last turn to his parents' winery.

Gloomy twilight hung in the air. Clouds scudded above, so dark and thick they choked out any semblance of the setting sun. Shadows cast by the oaks and pines of the Greenleaf Forest lay across their path, making the road in the distance near invisible before it disappeared at the next bend. Thicker still was the silence around them.

Kachien dismounted next, her eyes flitting from side to side to take in their surroundings. Ancel and Guthrie followed soon after. The innkeeper secured their mounts before leading the animals among the trees, returning a few moments later. Charra remained next to Ancel, his gaze riveted on the woods.

"What does my mother have to do with any of this? Why would shadelings be after her?"

"Everything," Galiana answered, her white dress standing out within the darkness of the area.

"I don't understand," Ancel said.

"You soon will," Galiana said. I—" She stumbled on the uneven ground.

Guthrie caught her. "Are you sure you're up for this, Shin Galiana?"

Sagging against Guthrie for a moment, Galiana squeezed here eyes tight and took several deep breaths. When she opened them, she spoke again, her voice a hoarse reflection of itself. "There is no one left but me who could do this. Now I know why they attacked at the Spellforge Hour. It was to tempt us into expending as much power as possible to save Eldanhill. It will still be another day before any of the other Matii are recovered as much as I am. Whoever or whatever that man in black was who defeated Stefan, he will return. After all, dawn is when power waxes greatest for males. Whatever he plans will happen soon."

"Let's rest for a moment," Guthrie implored.

Galiana gave the innkeeper's hand a gentle touch and a squeeze. "A moment we do not have. Follow." She pushed herself from Guthrie's arms and headed toward the winery. "As for your mother's purpose, let me ask you. How does the sword feel?"

Ancel glanced to his hip tentatively. "I–I–It feels like it belongs." More than that, the sword felt like an extension of his own body.

"Like your mother, the weapon is a Key. A Key only certain Setian can be bonded to."

Setian? Kachien's words to Jillian came flooding back and his stomach knotted. "What do the Setian have to do with us?"

"Most of Eldanhill's Council are Setian. Most folk in Eldanhill are either Setian refugees or from one of the old clans before the Shadowbearer War."

Ancel felt dizzy. He stopped in his tracks. "Th–That's impossible. The Setian no longer exist." A nudge from Charra set his legs moving again.

"Oh, we do," Galiana said. "But you and most others have always been taught differently. Seventy years of teaching such a thing all across Denestia can beget such a belief."

"The Devout?" Ancel whispered, wide–eyed.

"Yes. You've always been the smartest of my students." The pride in Galiana's voice was plain. "That's but one of their roles."

Ancel swallowed. How much of what he'd learned had been a fabrication? "If we're Setian, why hasn't he Tribunal killed us? Surely they know?"

"They do, but they need us as we need them."

"Why?"

"How has the Tribunal ruled for over a thousand years?"

In his mind, Ancel leafed through books on Tribunal politics. "They maintain a hold and involvement in Granadian politics, through the use of Ashishin to enhance everything from inventions, education, trade, crops, mining to health to even military stability. By establishing the Streamean religion here in Granadia, they united the once feuding kingdoms under a common premise of enlightenment through worship while still maintaining individuality. They quelled any upstart rebellions, destroyed the shade in numerous wars, flung back every invasion from the Erastonians to the Everlanders, and Granadia has prospered ever since.

"They appoint new Exalted every fifty years who are staunch backers of all it means to be a High Ashishin of the Tribunal. Through rigorous trials, their Order is maintained. None can become Exalted without the trials."

"True, indeed. But it is more than just an appointment. The Exalted have been the same High Ashishin for the past five hundred years."

Ancel frowned. She couldn't mean the same exact people could she?

As if sensing his uncertainty, Galiana continued, "The Tribunal procured a method to extend their lives. But not without a price. Their method required them to take a life, but it cost them their youth, their vitality. The need only increased with each use. In the end, driven by this need, the Tribunal started war after war to procure the necessary sela. Sometimes, they resorted to attacking villages in the wilds of Ostania under the guise of slavers or raiders."

Speechless, Ancel could only stare. Galiana's words made the Tribunal out to be much like the shadelings.

"Until they discovered we Setian possessed the secret of using essences absorbed and reproduced by kinai to halt aging altogether. Then came the Shadowbearer War. In return for our safety, for the preservation of our race, we agreed to serve the Tribunal, providing them with our Forging."

Ancel's fist clenched on the sword's hilt. In essence, his people were little more than slaves. He looked over to Kachien, but she showed no reaction as if all this was old news to her. "What has all this got to do with my mother and the shadelings?"

"Immortality is a thing all dream of, even those who serve the shade. Our Forging is the closest thing to it. In our Forging, your mother is the Key. Like few among the Setian and other races, she possesses a special Gift. As do you. Her Gift is the ability to Forge every essence into one to form Prima Materium. The primordial origin of Mater itself. It's a requirement for the life extension to work. Her Gift is unique."

Galiana stopped and turned to Ancel. She held his gaze. "Not only does the shade want her for this, but they seek you, Ancel. You see, the Setian are the descendants of the Eztezians."

This time, Kachien started.

Ancel's mind reeled.

"Kachien told me your power manifested. The colors you see around any living thing is called an aura. It signifies the Mater possessed by that creature. With it, you can identify anything from lifeline to intention, good to evil. And that's just the cusp of what I know. No one knows what else you can do. According to the Chronicles, such power shows in those who become Eztezian Guardians. If a Bloodline Affinity is perfected, such a person's mind can be delved into and provide the locations of the Chroniclers—the great men and women who could see all events and possibilities, past, present, and future. In turn, this would lead to the discovery of the remainder of the Eztezian Guardians.

"We could not only face another Great Divide if they are unsealed, but we must consider that a way has been discovered to use the Eztezians to break the seals they placed on the Nether. The very seals which have already been weakening. We know the Tribunal learned their Forge from one of the few Skadwaz who escaped the sealing three thousand years ago. But we never knew if we had destroyed them all until recently. We—

A screeching wail resonated through the air, followed by several screams. Charra's loud, grunting bark answered.

The wail and screams came from the direction of the winery.

Ancel broke into a run.

CHAPTER 49

The thrill of battle energy surged through Ryne. He, Sakari, Irmina, Jerem, Varick, and Refald stood at the front of the army massed to depart below the Vallum of Light. The flood of auras from the tens of thousands of soldiers filled his vision in waves.

Jerem had brought an entire legion of crimson–garbed Ashishin. One cohort accompanied Ryne's group destined to defend Castere. The other nine cohorts were stationed with Clovis, Strom, and the other Knight Captains for their defense of Cendos and Bastair. Ryne's group consisted of an additional two legions of infantry led by Varick and Refald. The clink of armor and weapons and the mutterings of thousands of voices ran down the ranks as soldiers shifted impatiently while they waited.

"All are in order," Varick said.

"Good," Jerem said, his wrinkled face a mask of concentration. "Remember, allow the Ashishin to engage first."

"I'd still rather you be there to command them and to help," Varick said, ready to argue once more that having a High Ashishin with his men would be invaluable.

"There are other more pressing developments that need tending to. Rest assured, my Ashishin will follow whatever commands you give."

Varick bowed.

"Ashishin, prepare," Jerem called, his voice reflecting the strain of whatever he did.

Ryne reached through his Scripts to touch his

Matersense. All around him, he felt every Ashishin do the same. He immediately fled into the calm center of his mind, locking away both his bloodlust and the warring voices. His battle energy built to a sweet resonance to match his thumping heart. A grim smile parted his lips.

"We depart," Jerem declared.

As before, first came the tearing sound as if the world itself around them ripped. Wind howled. The air in front of them coalesced until a slash formed, and the falling sensation struck.

Seconds later, there was a deafening roar. The ground below them heaved. Lightning split the air. Fire lit the night, and heat washed over them in waves. Ryne squinted. Men and animals screamed.

They stood on a wall lit by sputtering torches, lamps, and dying flames. Not just any wall. The battlements of Castere's Inner Ring.

Blue armored Astocan soldiers covered the ground, many with gaping wounds, some groaning and others shuddering in the final throes of death. Among them were Amuni's Children, their black armor showing great rents that oozed bodily fluids. Darkwraiths and wraithwolves stood out among the dead and wounded; the former like slimy puddles in the shape of men. The reek of spilled innards and burnt flesh was still fresh.

Spread from where they appeared, out into an ever widening circle, the ground was scorched and blackened, flames still roaring up into the main flagstoned avenue of the Inner Ring and down into the Mid Ring. Where Jerem had placed them, above the single gate to the Inner Ring, not a single being stood that didn't belong to the Granadian army.

Ashishin spread out into small groups with deadly efficiency, burning whatever moved to a crisp. Dagodin swept out, some forming a circle around Varick, Refald and the Knight Captains, while others went about the task of taking swords to anything moving not dressed in Granadian colors. Howls and wails echoed from below.

"Man the battlements!" Varick yelled.

Farther along the bulwark, Astocans fought Amuni's Children and shadelings. The Granadians struck from behind, tearing into the enemy. Bolstered by the attack, the Astocans surged forward. The shade army disappeared beneath the crush of the two armies.

Up the avenue, within the Inner Ring, the Forged flames died. The Astocan army rushed back down toward the gates. Within the Mid Ring, the same occurred, but it was the shade's minions that surged up through the open gates, spilling into the courtyard and avenue.

Behind and below them, the city boiled black with Amuni's Children and shadelings. Out in the Rainbow Lakes, warsailers and a myriad of other vessels burned. All along the walls that stretched into the water, Namazzi Forged great gouts of liquid into huge waves in an attempt to decimate incoming enemy ships. Shadelings Blurred up onto the walls, tearing the Astocan Matii apart. The Outer Ring was a mass of burning structures. Gigantic spears of flame sailed into the air and flew deeper into the city, sparking new fires within the Mid Ring. Smoke billowed into the air, blotting out the stars and painting the dark sky black.

Ryne turned his attention back to the chaos at the gates. If they lost the gates, their attack would fail. "Irmina, Sakari, with me," he commanded.

Not waiting to see them comply, Ryne leaped from the battlements into the Inner Ring's side of the wall. While falling, he drew his sword, touched his Scripts and fed light and fire essences into them. As his feet touched the ground, he also took a hold of earth essences. He landed among several thousand shadelings and Amuni's Children. Glowing red and green eyes regarded him for a moment, the expressions on every face one of stunned silence.

Not waiting for their recovery, Ryne slammed his sword into the ground. At the same time, he drew on his Scripts again, picturing the same bubbles around the men and women in battle drawn there. Similar bubbles sprang up around himself, Irmina and Sakari as they landed beside him. Ryne triggered his Forging through his weapon.

In a ring and a roar, the ground exploded. Debris, men and shadelings were hurled into the air.

The earth became a living thing with dirt and stone for hands and teeth, ripping men apart. Fire and light rippled out in a thousand tongues, scorching all Ryne had targeted as he'd fallen.

The rubble, blood, and gore struck against the shields Ryne had Forged. As the earth died to a mere undulation, and the flame and light subsided, he leapt forward onto any enemy still standing before the gates.

Beside him, Sakari was a whirlwind of movement, sandy hair streaming as his sword licked out, lopping off arms, legs and heads like mere twigs.

Irmina's hand glowed. Flames leapt forth from it in circular balls. Where they struck, they punched through armor and flesh alike. Any man or creature that managed to get close to her met death at the end of her blade.

Within moments, no living enemy stood inside the gates.

Ryne looked back to see the Astocans streaming down to the courtyard. "Close the gates," he yelled.

Several men rushed to a gigantic winch on the side. Metal rang on metal, followed by skin crawling screeches and the clang, clang, clang of gears rusty from nonuse churning against each other. The gate rumbled shut a few agonizing inches at a time.

Irmina continued to shoot her flames into the army roiling outside the gates. From above, lightning tore into them, called down by the Ashishin lining the battlements. The ground heaved under the shadeling army a few times and toppled many from their feet.

When the gate crashed shut, a huge cheer went up. From the Astocans came awed whispers of Blessed Ashishin. Many bowed. Within the next few minutes, Refald's infantry stood at the head of the Astocans before the gates.

A familiar figure with a head wrapped in bloody bandages stepped forward. "They've taken the keep," Rosival said. "It was Voliny himself. He betrayed us. We've managed to secure the way."

"Go, Ryne," Varick yelled from the walls above. "We shall hold this until the last of us falls or you complete your task. Go!"

Taking Sakari, Irmina and several Ashishin, Ryne raced toward the keep.

Ancel battled against the Sendethi soldier in front of him. Deep within the Eye, he barely heard or noticed the other soldiers nearby or the howls and cries of the shadelings.

His opponent forced him to use every trick he'd learned. Ancel dodged, twisted, parried, and changed into every defensive Stance he knew. Not once did the Sendethi allow him a chance to attack. Sweat beading his forehead, Ancel was pushed farther back until he stood on an incline.

Breathing hard, Ancel waited for the man's attack. Confidence shone in the soldier's eyes as bright as the flames licking out from the winery. The Sendethi's sword slashed.

Ancel leaped. But not away, toward the man. He judged the distance perfectly. His foot landed on a gauntleted fist, and just as it touched, he pushed off, flipping into the air, sword swinging. Ancel's weapon cleaved helmet and head in a shower of blood and brains. As the soldier was falling to one side, Ancel landed and rolled, coming up in search of another opponent.

In the middle of the fracas, Shin Galiana stood, fire streaking from her hands in multiple fist–sized balls. Occasionally, lightning split the sky to strike shadelings close to the winery. On the ground lay the ravaged bodies of the servants, eyes wide in horror, chests, and throats mangled. Those who'd tried to run were face down, backs mauled and ravaged, rents torn into their skin, dark puddles oozing around them.

Off to one side Kachien darted with that uncanny speed of hers, black blades near invisible as she carved through man and beast. Guthrie strode among the enemy, swinging his two–handed greatsword. Anything in its path was sheared in two. Every kill the man bellowed, "In Ilumni's Name!"

Charra stayed close to Ancel, hamstringing men, or diving bone hackles first into shadelings. His great jaws and knife–like claws tore fur, flesh and gouged armor with impunity. He did enough to maim before retreating to defend against any who approached Ancel.

Abruptly, lightning rained down from the sky in great, jagged lances, so incandescent, that for a moment it blotted every form from sight and etched every shadow in sharp edges. A noiseless concussion thumped Ancel in the chest, almost knocking him from his feet. He flung a hand up to cover his eyes and used the other to maintain his balance. Spots danced through his vision, afterimages burnt into his retinas. When his sight cleared, shadeling and men lay dead all around Galiana, brunt to a crisp, the aroma of their scorched flesh and the metallic scent of the lightning bolts heavy in the air.

Galiana collapsed to one knee. Roaring, Guthrie rushed to her side. He was able to help her to her feet before Ancel reached them.

Ancel's head whirled around to a crackling sound. Flames licked out the windows of the winery and timber crumbled. A roof collapsed. A lump rose in Ancel's throat. He cried out.

His mother was trapped inside.

"No," Galiana said in a weak voice as Ancel stepped forward. "You cannot help her. Look, but not with your eyes."

Ancel opened his Matersense. Essences spilled about the winery, dancing and zipping in and out of any opening. Flashes of light and fire shot through before being repelled by shade and air. The force from them buffeted him.

A battle raged inside his home.

As if they sensed what was happening the remaining shadelings and Sendethi had retreated until they stood at the far side of the field. Green and red eyes stared at the burning structure.

"Your mother is one of the strongest Ashishin I know, but against whoever she is fighting inside, you cannot help," Galiana whispered.

A hollow boom sounded, and one of the walls blew outward. From the smoke and debris strode a man swathed in all black. He dragged the limp form of Ancel's mother from the building by one arm.

CHAPTER 50

In Castere, they bypassed the villas, spires, and fountains along the main avenue of the Inner Ring undisturbed. Ryne kept a vigilant eye out for any enemies, but the soldiers they saw were Rosival's men, most wounded, many dead or dying. A few Namazzi, blue uniforms sporting the Waterwall insignia, joined the once small group that had grown on its way to Castere Keep.

At the castle, not a single Waterwall flag fluttered in the slight breeze. The keep's silver–blue walls and towers reared in the dark before them like a great monolith, battlements unlit, windows black uninviting pits.

"Use the columns to keep cover," Ryne instructed as they crept down the colonnade before the keep's entrance.

In quick bursts, they darted from one column to the next until there were no more pillars left. Breaths echoing into the night air, they hid behind the last few. Ahead, the twin barbicans loomed, dark and foreboding. The heavy gate and spiked portcullis they protected was closed.

Two Ashishin whispered to each other then stepped from behind their pillar at the same time. They raised their hands.

A faint buzz thrummed through the air. Soft, wet thuds followed. Choking sounds issued from the Matii as they folded over, clutching at their chests and necks where several dozen crossbow bolts protruded from their bodies. The men crumpled to the ground, blood pooling beneath them.

"Fools," Ryne muttered.

"So what's the plan to get inside?" Irmina asked. "A few archers can hold that gate against us indefinitely."

"Against normal men or Ashishin, maybe, but not against me. Sakari, you take the left barbican, I'll take the right. You Ashishin, on my signal illuminate those towers. Namazzi, your targets will be lit then." Ryne nodded to the two dead Ashishin. "Use their blood if you must."

"What will the signal be?" One of the Ashishin asked, a slim man whose uniform hung about him loosely.

"When we charge the wall."

"You're mad," another Matii said.

Ryne smiled grimly and reached for the Forms. Below him, the earth provided more than enough fodder for what he intended. Flagstones cracked, rippled, and clacked against each other as he Forged four constructs of himself, keeping them hidden under the avenue. Sharp intakes of breath escaped from the other Matii.

At the same time, Ryne linked with Sakari. "When I send them, we Shimmer to the top of the towers."

"As you wish."

Making sure he was seated deep in the calm pool of his mind, Ryne touched his Scripts once more. Light surged up into him. In that moment, he summoned the constructs from the earth.

In a rumbling shower of stone and earth, the flagstones tore apart as the eight–foot replicas pulled themselves up. Scores of arrow bolts thrummed through the air, bouncing off the constructs' cobblestone skin with sharp pings. Ryne sent the constructs careening toward the gate, their footsteps a deep rumble.

Light bloomed above the barbicans. Picking out the Streams, Ryne Shimmered, reappearing behind several dozen stunned men in black armor—Amuni's Children. Or so he thought until he saw the painted faces.

Alzari.

It was a trap.

Ryne's smile never touched his eyes as he danced among the men. Disconcerted by the light, and distracted by the constructs barreling into the gate with loud thuds and crashes, most of the mercenaries never saw when death took them. Ryne's sword sheared through bone, sinew and armor as if slicing air. Blood and limbs flew, followed by the screams of the dying.

As the Alzari began to understand what was happening, Ryne delved into the Forms at his feet, deconstructing the mortar between the bricks. The substance came apart like sand.

The entire roof collapsed. Those who hadn't been screaming yet, screamed then.

The soldiers in the rooms below tried to flee, but there was nowhere to go. Debris bombarded them, burying them under suffocating mounds of brick and pestle. Winding stairs led down, every few flights with a landing and murder holes manned by more soldiers. Brick and dirt rained down the hollow center of the building. Men leapt away from the opening.

Ryne sprang over the banister, his greatsword pointed down. The earlier shield he'd used formed around him, its blue tinge lighting the dark interior of the barbican. Swords and arrows bounced of its surface as he fell. He hit the floor among a milling mass of men still struggling to comprehend how the roof had fallen in. With the force of the fall behind it, the greatsword sunk into the ground as if the surface was mud instead of brick. The metallic clang of the silversteel penetrating stone echoed a death knell. Ryne triggered his Scripts.

The floor, walls, and pillar supports exploded, showering stone and mortar in a white smoky, mist. With a groan, then a thunderous rumble, the tower collapsed around Ryne, rubble bouncing off his shield.

Still linked with Sakari, Ryne saw the carnage the man waged as he'd fought his way from the roof and down the stairs. The steps ran red with rivulets of blood. It poured off onto the soldiers clamoring below. Those who rushed up the steps died. From somewhere, Sakari had gained a second sword and this he used to knock away any incoming bolts. The man fought more like a daemon than a man. Ryne frowned before his eyes shot open at a strange sound from Sakari.

He was laughing. A high, mad, cackle that rang out in peals.

Pushing the sound to the back of his mind, Ryne turned back to what he'd left in his wake. White smoke from the debris choked the air, moans and groans echoed, and here and there, rubble shifted. Men called for help, often followed by a hand reaching up from the stone and dirt. Covered in white residue and looking like an avenging spirit, Ryne found what remained of the main door and strode through the crumbled wall into the hall that held the winch for the portcullis and gate. No one attempted to stop him. He unhitched the chain and pulled.

Slowly, gears churning and clanging, the gate and portcullis rose.

"Mother!" Ancel screamed, his mind battering against the Forge that prevented him from touching the essences spilling about them in waves.

It was Shin Galiana's Forge. The old woman, her silver hair hanging in wild wisps that stuck to her forehead and cheeks, leaned heavily on Guthrie, her hand held out before her, and her brow furrowed and slick with sweat. She'd stopped Ancel as soon as he tried to lash out at the dark-garbed man who held his mother prisoner.

His mother lay unmoving at the man's feet. Swathed in shade and in clothing as black as a daemon's maw, the man had responded to Galiana's own attack without so much as a wave of his hand and now faced her. Mater battered whatever barrier Shin Galiana had erected between them. Essences slammed and sliced incessantly, but to no avail.

Ancel could see the man also maintained a complex Forge around his mother. Similar to the one Galiana used to keep him from touching the essences. Ancel's chest burned with the need to help, the need to rush to his mother's side, the need to find out if she still lived.

"Calm yourself, boy," Guthrie instructed. "Seek the Eye. You can't help here."

Ancel had tried for calm several times, but every time, he'd failed. Now, he no longer wanted to be under control. He wanted to lash out with everything he had. A hand brushed his shoulder.

"I know how you feel. I have seen my loved ones taken. But this man and them," Kachien nodded toward the shadelings at the other side of the field. "We cannot handle. Not now. Not like this."

"I won't leave my mother." Ancel gritted his teeth against the tears streaming down his face and the pain that tore at his chest. "I won't." Mind racing, he sought a way to help her. Without the ability to reach the Eye, the voices he'd heard in his head before came alive.

"Our power is yours if you want it. Take it. Use it to crush all who stand in your way. None can stand before you. Not even him." On and on the voices raged, but still Galiana prevented him from touching the essences.

Ancel reached for his sword. As he touched its hilt, Kachien's hand stopped him. Scowling, he shrugged her off, and his hand closed around the handle.

The sword's bond solidified. Whereas before he could feel it in his mind, now he felt the sword's bond as if he and the sword were one and the same. He *was* the sword. Power rushed through the weapon into him. Glowing hot, it tore through him and his back arched.

He felt them then.

Hundreds of pinpoints of energy, of essences, one nearby, and the others spread far and near. He opened eyes he hadn't realized he'd closed and looked toward his mother.

Her gaze met his. She smiled.

The man in black shook his head, or the shadow representing his head. Red eyes glanced down at Ancel's mother before his gaze locked on Ancel and the now glowing sword. The eyes narrowed to slits.

***

Sword in hand, Irmina edged around the corpses and past the last pillars in the Audience Chamber. From the door to the dais at the room's center, bodies in the rigor of death lined the floor. Near the dais, the dead were piled in an oozing heap, their chests gaping holes of flesh and bone. The very air buzzed with power. Even without touching her Matersense, she felt the tingle of essences coursing around her in short bursts. Never before had she experienced such.

A man garbed in charcoal clothing sat upon a throne.

Scars marred one side of his face and he had only one eye. On the same side of his body, his arm was nothing more than a stump. She recognized the man's face.

Mayor Bertram.

Sitting on the mosaic floor tiles in front of the man were several Astocan nobles, their clothes dirty and disheveled. They stared with wide, uncomprehending eyes.

Around Bertram's throne stood two ebony beasts standing on spindly legs with small, humming insect–like wings on their backs. Long hair twisted like rope hung down to their waists. The daemons made keening noises, their gazes locked on Ryne.

Wraithwolves and darkwraiths appeared around the room. The Matii stopped abruptly, hands raised toward the shadelings. Having long ago embraced her Matersense, Irmina waited. Beside her, Ryne's face was a mottled mask of rage.

"You, Bertram? Or Voliny, or whatever your real name is. You sacrificed Carnas for this? For revenge?" Ryne's quiet voice cut through the spacious hall.

Bertram threw his head back and laughed. A scornful, vile sound. He brought his one–eyed gaze to bear on Ryne. "You would think that way. Forever naïve despite all you've done yourself. There was a time this was about revenge. About settling the score with the Tribunal, about what losing my family meant, about you costing me my son. But then, it became so much more. I realized Ilumni had failed us. I saw a way to recapture all Ostania had ever been and more. A way to make myself a god among men. A chance to succeed where you failed, Nerian."

Ryne's brows drew together in confusion. Irmina frowned. Why had he just called Ryne, Nerian?

"Ah," Bertram said. "He still doesn't know." Around the room grunts and whispers rose from the shadelings that sounded too similar to laughter. "Let me ask you, Ryne *Thanairen* Waldron, why do you think they," he nodded to the daemons, "didn't attack you? Why has the shade always found you? Coincidence? No. And you must know by now it had nothing to do with your little Ashishin there."

"What in Ilumni's name are you talking about," Ryne said. "You lie. Just like you lied in Carnas."

"Do I? What about your dreams? Your lost memories?

The killings you do remember? The voices that war within you? The reason you slayed so many innocents? The reason you hid in Carnas in the first place. The thousands of reasons you seek redemption." Bertram made a circular gesture with his hand. "Here, let me help you past the fog clouding the memory you try to reach."

The Astocans on the floor gasped and crumpled. In front of Bertram, a light blue globe at least six feet in diameter appeared. At the same time, Ryne groaned and dropped to his knees.

An image bloomed in the globe. It showed a giant man about Ryne's height garbed in resplendent black armor that seemed to drink in any light. Another image displayed the same man in golden armor, slamming a Lightstorm standard into a pile of bones and bodies. She couldn't see the tattoos but Irmina knew by the eyes and hair both men were Ryne. The first one was also a picture she'd seen in a Tome of the Chronicles.

A portrait of Nerian the Shadowbearer.

Tears streaming down his face, Ryne choked back a sob. "All this time, you fucking bastards. All this time…"

"Yes." Bertram laughed scornfully. "All this time. You've always been my master's tool. He uses you then wipes your memories. You've fought on every side, but always for us. Always for his purpose. And every time, I've gotten the pleasure of revealing this to you. It still brings a thrill you cannot begin to imagine."

Irmina gaped. Here before her, on his knees and vulnerable, was the cause of her family's pain, her people's past, the death and suffering that haunted her in her dreams. The man who the Dorns served all those years ago when they began to wipe out her family, when with the final stroke, they had her parents killed. Here, she could exact ultimate revenge.

Jerem's words came back to her then. *"This mission will be your final test. This task will force you to make the most difficult choice you have ever had to make. It will define what path you take. Regardless of your choice, you will be scarred for the remainder of your days."*

Irmina reached out to the Mater coiling in the air. When she touched it, the power flooded her in too many individual strands to count. Behind it all, she sensed something familiar, something she knew. Realization dawned on her. The pinpoints were people and places all drawn together in one enormous Forging. For some reason a picture of Ancel came to her mind, his dark hair flying behind him, a glowing sword in his hand and Mater shooting up into the sky.

Irmina stabbed.

The world slowed to a standstill for Ancel. The essences around the man waxed and waned as he struggled against not only his mother's Forge but Galiana's and Kachien's also. In Ancel's hand, the sword vibrated, power surging through it. The first pinpricks now connected to too many tiny pockets of power for him to count. There were thousands upon thousands upon thousands of them.

The shadowy man's other hand rose, and a long, silvery, horizontal slash appeared in the air. It snapped open in the shape of an eye. Beyond the opening, a night–black hall with red carpets and several torches burning with strange, black flames led to a throne.

The man snatched Ancel's mother by the arm, stepped into the portal, and dragged her in behind him. The slash snapped close.

Ancel's charm, the link that told him of his mother's presence, cooled against his neck. Ancel screamed. In a desperate act, he snatched at the pinpricks of power. At all of them.

"Nooooo!" Galiana croaked.

Mater flooded Ancel in a burning white torrent. It flashed through the sword, struck a wall of the winery, and disintegrated the structure. Beyond was a tall spire of silversteel. The bar of Mater struck the spire and shot into the air in a thousand directions.

Ancel felt it then.

One by one, in every town or city, the power touched a temple. Religion made no difference, whether Streamean, Formist, or Flowic. It touched them all before ricocheting into the night sky, lighting the heavens like the noonday sun, connecting to other points in a wide band.

Ancel pictured the portal he'd seen the man use. He

needed to follow. He had to follow. There was no choice if he was to save his mother. His need overpowered all else.

Charra roared. A bloodcurdling sound that drowned out everything.

Another slash appeared in the air, two times the size of the prior one. Like the other before it, the slash opened up into the shape of an eye. Inky darkness lay beyond the opening. Trembling with elation, his mouth a slit of a smile, Ancel took a step forward.

A black tentacle reached out from the portal. Then another. Dark mist billowed forth. It stretched up until it towered thirty feet into the air. Slowly, the blackness congealed like thick syrup poured into a mold and began to form a torso. From the back stretched gigantic, oval plates honed to a fine edge, each glinting with blackness. Armor of the same texture appeared to cover the chest. The tentacles split into four along the ribs, shortening and solidifying into arms with skin so shiny it glowed where it stretched over bone at the joints. Claws tipped each four digit hand. Slits opened where a head should be to reveal eight milky white eyes, and as Ancel watched, the face formed, jaw stretching out into a eel–like countenance but with fangs that never belonged to any eel Ancel knew. A horn stood out on the forehead, and two others stretched back where there should have been ears. Worm–like beings swarmed around the creature, floating in the air, each about five feet long, their facial features matching their giant counterpart.

Voices whispered through Ancel's head as he gaped.

"Your power, your need has summoned me, boy," a guttural voice said from deep within the creature. "You have ascended as the seals have weakened. You have been found worthy of our gift."

The voices in Ancel's head whispered again. They told him what it was he faced.

Netherling.

From the corner of his eyes, on his knees, Ryne saw and felt a sword go through a chest. No. Not his chest. Sakari's.

Eyes wide, Sakari looked down at Irmina's weapon

protruding from his chest and folded over. An aura appeared around Sakari then. Black as the pits of the Nether itself, shade circled Sakari in waves as he fell. Skin peeled from his human body to reveal black tentacles where there should be limbs.

An enormous torrent of power, of essences in hundreds of thousands of strands, shot through the air into Ryne's body. The elements were as primordial and powerful as those in an Entosis.

Ryne stood; his link with Sakari broken. From somewhere else thousands of miles north and west, he felt another link to another person. The fog that once hid his memories burned away.

He knew who he was now. All of his other personas. Not just Nerian the Shadowbearer, Ryne Waldron, or Exalted Thanairen but the hundreds of others. All from legends and myths several thousand years old. He saw all his lives unravel before him.

From the pillars around the room, Bertram's Royal Guards appeared. So did several hundred Alzari. The shadelings prepared to pounce, while the daemons, Bertram, and the Alzari all drew on Mater.

A thousand Forges bloomed around the room, all directed at Ryne.

In Ryne's mind, a man appeared. At least a foot taller than Ryne, he had blonde hair done in a long braid with gold wire worked into it. Scripts covered his body and armor. His face reminded Ryne of himself.

"Brother," the man said. "I see you lost your way again."

"No, Damal," Ryne corrected. "I found it." He caressed his Matersense. What he once thought was his bloodlust, a craving to kill, clung to him like an extra layer of skin and he allowed it to. The voices in his head were different sides of an argument like magistrates at court. They were the living entities that inhabited Mater itself arguing who should live and who should die. And Ryne was the final judgment.

Bars of shade flew toward Ryne from the daemons. From Bertram shot forth a streak of black lightning turned sideways. The ground rumbled as the Alzari worked the Forms sending stone, tiles, and the earth itself rippling toward Ryne, tossing corpses unceremoniously aside. In leaping bounds and gliding gaits, the shadelings rushed toward Ryne, howling and wailing with their eagerness to tear him apart.

Around Ryne, his Scripts shone bright. No, not Scripts. Scripts were what Matii could once do on *divya* to add more power. On a living being, these were Etchings, and only a netherling could do such an imbuing.

Defensive Forgings from the Namazzi and Ashishin flew out to meet the incoming attack. Air, in gale force winds, howled from the Namazzi, and light and fire from the Ashishin. The opposing essences collided, followed by a roaring boom.

The force of the explosion blew Ryne off his feet. Matii, soldiers, and shadelings were thrown back, arms and legs mangled, bodies gashed. Some slammed against what remained of the walls and pillars that leaned listlessly. Smoke billowed and flames licked around the room.

Blood streaming from his ears and nose, and rasping for breath in the hot air, Ryne struggled to his feet. Irmina lay near him, her face and clothes blackened messes. Her chest rose and fell in barely discernable increments. Of Sakari, there was no sign.

Swaying as he stood, his face impassive, Ryne touched his sword's hilt. A gash ran down the side of his face, opposite the old claw marks, and cuts and burns marred his body. His Etchings worked to mend him.

Bertram and the daemons crawled to their feet. So did a few of the Alzari and whatever remained of the shadelings.

"Brother," Damal said. "They come. Are you ready?"

Ryne gave a weak nod. Bracing himself, he reached toward his new link. Mater flooded him from a thousand, no, a hundred thousand, no, from more sources than he could count.

Time slowed. Forges flew out from Bertram and the daemons. Forms tore the ground from the Alzari. Lightning, bars of shadow, fire, and earth flew forth. Death raced toward Ryne.

"Recite with me," Damal commanded.

"Light to balance shade. Light to show honor. Honor to show mercy," Ryne said in concert with Damal. Ryne's Etchings bloomed brighter than ever before.

"Shade to balance light. Mercy to Gift death. Death to those found wanting." Shade billowed within Ryne's Etchings.

"The elements of Mater must exist in harmony." Ryne's voice rose with a wind that howled through the air.

"Why do we exist, brother?" Damal shouted.

"To help the helpless. To defend. To build. To destroy. To judge." Ryne's voice echoed above the groans of the dying, above the wind, above the elements streaking toward him.

"Declare judgment," Damal whispered, and he disappeared.

Ryne thrust all the power roaring within him and without into his Etchings. He chose the ones depicting an army of giants facing down a vast gathering of shadelings.

The shapes of the giants leaped from his body. One by one, they grew until they stood twenty feet tall, heads reaching past what pillars still stood. Etchings covered their bodies. One bowed to Ryne.

It was Damal.

The Eztezian Guardians turned toward the surging Forges and Amuni's servants before them. Massive greatswords bounded into their hands.

The world became a white blaze as the Eztezians unleashed their power in the Audience Chamber and all through Castere. Wherever they appeared, anything serving the shade perished.

CHAPTER 51

A ncel stood before the netherling with his head bowed. So did Galiana, Kachien, and Guthrie. With a mere wave of its hand, the creature had swept the shadelings into ash.

"I know you feel the link to your new master. He will teach you all you need to know of your Gift," The netherling said, his voice a deep growl. "There are a few of us here in your realm. Not all represent the interests of your kind. You must seek them out while you learn. Use your pet." White eyes regarded Charra. "He himself is one of us."

Ancel gaped. *Charra, a netherling?*

"And now for your Gift," the netherling announced. "There are twelve sets of these. We provide you with ten. The other two we do not know how to obtain and have never possessed them. We do know they will be required for you and your people to prevail. Hold out your arm."

Ancel reached a tentative hand out, his palm up, expecting to receive weapons of some sort. Instead, throbbing pain shot through his arm. Back arching, he screamed. The pain increased until white danced before his eyes, blades and fire scoured his skin, and his head pounded as if it would burst. He would have fallen to the ground, but somehow the pain itself kept him erect.

"This is the first set of your Etchings. They represent the essences of light among the Streams. Like the other essences, they will speak to you from time to time. Heed what they say, but the choices you make are yours. This is my Gift to you. As you master it, others will come to you to pass on the other Gifts."

Tears streaming down his face as the pain subsided, Ancel glanced at his right arm. His clothes had been shorn from half his body and hung in tatters about him. Up his arm and across his right chest was the most beautiful artwork he'd ever seen. The Etching displayed the sun, moon, and stars in various scenes, sometimes with lightning illuminating dark skies. The Etching writhed and throbbed.

A slash appeared in the air again. Behind it, what was left of the winery still smoked, timber, stone, and brick black to match the ground for thousands of feet. As before, the slash formed into an eye that opened onto a void.

The netherling stepped through, the armored plates on its back chiming with his movement, and the portal closed.

Ryne stood outside what remained of Castere Keep. Below, most of the fires were petering out and smoke rose in the air. The twin statues of Aeoli and Hyzenki still stood tall in the great lakes. For reasons, he couldn't quite place, he felt no elation at having destroyed Bertram and the threat from the shade's army. The victory seemed hollow, incomplete. The innocents slain in Carnas and elsewhere were still dead. Nothing would change that. Not even if he swept the land with the rest of the allied Granadian and Ostanian forces to hunt down what remained of the army. He looked northwest to where he felt his new link out across the sea in Granadia.

"So what now?" Irmina asked. Her Ashishin uniform was torn in too many places to count, but at least she'd been mended.

"I must seek him out as Halvor said. He needs me."

"Who?"

"The one who provided me with the power I needed. He will need you also. After all, you saved me. I cannot thank you enough for that," Ryne said. A shadow crept across Irmina's face. Ryne assumed it was from the pain.

"I just did as was needed." Her shoulders drooped, and with a sigh she asked, "So who is this person?"

"A youth named Ancel."

Black rain fell around Sakari. He reached for the barrier, wincing, expecting the normal pain that would have prevented his passage. None came. The Kassite had already thinned here. Untouched by the torrential downpour of inky rain, or the storming winds, he drew from the abundance of shade coursing around him. Forging a rift at the thinnest point of the Kassite, he stepped through. He Materialized, already kneeling, in the absolute black of several shadelamps. The near blinding umbra forced him to bow his head and close his eyes. He took a moment and gathered himself. He still hadn't fully adapted to his ability to see within the dark as clear as a bright, sunlit day.

Sakari remained on his knees in the middle of a red–carpeted, marble walkway. At first, the malefic form seated upon the throne didn't react to his presence. A gray haired woman with wild, silver–blue eyes lay at the form's feet. Normally, Sakari wouldn't have ventured this far in, but the Master had demanded he come directly to him as soon as the battle concluded. He kept his head down.

Something cold brushed against his skin, and he forced the thudding beat of his heart to a tenuous vibration. Freezing tendrils of Kahkon's shade touched him, probing, begging for him to flinch away in fear. Bumps crept along his skin where it touched, but he didn't budge. To do so meant death. He had no intention of feeding his Master's hunger.

"You bring news?" asked Kahkon's disembodied voice in a near chuckle. The voice came from everywhere and nowhere.

"Yes, my Lord," answered Sakari. "It has happened as you prophesied, sire. Prima Materium has been released. Eztezian Bertram perished in the undertaking. The first seal is broken."

A soft laugh issued from the roiling darkness on the throne. "He lost control when she wounded you, didn't he?"

"Yes, my lord," Sakari said, maintaining a neutral tone.

"And the sword?"

"The young man still possesses it." Why would a sword be of any concern to one such as his Master? Sakari dared not ask. Instead, he made a mental note of it.

"Good. Take a contingent of Vasumbral with you to establish our reign here. Scour the land until you find the boy and his ilk. Kill them all. Bring this pitiful world to its knees. Feed the advent of Amuni." The malevolent cackle of Kahkon's voice echoed within Sakari's head before dwindling away just as the darkness sitting on the throne faded and the tendrils of shade and the woman with it.

Sakari stood as the blackness congealed, somehow making an even darker blotch within the umbra.

A sound drifted through the air like a dry rasp of metal on leather mixed with the crackle of a fire. Tentacles stretched out, followed by a long, slithering body as broad across as a wagon. The form writhed and coiled and stretched, at times appearing to be joined by vertebrae, but no beginning or end came into sight. Hundreds of miniscule feelers fluttered under the bellies of the beasts, some touching the ground to drag, while others appeared to sample the air. Sakari spat. He didn't like them, but like any other tool, the Vasumbrals would be used.

ORIGINS

From the notes of Jenoah Amelie – First of the Exalted

In founding the Tribunal, we hope to give the peoples of Denestia a basis to understand that harmony must be maintained among not only the many races that populate each continent, but between Mater itself and the ensuing religions.

Mater is the core elemental power which exists within everything. It makes up the three elements the gods represent and their individual essences. Mater is more than just the elements driving one world. It drives all worlds. The three elements are the solids of the Forms, the liquids of the Flows, and the energy of the Streams. Those are further broken down into separate essences. For instance, earth, wood and metal are a part of the Forms. Heat, cold, light and shade are a part of the Streams. Water and air are a part of the Flows. These are intermingled to produce things as an example of harmony. Take for example ice. It's a combination of cold essences and water. Mud is a combination of water and earth within the Forms. The list goes on. Finally, there's sela essence, a combination of life and death which sits outside the three elements and is required for anything to live or die.

From these and the gods they represented, man derived three main religions: Streamean, Formist, and Flowic. There are many other minor religions and gods, but these are said to be the original ones developed from the beings created by the primordial essence of the One God.

Mater is more than just elemental power. It's compromised of living entities. These entities range from malevolent to good. One constant among them is that in order to live, they, like us, must feed. They feed on sela essence. In order to gain sela, death is necessary. These entities inhabit people, plants, or creatures strong enough to use the actual forces given off by the essences in physical or mental acts in what's called Materforging or simply Forging.

However, once one has Forged, it affects the psyche and slowly erodes one's sanity, causing sela to begin leaking. To stem the tide of this effect and stabilize the mind and body, one is forced to kill to feed Mater itself. This cycle continues until the person goes completely insane, unleashes all their power, and dies. In turn the entities of Mater get what they want most. To feed. Yet, we believe a balance must be maintained here, as we doubt the essences could survive without us, and in turn us without them.

Mater is also linked to the Matus, (one who can wield Mater), emotionally. Strong emotions can trigger its use. The entities then harness that in a form of bloodlust to encourage the Matus to kill. The main extremes of emotions like rage, love, intense fear, grief and being overjoyed reflect the state of the entities and what they represent from malevolence for the darker emotions, to benevolence for the lighter ones. The one type of Matus this seems not to affect are the Dagodin, who can sense Mater and wield items imbued with it, but they themselves cannot Forge.

For Forgers, this is where the Shunyata, or the Eye as it is called in some places, is of teh utmost importance. To gain emotional control of oneself, you attain the Shunyata. However, the Matus cannot always remain in the Shunyata. If they did, the entities would deplete their sela to such an extent that the Matus will either go insane, die, or both. Performing a Forging that's beyond the Matus' means can tear the aura that surrounds his or her body, causing sela to begin leaking. An almost irreversible process.

It has been found that by embracing the essences, your emotions, remaining in control, and only feeding the essences a bare minimum, one can almost stave off insanity indefinitely.

This is part of the harmony. However, one crack of weakness, one surrender to the promises the essences offer, one Forging outside the Shunyata, and the road to doom is paved. For this we developed, the Pathfinders—Matii who are powerful enough and have shown the utmost control and skill. Their jobs were to hunt down and eliminate wayward Matii.

It is with such knowledge that we now decide on which Matii should lead us.

GLOSSARY

Alzari – Matii who wield mostly the Forms, strongest in earth essences and metal. Ancestors of the Setian.

Amuni – One of the gods of Streams, specifically, shade. Brother of Ilumni.

Ashishin – Matii who serve the Tribunal and often represent the god Ilumni and the Streams, specifically light and heat. Most of the Granadian peoples are descendants of the Ashishin. They often bear the title of Shin or High Shin.

Astoca – A kingdom within south central Ostania. Their people, the Astocans, are cousins to the Cardians. (See Namazzi)

Bana – A kingdom in eastern Ostania. Their people are the Banai and worship Humelen and the Forms.

Bastions of Light – Towers along the Vallum of Light and located at strategic points within Granadia that can be used to send warning of an impending attack to the Tribunal.

Cardia – A kingdom far south in Ostania. Their people, the Cardians, are related to the Astocans. (See Namazzi)

construct – A sentient entity created from essences.

Dagodin – A Matus who cannot Forge but can wield items imbued with Mater called divya.

Darkwraith – A type of shadeling created by merging the sela essences, spirit, and shade of a Matus.

dartan – A massive beast of burden, bigger than any horse. It has 6 legs, hardened skin, and a shell into which it can withdraw its legs. It also has a long snake-like neck and is a meat eater. Originally created during the Luminance Wars.

Deathbringer – A type of Matii used by the Felani and others, said to be already crazed Matii. Only the Felani know how they're controlled.

Denestia – The world where this story takes place, said to have been the crowning achievement of the god Ilumni who defeated his brother Amuni for its possession.

Devout – A priest who serves Ilumni and goes on pilgrimages to do the Tribunal's bidding, often preaching the word of Streamean worship and its virtues.

divya – An item imbued with Mater.

Dosteri – A race originating in Everland who later inhabited Granadia.

Elements of Mater – The completed essences that make up the Flows, the Forms, and the Streams. (See Mater)

Erastonia – A kingdom in Everland.

Erastonian – Powerful warriors from Everland, specifically from a place called Erastonia. They possess some of the strongest Matii within the known world. Their main task is defending the Great Divide and killing any shadelings that happen to escape from the prisons contained with the Divide.

Essences – The individual strands of power that make up the elements of Mater.

Everland – The northernmost continent in Denestia.

Exalted – Mythical leaders of the Tribunal.

Eztezian – The Eztezians were the descendants of the gods. Great warriors and the most powerful Matii to grace Denestia. They were tasked with protecting Denestia from the shade and from itself. Driven mad by their overuse of Mater however, they almost destroyed the world. They created the Great Divide, which brought about the shade's defeat. Then they turned on the gods, sealing them in the Nether to prevent future wars and the creation of more creatures like the shadelings.

Felan – A kingdom is western Ostania. Their people are known as the Felani.

Flowic – The religions named after the elements of Flows and its gods.

Flows – The combination of two essences—primarily water and air that make up liquids known as the Flows. There are other variations that involve other essences. E.g Water and cold to form ice. Heat, air, and something flammable to create fire.

Forger – A Matus who can Forge essences of Mater

Forging – See Materforging

Formist – The religion named after the elements of Forms and its gods.

Forms – The combination of three essences—earth, metal, and wood, that make up solids known as the Forms. There are other variations of solids that can be enhanced by using other essences, as well as other essences not in this umbrella that can be used to form solids. (See example in Streams.)

Gerde – Stoneform beasts with eight-legs that bear similarities to crabs, but were the size of ponies.

Granadia – The Western continent of Denestia. Have been at conflict with most of Ostania for millenia.

Harna – A kingdom in northern Ostania. Followers of Formist religion. Descendants of the Sven.

Humelen – One of the Gods of Forms, specifically earth.

Hydae – A world formed by Amuni when he lost to his brother Ilumni.

Ilumni – One of the gods of Streams, specifically, light. Brother of Amuni.

Imbuer – A Matus who can imbue properties of essences into an item to create divya.

kinai – A special plant that draws on essences, used in many healing formulas and potent drinks. Said to enhance the user's strength, stamina, and agility.

Luminance War – An ancient war when shadelings escaped the Great Divide and swept across Ostania.

Mater – Mater is the core elemental power which exists within everything. It makes up the three elements the gods represent and their individual essences. Mater drives all worlds. The three elements are the solids of the Forms, the liquids of the Flows, and the energy of the Streams. Those are further broken down into separate essences. For instance, earth, wood and metal are a part of the Forms. Heat, cold, light and shade are a part of the Streams. Water and air are a part of the Flows. Finally, there's sela essence, a combination of life and death which sits outside the three elements and is required for anything to live or die. (See

Streams, Flows, Forms.)

Materialize – Ability to Forge a portal between two places for travel.

Materforging – The act of wielding the essences or elements of Mater.

Matersense – The ability to open up one's mind to be able to sense or see nearby essences within the elements of Mater.

Matus – One who can sense Mater (Plural – Matii) Not every Matus can manipulate or Forge Mater. What essence a Matus is strongest in is often determined by bloodline. However, one can train to become adept in other essences. It is difficult and takes powerful Matii to wield essences from two separate elements simultaneously. It is considered to only be an ability of the netherlings or gods to wield all essences within all three elements at the same time.

Mystera – Schools built throughout Granadia for the purpose of teaching and recruiting Matii.

Namazzi – Matii who wield mostly the Flows, ancestors of the Cardians and Astocans.

Netherling – Primordial beings from the Nether, said to have been the ones to bestow their power on the Eztezians in order to save the world. This act was part of their revenge against the gods for their experiments.

Ostania – The Eastern continent of Denestia. Have been at conflict with most of Ostania for millenia.

Pathfinder – Powerful Matii, trained by the Tribunal, who have passed the ultimate tests of control over their emotions, which ensure they will not succumb to the temptations of the power the essences promise. They are used to hunt Matii who break the laws governing the use of Forging or those who go insane. They often accompany Ashishin to protect the Ashishin from attackers and from themselves.

Raijin – An elite assassin corps within the Tribunal.

Sanctums of Shelter – Similar to the Bastions of Light but more powerful and arrayed along the mountains in Northern Granadia to protect from any direct incursion by the shade through the Great Divide.

Scorpio – A massive crossbow–type weapon that fires large metal projectiles.

Senjin – A sport played with a leather ball, featuring

14 combatants, 7 per side, on a field spilt into 6 parts, with two halves. The team to score three times first, wins.

Seti – A kingdom in north western Ostania. Their people the Setian are descendants of the Alzari. (See Alzari)

Shadelings – Creatures created in the God Wars, primarily by the god Amuni, and his followers by experimenting with netherlings and the essence of shade. The effects of the couplings can be seen within some of the strange beasts within Denestia.

Shin – The respectful title given to Ashishin Matii.

Shunyata – A place within each person where they can separate and control their emotions. Also the place where sela essence is stored within any living being. Also known as the Eye.

Streamean – The religion named after the elements of Streams and its gods.

Streams – The combination of four essences—light, heat, cold, and shade that make up energy. The energy can be used in the forming of the other elements e.g cold is needed to form ice which is part of the Forms and part of the Flows.

Sven – The earth elemental peoples that inhabit the Nevermore Mountains in north eastern Ostania. Descendants of the Svenzar.

Svenzar – Form elementals that reside in mountainous areas. Their power resides in earth, metal, and wood.

The Aegis – Said to be a power or a person who would help either protect the gods or defend against their resurgence.

The Chronicles – Said to be sacred tomes written by the Eztezians themselves and their descendants, dictating the past and the future of the world.

The Disciplines – A set of rules and pointers on how to govern and lead soldiers.

The Eye – See Shunyata.

The Great Divide – A massive rift in the land created by the Eztezians to defeat the shadelings. It runs from north to south across central Everland, and is guarded by the Erastonians.

The Iluminus – Named after the god Ilumni, it is the central city, learning hub and home of the Tribunal and its Matii.

The Nether – A realm between the worlds thought to be the origination of Mater, the gods, and netherlings.

The Stone – The great hidden city where the Svenzar and Sven live in northern Ostania.

The Unvanquished – Stefan Dorn's elite troops in Ostania.

Travelshaft – Tunnels developed by the Svenzar using the Forms, where time is slowed and speed increased to allow travel between large distances in a small amount of time. Said to somehow be constructed between the Planes of Existence.

Tribunal – The founding society of Ashishin among the Matii. They determined what was needed for the Matii as a whole to function in their proper roles as protectors and mediators. Eventually, the different Matii split apart due to conflicts in ideals, philosophies and religions. The Tribunal rules in Granadia. They left Ostania where most of the other Matii fled, to fend for themselves.

Vallum of Light – A massive wall imbued with Mater and erected by Eztezians within the Tribunal to separate Ostania from Granadia.

Warping – A Forging by powerful Matii, using the sela essences of something recently killed, to twist the essences in a specific area, thus rendering them unusable for a period of time.

Wraithwolf – A type of shadeling using a combination of wolf or other canine type beast, as well as the sela of a person, and essences of shade.

Zar – The respectful title given to Alzari Matii.

Message from the Author

In writing this first book, and series, I hope to have created a world my reader will lose themselves in. One where you can smell the scents, feel the textures, see the scenery, engage in the wonders of the world, cringe at its beasts, revile the evil of men and monsters, engross themselves in its history, celebrate the victories, weep at the defeats, feel the characters, love them, hate them, smile with them, laugh and cry with them, tremble, rage, scream with them, cackle with them in their insanity. I could continue to wax poetic. I've tried to weave my world around all these elements and a group of characters that can evoke those feelings while they traverse this world it took over ten years to create.

As an author nothing is greater than the reader. I humbly ask for your opinions. Your honest review will help me to know if I am doing the things mentioned above, where I'm weakest, where I'm strongest and help push me to new heights as I continue to hone my craft to the best it could possibly be and give my readers a promise of something they will always enjoy when they see my name attached.

Even if it's only one line, posting a review on Amazon, Barnes & Noble, Smashwords, Goodreads and similar sites will go a long way.

Don't forget to come visit my blog, Ramblings of a Fantasy Author and become a fan on my facebook page, TCSimpson on Facebook, if it so moves you. Insightful comments are always welcome. So come on, take the journey, help increase this vision of a whole new world.

Terry C. Simpson.

Novels By Terry C. Simpson

AEGIS OF THE GODS
Prequel: The Shadowbearer
Book 1: Etchings of Power
Book 2: Ashes and Blood (Coming Soon)

Fantasy works from Alexandria Publishing Group

By David M Brown
Fezariu's Epiphany

By Valerie Douglas
Song of the Fairy Queen
The Coming Storm Series
Setting Boundaries
Not Magic Enough
The Coming Storm
A Convocation of Kings

By Paul Kater
Hilda the Wicked Witch series
Hilda the wicked witch
Hilda – Snow White revisited
Hilda – The Challenge
Hilda and Zelda
Hilda – Cats
Hilda – Lycadea
Hilda – Back to School
Hilda – Dragon Master

By Stephen H. King
Cataclysm: Return of the Gods

Ascension: Return of the Gods

By Jonathan Gould
Doodling
Flidderbugs
Magnus Opum